A Gift of Jacinth

Wishes & Dreams
Book 2

ALLIE McCORMACK

McCormack, Allie

ISBN-13: 978-1-7371979-6-6

A Gift of Jacinth / Allie McCormack

Visit Allie's website at www.alliemccormack.com
Cover Art designed by Dar Albert at Wicked Smart Designs
http://www.wickedsmartdesigns.com
Copy editing by Chrissy Bixby

Published by Amazon

Fiction

Printed in the USA

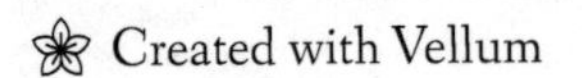

ACKNOWLEDGMENTS

ACKNOWLEDGMENTS

I want to give a really big shout-out to my wonderful Beta Reader Team, who read through my manuscript and sent me tons of thoughtful feedback. I couldn't have done it without them!

Cassandra Wengewicz
Dianna Evans
Lindsey Philipson
Michelle Zeppieri

Also to a very dear friend, *Kathleen Crapse,* for reading my manuscripts and encouraging me to write, and always wanting to read more!

BOOKS BY ALLIE MCCORMACK

Multicultural Romance

Sons of the Desert series:

SwanSong

Castles in the Sand

Paranormal Romance

When Darkness Falls: The Trilogy

Wishes & Dreams series:

Wishes in a Bottle

A Gift of Jacinth

A Cat for Troy

Contemporary Romance

Truck Stop

Boxed Sets (Ebook Only)

Wishes & Dreams Boxed Set

(Books 1-3)

If of thy mortal goods thou art bereft
And of thy slender store two loaves
alone to thee are left
Sell one, and with the dole,
Buy hyacinths to feed the soul.

Rubaiyat of Omar Khayyam (1048-1123)

PROLOGUE

From the moment the tingling anticipation awoke her from a languorous slumber this morning, Jacinth had known today was the day. In the hours since then, she'd watched customers come and go in the antique shop. Old and young, rich and not-so-much. None of them had been the one. It was almost five o'clock now, and soon the lanky, rather dim-witted clerk Julian had hired would go for dinner. Then she'd have to wait another hour before Julian came and re-opened his shop for the evening.

Still, she was unable to relax her vigil, hugging her knees as she watched the door of the antique shop through the shimmering silver walls of her teapot. Djinn could use anything as a vessel, not just the oil lamp in the Arabian Nights story. Hers was a teapot of the purest silver, tall and slender. It had been crafted for her by a silversmith in her Djinn homeland of Qaf eight hundred years ago, when she had first become a Wish Bearer. Outside it looked like a lovely, graceful teapot with decorative flowers etched into its silver surface, but inside... ah, inside it was like home!

She propped her chin on her hands and sighed, bored with the hours of waiting. Ruefully she admitted that patience had never been one of her virtues. She was consumed with curiosity, eager to meet her teapot's new owner. Even after all these centuries as a Wish Bearer, granting wishes to mortals, she never lost the sense of excitement, the breathless suspense, of that first meeting with a new *Sahib*, the Master of the bottle, to whom she'd grant three wishes. She wondered who the *Sahib* would be this time. A woman, full of hopes and dreams? A man, dark and brooding from injustice, like her poor Julian?

She'd been feeling oddly restless lately. Almost... well, not lonely, precisely. Perhaps it was because it was strange not to be able to pop in to see Julian whenever she wanted. A fourteenth-century Mage whose spell had gone spectacularly wrong, Julian had been bound to a Djinn vessel, granting wishes for six hundred years. Jacinth had been assigned by the Djinn Council to act as his mentor, teaching him their ways and helping him through the difficult centuries. Then a few months ago he had met Alessandra, who'd been able to free him from the spell. They'd just gotten married, and it wasn't right for her to keep dropping in all the time when they were building their new life together. Even before then, though, she'd begun to feel adrift, without a purpose. So she'd retrieved her Djinn vessel from Qaf and put it in Whimsies, Julian's antique shop tucked away on a side street here in Manhattan, for just the right person to find.

She jumped to her feet, the restless energy making her unable to sit still any more. She wanted her *Sahib*, the one who would buy her teapot and call her forth, to come *now*. She paced the length of the vessel and back. Chimes sounded in the shop as someone entered, and she rushed to the wall, the silver cool and silky beneath her fingers. Disappointment shot through her even before she saw the elderly woman's face. This was not the one. She resumed her pacing.

Almost on the stroke of five o'clock, the door opened and he walked in. There was nothing about him to indicate that he was to be her next *Sahib*, but she knew... she always knew. Eagerly she studied him as he looked about the shop. A shade over six feet, he had thick hair of mingled brown and blond, like sun-streaked toffee. It was a bit long and rather shaggy, in need of a trim. The face was tanned, as if he got lots of sun, with a strong nose and chin and well-shaped lips. No, not dark and brooding like her poor Julian. But there must be something, some reason he was to be her *Sahib*.

As he came closer she saw his eyes were a cool blue, almost aquamarine, under well-shaped brows. A plain cotton shirt stretched across broad shoulders, the sleeves rolled up to show strong forearms. It was tucked neatly into a pair of faded jeans that hugged his hips and thighs. Jacinth would bet her stack of gold bangles that he had a great butt. He was also terrifically handsome. Not that she was interested in that way, but there was nothing wrong with appreciating.

His jeans were dusty, as were the black work boots he wore, and she thought he might be in construction. He didn't look at all like the type to be interested in antiques. Of course, they rarely did.

"Over here," she whispered, as if she could urge him closer, even though she knew he couldn't hear.

The man drew near, stopping before the low table on which her teapot stood. Looking a bit bemused, he reached out to pick it up. Although not a mind reader, Jacinth could feel the flow of his emotions, channeled through his touch on the pure silver of her Djinn vessel. Confusion, of course. He was wondering why he was looking at this elegant teapot, and why he was here in this antique shop at all. Ah, there it was. Sharp edges of anger, long suppressed but no less acute for all that. The sense of desolation, of despair. Grief and longing. This, then, was why he was here. He needed her.

Satisfied, Jacinth could relax now, reclining on her chaise lounge as she prepared to watch events unfold, and wait for him to call her forth.

CHAPTER 1

He was out of his mind.

Pulling into his driveway, Douglas glanced sideways at the passenger seat. A shaft of light from the porch shone through the window directly onto the elegant, slender teapot. It gleamed silver, standing out against the car's dark upholstery. It was tall with a curling handle and long graceful spout, and ornate designs were delicately etched into the smooth surface. It had to be at least a hundred years old, Douglas thought. Perhaps older. It just had that kind of look, from an older, more graceful era.

Which didn't explain how he'd come to waste fifty bucks on an old teapot, even if he had gotten what was probably the bargain of the century. He wasn't interested in teapots, or antiques either, for that matter. Not that he had anything against them, but he wasn't an antiques kind of guy. Killing time after an appointment in the city, he'd stepped into the shop on a whim, for no other reason than to prolong the moment of going home to his empty house on a Friday evening. The moment he'd caught sight of the teapot, though, sitting in solitary splendor on a mahogany table as dusty as any attic, he'd been drawn to it.

The etched silver was cool to the touch and satiny, like running water. Douglas thought it was a shame the thing was tucked away, forsaken in the musty shop. It belonged somewhere else; a museum for people to enjoy looking at, or as the prized possession of some collector. There were no markings, no silversmith's stamp. He knew some about such things from a childhood spent antiquing with his parents; he just hadn't ever been interested in them himself. The teapot was either very, very old, or it wasn't really silver. He was betting on the former.

He still couldn't believe such an old, obviously valuable item was only fifty dollars. When he questioned the lanky clerk, the kid had clearly been bored, impatient to close up the shop for dinner, and told him to come back later in the evening when the owner would be in. Personally, Douglas thought the owner needed to seriously revise his hiring policies. He'd found himself oddly reluctant to let go of the teapot, though, to put it back down on the dusty table. So he'd paid the fifty dollars and here he was, with a teapot he didn't have a clue what to do with, and questioning his own sanity. Maybe there was a full moon.

Carrying his new purchase, Douglas got out of the car and let himself into the quiet, darkened house. He'd had a long day at the clinic, longer still because of the trip he'd had to make into Manhattan. But it was better than sitting alone here in his silent house. It was bad enough getting off work at noon on Friday, with the weekend stretching unbearably long and lonely ahead of him.

Turning on the lights in the dining room, he was careful not to look down the dim hallway with its closed doors. Instead, he turned his attention to his new find. He lifted the silver teapot carefully and held it up to the light. An odd sizzling feeling ran through his fingertips, almost like electricity. It wasn't unpleasant, but faded as he tried to analyze the sensation. Maybe he should eat.

Feeling weary, Douglas went into the kitchen to rummage in the freezer. He picked a nice sirloin and put it in the microwave to thaw, then glanced at the phone. He ought to call the investigator, see if there'd been any new leads. Not that he expected there to be any... it had been one dead end after another for two immeasurable years.

The microwave pinged, and Douglas took the steak out and put it under the broiler. A salad would go well with it, if the lettuce hadn't wilted. Checking the crisper, he retrieved the limp ball that had been a head of lettuce a week ago. Hell. He tossed it in the garbage. Grabbing a potato he scrubbed it, then pierced holes with a fork, ready to go into the microwave to bake. Waiting for the steak to cook, he carried the silver teapot into the living room, putting it on the coffee table where he could look at it while he ate. Eating here on the sofa with his meal on the coffee table wasn't a blatant reminder of what he'd lost as sitting at the family-sized dinette in the other room.

Douglas sank onto the sofa cushions with a sigh. It did feel good to relax, to stretch his legs out before him. If only the silence weren't so profound. Long ago, children's voices had filled the house, their laughter ringing through the rooms. He shook off those thoughts and opened his eyes, focusing on the silver teapot. Just looking at it seemed to soothe him, something in the graceful lines of the thing. He still couldn't figure out why this teapot caught his interest so firmly. Of course, it *was* extraordinary. He'd never seen anything quite like it before.

He picked the teapot up, handling it carefully, enjoying the smooth, satiny feel of the silver against his fingers. It had been kept beautifully polished, he had to say that for whoever owned the antique store. The design etched in the silver was vaguely Oriental, although he couldn't make out any particular motif he recognized. No cherry blossoms or geishas or Mt. Fuji, for instance. Idly he traced the lines with one fingertip.

"Your steak is burning."

Douglas jerked upright, staring at the apparition that seemed to appear in front of him out of nowhere.

"What?" He passed a hand over his face, not sure he was seeing what he thought he saw. There was a petite young woman, rather scantily clad in some kind of Arabian Nights costume, standing in the middle of his living room floor. "Who are you?"

"Your steak," the apparition repeated patiently. "It burns."

Douglas came off the sofa as the smell of charred meat wafted from the kitchen. "Hell!"

Rushing into the kitchen, he grabbed a potholder and pulled out the broiler pan, only to miscalculate and grab the top of the pan with his bare thumb.

"Ouch!" He tossed the pan onto the top of the stove, shaking his hand. "Damn, damn, damn!"

"Oh, let me look." The woman had followed him into the kitchen, and reached for his hand. He snatched it away from her, turning to hold his thumb under water from the faucet.

"Who the hell are you?" he snapped over his shoulder. "And what are you doing in my house? How did you get in?"

"I am Jacinth. I'm a Djinn," she said cheerfully, as if that explained everything. Her voice was lilting and charmingly accented, although he couldn't quite place it to any particular region. He could only stare at her, but she seemed more concerned with peering into the sink to check on his injured thumb.

Douglas promptly forgot all about the thumb as her words belatedly sank in. "A... what?"

"A Djinn... you know, a genie."

She was mental, that's what she was. Shutting off the faucet, Douglas counted to ten under his breath while gingerly patting his hand dry with a towel. He didn't need this. He had enough problems without a space case in his kitchen. Speaking of which, how did she get in here?

A dainty hand was laid on his wrist, her touch soft as silk. Brown eyes, the color of rich dark chocolate, peered up at him with earnest intent.

"From the teapot," she said, tilting her head to indicate the living room. Her hair, long and gleaming black, was gathered into a ponytail on top of her head, from which it spilled, curling wildly, to brush her hips.

"A genie from the teapot." Douglas leaned back against the counter, feeling a bit weak. Now he'd heard everything. It was safe to assume someone was looking for her... an official someone. He just hoped she wasn't dangerous.

"Look, miss..." How did one address a delusional... genie? "I've had a really long day, and it hasn't gotten any better since I burned my dinner. Maybe you could just... pop along back into your teapot and come back tomorrow."

Those big brown eyes made a discovery. "You don't believe me."

She sounded terribly hurt, and despite himself he felt like a complete villain for not believing her. He managed to stop himself from apologizing... barely... then found it wasn't necessary with her next words.

"That's okay." Jacinth nodded understandingly. "Many have a difficulty believing it at first. I will show you, because it was my fault."

A flick of her fingers, and all the pain vanished from his thumb. He looked at it in amazement and saw the bright red streak was gone as well. A tantalizing odor filled the air, and turning, he saw his steak still on the broiler pan... not charred, but done just as he liked it, brown and juicy. He stared at it, then looked back at his thumb, then at the woman watching him with wide, expectant eyes.

"The burned steak was not my fault, of course," she said, seeming to feel an excuse was necessary. "But I feel bad because I made you burn yourself so I fixed that too."

"How did you do that?" he demanded. Hypnotism? Had she somehow put him in a trance? He'd heard pain could be taken away under hypnosis... but the steak...

She heaved an exaggerated sigh. "I see you are going to be a difficult case."

"Lady, you're the case." He took a deep breath, fighting the urge to let the pent-up frustration of the last two years explode. Anger wrestled with his unfortunate protective tendencies. Even though this was his home and she was an intruder, she was just so damned cute. He found himself reluctant to hurt her feelings. Which was so stupid he couldn't believe he was worrying about her feelings. For all he knew she could be an axe murderer or something.

"I'm sorry, but I don't have time for this now. Could you please leave?"

"I cannot." She managed to somehow sound apologetic.

"Of course you can." Douglas pointed past her shoulder. "Right through that hallway, and out the front door."

She shook her head, the ponytail swishing vigorously.

"I cannot leave until I have granted you three wishes."

Three wishes. Right. Douglas grabbed her arm and led her

firmly to the front door. Yanking the door open, he pushed her through the opening.

"Goodbye."

He shut the door and locked it, then leaned his forehead against the glass pane, closing his eyes for a brief moment. A genie. Three wishes. Yeah, right! And pigs fly.

Straightening, he turned. And leaped back with a yell, crashing into the door behind him. In front of him stood the woman he'd just shoved outside.

"How...?" His voice sounded croaky, and he thought might have lost five years off his life. His heart still thudding uncomfortably, he shouldered past her into the kitchen, checking the door there, although she'd have to be superhuman to have run around the house and through the locked gate to the back yard in the few seconds since he'd closed the door. But the kitchen door was still locked. He went into the dining room and checked the patio door. Locked. Striding down the hall to his bedroom, he could see the sliding glass door there was also locked.

He turned to glare at the ... whatever she was... who'd followed him silently through the house.

"How did you get back in?"

"I am a Djinn." Her amused voice suggested she was humoring him. "You brought my teapot home, you rubbed it. I must grant you three wishes."

Douglas ground his teeth. "There's no such thing as genies."

"But I'm here," she pointed out, sounding eminently reasonable.

"That doesn't mean you're a... a genie."

Her brown eyes sparkled. Damn it, she was enjoying this! Douglas thought fast.

"If you're a genie, prove it."

Her face brightened as if he'd handed her a gift. She took him by his (now pain-free) hand and led him, unresisting, back into the living room. His plate sat on the coffee table, the steak steaming gently beside a baked potato heaped with a generous dollop of sour cream and chives. Next to the plate, a bowl was piled high with a crisp salad.

He swore an oath.

"Okay, that's it. I'm outta here." Douglas turned toward the door. He'd been working way too hard, that was obvious. He'd find a nice, friendly hospital and have them check him in. He grabbed the woman by the wrist and dragged her behind him while he dug with his other in his pocket for keys. He released her once they were outside and, locking the front door, headed for his car.

"Where are you going?" She was one step behind him.

"To the hospital. I'm convinced, okay? You haven't lost your mind. I've lost mine."

She put her hand over his, stopping him when he would have opened his car door.

"You have not lost your mind. And I am not in league with anyone to play tricks on you."

How'd she known that's what he was thinking? She peered up at him with an earnest expression.

"I will prove this."

The car before him shimmered, and the next moment, Douglas found himself standing back in his living room, the genie at his side.

He sank onto the sofa since he wasn't sure his legs would hold him. He knew he had been outside, standing next to his car. He *knew* that. He looked up at the... genie? ...who was watching him with the oddest look of anxiety. As if she actually cared whether he believed in her or not.

"So, okay. I think I'm convinced."

With a brilliant smile lighting her face, she sat in one of the easy chairs across from him and gestured at the coffee table.

"Eat your dinner now. I think you are tired as well as hungry, or you would not be so difficult."

He hadn't eaten all day, and the wafting aroma of the steak was making him hungrier by the minute. He sighed, surrendering, and picked up his fork and knife and cut into the steak.

"Why me?"

"Because of the teapot," she explained, her light accent putting an upward lilt on certain syllables. "Like the story of Aladdin's lamp. You found it and rubbed it, and here I am, to grant you three wishes."

Douglas thought it over while he ate. The steak was perfectly done, tender enough to cut with a butter knife. The potato was perfect too, and the salad cool and crisp.

She tilted her head, studying him. "Don't you have any other questions?"

"Yeah. Where were you when I needed you?" Douglas muttered around a mouthful of potatoes.

The genie... Jacinth... straightened, looking interested.

"What was that?"

He swallowed. "Nothing."

She studied him through narrowed eyes for a moment, then apparently decided to let it pass. She stood up, and he watched her wander about the living room while he ate. He wondered what she made of the room. It was spartanly furnished with the sofa and coffee table, and two easy chairs. He and Lilian had bought paintings for the walls, and the little shelves and knick-knacks she delighted in, but she'd taken those when she moved out. After the divorce he'd hung pictures of the kids above the fireplace, but after she'd taken them away, eventually it hurt too much to have the painful reminder, and he'd taken them down. Looking about now, seeing the room as a stranger would, Douglas thought it looked bare and ugly. He shrugged, not really caring. He spent as little time at home as possible.

He turned his attention to the alleged genie. She was extraordinarily pretty in a piquant sort of way, with a kind of creamy gold skin, her face an oval with a little straight nose and luminous brown eyes. Her figure was phenomenal, with curves in all the right places that showed to advantage in the skimpy Arabian Nights type costume. It was similar to what belly dancers wore, with a velvet top and a matching heavy sash about her hips, and some kind of sheer material encasing her slender arms and legs. It was much richer than the little he'd seen of belly dancers, though. The deep green fabric set off her coloring well, as did the stack of heavy gold bangles on her slender wrists and a dainty anklet with tiny bells that chimed when she moved.

Finishing his dinner, Douglas pushed the plate back. It was a very good meal... the best he'd had in a long time. He wasn't very handy in the kitchen. Along with everything else, he hadn't had a potato in the house, nor sour cream either. And he distinctly remembered throwing away the soggy, wilted head of lettuce just a short while before. Okay, so maybe she was a genie. Still...

"All right," he admitted. "I believe you're a genie. But I'm just not ready for this. It's been a rough couple of years, and I really don't need anything else to deal with right now."

The brown eyes watched him steadily, not without sympathy.

"Has it occurred to you," she suggested in her warm, lilted

voice, "that perhaps I could help? That I may improve things for you?"

Like that was going to happen. It'd take more than even a bona fide genie to put things right in his life. More than the Easter bunny, the tooth fairy, and even Santa Claus with all his elves put together. So far even God hadn't answered his prayers, although Douglas never lost faith. After all this time, though, faith was stretched a bit thin.

"I don't want you to take this personally," he told her. "But I really need you to disappear back into your teapot now."

"Okay." Jacinth smiled agreeably, and vanished.

"Hallelujah," Douglas muttered under his breath, having expected another argument from the very determined woman. Genie. Whatever.

He picked up the teapot and tucked it under his arm, heading for the front door. This was going back where it came from.

SOMEWHAT TO DOUGLAS' surprise, the antique shop was still open, although it was almost eight o'clock. There was a different man behind the counter, though. Appearing to be about Douglas' own age, he was dark in an Italianate kind of way, with a brooding look about him. On spotting the silver object under Douglas' arm, one black eyebrow flew up.

"Good afternoon," The man's voice was very faintly accented, Italian perhaps. "Welcome to Whimsies. May I help you?"

Douglas stalked forward and set the teapot on the counter. "I bought this here this afternoon. There were a few things your clerk forgot to mention."

"I see." Blue eyes in a deeply bronzed face studied him, then shifted to the teapot. A corner of the man's mouth twitched. "I'm sorry you aren't happy with it. We don't generally get returns on this particular item."

"I don't care about the money," Douglas all but snarled. "I just want the damned thing out of my life!"

He didn't wait for the man's reply, but turned on his heel and stalked out of the store.

Walking to his car, parallel parked two blocks away, Douglas found his thoughts returning with some regret to the lovely young woman. She'd been so young, perhaps in her early twenties. No grief shadowed her mahogany eyes, no pain had left its mark on her cheery outlook. By contrast, Douglas felt every second of his thirty-one years.

The beginning of an old poem popped into his head. "Had we but world enough, and time..." Okay, so the rest of the poem didn't fit, something about a coy mistress, but the first line echoed over and over. He shook his head to clear the refrain from his mind as he reached his car. A few minutes later he was on his way, back to his quiet, safe, very lonely home. He wasn't sure if the sigh that escaped him was relief, or regret.

A few blocks along, slowing to make a right turn at a brightly lit intersection, the streetlights reflected off a gleaming, silver object on the passenger's side. The teapot!

"Damn it!"

Douglas hit the brakes, heard them squeal in protest. He made a quick turn into a gas station, turned around and burned rubber out of the driveway, heading back downtown.

This time there was a pretty woman with long, honey-blonde hair behind the counter with the dark man. She looked around curiously as Douglas stormed into the shop. Douglas didn't bother addressing either of them. He set the teapot on the counter firmly and pointed his finger at it.

"Stay!"

Turning on his heel, he strode out the door and crossed the sidewalk to look into the passenger seat. Sure enough, there was the teapot. He grabbed it and stomped back to the store. The couple watched him, not saying a word. Douglas held up the teapot.

"Do you see this?"

They nodded in unison, the woman's eyes wide as she stared at the teapot.

"Good. I do not. I absolutely do. Not. Want. To see this in my car when I leave this place. Are we clear on that?"

The man cleared his throat, shooting a warning glance at the woman, who appeared to be struggling with suppressed laughter.

"Perfectly clear," he replied solemnly.

"Fine."

Douglas handed him the teapot and left the store. Back at his car, he scrutinized it carefully. There was no teapot in the front seat. Suspicious, he peered into the back seat. Nope. Opening the trunk, he rummaged through the various emergency supplies he kept there. No teapot.

With a feeling of relief, he got into the car and headed for home. He'd just forget this whole day ever happened. He made the rest of the drive home in a reasonably normal frame of mind, forcibly squashing thoughts of the appealing woman who'd invaded his life only a couple of hours earlier. Wouldn't it be nice, he thought wearily as he pulled into his driveway, if his problem could be solved as easily as making a wish? He gave a short laugh as he turned off the engine, rubbing his hands across his face.

"Yeah, right. Just make a wish and bingo, everything's fixed." He got out of the car. "And now you're talking to yourself. You've finally gone around the bend. Way to go, guy."

He opened his front door and headed into the living room, intending to pick up his dirty dishes from dinner, and stopped dead in his tracks.

Jacinth sat on the sofa, her lower lip caught between white teeth, looking up at him with a mixture of amusement and guilt on her piquant face. The teapot rested on the coffee table before her.

Douglas threw up his hands in surrender.

"Right. You want my house? You can have it."

Hell, he hated the place now anyway. He'd find a motel to stay in. He headed toward the door.

"No! Don't go!" Appearing at his side, she caught his sleeve, tugging him back. "Wait. Just wait. There must be something you want... something you desire more than anything else in the whole world."

That caught him unaware, like a blow to the gut. *More than anything else in the whole world...*

"My kids," he whispered. "I just want my kids."

CHAPTER 2

"Mmmm." The young woman's... genie's... expression was thoughtful, her mouth forming a moue of uncertainty, drawing his attention. A dusky rose color, her lips were generously curved. Even tempting. Douglas shook his head slightly, pushing the thought away, and concentrated on her words.

"Maybe you should explain a little more," she said. "Come sit down, and tell me about them."

Why was he doing this? Douglas wondered as he followed her to the sofa. One of them... and he wasn't quite certain anymore which one it was... needed help. Badly.

"Now." She made herself comfortable on the sofa, tucking her legs up under her as she faced him expectantly. "Tell me about your children."

God! The longing for them was so strong, a constant ache that never left him. Looking into her face, he saw only sympathy and an intent interest. After all this time, someone who actually seemed to care. Sure, the cops, the social workers, even his investigators were on it. They were all professionals. It was their job to deal with these kinds of things, though; it wasn't a personal involvement. Douglas could even understand that, since Molly and Benny weren't considered to be seriously at risk. What was a little neglect, he thought, fighting back bitterness, when set against unspeakable acts committed against so many children kidnapped by murderers, and worse?

He hardly ever talked about his kids anymore to anyone, preferring not to share his pain, but the brown eyes watching him so compassionately invited him... almost compelled him... to confide in her. Douglas reached into his back pocket for his wallet with the pictures he carried with him always. He opened it, gazing at the young faces for a moment before passing it to her.

"Molly," he managed to choke out his daughter's name. "And Benny. Molly's about four now. And Benny's six... he should be starting first grade this year."

"Should be?" she prompted, her voice gentle.

"Yeah. I haven't seen them in two years. Molly... I guess she wouldn't even remember me by now. My ex-wife was an alcoholic. We got divorced, and when I found out she was neglecting the kids, I sued for custody and won. She was supposed to be in detox, the judge ordered it. I didn't mind sharing custody if she'd sober up, but she didn't take care of the kids when she was drinking. But then one day while I was at work, she showed up at the babysitter's and took them. I've never seen them since."

Anger and pain surged through him all over again.

"I just wanted what was best for the kids," he ground out. "I wasn't trying to take them from her or keep her from seeing them. I didn't want them hurt, that's all."

He picked up his wallet from where the woman had placed it on the coffee table, feeling the familiar heavy weight in his chest as he looked at the young faces laughing at him from the plastic sleeves. "I miss them so much. There's not a day that's gone by that I haven't wished for them back."

Close enough, Jacinth decided. He was speaking more to himself than to her, but it would do for a bona fide wish. It would be helpful, though, if he had investigators were on the case, reports, pictures, and fliers.

"You've tried to find them?" She prodded gently, hoping for more information.

"Tried? I've had a private investigator on the case for two years. Every time we think we're getting close, they vanish again. I don't know if they're well, if they're happy. I don't know if they remember me at all, or miss me. What if they think I didn't want them, told her to take them away? I guess..."

"So there are official reports out? Missing children fliers, and all that?" Her voice was quiet, soothing, encouraging him to continue.

"Yeah." He broke off, dropping his head to his hands. "I guess I know they're alive. I have to believe they're still alive. If they're dead... but they're not."

Douglas steadied himself, taking a deep breath and raising his head. "She keeps moving. My ex-wife, Lilian. We keep getting reports of them, but when the authorities get there, they're gone. We're always just one step behind, it seems."

The deep brown eyes watching him so closely were sympathetic, and she nodded in understanding.

"Okay," she told him.

Douglas raised his head from his hands. "What?" he asked blankly. "Okay, what?"

The delicate black brows lifted, and her brown eyes sparkled at him in obvious pleasure.

"As in okay, I can get your children back for you."

Douglas stood up swiftly, almost knocking over the coffee table as hot anger flashed through him. He'd fallen for her soft sympathy, spilled his guts to her, and now she sat there mocking him.

"Lady, you're out of your mind. Look, just get the hell out of here. Now!"

She didn't move, and her eyes sparkled brighter. "Answer the phone."

"What?"

"Your phone is ringing."

Swearing, Douglas swung around, striding across to the kitchen where he'd left his cell phone back when he'd first been scrounging for dinner. He wanted this lunatic out of his house. He'd get rid of whoever this was, and then he was calling the cops. Whatever it took, he wanted her gone, *now*.

"Hello?"

"We've got them!" The excited shout almost broke his eardrum. Douglas winced, holding the phone away from his ear.

"Got who? Who is this?"

"It's Arnie. Get a grip, man, who did you think it was?"

"Arnie?" His investigator. Incredible hope flooded through him. Impossible, impossible. "What have you got?"

"Your kids, man. C'mon, Doug, snap out of it. We've found them!"

His kids? Douglas slumped against the counter, his knees turning to jelly.

"My kids?" he whispered.

"Molly and Benny," Arnie confirmed. "They're safe. You know we had their pictures on those websites for missing children, and the woman who was babysitting them for the evening recognized them. I got called right away. The cops are on their way to her house with a social worker to get them in protective custody before Lilian gets back, but you need to get out there as soon as you can."

"Where?" Douglas asked hoarsely. "Where are they?"

"In California, dude. Los Angeles. Check your fax, I'll send over the particulars in a few minutes, they're faxing them from California and I'll send them on. You can catch a redeye flight and be there first thing in the morning. Take everything you've got, the divorce and custody papers. There's plenty of documentation that Lilian took the kids illegally, so no question there. And you've got one helluva bill from yours truly to show that you've been searching for them for the past two years."

Douglas closed his eyes. Thank God! They'd been found, they were safe. Benny and Molly... he'd be with them again tomorrow. He'd see them, hold them. Bring them home.

"Be sure to send me your flight info. The social worker's going to meet you there at the LAX."

Douglas held his phone out to stare at it with a puzzled frown. Seriously?

"Meeting me at the airport?" he repeated.

His glance fell on Jacinth, who just gave him that mischievous smile, her slender shoulders shrugging a little.

"I'll be there. Thanks, Arnie."

He hung up the phone and turned slowly. Jacinth was still seated in her corner of the sofa, staring up at him expectantly, a mischievous smile quivering at the corners of her mouth. Douglas stared back.

"How the hell did you manage that?"

Her laughter was like tinkling bells. "Just a wee bit of pizzazz... is that the right word? ...to make things go smoothly."

In the bedroom that served as a home office in the back of the house he heard the fax line ring, then silence as the machine picked up. California! He needed to make a plane reservation.

Fixing Jacinth with his best intimidating stare, he pointed a finger at her.

"I want to talk to you. Don't go anywhere."

The lush mouth curved in a sweet smile, and her dark eyes gleamed. She appeared to be enjoying herself.

"Of course not." A small demitasse cup appeared on the coffee table, and the enticing aroma of rich Turkish coffee filled the air. She leaned forward to pick it up, and sipped daintily. Laughing eyes regarded him over the rim of the cup. "You go do what you have to do."

How did she *do* that? Douglas spun on his heel, stalking to the back of the house to turn on his computer. A *genie*! Hell.

A quarter hour later he had a round-trip e-ticket to Los Angeles and two children's tickets back to New York. He hung up the phone and stood uncertainly. He had to pack, although there was plenty of time, the flight didn't leave until 3 am. He'd made the return reservations for the same day, late in the evening, but he had no idea in fact how long it would take to get possession of Benny and Molly. He assumed there would be a lot of red tape, and it was possible, even probable, that he'd have to appear before a judge on the coming Monday. He could change the plane tickets, no problem, but he was unsure of how much to pack. And... oh, God! The kids' rooms!

"Geez," he muttered, heading for the hallway. "How the hell am I going to do all this and get to the airport by three in the morning?"

He opened the door to Molly's room and switched on the light. In the beginning he'd kept the rooms up, expecting the children to be home any day, but this last year hope had become more of a dream, and it had hurt too much to see their things. He'd finally shut the doors and stayed out. Now he looked around and sighed, knowing Benny's room wouldn't be much better. The rooms were basically clean, but the sheets had been on the beds for months, and there was dust everywhere. Plus they'd been shut up for so long in the stifling midsummer heat, they were musty and over warm.

"Ugh. It seems more like a museum than a bedroom." Jacinth leaned around his shoulder to peer through the door, wrinkling her pretty little nose.

Douglas couldn't object to her assessment.

"An untended museum," he admitted with a sigh. "It was so hard to come in here, though... I started letting things go."

"Oh, what a lovely doll!" Jacinth slipped past him into the room, picking up the china doll that lay against Molly's pillow in royal splendor. Yards of cream lace spilled over her arms as she cradled the doll in her arms, stroking the golden curls.

Pain lanced through Douglas' chest.

"Yes," he managed to say. "Isabel. It was her favorite, even though Molly was so small. Lilian told me it was too fancy for a toddler. But Molly loved it the instant she set eyes on it."

"Take it with you," Jacinth told him, sounding decisive. "She is so young, she will be confused. Having something familiar and beloved that she may remember from before, it would help."

She came to stand before him, holding the doll out. He took it, noting that his fingers shook slightly. Molly... was he really going to see her again? Bring her home, after all this time?

"Is this really real?" he asked her abruptly, needing to know. "Or is this some dream I'm having... some hallucination?"

"Go look at your fax machine," she suggested, apparently unoffended. How could she be so... so casual about all this? Douglas felt like he'd been dropped down Alice's rabbit hole and hadn't hit bottom yet.

He stood looking down at the genie, really seeing her for the first time. He was startled to realize how petite she was, her head barely reaching his shoulder as she stood at his side. Somehow she'd seemed taller at first. Although her face was almost classically lovely, oval with smooth golden skin, her expression made her look rather pixie-ish along with the constant mischievous gleam in the dark brown eyes. Black brows arched delicately over those eyes, and she had a wide, shapely mouth, her lips soft and oddly vulnerable. Despite her petite height, curved breasts swelled softly above a slender waist and rounded hips. Her small feet were bare except for the anklet she wore. She looked as delicate as the porcelain doll in his arms.

"I don't believe in genies. Or in wishes, or in magic." He had to make her understand that somehow. "I don't believe in *you*."

Her smile was comforting, and she patted his arm.

"It's okay. You will. Not to worry about that right now. We must get these rooms into shape. You don't want to bring the children back to this."

She was right about that, Douglas thought, surveying Molly's room with a grimace.

"I'll dust," Jacinth told him. "You change the beds and vacuum. We'll open the windows to let some air in, and close them before you leave in the morning. Open the air conditioning vents, and they'll be fine by the time you get back."

Nodding, Douglas turned and took a step away, toward the hall closet where he kept the vacuum, then paused to look back.

"You're really going to dust?"

The brown eyes blinked inquisitively.

"I mean, you're not going to... you know..." Douglas put his finger on the tip of his nose, wriggling it like Samantha in Bewitched.

Jacinth burst into laughter, a joyous trill.

"No, of course not!" She twinkled at him in delight. "Do you like those old shows, too? They're so fun!"

"Yes, they are," Douglas agreed, walking off to get the vacuum. "I just never thought I'd find myself in the middle of one."

He went into Benny's room, flinging open the curtains and sliding back the window, letting the evening air in. This room was larger than Molly's, and not quite so stuffy. He'd have to get rid of the clothes in the small dresser, he mused as he ran the vacuum over the floor. They wouldn't fit Benny any longer. He could do that when he got the kids home, though. Turning off the machine, he moved the rocking horse so he could vacuum under it. With the sudden absence of the motor's sound, he could hear odd noises came from down the hall.

Now what? He wondered, heading for Molly's room.

The lacy little-girl curtains had been taken down from the window and the screen pushed out. Jacinth was standing on a chair leaning out the window, thwacking the curtains against the side of the house. Despite himself, Douglas couldn't help admiring the enticing curve of her rounded derriere, the smooth golden skin of her exposed back above the low-cut trousers. He'd always thought men who smacked women's bottoms were neanderthal and incredibly obnoxious; therefore, the sudden urge he had to do just that was an unpleasant surprise.

He stuffed both hands in his pockets, removing the temptation. With an effort he reminded himself that he needed to get the children's rooms ready, and himself ready as well for the trip to California. Furthermore, he hadn't quite figured out yet what was going on with this woman who not only claimed to be a genie but had presented fairly unarguable proof. He was still struggling with that.

With a mental sigh, Douglas went back to the room he was working on.

The vacuuming finished and the twin bed freshly made with plain sheets... somehow he had a feeling Benny would no longer care for his beloved purple dinosaur sheets... Douglas wheeled the vacuum cleaner down the hall to Molly's room. He stopped at the doorway, surveying the room in surprised approval.

Besides dusting the shelves, dresser top, curtains, and books, Jacinth had gathered all of the prettiest dolls from Molly's toy box and sat them carefully around the room. Some were arranged on the bed, and some seated around a small grouping of chairs at the child-sized table. The lamp which had been on the tall dresser now sat on the bedside table, ready for Molly to turn on and off. A huge overstuffed rabbit... a gift from the Easter bunny that last Easter... sat on top of the toy box, a picture book open on its lap. Jacinth had taken a pair of glasses from Molly's pink and white costume chest and perched it on the rabbit's nose, giving it a rather regal, intellectual look. A feathery pink stole from that same chest was draped about a ballerina doll, standing poised on the dresser.

There wasn't anything special, nothing that hadn't been in the room already... but Jacinth had turned the simple bedroom into a little girl's dream.

Douglas raised his head, sniffing experimentally. There was a slight scent of roses. He glanced at Jacinth suspiciously. She met his look with a guilty smile, holding up her thumb and forefinger to show him a tiny measure of space.

"Just an eensie bit of magic. To freshen the room up."

Molly loved roses. He used to call her his little flower child.

Douglas experienced a moment of pure panic. What was he going to say to his children? What would he do with them? He had no idea what Lilian might have told them. Would they want to come home with him, even if they remembered him? He didn't know anymore what they liked, what their favorite foods were, what they liked to watch on television. Molly had been little more than a baby when he'd last seen her, while Benny had been just a toddler, and now he was about to start school!

"Come with me." The words were out of his mouth before he'd had time to consider, but having said it, it felt right. "Help me with Benny and Molly. They won't know me, and I don't know what Lilian's told them, what they will think. I... I need you."

Jacinth's brown eyes widened, and her lips formed an "O" of surprise. After a moment, her expression turned thoughtful.

"How would you explain me?"

Douglas thought about that, possibilities racing through his mind.

"The nanny. I'll say you're the nanny I've hired to take care of the children and the house while I'm working."

Jacinth nodded. "Yes, that will work. I'll bring some references, in case the social work people there ask."

References? Douglas stared at her.

"Douglas." She spoke slowly, as if to a somewhat obtuse child. "I have resources, other people I've known through the years, and other Djinn. Yes, I can get references. I'll make some calls, and have them faxed here."

Djinn... genie? "You mean... there are *more* of you?"

She laughed. "Of course. Now give me your fax number, or your email if you prefer, so I can get those references."

He told her, then hesitated.

"Do you, uh..." He tried to think of a way to put it tactfully but failed. Oh, the hell with it. "Have you got something else you could wear?"

Jacinth looked down at the exotic costume she wore and giggled.

"Oh, this. Sorry, I forgot."

She swept her hand downward, and before he could blink, she stood before him dressed in navy trousers and a silky blouse of pale blue neatly tucked into the waistband. Her beautiful blue-black hair was swept up into a neat clip at the back of her head, the loose hold allowing soft waves to frame her face. She wore a pair of low black sandals, from which polished toenails peeked. Despite her small stature, she looked both competent and friendly... perfect for dealing with young children.

"So, uh... does asking you to come with me, count as a wish?" Douglas asked, feeling awkward. He didn't know how this whole thing worked, or what to expect. It was unsettling, to say the least.

Jacinth shook her head, the dimple at the corner of her mouth appearing.

"The wishes are only if there is magic involved. I don't have to agree to any request, you understand. Only the wishes. But I like to help, it is why I am a Wish Bearer. Besides, I like children. We have many at my village in Qaf. Call it a favor if you like." She tilted her head, regarding him with curiosity. "I know you don't want to wait until morning to go to California. Why have you not wished for me to send you there right away?"

"Not because I didn't think about it," Douglas said ruefully. "But I need everything to be on the up-and-up. I need to be on that passenger manifest, just in case anybody checks."

She waited, her gaze steady, until he shrugged somewhat uncomfortably. "And a part of me still doesn't believe it."

Nodding, she laid one hand lightly on his arm. "That's okay. It takes everyone a little time to get used to the idea." She aimed one of those candle-bright smiles at him. He'd never met anyone so... accepting. It seemed like everything was okay with her.

"How old are you?" he asked, suddenly curious.

The mischievous twinkle returned in an instant, and she shook her head.

"You don't want to know. Trust me on that. At least, not while you're still having trouble just believing I'm real."

Well, that was fair.

"If you're going to California tomorrow, isn't there anyone you need to let know?" She asked. "Your job?"

"Right. Gotta call the clinic." He couldn't believe he'd forgotten about that. A quick glance at his watch showed that it was almost ten. He'd call Troy at home. "I'm a veterinarian. There are three of us, my partners will be able to cover for me for tomorrow and Saturday if need be. Sundays we're open half day, but we take it in turns."

Jacinth's face lit with interest. "A veterinarian! How wonderful! Do you specialize, or what?"

"I take care of horses, mostly. Livestock. There are lots of farms in this area, and large properties where people have horses. Riding, training, horse shows. My partners see dogs, cats and birds, and other kinds of household pets."

The genie rubbed her small, straight nose, appearing thoughtful. "Will it be a problem, taking off so suddenly like this?"

Douglas chuckled. "Nope. If they thought for one minute that I would hesitate to dump my patients on them to get to Ben and Molly, Troy'd be kicking my butt while Suzanne got on the phone and made the plane reservations herself."

He glanced around the room, running his hands through his hair. He'd planned to get Benny a pony for Christmas the year Lilian had stolen the kids away, and he'd asked Suzanne to keep an eye out for a likely puppy as well. Then the kids were gone, and he'd been alone. What would it be like? Would they still be a family, or would it take him months... maybe even years... to reconnect with his children? He knew Benny would have changed in so many little ways, like whether or not he'd outgrown big purple dinosaurs. And Molly had been so little when he'd seen her last. He had to face the fact that she likely wouldn't remember him at all.

"Let's switch bedrooms," he suggested. "I need to vacuum in here, and change the bed."

Jacinth nodded and disappeared down the hall, although her floral scent lingered, mixing pleasantly with the rose fragrance in the small room.

At least Molly wouldn't have outgrown her bedding, he thought, stretching out the elastic bottom on a pretty rosebud strewn sheet to slip over the mattress edge. It seemed almost unreal, that they'd really be back here with him... if not tomorrow, at least soon. Tomorrow he'd actually see their little faces, hug them to him. Maybe he was dreaming. Or hallucinating.

He slipped out of Molly's bedroom and stole down the hall to his office. There was the fax from Arnie, as he'd expected. The address and phone number of the precinct, the cop who'd gone to pick up the kids. The social worker's name and phone number. An email had come in from Arnie as well, saying he gotten Douglas' airline reservation and called that information to Los Angeles. The social worker would be waiting for him at the airport. Of course, Arnie had copies of all the legal documents, but still, he must have done quite a bit of talking in the last two hours to have convinced the authorities to hand the children straight over to Douglas. That is, *if* they were convinced, but it was a good start. He was grateful for that. Not that he wouldn't jump through any hoops they required to get his kids, but to know so much was taken care of was a great relief. He couldn't know what else was required until he got there.

A part of him whispered that it couldn't be this easy, that there were going to be immense hurdles before him in California, but he pushed away the warning voice. He didn't care. To see his kids... to have them back... that was all he wanted. He'd do whatever it took, because nothing was as important as his children.

The fax line rang again as he stood studying Arnie's email, and he picked it up curiously. It was Jacinth's reference, as she'd promised. He looked it over curiously. From the "East Wind Nanny Service," it showed Jacinth Khayyam, age 24, with a BA in childhood education. Her references were impeccable, her length of previous employment through the agency was two years, and her job performance at her previous post completely satisfactory.

Douglas sat down at his computer to purchase another plane ticket... *"for a genie,"* his mind taunted him... then wandered back down the hall, paper in hand. He stopped at the door to Benny's room, where Jacinth was stretched out on the floor, engaged in meticulously laying a toy train track around one leg of the bed.

"Is there really an East Wind Nanny Service?" he asked in some curiosity.

She looked around, a question in her eyes. Seeing the paper he held up, she nodded.

"Of course. We have some Djinn who work exclusively with children, you know. I thought an agency would be a useful thing to such Djinn, so I checked to see if we had contacts with one, and we did, and there's the reference."

She seemed inordinately pleased with herself for thinking to check to see if there was a genie-affiliated nanny agency, and Douglas chuckled. The brown eyes gleamed in response.

"That's the first time I have seen you smile," she confided. "You need to not be so serious."

Serious? His life had been as bleak as the Gobi desert since he'd come home that fateful afternoon and discovered Molly and Benny gone.

"Just let me get my kids back," he promised her. "That'll go a long way towards fixing just about everything."

LATER THAT EVENING, Jacinth lowered herself onto the silken covered lounge cushions inside her bottle. Douglas had gone to his room to get a couple hours' sleep before they had to leave for the airport. He was wound up tight as a tick, and she suspected he wouldn't get much sleep, if any, but at least he was resting.

Stretching one hand to the wall, she lay her palm on the shimmering silvery surface. "Mother?"

There was a ripple, and Zahra's serene features appeared on the shining silver. "Yes, daughter?"

Jacinth drew up her knees, her arms hugging them while she grinned at her mother in delight. "I have a *Sahib*!"

"Already?" Her mother's delicate brows rose in surprise, and her eyes, green and sparkling as emeralds, sharpened with interest. "That was very fast, you'd only gone into your vessel a week ago. So tell me!"

Briefly, Jacinth related the events of Douglas trying to take the teapot back to the antique shop, and they both had a good laugh.

"I've never heard of anyone trying to return their vessel before!" Zahra shook her head. "So he is leaving soon?"

"We," Jacinth corrected. "He's asked me to come along to help him with the children. As the nanny," she added with a mischievous sparkle.

"Really? I didn't know you knew anything about children?"

"Well, no, I don't," Jacinth admitted. "But I've got my laptop plugged into the internet, and I'll do some research. I figured I'd start with some YouTube videos on parenting. Besides, it's only for a short while, until he finds someone suitable to watch the children."

She grabbed a cushion and dragged it to her, hugging it tightly. "I had so much fun arranging Molly's room. I feel... oh, I don't know. Excited and interested. I'm looking forward to flying on an airplane, too. I've never done."

Zahra winced. "I can't imagine how anyone can travel that way, packed like sardines into a metal can."

Jacinth twinkled at her mother responsively. "It won't be that bad. Douglas booked us seats in business class... I checked."

"I'm so glad. I've been worried about you."

Jacinth stared at her mother's reflection in the silver surface, blinking at her in complete surprise. "Why? I'm fine!"

"You are not, dearest," her mother corrected gently. "You have isolated yourself from everyone."

"I have not!" She denied hotly, dropping the pillow and sitting upright on the low cushions. "I've been... well, I've been busy."

"Busy with what?"

She'd been busy trying to find something... anything... that would interest her enough to keep her waking up every day. But she couldn't tell her mother that, of course.

"I've been helping Julian," she said defensively. "He was having a rough time of it."

Her mother's expression softened a bit. "Yes, I do know. But that's been some weeks now, and he's settled in with that young woman, Alessandra." Zahra studied her, making Jacinth squirm uncomfortably. "Are you sure you're all right with that? I had often wondered, over these last centuries..."

Jacinth stared at her a long minute, then laughed suddenly.

"Oh! Oh, no, it was never anything like that between us." She smiled fondly, feeling the sudden rush of affection for the mage she had mentored for so long. "Poor Julian, he was so very unhappy. He never wanted to be one of us, nor would he have been happy married to one. He wanted his human life back. And for me... Oh! Julian was the younger brother I never had, someone to watch over and care about, and pick him up when he stumbled and fell. Alessandra has become a very good friend as well. The reason I've distanced myself from them since they married was to give them privacy. They needed to start their lives together without me dropping in every other minute."

She settled back against the cushions, tucking her feet under her. Again she felt the glow of excitement.

"I'm looking forward to this, so much," she confided to her mother's image. "Douglas showed me pictures of the children. The little girl, Molly, she's the most adorable thing you ever saw, with golden curls and big blue eyes. Ben, that's the boy, he looks just like his father with dark hair. His eyes are blue too but different, more like aquamarine. The children were much smaller when the pictures were taken, of course. They're four and six now."

Zahra's delicate brows drew together as she thought that over. "This situation must be awfully hard on the children."

"Yes," Jacinth agreed. "I think that's what has Douglas in

such a sudden panic and why he asked me to come along. He has no idea what to expect, either from the children or from the legalese required. I've done what I can to smooth the way for the legal process, at least."

"It's probably a good thing you'll be going along," Zahra remarked. "You can be right there to take care of any problems as they come up."

Jacinth hugged her knees again, nodding. "That's what I was thinking. It's a tough situation, and none of them need more stress at this point. Douglas plans on us all flying back as soon as the legal part is cleared up." She made a little moue of regret. "I rather wished we could have stayed and gone to Disneyland. I've never been. It would be so fun, especially with children along to enjoy it with."

Zahra shook her head. "It would be far better for the children to return to their home right away and get some kind of routine established. Later perhaps you could prevail upon your *Sahib* to take them on a trip to that place in Florida."

Brightening, Jacinth nodded. "Disney World! Yes, that's a good idea. I like that!"

A faint sound intruded from outside the teapot. Tilting her head, Jacinth listened carefully. "That's Douglas' alarm clock, I think. We'll be leaving for the airport. I have to go, Mother."

"Very well. Keep in touch, dear one, and let me know how things go."

The silvery walls shimmered, and her mother's visage faded. Jacinth stood up, drawing in a deep breath and feeling a little shiver of delight. This was going to be so much fun!

CHAPTER 3

Douglas came to an abrupt halt as he emerged from the narrow hallway of arrivals into the bright lights and soaring ceilings of the terminal lobby at Los Angeles International. To one side of the waiting area stood an older woman, obviously watching for him. Clinging to her hands, one on each side, were two wide-eyed, scared looking young children. *His* children.

"Don't rush it." Jacinth's low voice advised from behind him. He nodded shortly as he moved forward, scarcely able to tear his eyes from his children to watch where he was putting his feet.

"Dad!"

Benny, his fair hair tousled and shaggy above bright blue eyes, clung to the woman's hand, eagerness clearly warring with doubt.

"Ben!"

A lump in his throat, Douglas knelt down, spreading his arms wide. The boy launched himself forward, and Douglas caught him, hugging him tightly, closing his eyes tight against the tears that threatened.

"Benny," he whispered. "I've missed you so much. Thank God I've got you back safely."

He stood, still holding Benny, who clung to him like a limpet. Molly didn't recognize him. He'd braced himself for that, but still, it was hard. She hung back, peeking at him from behind the social worker's legs.

"You certainly must be Mr. McCandliss." The woman held out her hand. "I'm Susan Perrin."

"Yes, I am. Hello." He took her hand, shaking it, but his eyes were all for his daughter. A touch on his shoulder made him remember Jacinth, and he turned. She put the doll she carried into his free arm with a smile.

"I don't know if you remember Isabel?"

He offered the doll to the shy girl. Molly was pretty as a picture, much like a porcelain doll herself, her fine blonde curls and blue eyes like Benny's but daintier. There was recognition in those big eyes as she looked at the doll, but her uncertainty about him was clear.

Benny squirmed to get down. Douglas placed him on his feet, and the boy went to his sister, taking her by the hand. As serious as a judge, Benny took the doll from Douglas and pressed it into Molly's arms.

"It's Daddy, Molly. Don't you remember Daddy? and Dolly?"

Douglas sought to reassure him. "It's okay, Benny. She was very little when... when you went away. She probably doesn't remember."

"Give her a little time," the social worker told them. "I'm sure she'll remember once she's back in familiar surroundings. Mr. Belmont said you still live in the same home?"

He nodded, then followed her questioning glance. Jacinth stood a little behind him, waiting patiently. He beckoned her forward.

"This is Jacinth Khayyam." He stumbled over the last name that had been on the reference. He should have asked her how to pronounce it. "She's a licensed nanny, from the East Wind Nanny Service."

"Oh, yes." The older woman looked relieved. "I'm so glad you thought to hire someone. I don't think anyone was aware when they spoke to Mr. Belmont, your investigator, last night, but... well, it seems that Molly doesn't speak."

Douglas just looked at her, feeling blank astonishment. "Molly? She babbles like a little brook."

He felt a tug on his hand. Benny was looking up at him, his expression oddly anxious for a six year old.

"Molly didn't talk for a long time," the boy confirmed. "I tried to take care of her, Dad, just like you'd have wanted."

Douglas knelt again and swept Benny into his arms.

"I'm sure you did, son. I'm sure you did. And now we're all together again, maybe Molly will feel like talking to us soon, okay?"

He cast a helpless glance up at Jacinth. Molly didn't talk? What the hell had been happening with his kids?

"We need to go someplace we can talk," the social worker told him. Douglas agreed fervently.

"Can we go to McDonalds?" Benny piped right up, his little voice excited. "One of the ones with a playground?"

"What if I come with you and Molly on the playground," Jacinth asked Benny, "while your daddy and Mrs. Perrin talk? Will that be okay?"

Benny gave her a doubtful glance, and reached for his

father's hand, holding on tight. Douglas ruffled the boy's hair, glancing at the social worker to see her nod of agreement.

"It's okay, Benny. I'll be right there at the table with Mrs. Perrin. I won't be out of your sight for one minute." *Nor you out of mine*, he thought with grim determination.

That seemed to be all the reassurance Benny needed. He grasped Jacinth's hand with his free one, and grinned up at her.

"Okay, sure!"

Molly went to the genie, holding out her dimpled, chubby hand for Jacinth to take, the other hand clutching her doll. It was that simple, Douglas thought ruefully, and she'd won both kids over. In fact, she won Molly over so thoroughly that the little girl refused to be parted from her, clinging stubbornly when they reached the social worker's car.

"Why don't you let Benny go with Douglas?" Jacinth suggested to Mrs. Perrin finally, "Molly and I will ride with you, I can sit beside her in the back seat."

Douglas didn't blame the older woman for not wanting to let him leave the parking lot with both children. It was her job to watch out for them, after all. He held his breath as she considered, then let it out in relief when she nodded her consent.

"Yeah!" Benny leaped into the air, yelling in excitement. He bounced up and down, still hanging onto Douglas all the while. "I get to ride with Dad!"

Molly's lower lip trembled; clearly she wasn't sure she wanted to be parted from her brother. Douglas watched Jacinth lean down to whisper something in the little girl's ear, and the pout just forming disappeared, to be replaced with a wide smile. Molly held up her arms to Jacinth, who lifted her without apparent effort and strapped her into the car booster seat in Mrs. Perrin's car.

"Could you meet me at the rental car lot?" Douglas asked Mrs. Perrin. "I don't know the area, I can follow you to the McDonald's."

At her nod, Douglas strode off towards the area where his rental car waited, Benny jumping about at his side.

He let Benny chatter freely, not asking the boy any of the hundreds of questions that were foremost in his mind. Where had they been? Had Lilian taken good care of them? They were dressed in clean clothes, and were well-scrubbed; was that Lilian's doing, or had the foster people they'd spent the night with done that? What had Lilian told them about him? Had they known that she'd stolen them? Did they think he hadn't wanted them?

"It's way cool we've got a nanny, Dad," Benny was saying. "I never knew anybody who had a real nanny. Will she live with us?"

"Um..." Douglas hadn't even thought of that. He opted for what little truth he had to go on. "I don't know, Benny. This all happened so suddenly, I haven't had time to talk to her at any length. We'll work it all out, once we're home."

"UNFORTUNATELY, WE DON'T KNOW MUCH," Mrs. Perrin told Douglas once they were seated alone. The children had eaten breakfast, and Jacinth had taken the trays with the litter of wrappers and napkins off the table before herding them out to the enclosed play area, leaving Douglas and Mrs. Perrin to talk. And Douglas to sign a veritable ream of official paperwork.

"Your ex-wife never came back to the sitter's house last night. It's possible that she came earlier than she'd planned, saw the police there and ran. But Benny doesn't know their address, and Molly of course isn't talking. The children are in good health, though, as you can see."

"Is there any problem about my taking them home? What do I need to do?" Douglas asked. "I didn't know if there might be red tape to go through, or if I'd need to go before a judge. Anything like that. I'll do whatever it takes, however long it takes. What am I looking at?"

Mrs. Perrin, bless her, shook her head. "The paperwork your investigator faxed over last night was quite complete, and we received an extra set from your lawyer this morning as well. There's no doubt you have court-ordered custody and that Mrs. McCandliss acted illegally in kidnapping Benny and Molly, and that you've been actively searching for them ever since."

She seemed to hesitate, and Douglas felt his muscles tense. *Here it comes,* he thought.

"We're extremely concerned about Molly. That's the main reason I wanted to speak to you in private." She cast an amused glance about the crowded fast food restaurant. "Such as it is. Your nanny seems very young, although the East Wind Nanny Service has an outstanding reputation. We have no idea why Molly may not be speaking. Neither child shows evidence of trauma or abuse, and if Benny knows why his sister won't speak, he isn't saying. It's clear he has established himself in the parental role and is protective of her. I'd be much more comfortable if I had your assurance that if she doesn't begin speaking again in a very short while, you'll seek counseling for her."

Douglas grimaced. "It's already on my agenda, believe me. I knew there would be a period of adjustment, even without this. I wish I knew what Lilian told them. Benny seems to have no problem accepting me, at any rate."

"Yes, that was a relief," the woman admitted. "We didn't

know what to expect. They were already asleep when we picked them up last night, in no case to be questioned. This morning, what with getting the children up and bringing them to meet you, there's been no time."

"Whatever it is, we'll deal with it."

Douglas looked around, spotting Benny as the boy scrambled into an oversized plastic tube. Molly wasn't playing, and had Jacinth's hand firmly gripped. She didn't look unhappy, though, her doll held tight, treasured. Her little face was bright with pleasure as she listened to whatever Jacinth was telling her.

"Molly certainly has taken to your nanny," Mrs. Perrin commented, rising from the little table, her briefcase in her hand. "That can't be a bad thing. Well, I'll be on my way, Mr. McCandliss. Contact us if you get any information that might help us to find your ex-wife, and let us know if we can help in any way."

Douglas rose as well, holding out his hand. "I will. Thank you, Mrs. Perrin. Thank you so much."

"You're very welcome."

With a smile, and a last approving glance at the children she was gone. Douglas watched her walk away, feeling his heart pound. Was that it? He couldn't believe it was so easy. Wasn't there more he had to go through before the kids were really his to take home? The legalities, red tape... maybe an intense scrutiny of his ability to care for the kids. A court appearance.

"Is this your doing?" he asked Jacinth, joining her and Molly in the play area.

She didn't pretend not to know what he was talking about.

"You didn't need more hassles," she told him. She smiled down at Molly, squeezing the little girl's hand reassuringly. "Nor did they. They needed their father as much as you needed them. You yourself made things easy, Douglas, by having been actively searching. A matter of preparation meeting opportunity."

"Hey, Dad!" They both looked up, to see Benny waving at them atop a slide. "Watch me!"

With a push, he was off, sliding down and around through the plastic tube, to land in a triumphant heap at their feet. Clambering up, Benny bounded to Douglas' side.

"Cool, huh?"

"Absolutely," Douglas assured the boy, then glanced at his watch.

"It's eleven o'clock now. We don't leave until eight this evening. What should we do until then?"

Benny's eyes lit like fireworks.

"Can we go to Disneyland? We've never been. Please?"

When Douglas shook his head, the children weren't the only ones to look disappointed, he noted. Jacinth's brown eyes looked at him reproachfully, as if he had rained on her parade.

"We don't have enough time," he explained. "Disneyland is at least an hour's drive from here. What about the zoo?"

The faces around him brightened.

"Cool!" Benny said. Apparently that was his favorite word.

Douglas squatted on his heels before his daughter so that he was on eye level with her. She'd hung back the entire time he'd been talking, watching him shyly from behind Jacinth's dark slacks.

"What about you, Molly? Would you like to go to the zoo? See the animals... lions and tigers, and elephants."

"They have a koala exhibit, too," Jacinth told the little girl. Douglas didn't know how she could know that, but he had no doubt they'd find koalas at the zoo. "Pretty koala bears, Molly.

And a petting zoo, where you can feed baby goats and sheep, and even little tiny horses."

There was fascination in the limpid blue gaze raised to Jacinth, and the child tipped her head in an infinitesimal nod.

"The zoo it is," Douglas said decisively, satisfaction flooding through him. "Everybody, let's go!"

HE STILL COULD HARDLY BELIEVE it. Watching Molly, who'd with difficulty been persuaded to leave her beloved Isabel in the car, petting the dwarf goat not much bigger than her, while Benny went into raptures over a pot-bellied pig, Douglas had to keep shaking off the feeling that he was going to wake up any moment and find himself back at home, alone in his big house, his children still missing.

"Thank you," he said to Jacinth, who was standing at his side. "I can't begin to thank you enough."

Her dark eyes sparkled in pleasure, and she glanced at the children.

"I'm glad I could help. And coming to the zoo was a good idea."

He grinned at her. "Even if you'd rather have gone to Disneyland, like the kids."

Her trill of laughter was infectious. Douglas saw people nearby them glance over, smiling themselves. He'd noticed that on the airplane this morning, and in the crowded terminal of the airport. She cheered everyone up, he thought. Whoever she came in contact with, left just a little lighter of heart.

He glanced at Molly, awe in her little face as she stroked an affectionate goat that shoved its nose at her.

"Could you..."

His impulsive question was silenced by the touch of her fingers against his lips. They were warm, and oddly vibrant.

"No." Jacinth's eyes met his, intent. "That is... yes, I could use the magic. But don't wish it. At least, not yet. Sometimes the easiest road is not necessarily the best one. I truly think she will start to talk again once she's home, in familiar surroundings. Once she feels secure. If you must wish it, I will make her speak... but I think you would do better to wait."

The sigh came from the very depths of his soul.

"Okay. I hadn't thought... but you're probably right."

"I would have let your legal process about the custody take its course," Jacinth told him, her face serious. "Often the natural way is best. Molly not speaking changed the situation, though. Once she told us that, there wasn't any way I was going to allow things to drag on. And," she added with her mischievous twinkle, "it was totally within the scope of your wish, which was to have your kids back."

He looked at her with renewed curiosity. "I haven't had time to even think about that. Is it really three wishes, like in the story? And is there a time limit on these wishes?"

"Nope," she replied cheerfully. "That is... yes, three wishes, and no, there's no time limit. Take all the time you need, Douglas. One wish down, two to go."

He grinned at her. "Don't you have to call me 'Master?'"

Jacinth aimed a steely look at him. "Not in this lifetime, buddy."

They both laughed.

"I think I'm actually starting to believe it," he said ruefully, running his fingers through his hair. "I know it's impossible... but here we are, and there are my kids. It's hard *not* to believe. Even when Arnie called and said they'd found them, I couldn't believe it would be so easy."

CHAPTER 4

IT WASN'T GOING to be all *that* easy, after all, he thought as he looked at Benny's scared, apprehensive face a few hours later.

"Benny." He squatted down to the boy's level, holding his gaze reassuringly. "It's very safe. Planes don't usually crash, or fly into buildings, I promise. Those were accidents."

"Mom said they did," Benny told him, fear in his voice. "She was always watching plane crashes on the news. She watched them over and over."

Was that how Lilian had planned to keep him from taking the kids if he found them? Douglas had to wonder. Certainly, she'd always had a taste for the morbid and the sensational, but to deliberately implant a fear of flying in a young child when she had taken the children the width of the continent away from him, was going too far. Molly looked scared too, even abandoning Jacinth to cling to her brother's hand. Tears welled up in those bottomless blue eyes, and her lower lip trembled ominously. If he was going to put these two on the plane, it was going to have to be by brute force.

Exchanging a glance with Jacinth, he saw his opinion mirrored in her face. They had two choices. They could find another mode of travel to New York, or carry two screaming, terrified children onto the airplane. Douglas had never considered himself lacking in courage, but his nerves quailed at the graphic image that conjured up.

"Okay, okay, don't panic," he told them. "Give me a couple of minutes here and I'll think of something."

He moved a few feet away from the car where they all stood, still in the parking lot at the zoo. Jacinth followed, and he lowered his voice to consult with her.

"What am I supposed to do? Dammit, we're three thousand miles from home! Did Lilian do this on purpose?"

Jacinth gnawed on her lower lip, feeling her brows pull together as she pondered.

"Probably," she agreed. "I think you're going to have to rent the car all the way to New York, Douglas."

His grimace was rueful. "That distressing possibility occurred to me. At least that would be better than taking the bus or the train, which are our only other options. Four days in a car with two young children, though, is my idea of a nightmare. They're so little, and it's been so long since we've been together, we're complete strangers to each other. This is definitely not how I'd choose to get to know each other again."

Jacinth twinkled at him. "You have a nanny," she reminded him. "And once you're home, you have your job to go to. This might turn out for the best for both you and the children. By the time we get to New York you'll have established a rapport with them.

Enthusiasm fired in her, and she felt a burst of excitement. "It'll be fun, Douglas. We can play car games, and I can read them stories, and we'll buy some of those children's sing-along CD's.

We can eat at truck stops and roadside diners along the way, then stop at motels in the afternoon. The children can nap, then we can go to dinner, and maybe swim in the motel pool in the evening. We can buy postcards and a camera and take lots of pictures."

She watched Douglas hopefully as he thought this over. Driving across America wasn't something she'd ever have thought of doing, or even wanting to do, but now she was seized with a great longing. Perhaps it was because of the presence of Douglas and the children, having someone to share this great new adventure with.

"It doesn't sound like such a bad idea, when you put it that way," Douglas admitted. "Maybe this could work after all."

Hope sprang up in her breast as another thought occurred to her. "If we're not going to fly out from here tonight, could we stay one more day and go to Disneyland tomorrow?"

Douglas broke into laughter. "Okay, yes, we'll go to Disneyland."

Hearing him, Benny let out a whoop of excitement, and Molly's eyes shone like stars. Douglas held up a hand for silence.

"But we're not staying late," he warned them. "I'm not fighting this kind of traffic on a Monday morning. We'll leave Disneyland before it gets dark so we'll be well out of the city before we find a motel for the night. No arguments when I say it's time to leave. Agreed?"

He noted with amusement that Jacinth joined in with Benny in assuring him that was fine, while Molly nodded her head vigorously, the curly blond bangs flopping in her eyes. She was so adorable, he wanted to scoop her in his arms and hold her tight. His chest constricted, and his eyes stung a little as he looked at his kids. He loved them both so much.

"I owe you," he told Jacinth, his voice hoarse with the emotion he couldn't suppress. "I owe you a lot. There's nothing in the world that means as much as my kids."

After getting the children seat belted into the car, Molly in the booster seat he'd requested from the car rental agency, Douglas' brain began to clear and to plan. He'd had so little time to think through all of this, he felt like he was being thrust inexorably forward, with no chance to catch his breath or figure out what was happening to him. One way or another, he'd been racing since the moment last night when a woman's voice had announced his steak was burning. It was time, he decided, to regain a little control over the situation.

Getting into the car, he looked around before turning the key in the ignition, holding up a hand for attention.

"First things first," he announced. "We have to get you kids some clothes."

There was a groan from the back seat, and Benny rolled his eyes expressively.

"Clooothes," he whined, drawing the vowel out plaintively. His daughter seemed equally unmoved, regarding Douglas with an unwavering stare.

"I think it's a good idea," Jacinth told Benny, clearly trying to be conciliating. "You can't wear those same clothes for days on end."

Benny's brow clouded in something close to a pout.

"I like these clothes," he insisted.

"Yes, and they're very nice." Jacinth managed to infuse more admiration in her voice than Douglas would have been able to, and he stared at her in appreciation for her tactics. "Have you had them for long?"

"That lady brought them for us this morning," Benny told

them proudly. "She said the ones we had on were un... un... un-something."

Probably unspeakable, Douglas thought grimly, if Lilian had still been spending every available dollar on her liquor and neglecting the kids' well-being the way she had before he'd gotten custody.

Unenthusiastic silence emanated from the back seat of the car during the short drive to a nearby mall Douglas had seen off the freeway on their way to the zoo. Once inside the mall, however, Benny gripped Douglas' hand tightly, staring around in awe.

"*New* clothes?" the boy asked, as if it were something wonderful. "You're going to buy us *new* clothes?"

At Douglas' nod, Benny let out a whoop of ecstasy. "Molly, did you hear that? Dad's going to buy us *new* clothes!"

Molly just looked, her eyes even bigger as she stared about her at the myriad of shops, the bustling people. Douglas noticed that her clutch on Isabel tightened, and she looked more than a little scared. It was pretty clear, Douglas thought, biting back a rising fury, that they'd never... or at least, rarely... seen the inside of a mall. Much less had anything bought for them there. Beside him, he noticed that Jacinth was blinking away faint moisture from the corners of her eyes.

An hour later, trudging from the mall under the burden of dozens of bags and various assorted items... not all of them clothing... they were almost to the parking lot when Benny came to a sudden halt.

"Dad! We didn't get any clothes for Miss Jas."

Benny had struggled so hard with Jacinth's name, she'd told him earlier just to call him Jas.

"Oh, no," Jacinth replied sunnily. "I don't need any. I have plenty of clothes in my suitcase in the car."

Caught off guard, Douglas responded instinctively. "You do?"

Benny gave him a questioning look, but Jacinth's eyes twinkled responsively.

"I do now," she told Douglas *sotto voce* a few minutes later. "It's a good thing he hadn't had a look in the trunk before he mentioned it, though."

"A very good thing." Douglas' response was heartfelt.

Arriving in Anaheim, Douglas chose one of the large hotels at random and booked them a small suite with a living room and kitchenette, and a bedroom with two queen beds.

"Gals in one bed, guys in the other," he told his small family, gesturing to the beds with a sweep of his hand. "Molly gets first pick."

Benny narrowed his eyes suspiciously.

"Does she always get to pick?"

"Of course not," Jacinth jumped in. "We'll take turns. Tomorrow you get to choose."

"Okay." Apparently satisfied, he lost interest in the proceedings and wandered into the kitchenette to look inside the small refrigerator there.

Molly, who'd begun to droop, crawled onto the nearest bed and curled up, her thumb going into her mouth. She was tired, Douglas thought with sudden guilt. She was so small, and they'd been on the go all day long. He'd been so caught up in enjoying being with them, it hadn't occurred to him that she'd need a nap, or that it had been a very long day for a four-year-old. She'd even forgotten her beloved doll, leaving Isabel on the sofa in the living room. He turned at a light touch on his shoulder.

"I'll get her bathed and changed," Jacinth told him, her lovely lips curving in a smile. "It might be best if you sent out for some food, or you and Benny could get an order to go from that restaurant we saw on the corner. We'll eat here and she can go straight to sleep."

"Thank you." He cast a worried glance at Molly, seeing suddenly how tiny she was. "I didn't think... I didn't realize..."

"There's no harm done. She's just a little tired. She had a wonderful time. Don't beat yourself up, Douglas. But go get some food so she can eat before I put her to bed."

With a firm push, Jacinth turned him and propelled him into the living room. The door to the bedroom was shut firmly behind him.

"Well, Benny, what shall it be?" Douglas asked. "Do we order pizza to be delivered, or go see what the restaurant has?"

"No pizza," Benny begged, wrinkling his nose in distaste. "I hate pizza."

The fervent passion in his voice, the pleading in Benny's blue eyes, so like his sister's, told Douglas more than words of too many nights of delivered pizza. Too many nights when Lilian, driven to distraction by the pleas of her hungry children, had impatiently phoned for pizza delivery. It had been a whopping three hundred dollars owed to a local pizza company in one month that had finally alerted Douglas to his wife's neglect of the children. They had already been divorced by then, but he hadn't fought her for custody initially, believing that the children were better off with their mother. The accountant for the pizza company, looking for payment for an impressive stack of bounced checks, had contacted Douglas. Only a brief investigation had been needed to uncover the real state of affairs. Douglas had paid for the checks and the huge fees, not wanting to see his children's mother go to jail for kiting checks, but he'd immediately filed for custody.

"The restaurant it is," Douglas announced, tweaking the

boy's nose. Benny's delighted laugh filled him with satisfaction. He'd missed the children's voices, their laughter, these last two years.

THE BATH APPEARED to revive Molly somewhat, and Jacinth dressed her in the cute pink sleeper with white lambs that they'd gotten at the mall, and brushed out the silky golden curls.

"There!" She pronounced, sitting back on her heels. "All ready for dinner once your dad and Benny get back."

Her heart seemed to almost overflow as the little girl stretched out her arms to be held. She rose, and sat on the bed, pulling Molly into her arms, nuzzling the curly, damp mop of hair as the child cuddled against her. It was sweet to sit here with Molly, rocking back and forth a little and crooning an old Persian lullaby. When they got home, she'd see about getting a rocking chair.

It wasn't much longer before Douglas and Benny returned with a huge sack of hamburgers and fries. Not particularly great nutrition, and it was probable that Disneyland wasn't likely to be much better. Tomorrow evening she'd talk with Douglas, and they could plan ahead and make sure the children got proper meals.

"It's a summer evening, across the street from Disneyland," Douglas told her in an undertone as he cut one of the burgers into quarters for Molly. "Every restaurant is full to capacity, and anything other than hamburgers was going to take a while."

"At least these are proper hamburgers, thick and juicy." She took a large bite of hers, humming with approval. "And the fries are nice and crisp outside, and soft inside."

When Benny slid from his chair after demolishing his burger, announcing his intention of watching television, Molly instantly joined him. Worried, Douglas stood up, intending to put her in bed, but Jacinth shook her head at him.

"It won't hurt her to stay up a little longer. It will be better for her not to sleep so soon after eating. She will fall asleep in front of the television very quickly, and then we can tuck her into bed."

Half an hour later they were carrying into the bedroom not only Molly but Benny, too. Both children were so worn out that neither of them stirred as they were put to bed.

"How do you know so much about children?" Douglas asked after they returned to the living room.

"Don't ask," she warned laughingly. "And no... I have never had children. I will, one day. When I am ready."

"Oh and by the way... Nice catch there in the parking lot," Douglas said, rubbing the back of his neck. "I almost blew it."

"Me too." She grimaced, feeling rueful at the memory. "I forgot I'd need to have more clothes too."

She shot him a mischievous look. "Unless you wanted me wearing this same type of clothes? As befitting the nanny?"

Douglas looked at the pantsuit outfit she still wore, feeling distaste. While undoubtedly professional looking, it did nothing for her.

"I liked what you wore when I first saw you better," he commented, unable to resist teasing her. "It was so... uh... Hollywood."

Jacinth laughed aloud, her eyes sparkling in delight. In a twinkling she had changed into faded jeans and a loose-fitting t-shirt of a bright fuchsia color, settling herself comfortably against the sofa cushions. From nowhere a hairbrush appeared in her hand, making Douglas blink, and she began to brush her heavy mane of ebony hair with long, firm sweeps of the brush.

"Isn't it awful?" she agreed. "The other Djinn always tease

me. But I think the costume makes it easier for people to accept me when I first appear, because I look like what they'd expect a genie to look like. As hard a time as you had believing in me last night, what if I had shown up dressed like this?"

She indicated the t-shirt and somewhat shabby jeans with a sweep of her hand. There was something in what she said, he decided. Still...

"But when you're dressed like that doesn't it give some guys ideas? I mean, what if you have to obey a wish for... well..." Douglas fumbled to a halt, not knowing how to put the question tactfully. Jacinth, however, appeared to understand what was in his thoughts.

"The kind of men that would make such a wish would not find my bottle. Wish Bearers choose the type of wishes we grant, but in a round-about way. Basically, the magic of the vessel attracts the kind of person who would make the wishes that the Djinn inside it would choose to grant. If you understand?"

Douglas pondered that a moment. "So you go about helping single fathers get their children? Do you help single mothers too?"

The dark head tilted, and he got the impression that Jacinth was studying him intently.

"Actually, no, I don't. You were a surprise to me. There are Djinn who specialize in such concerns, who work exclusively with children. It is very odd that you didn't pick up the vessel of such a one."

"So what is it you specialize in?"

"People in need," she said simply. "Good people who are desperate, who need only a helping hand but cannot find one. People who have the capacity to be happy, if the barriers were removed. Me, I remove the barriers."

Douglas' gaze went to the door of the bedroom where his children slept, little mounds under the covers.

"I can be happy... with my children. It's all I wanted."

His attention turned back to the vibrant young woman before him, and he studied her curiously.

"What about you, Jacinth? What is it you want?"

She pondered this, putting away her brush and tucking her bare feet with their daintily painted toenails under her and curling up in the sofa cushions rather in the manner of a cat. It seemed to be her favorite position.

"I like to help. I like to make people feel good. To know that I've made a difference in their lives. I like being Djinn."

"So which is right, Djinn or genie?" He asked, curious. "You seem to use them interchangeably."

"Okay." She grinned at him, tucking a long strand of hair behind one ear. "Djinn Etymology 101. Either is correct, genie is the anglicized version of the Arabic word Djinni, a single Djinn. But the word Djinn is both the plural, and the collective term; that is, more than one Djinni is Djinn, but also you would use Djinn to speak of the race of Djinn, the way you would use the word man when speaking of mankind."

Her eyes sparkled. "There's also a word for a female, Djinniri. But to keep it simple amongst English speakers we just use Djinn."

Holding up his hands in surrender, Douglas laughed. "Djinn. Got it."

He glanced into the darkened bedroom. "Benny hasn't said a word about his mother."

"Don't ask him. He'll tell you about things when he's ready."

With a sigh, Douglas nodded. "It's so hard, not knowing..."

Jacinth leaned forward, her slender fingers clasping his hand.

"They weren't abused, Douglas." Her eyes were steady and earnest. "I can't read their minds... some Djinn can, but that's not one of my talents. But I would know. The most that they've missed, has been love. Just love them. Let them know you want them and that you care. That's what they need most from you."

CHAPTER 5

IT HAD BEEN years since Douglas had been to Disneyland. He'd spent his first summer break from college with his dorm mate and best friend, Troy, touring the country in an old beat-up Chevy van. That vehicle would have made his parents proud, he recalled with a fond grin. They'd done all the usual tourist stuff... the Arch in St. Louis, Graceland in Memphis, the Painted Desert and the Grand Canyon, the Alamo in Texas... and they'd gone to Disneyland. It was a wonderful summer, the last real vacation he'd had. The next semester at college he'd met Lilian, and they were married the summer he graduated.

"Dad! Hey, Dad!" Benny's voice jerked him out of his reverie. "Can I have a Mickey Mouse balloon?"

Both children looked at him with such pleading eyes, it was hard to resist. Past experience came to his rescue, and he hardened his heart.

"Not just now," he explained, kneeling down to look them in the eyes. "We're going to be going on rides, and the balloons will be in the way, maybe even get popped or lost."

"We could get them on the way out, when we leave," Jacinth suggested. He gave her a grateful glance as his kids agreed with enthusiasm, Benny cheering and Molly bouncing with excitement, joy on her little face.

"In the meantime," Jacinth continued, casting Douglas a look that he had already learned meant mischief, "let's all get mouse ears."

Douglas gave in with good grace, chuckling at Benny when the boy danced ahead of them into the huge building that housed a myriad of Disney toys, clothes, jewelry, and who knew what else.

"All of us?" he murmured under his breath, for Jacinth's ears. Her warm laugh had him tingling right to his toes, as did the sparkling smile she sent his way.

"All of us."

"It'll be a cold day in..." he glanced at Molly, clinging to his hand as she gazed about her in wide-eyed awe, "in a hot place before I wear mouse ears."

Jacinth just grinned. "We'll see."

He shot her a sideways look, as new possibilities regarding Djinn magic occurred to him. Could she do magic that he did *not* wish for? He'd have to remember to ask her. In the meantime, the only way he was wearing mouse ears would be if she magicked them onto him.

Speaking of mouse ears... he realized with a start that he had lost sight of Benny. Heart pounding, his ears ringing, he looked around wildly, pushing forward through the crowds of people around him looking for the small tow-headed boy. A hand tugged at his elbow and he looked around. Jacinth shook her head at him.

"It's okay. You don't have to panic, Douglas. Nothing can happen to the children when I am here. We will speak with them about this, however."

Her lips curved in a warm smile, and she slid her hand down his arm to clasp his fingers, squeezing reassuringly. She tilted her head off to his right, and he looked in that direction. A few feet from where they stood an elderly lady turned away from the cash register, and with a sigh of relief, Douglas saw his son at the counter, peering at a display of watches.

"I didn't think... I know how important it is," he drew an arm over his damp brow. His heart was still thudding with the remnants of panic. "How could I have forgotten not to lay down that law with them? There's nothing more important, and I forgot."

She pointed through the doorway. "Let's take them out to that cafe in the square. You get a table and get them settled, while I get us all some lemonade. Then we'll all have a serious talk about safety."

"That's a plan."

The talk turned out to be considerably easier than he'd expected... and far more disturbing. Hardly had he launched into a carefully--if quickly--planned speech, than Benny interrupted.

"Oh, I know. So we don't get taken by a ped... pedo... something."

Douglas felt his jaw drop as he stared at his son. Beside him, he heard Jacinth's horrified gasp.

"Mom likes to watch all those crime shows," Benny went on, apparently unaware of the consternation his casual words had caused. "I always took really good care of Molly to be sure those bad guys didn't get her. I always make her hold my hand when we're out. Except now," he added, "'cause she's holding your hand or Miss Jases."

Gathering his wits, Douglas nodded in approval. "That's

good, Benny. But you need to stick with us, too. You don't have to be holding our hand all the time, but you do need to stay right by my side. It doesn't take any time at all for someone to... to abduct a child."

"Seven seconds," Benny stated knowledgeably, again leaving Douglas speechless. "But I'd scream if somebody tried. I'd scream real loud."

"If you had a chance," Jacinth put in gently. "Sometimes they don't give you that chance, you know."

Benny looked thoughtful. "Oh."

"If you can't see us, we can't see you," Douglas told him. "Especially in a crowded place like this. When you were over looking at the watches, we couldn't see you. People had gotten in between us."

"Think if you were out with Molly, and you looked around and she was gone. You couldn't see her anywhere. How would you feel?" Jacinth prompted gently.

Benny visibly paled, his eyes widening in alarm. "Scared! I'd be about half crazy to find her."

Jacinth nodded. "And that's just how your dad felt for that one instant he couldn't see you, a few minutes ago."

"Wow." Benny's apologetic gaze met Douglas'. "I'm sorry, Dad. I won't do it again. I'll be real careful, I promise."

"How about you, sweet girl," Jacinth touched Molly's nose, making the little girl giggle. "Do you promise to stay right with your dad and Benny and me, and not get out of sight?"

Molly nodded, her golden curls bouncing. The subject changed to what section of the park they'd visit next, but across the table, Douglas' eyes met Jacinth's. Words weren't needed, Douglas thought, to know that they were thinking the same thing. What the hell had Lilian been doing, exposing the children to such shows? Yes, kids needed to know to be safe and stay with a responsible adult at all times but for God's sake...!

"Dad? Hey, Dad!" Benny pulled on his shirt, catching his attention. "Can we go to Fantasyland first? We want to go on Peter Pan ride and the carousel. Can we?"

Douglas laughed, reaching out to ruffle his son's hair. Pure joy at being able to do so rushed through him. How long had it been since he'd felt this happy?

"Of course we can."

LOOKING like mother and daughter in their jeans and identical Mickey Mouse t-shirts, Jacinth and Molly went around on a ribbon-bedecked carousel horse, Molly firmly lodged in Jacinth's lap. Their dark and fair hair, both caught up in pigtails, mingled over the bright red shirts. Molly was laughing, as was Benny on the prancing pony beside them. Douglas stood outside the rail taking pictures. He couldn't get enough pictures of them. It was past noon, and already he'd had to make a trip to the camera shop to get another memory card for the digital camera he'd bought at the mall the day before.

After adjusting his mouse ears, which always seemed to be sliding off to one side or the other, he turned the LCD screen on and scrolled back to the one he'd taken of Jacinth. She'd been sitting alone on the carousel horse, waiting for him to hand Molly up to her. With red yarn tying her hair into two long ebony pigtails and her small feet stuffed into tennis shoes, she hardly looked older than the children. But there was a rounded curve to her hips that was far from childlike, and the thin cotton shirt clung lovingly to her high, full breasts.

Even preoccupied with his children, Douglas had a hard

time taking his eyes from Jacinth's enticing form. It wasn't just the sexy curves, the slumbering sensuality in her dark eyes and full lips that drew his eyes to her time and time again. She had an innate joy of life, experiencing everything to its full and reveling in it. As for the magic, he still wasn't sure about that. He had to accept that she was what she said. It was beyond dispute by now. The problem was, she seemed so alive, so vital, he kept forgetting that she wasn't going to be here always. That she'd only be here until she'd granted him two more wishes. Forgetting that she was not, in fact, a human woman.

"Dad! Dad!"

Jolted out of his thoughts, Douglas realized the carousel had stopped, and Benny was running towards him. Jacinth wasn't far behind, Molly propped on her hip. It seemed utterly natural to him to gather her into his arms, child and all, and drop a light kiss on that lush, inviting mouth.

He felt her instinctive response, the soft lips molding to his, her slight form pressing against him as she leaned into his embrace for a long moment.

"Oh!" With a gasp she fell back, her eyes wide and startled. She looked almost scared, poised as if she wasn't sure whether she should run.

"I'm sorry," he told her. "I shouldn't have done that. It just... it seemed so natural. You and me, and the kids."

"Like family." She nodded, settling Molly more comfortably on her hip, her expression serious. "But you mustn't forget. There can't be anything between us."

"Miss Jas! Miss Jas!" Heedless of their conversation, Benny tugged at her hand.

"What is it, honey?" Jacinth ruffled the boy's tousled hair affectionately.

"How come you've got different shoes on?" he wanted to know.

Instinctively Douglas looked down. He hadn't even realized that she'd changed, even though he'd noticed the sandals she'd worn this morning when they left the motel. He'd particularly noted how they'd shown off her small, well-shaped toes, with their pink nail polish. Now she wore pristine white sneakers.

Jacinth smiled at Benny.

"I carried these in my purse in case my feet got tired." She didn't even bat an eye as she lied without hesitation. "I changed them while we were on the Peter Pan ride."

Douglas eyed her purse. It wasn't very big, but then, neither were the sneakers. Benny, though, accepted her explanation without question.

"Nice catch yourself," Douglas whispered to her as they followed the boy through the crowd.

"He's very quick," Jacinth admitted. "I didn't think he'd notice. I did wait until we were in the darkest part of the ride."

"He always was as sharp as a tack," Douglas said, feeling a surge of pride in his son as his eyes rested on Benny's eager face and bright eyes as the boy waited for them at the entrance to the next ride.

"I'll have to be more careful. I have a tendency to not think before acting," Jacinth confided, rather unnecessarily. Douglas had already figured that out and had to bite back a smile.

As they stood in line, Jacinth told him that she'd never been to Disneyland.

"It's one of those things I always meant to do, but never got around to," she confessed, wrinkling her small nose.

He wondered why she hadn't just popped right into the amusement park if she'd wanted to see it. Were there some sort of rules against that kind of thing, he wondered? He had so many questions he wanted to ask her, but couldn't with the children about. Even in the hotel suite, he couldn't be positive that one or both children might not be awake, listening. Little pitchers have big ears, he remembered his mother saying.

Jacinth chatted happily with Benny and with other people as they waited in line, and teased Molly to make the little girl giggle. She appeared to have forgotten the embrace, but Douglas couldn't stop thinking of it. He remembered clearly how natural she'd felt in his arms, her soft warmth against him, the feel of her lips against his, her vibrant response.

She was an honest-to-god, card-carrying genie. Could things get any more complicated?

CHAPTER 6

By the time the SUV nosed around the corner onto Douglas' street late at night four days later, Jacinth was ready for a long bath and a much longer sleep. Preferably in her own chaise lounge with its silken throw and down-filled pillows, flickering candles casting shadows about the walls, and incense wafting from the brass brazier that hung overhead.

Douglas turned his head as she sighed. "Tired?"

"A little," she admitted. "It's good to be home finally."

Home? Where did that thought come from? This was Douglas' home, not hers. Yet, the door to the room in her thoughts opened onto the hallway in Douglas' house.

Douglas frowned. "We didn't think to make a room up for you. Can you sleep on the sofa for tonight? Tomorrow I'll arrange to have a bedroom set delivered for the guest room."

She burst out laughing. "Douglas, have you forgotten? I've got somewhere to go. Let's just get the children into bed."

Douglas' low laughter joined hers as he pulled into the driveway and killed the engine.

"Yes, I guess I had forgotten," he admitted. "I do have a spare bedroom though, and we have to consider the kids. How do we explain if one of them comes looking for you in the night and you're not there?"

He hesitated, his look questioning. "That is... if you're going to stay a while longer? I don't know we didn't talk about..."

Jacinth reached over to pat his hand, and opened her door. "Let's get the children into bed first. Then we'll talk."

Molly scarcely stirred as Jacinth lifted her from the car seat and carried her into the house. Douglas supported Ben, who stumbled sleepily, rubbing his eyes.

"Do I still have my own room?" The little boy asked as Douglas opened the front door.

Jacinth saw Douglas' jaw set at this reminder of what his ex-wife had put them all through these last two years.

"Yes," he told the boy. "It's just the same, and Molly's too."

"Cool." Ben yawned mightily.

It didn't take long to get them tucked into bed. Molly never did wake up, even when Jacinth undressed her and put her into her pajamas, and Douglas reported that Benny was asleep before the lights were out.

"Man, it's good to be home." Douglas collapsed on the sofa with a sigh of relief, then pulled himself up. "Oh, geez, I need to call Mom!"

He pulled his cell phone from its holder on his belt and dialed, then after a bit, he hung up.

"Nobody's home. They either went to bed and turned off the ringer, or they're out dancing somewhere."

"Out dancing? That's sweet." Jacinth imagined Douglas' parents twirling around the dance floor in a waltz, or jitter-bugging across the floor. Although, it was unlikely his parents were much older than their mid-fifties, so it was far more probable they'd be rocking around the clock to Elton John. She liked Elton John herself.

Jacinth tucked her feet up under her in the over-stuffed chair she'd curled up in, and conjured up some steaming Turkish coffee for them both. Douglas jumped as a cup appeared on the coffee table in front of him, and swore under his breath.

"Geez, you could give a guy some warning," he grumbled, but reached for it gratefully. He sipped, closing his eyes in ecstasy. "Mmmm. This stuff is good. I may never sleep again, however. I think I feel my toes curling."

She laughed, enjoying her own taste of the rich brew. "It's my mother's recipe. Nobody makes coffee like the old desert bedouins."

Douglas looked at her with interest. "A bedouin? Is that what she was?"

"Mmhmm." Jacinth sipped her coffee, feeling the warmth of it spreading through her veins. "A thousand years ago the Persian Empire was the center of knowledge, but outside the cities, the people were either settled farmers or desert nomads.

"And...?" he prompted, wondering where she was going with this.

"She was born to a Djinn who'd served in one the nomadic tribes for centuries, and she grew up with them."

She was watching him expectantly, and Douglas struggled to put the puzzle pieces together. "Oh, now, wait a minute... You're not telling me..."

Jacinth nodded, her eyes holding that mischievous twinkle that warned him she was about to say something outrageous.

"My mother is a thousand years old. She was only a hundred when I was born."

"You..." He stared at her, words failing him.

"I'm nine hundred years old." She twinkled at him, holding up one hand, with the thumb and forefinger held slightly apart. "And a little bit over."

Douglas closed his eyes briefly. "I so did not want to know that."

He leaned forward, pinning her with the sternest look he could summon.

"I ask you, do I look like a fairy tale kind of guy? Magic lamps and genies and all that stuff? These kinds of things just don't happen... and if they do, they don't happen to guys like me. I'm a working man. I'm a veterinarian, for God's sake. You don't get more ordinary than that."

"But it did happen to you," she pointed out with the utmost simplicity.

Douglas stared at her for a long minute, digesting that.

"Yes. I guess it did. So... now what?"

"I don't mind staying a while, helping Molly and Ben to settle in, and give you a chance to find the right person to care for them. I'll stay in the extra bedroom so it seems normal to the children and any of your friends and family who come by." Her dimples appeared. "And you still have two more wishes, of course."

"Um, this wish business," Douglas began, choosing his words carefully. "Do I have to be careful what I say or the next person I get annoyed with will wind up with a carrot attached to his ear or something?"

Her laughter was clear and joyous. He could have listened to her laughing forever.

"No," she finally managed to gasp. "No, Douglas, I can tell wishful thinking from a true wish. A true wish has to be from your heart."

"Is there some kind of time limit on this?"

Jacinth shook her head. "No. But if you know your wishes, Douglas, then make them, without fear that I'll leave you in the lurch. I'll stay and help you with the children until you don't need me, regardless of the wishes."

"Well, that's just it. I don't know what to wish for." Douglas sat back against the sofa cushions, his coffee finished. "I've thought about it a lot these last few days while we were driving across the country. I mean, who wouldn't think about it. But it's not so easy. People always joke around, what would you get if you could have anything you wanted? I always said I'd wish for a Lamborghini. But now that I could have one... when I have just two wishes for anything I want in the whole world... in the greater scheme of things, a Lamborghini somehow doesn't seem so important. And I don't know what I do want."

"And then, too," he continued, "if I use my two wishes and get anything I want, and later Lilian comes and kidnaps the children again, what the hell good would a Lamborghini do me when I could have saved those wishes and instead had you to find them again for me? But then again, I can hardly ask you to wait around for the next decade and a half until Molly turns eighteen."

Jacinth's piquant face lit with amusement, her eyes twinkling at him. "That's not so long. I was stuck for a whole century in the house of this dreary family of Spaniards, very cold and austere, and utterly joyless. Then one day a maid was polishing my teapot and stroked it in just the right manner. She was very pretty, and she loved the oldest son of the house. I granted her wish to marry the young man. They had beautiful children, and everyone was much happier after that, not dismal anymore, and I was finally able to move on."

Douglas wasn't sure if he was fascinated or horrified. Maybe a bit of each.

"You lived all that time with them, and they didn't know you were a... a genie?"

"Oh, no." Jacinth shook her head with a frown. "They didn't know about me at all, except, of course, the maid at the end. I stayed in my teapot. It was a very bad time then, when all that was happening with England and Spain, and Elizabeth reviling Philip, and the Inquisition and all. Possibly it was just as well that no one knew; anyone I helped then might have been burned at the stake for a witch if any wish that I granted made them suspect."

She was talking about the fifteenth century, Douglas realized somewhat belatedly. Columbus was just discovering America! Incredible!

"So just owning the teapot isn't enough?"

"It's part of the magic," Jacinth explained. "The vessel is enchanted to attract only those I wish to serve. For me, I don't like those who are hungry for power or money, or who are unkind. I enjoy positive people, and good people who are needy. The bad ones, when they see my teapot they have no interest in it. They won't buy it and take it home, or try to use it. It attracts only the right kind of wisher for me, do you see?"

"So what if the right person is attracted to your teapot, but gives it as a present, a wedding gift or something, to the wrong kind of person?"

"That's how I wound up with that Spanish family." She made a moue of distaste. "They'd acquired my teapot as a gift, and passed it down from generation to generation as an heirloom which they thought was hideously ugly, but very valuable, so of course they kept it. I thought I would never get out of there! But it all turned out well in the end."

"The family stayed very happy," she added with an elfin smile. "I checked on them, their descendants, you know, now and again through the centuries, just to see how it was working. All my magic does well."

"So how did I end up with your teapot?" Douglas wanted to know. "I didn't even believe in magic."

"Yes, but you were just the kind of person that my teapot's magic would attract," Jacinth pointed out. "Perhaps you didn't believe, but that is not so important. You were a good person who was in desperate need and out of options. You needed something more."

"I needed a miracle," Douglas admitted. "I just didn't think I'd get one."

"Exactly! And voila! Here we are." She smiled at him and took a sip of her coffee, apparently satisfied.

Exhaustion was slowly creeping over him and he rose, stretching his back.

"We've got to get you set up for the night."

"Just show me the room, and I'll make myself at home," she assured him, rising gracefully. It still surprised him how small she was, for someone with such an indomitable will. She barely reached the top of his shoulder.

He led the way down the hall and opened a door at the far end, opposite his own. He grimaced, looking at the stacks of boxes scattered around.

"I always meant to organize these, get them into the storage shed out back," he said apologetically. "If you wouldn't mind, just for tonight... you know... zapping yourself a bed or something. Tomorrow I'll clear it out and get some furniture for you."

"I'll be fine," she assured him, tongue firmly in cheek. What Douglas didn't know wouldn't hurt him.

Douglas nodded. "Goodnight, then."

He stood looking down at her, as if reluctant to leave. She

felt the same pull, wanting to extend their time together, time alone. But it wasn't wise at all. She took a step back.

"Good night, Douglas."

Loud sobs slowly penetrated Douglas' sleep. Molly! He struggled up, pushing aside the fatigue that weighed him down. Not wasting time trying to find his slippers in the dark, he headed for the doorway. Just as he reached it, the hall light came on; Jacinth was awake too, pulling up the collar of a downy robe against the coolness of the early morning. She entered Molly's room two steps ahead of him, turning on not the bright overhead light, but the small lamp on the nightstand.

Molly was sitting up in bed, looking around with wide, scared wet eyes. Seeing Douglas, she held out her arms to him. Poor baby, Douglas thought, picking her up. He sat on the bed, holding her across his lap, and Jacinth sat beside them.

"Did you wake in the dark and not know where you were?" Jacinth asked.

The curly head nodded, Molly's face against Douglas' chest. He felt guilty. He hadn't thought of a night lite, or that Molly might wake in the night in a strange room and be afraid.

"We'll get a night lite for you tomorrow, honey," he assured her, stroking the soft curls. "If we leave the hall light on, do you think you could go back to sleep?"

Molly nodded again, slithering off his lap to curl up in the bed. He pulled the covers up to her chin, and leaned down to kiss her downy, slightly damp cheek.

"Good night, then. Sweet dreams."

He clicked the lamp off, and left the room. Jacinth was waiting for him in the hallway, looking not much older than Benny in the quilted robe that swathed her slight form, her long blue-black hair tumbling loose in waves to her waist. She looked as sleepy as Molly.

"Thank you," he said, resisting the urge to lean down to kiss her cheek too.

Jacinth looked surprised. "For what? I didn't do anything."

Lilian had never gotten up when the children cried out in the night. He'd been the one to comfort the nightmares, to sit up with them when they were ill.

"Thanks just for being here, and supporting me while I get the hang of being a daddy again."

Jacinth nodded, yawning like a lazy cat. Douglas smothered a chuckle.

"Go on back to bed," he told her. "I'll see you in the morning."

She stood by her door, hand on the knob, as he passed her and went into his own room.

"'Nite."

THE SOUND of giggles and high-pitched squeals from across the hall woke him. The sun was up, shining bright and warm with a sunbeam slanting across the bed covers. Douglas stretched, wiggling his toes under the blankets, enjoying the sensation of waking up at home, in his own bed, to the sound of his children's laughter. Molly and Benny. He let their presence in his home wash over him in a warm rush of happiness. His first day at home with his kids. It was a beautiful day.

A movement near the doorway caught his attention, and he turned his head to see blonde curls and a pair of deep blue eyes peeping around the door jam. He smiled.

"G'morning, honey." He held out his hand in invitation. The little girl ran across the room, clambering up onto the bed. She submitted to his fierce hug, then pulled back. She tugged on his hand, her little face alight with excitement, the big blue eyes beseeching him.

"Okay, okay." Douglas yawned mightily before throwing back the covers. "Give me a minute."

Molly tucked her legs under her, sitting cross-legged on the bed as he sat up, running his hands through his hair. She giggled, and he grinned at her.

"My hair's standing straight up, huh?"

She giggled again and nodded. He finger-combed it and stood up, his body protesting. Four days in a car did awful things to the joints. He shrugged his robe on over his pajamas and held his hand out to Molly.

"C'mon, let's go find the rest of the family."

Her little hand firmly clasping his, Molly led him across the hallway to Jacinth's room. Douglas came to an abrupt halt in the doorway. He blinked, looking around, wondering if he was actually still asleep and dreaming.

This wasn't the same room he'd left Jacinth in last night. Well, it was, technically. But it certainly didn't bear any resemblance at all to the jumbled storage area it had been. The boxes were gone... every last one of them. He assumed they were now in the storage shed he'd mentioned. Persian carpets covered the floor, their various patterns overlapping. Deep reds and glowing blues and greens combined to create a collage of colors. Douglas was no expert on carpets, but he rather thought these were in the "priceless" range should any be offered at, say, Christie's. Long cushions lined two walls, forming a kind of low L-shaped sofa. Pillows of various sizes, shapes, and colors were scattered along its length. A chaise lounge, in all its opulent Victorian glory, stood to his right.

In the far corner of the room, draperies hung from some kind of attachment on the ceiling and flowed to the floor, curtaining the bed. Low and wide, the bed also was overflowing with bright pillows, and the jumbled sheets and covers in jewel colors looked to be some kind of silky material. He had a sneaking suspicion they probably were real silk. A round table stood beside the bed, holding an oil lamp and an alarm clock, incongruous in this lush Middle Eastern ambiance. A brass bowl hung from the ceiling from which smoke lazily drifted upwards, accounting for the faint scent of sandalwood in the air, and a brass lamp was suspended above the sofa.

Jacinth and Benny were on the sofa, their heads together over a large picture book in Jacinth's lap. As Molly let go of Douglas' hand and ran forward, they both looked up. Jacinth smiled in welcome, managing to look both mischievous and guilty. And well she should, Douglas thought, fighting back his own smile.

"Hi, Dad!" Benny was totally unconcerned. "Look, we're reading Aladdin's Lamp. It's my favorite, and Miss Jas says it's her favorite too."

"Imagine that," Douglas muttered under his breath.

Jacinth, hearing, twinkled up at him.

"Did you sleep well?"

With a sigh, he surrendered to the inevitable. Going with the flow seemed to be the status quo around Jacinth, he decided. He came forward, lowering himself to sit beside her on the sofa. Instantly Molly cuddled into his lap, and he hugged his daughter to him. She smelled sweet and fresh, her curls soft and just a tiny bit damp. Jacinth must have given her a bath. The little girl wore a pink shirt and white overalls, but Benny was still in his pajamas.

Jacinth closed the book she held, smiling down at Benny.

"I'll tell you what. Why don't Molly and I go start breakfast, since we're both ready to go, while you two guys get showered and dressed?"

"What are we going to do today?" Benny wanted to know.

"It's Friday," Douglas answered. "I have today off, and the weekend, but I have to go to work on Monday. I thought today we'd go take a look at your school and get you registered for this fall."

A shadow crossed Ben's face. "Mom said I didn't have to go to school. She said I wouldn't like it, that the teachers were mean and strict."

What the hell? Douglas choked down the familiar surge of anger. Fortunately Jacinth responded, because he didn't think he could trust his voice.

"Everyone has to go to school, Benny. Maybe your mother had teachers that weren't nice to her, but that was a long time ago. You'll be in first grade, with other boys your age, and you'll have loads and loads of fun."

"Mom said I didn't have to. She said the other boys would beat me up." Benny's jaw set in a stubborn, mulish line. "She said she'd home... home..."

"Home school you?" Jacinth finished for him, and he nodded.

She sent Douglas a questioning look, and he shook his head. No way would Lilian be the least bit qualified to home school. More likely she didn't want the responsibility of getting Benny up every morning and get him off to school. And she'd have had to wash and dress him decently, and make him a lunch to take, if she didn't want to call the attention of social services. But what had she thought she was going to do? Let both kids grow up running wild while she slept all day and drank all night?

Benny looked up at Jacinth, blue eyes wide and pleading. "Can't you teach me, Miss Jas?"

Jacinth's startled gaze flew to Douglas. This was a complication they hadn't envisioned. He thought fast. This wasn't the time to tell the children Jacinth wouldn't be staying. They'd only just arrived, and now this complication of Benny's reaction to school. The kids had had enough upset in their lives. He shook his head slightly.

"Later," he mouthed silently.

She nodded, and turned her attention back to the boy at her side.

"How about if you wait a bit and see what you think? We'll go and meet the teacher, and you'll get to look at the school and the playground, see how the other kids there like it. Maybe, if it's okay, we could stop by the kindergarten class..."

Where, Douglas thought grimly, Benny should have already been this year.

"...and meet some of the boys and girls who'll be in your class in September." Jacinth continued. "Maybe some will live nearby and you can make friends. Then you'll have all summer to play and get to know them before school starts."

To Douglas' relief, this seemed to interest Benny enough to erase the scowl from his face. Apparently the prospect of having friends made the idea of school more palatable. Had the children not had any friends, there in California? What the hell had gone on out there? His frustrated glance rested on Jacinth. She patted his arm, her light touch soothing.

"Let's get going," she said suddenly, dumping Benny off her lap onto the floor. She followed the boy down, tickling him while he rolled back and forth on the carpet laughing. In a flash

Molly squirmed off Douglas' lap and joined in the fun. There was nothing wrong with his daughter's giggle box, Douglas decided, even if she didn't speak yet.

He stood up, and Jacinth followed, reluctantly it seemed to him. She appeared to enjoy romping as much as his kids did, her cheeks flushed with pleasure and her eyes sparkling.

"Okay, up you go, champ." Douglas hefted his giggling son and tossed him over his shoulder. "Let's go hit the showers."

Hearing the house phone rang, he crossed to his bedroom, with Benny laughing like a loon and kicking in mock protest.

"Yo."

"Douglas?" His mother sounded as if she weren't quite sure it was him. He grinned, and lowered Benny to the floor.

"Mom! Hi. I've got news for you."

"Tell me that's Ben I hear in the background?"

"Yes. They were in California, I just got back with them last night. Their babysitter saw them on a Missing Children flyer and called the number, and the police and Social Services picked the kids up before Lilian could get back and disappear with them again."

"It's been so long. I can hardly believe it." She sounded like she was crying a little. Douglas smiled. That was so Mom. "We'll come right away, Douglas. Are you doing okay? We could fly out tonight if that's not too soon for you. Or do you need time with them alone? How are they?"

"They're fine, Mom. Take it easy. And yes, you can come as soon as you want, but, um," he cleared his throat. He was going to have some explaining to do. "You'd better come up in the RV."

His mother tsk'd impatiently. "Have you still not cleared that room out yet, Douglas?"

"Yes! I... that is, everything's in the storage shed." That was true enough, even if he hadn't been the one to do it. "The thing is, I hired a nanny for the kids. She's staying in the spare bedroom."

"A nanny! How wonderful. What's she like? Are the kids going to take to her?"

Douglas grinned, listening to the sound of pots banging merrily in the kitchen and the cheerful laughter that floated down the hallway.

"Yeah, just fine. She drove back from California with us. The kids love her."

His mother fumbled for words. "Is she... that is, she won't give them up to Lilian like that other sitter did, will she?"

"Mom. You can't blame the sitter for that. It never occurred to me--to anyone--that Lilian would grab the kids and run. The sitter had no reason to think Lilian meant to do anything other than take them for the afternoon. And no, this nanny won't. Forewarned is forearmed, and all that."

"Did you get references?"

Douglas rolled his eyes. "Yes, Mom. In fact, she came from an agency. The, um, East Wind Nanny Service."

His mother's appreciative laughter told him that she'd caught the nuance of that.

"Oh, how wonderful!" She was still laughing. "I hope she isn't planning to leave when the wind changes?"

Douglas glanced around the exotically furnished room, the very essence of Jacinth lingering in her absence. "I hope not, Mom."

Benny was tugging at his pajamas. "Is that Gramma?"

"Hang on, Mom, here's Benny."

He handed the phone over, listening absently to the boy's chatter as he picked out jeans and a shirt to wear today. He'd have to find some way to forestall having to put Molly on the phone. He didn't want Mom to worry, as he knew she would if he told her Molly wasn't speaking. Maybe Molly would be talking by the time they got here from Florida. He hoped.

He was saved from his quandary by Benny himself.

"Molly's in the kitchen, making breakfast with Miss Jas. We're going out after to look at my school. Here's Dad."

Benny handed him back the phone. His mother was laughing.

"What a boy! I'm so glad you've got the children back, Douglas. Is Miss Jas your nanny?"

"Yes, her name is Jacinth, hard for the kids to pronounce. But Miss Jas is a very popular person around here."

"I can certainly see that. Well, I don't want to interrupt your breakfast, so I'll let you go. See you in a couple of days."

"Okay. Bye, Mom."

He hung up the phone, shaking his head. The idea of his mom meeting Jacinth was kind of scary. The two of them together. And whoo boy! Was he going to have some explaining to do when his mom saw his nanny was a very beautiful young woman.

God forbid Mom discover she was a genie as well!

CHAPTER 7

HALFWAY THROUGH BREAKFAST, DOUGLAS' pager went off.

"It's the clinic," he announced. "I knew I shouldn't have called last night to tell them I got back into town."

He looked around the table at his children's faces. Both of them had worn an air of excitement throughout the meal. He suspected they weren't accustomed to sitting down and eating together as a family. Now the smile was gone from Molly's little face, and she seemed to have retreated into herself. Benny was equally crestfallen, but apparently resigned to the adults in his life leaving them alone at meal time. Douglas made a quick decision.

"We're going to have some rules here," he announced, surprising them. "Our first rule, which I'll expect everyone to abide by, is regarding meals. Breakfast and dinner are family time. There'll be no interruptions. No phone calls, no television. Just us, being together. Okay?"

Molly nodded, her eyes shining, but Benny was more doubtful.

"Does that go for you too?"

Douglas nodded.

"Definitely. I can look at this to see who's called," he held up his pager. "But I won't be answering it until the meal is over. Not unless it's an absolute emergency, okay?"

"Okay!" Benny shouted and bounced in his chair.

When breakfast was over, Douglas made his phone call while Jacinth organized the children, Molly clearing the table and Benny putting the dirty dishes to soak in soapy water. He hung up the phone, feeling disappointment.

"I've got to go into the clinic this afternoon," he announced. At Benny's protest, he held up a hand. "Just for a short while, to catch up on a few things, and sign the staff's paychecks, which can't wait."

"Isn't there a park just a couple of blocks away?" Jacinth addressed the children. "After lunch, we could walk over and check out the playground while your Dad works."

Benny seconded this with wild enthusiasm. Douglas was grateful for Jacinth's rescue. He didn't want to leave the children at all, not this first day. He had no intention of putting his work before his children's welfare, but he'd been gone for an entire week without any advance notice at all, and there were things that needed his attention. His partners had been great about covering him so he could take the week off to bring the kids home, and he owed them.

With both children excited--too excited, in Douglas' opinion--at the prospect of a visit to the park, it wasn't hard to herd everyone out of the house right away. There was a lot to be done before lunch.

The visit to Benny's school was a stunning success. The first-grade teacher was so young that Douglas suspected the ink on her teaching credential was barely dry. She was, however, bubbling over with enthusiasm, and it was clear that her young pupils adored her. Better yet, on the visit to the kindergarten class, Benny discovered an old playmate from two years ago who lived just down the street from them. Upon learning that the boy, Will, would be in the same first-grade class next year, school won Benny's enthusiastic approval.

"That's a relief," Douglas murmured for Jacinth's ears only as they followed an ecstatic Benny out to the parking lot.

"I was afraid we'd find an older, by-the-rules type of teacher," she confided. "After what his mother told him, we'd never have gotten Benny to accept school willingly."

Douglas set his teeth. "I can't imagine what Lilian thought she was doing."

He said no more, however, as they'd reached the car where Ben and Molly were waiting impatiently.

"Where to now?" Benny wanted to know.

"Now we get groceries. And no," he warned, giving the children a strict look as he and Jacinth fastened their seatbelts. "We are *not* getting a lot of junk food. No soda, chips, or presweetened cereal. No cookies or cakes or Twinkies. So don't even bother asking."

Two hours later, the car groaning under the weight of sacks upon sacks of food, dry, canned, fresh and frozen, Douglas pulled into the driveway. The children burst from the car like they were spring-loaded, squealing like banshees. Jacinth and Douglas exchanged a resigned look.

"No junk food, huh?" she asked, raising an eyebrow at him. "No soda, chips, or presweetened cereal. No cookies or cakes. Oh, and *definitely* no Twinkies."

Douglas winced.

"They were on sale," he defended. "It's cheaper to buy a big box than just a couple of those little packages."

"You're completely under their thumbs," she corrected with a smile, amusement glowing in her dark eyes.

"Daaaa-aaaa-aad!" Benny's shout could have raised the dead, if volume was all that was required. The children were waiting outside the front door.

"Okay, we're coming." Exchanging glances, Douglas and Jacinth got out of the car, Douglas going to unlock the front door and Jacinth opening the trunk.

By the time the groceries were put away, Douglas had to leave for the veterinary clinic where he worked.

"But we haven't even had lunch," Benny protested. Douglas tweaked the boy's nose.

"I don't usually eat lunch, champ. Especially not after a big breakfast like Miss Jas cooked us this morning. Maybe if you ask her nicely, she could put together some sandwiches and you could take them with you to the park for a picnic."

"Wow! Can we?" Ben turned excited eyes on Jacinth. Even Molly was anxious, tugging on Jacinth's hand and looking up, pleading evident in her little face.

Jacinth beamed at them, apparently as thrilled with the idea as the children. "I think it's a great idea. You children find the napkins and pick out a few pieces of fruit, while I make us some sandwiches."

Douglas produced a basket from the garage for them to use on their picnic before taking himself off, pleased with how things were going so far. His children were not only safe, but well cared for and happy.

Jacinth waited until Douglas had left, then led the children into the living room and settled them side-by-side on the sofa.

"Now." She sat on the coffee table facing them, making eye contact with each child.

"This is serious, and I want you both to pay attention. We're going to have rules for going to the park. Well, these are rules for going outside the house at any time, not just for the park. Remember the rules your dad and I talked to you about at Disneyland? The first, number one rule is, that you *always* stay within my sight, and you never go anywhere... not to the bathroom, not to a water fountain... without telling me. I want a solemn promise from both of you that you'll always obey me in this."

Both children nodded earnestly, looking apprehensive. She didn't want to scare them, but it wasn't a safe world sometimes. No one could take them from her, of course, but if she drilled safety into their heads, they'd stay safe once she was gone, when they were with whoever he hired to watch them after she left. She found the idea of someone else taking care of Benny and Molly was oddly distasteful. She chased the intrusive thought away.

"Okay. Just remember. If you can't see me, then I can't see you. As long as you can always see me... and no playing hide-and-seek with me, either! ...then you're fine. And you will always come when I call you, instantly. Okay?"

Both children nodded vigorously, so she bounced to her feet, holding out a hand to each of them. "Okay! So, let's get going!"

The park was within easy walking distance, just three blocks away. It was large, with green lawns and sprawling trees, and even a small lake with ducks. Near the street was a playground surrounded by benches and picnic tables

Only by putting her foot down firmly and the use of her best "nanny" manner (taking her role model from one of the

Disney films she was so fond of), was Jacinth able to persuade Benny and Molly to eat their picnic lunch before racing off to explore the playground. After wolfing down sandwiches and fruit in a manner that had to be bad for their digestion, the children raced off to the slides, while Jacinth kept an eye on them from the comfort of a bench under a shady tree. When they tired of the slide, she joined them at the swings, pushing them both, and later spun the merry-go-round for them, so that by the time the streets began to fill with mothers bringing their children after school, Jacinth was as worn out as the children.

"I think it's time to go," she panted, giving the merry-go-round one last turn. "We need to start fixing dinner before your dad gets home."

It was a measure of the good time they'd had that neither child objected. They went to retrieve their picnic basket and started back towards the street.

"Miss Jas, look!"

On a park bench, sunning itself lazily, was the largest house cat Jacinth had ever seen. It was a tabby, but an unusual type, its coat long and thick. Rich auburn swirls darkened to mahogany along the creature's spine, against a tawny ginger background that faded to cream on the large splayed paws. The cat slept, its head on one extended paw, but the long, beautifully plumed tail swept gently to and fro.

"Can we pet him?" Ben wanted to know. Molly clasped Jacinth's hand tightly, looking up at her. Impossible to know if the little girl was interested or afraid.

Jacinth decided to answer honestly. "I'm not sure, Benny. It's not wise to approach a strange animal, not knowing if it's friendly. It's often best to wait to see if it will come to you."

"But he's sleeping," the boy pointed out.

Jacinth smiled. "Not really. Just dozing in the sun. And it's a she. All calicoes are girls. See her tail, how it moves, the tip swishing back and forth? She's paying attention. If something came near that made her feel afraid or disturbed, she'd come awake fast enough."

Benny looked up at her with oddly wise eyes. "So if she's awake, then she knows we're here and she's not bothered by us."

The child's logic was impossible to refute. Still, Jacinth hesitated, eyeing the animal. That was one big cat.

Cautiously she quested the animal's mind, seeking to know the cat's nature, if it would welcome a friendly approach by children. She smothered an audible gasp when her mental touch was expertly blocked.

The cat stirred, opening great golden eyes that gazed at them in benign tolerance.

"*I don't mind the human kits.*" The low, husky voice in her mind was amused.

A shapeshifter? Jacinth knew of such, naturally, but she'd never met one before.

"I think she'll let you pet her, as long as you're careful," Jacinth told the kids. "Slowly now. Never rush at animals, even if you know them."

Benny approached the bench cautiously, and stroked the thick fur. The cat's eyes half closed in ecstasy, and the animal began to purr.

"She's soft," Benny reported. "Are all cats soft like this?"

Jacinth felt the familiar stirring of anger at their carelessly cruel mother. The cat too bristled mentally.

This is a day of surprises. A Djinn, with two human kits who have never touched a cat before.

It's a long story. Jacinth had never spoken on a mental pathway before, but she found it easy, perhaps because the shapeshifter had established the communication. *The mother is the culprit, and these two are no longer in her care. I'm helping them settle in with their father.*

Ah. The cat fixed its golden gaze on Molly. *The she-kit is afraid.*

Molly was indeed clinging to Jacinth's hand, watching her brother with wide eyes. Jacinth bent to the little girl.

"Molly, would you like to pet the kitty? I'll come and pet her with you, if you want."

At Molly's hesitant nod, she led the girl forward.

"Here. Pet her nice, like this." She took Molly's little hand in her own and stroked it along the cat's silky fur. The purring grew louder. "The kitty likes that, Molly. Hear her telling you?"

She took her hand away and watched Molly bury her fingers in the cat's thick coat, a look of wonder on the little face. Benny looked up at her.

"I want to keep her. Can we take her home with us, Miss Jas?"

Jacinth laughed, ruffling the boy's curly hair.

"No, Benny. This one clearly has a good home, and even if she didn't, cats belong to themselves."

I wouldn't mind an invitation to dinner. The cat's mental voice sounded lazily amused. *Can you cook, Djinn?*

Jacinth might not know shapeshifters, but she knew an insult when she heard it.

"Of course I can cook!" The words were out of her mouth before she could stop them. Ben and Molly looked at her in surprise.

"Who are you talking to, Miss Jas?" Benny asked.

"Umm... I was just thinking out loud."

Jacinth was aware of feline amusement. *Stop that!*

Have you a name, Djinn?

Jacinth. And you?

I am Cat.

Of course. Why didn't she think of that? Jacinth refrained from rolling her eyes.

The cat's amusement deepened. *Katerina is my human name. I do indeed go by Cat.*

"Miss Jas?" Benny was tugging on her hand. She knelt down to the children's level.

"We can't just pick up the cat and take it home," she explained. "We don't know if she wants to come with us or not. What we can do is walk very slowly and call her, and see if she'll follow us."

WALKING into the house a short while later, Douglas' eyebrows raised as he took in the huge feline adorning his sofa, two worshipful children in attendance.

Jacinth came from the kitchen with a welcoming smile.

"We have a guest for dinner."

"So I see." His lips pursed in a soundless whistle. "I'm no cat person, but that is one gorgeous animal."

The cat looked across the room at him, and he could have sworn the thing smiled. Jacinth tugged at his arm.

"Come into the kitchen."

Since his children were too wrapped up in their new friend to even notice he'd come home, he allowed her to pull him across the hall, where the tangy aroma of marinara filled the air. She moved away from him to give the bubbling spaghetti sauce a stir, and turned the heat down.

"Dare I ask, is our 'guest' staying?"

Jacinth shook her head solemnly, but there was mischief in her face.

"No. She has her own home."

Douglas waited for the punch line. Clearly, there was one.

Jacinth fiddled with the spoon she held. "She's not just a cat."

He narrowed his eyes, not liking the sound of that.

"She's... umm... well, she's human as well."

Taking a long breath, he counted to ten slowly. He was not going to lose his cool. Not, not, not.

Jacinth shot him a look, half wary, half amused. "She's a shapeshifter."

Douglas leaned his forehead against the door jam and squeezed his eyes shut. Maybe he was going insane. Maybe he was actually *in* a mental hospital and this whole last week was a massive hallucination.

"This is not happening," he stated definitely. "There's no such thing as shapeshifters. There's no such thing as genies. Djinn. Whatever. There's no such thing as..."

A sudden thought occurred to him and he spun around to stare at Jacinth in horror.

"Please. Please tell me there aren't really vampires or werewolves. At least tell me that much."

Jacinth's mahogany eyes danced. "Well...."

"No!" He clapped a hand over her mouth. "Never mind. I don't want to know. I absolutely do not want to know the answer to that."

She giggled and squirmed away from him.

"Douglas, really. You're letting your imagination get away with you."

"My..." Words failed him. He rubbed his forehead, which was beginning to hurt. "Okay, change of subject here. I thought maybe I'd take the kids to the mall tonight. And you too if you want, although maybe you'd like to take the evening off."

"Oh no! I love the mall," Jacinth hurried to assure him. "Why are we going?"

"Ben and Molly need more clothes than what we bought in California--an entire new wardrobe for each of them--and Ben's going to need things for school. Both kids need more bedding, and with Mom and Dad coming up, I thought it'd be a good time to replace all the old towels and linens with new ones. And the kids need toys, too; the ones they had from two years ago are too young."

He paused, thinking. "I also think I'm going to need more vacuum cleaner bags--lots more!"

Jacinth's clear laughter rang like chimes. She moved to the stove once more and cast a mischievous glance over her shoulder.

"And dish soap. And laundry detergent. And children's shampoo. And shower and bath gel. And bubble bath. And..."

"Stop! Stop!" Douglas raised both hands and backed up. "I give up already! Yes, we'll get everything we need!"

She laughed again. "I'll make a list, so we don't forget anything, like when we went to the supermarket. In fact, we need another supermarket trip, too."

"I was just thinking of food that time," Douglas admitted. "This has all happened so quickly..."

"I know. Don't worry, it will all come together. Give it time." She lifted the spaghetti pot from the burner and carried it to the sink. "Douglas, would you see that the children wash up for dinner? This is almost ready."

"What about Cat? I'm assuming she's going to be in her... uh... her cat form. There's no way we could explain it to the children otherwise."

"Of course she'll be in cat form." Jacinth lifted the colander from the pot and began rinsing the spaghetti under cold water.

"I'll cut some of this into small pieces into a bowl with the sauce on it. It'll be fine, Douglas. Don't worry."

"I'm not worried," he denied. "It's just... this is pretty weird, you know?"

"I know. I also know that if you don't go get the kids washed up, you'll all be late."

She planted a hand on his back and shoved him out of the kitchen as she spoke. With a wide grin, he went.

Jacinth rolled her eyes at his retreating back, then slid the tray of buttered and garlicked French bread into the oven. She put her hands on her hips and studied the dining room, mentally going over her checklist to be sure she had everything ready. Cat sauntered into the kitchen, tail held high.

Those are nice kits you have, Djinn.

Only a cat could make a compliment sound like an insult. Jacinth ignored that part.

"They're not my children."

The cat snorted, shaking her head vigorously. *Could have fooled me.*

The feline nose raised, sniffing delicately. *Smells good, Djinn.*

"Thank you. I hope you like it."

Here come the kits. Cat had a cat's hearing for sure. Jacinth barely had time to take the garlic bread from the oven before the children rushed into the dining room.

"Miss Jas, where's Cat going to eat?" Benny asked. Douglas must have warned the children not to touch the cat after washing their hands, but they hovered anxiously over her.

Yes, Djinn, where am I going to eat?

Jacinth suppressed the urge to stick her tongue out at the cat.

"Cat can eat over there," she pointed to the floor in front of the sliding glass door leading to the patio. "See, I've cut some noodles up for her, and put sauce on. As soon as it cools a little, I'll put it down for her and she can eat right here with us. Does that meet with everyone's approval?"

"Yeah, cool!" shouted Benny, while Molly nodded eagerly.

Works for me. Satisfaction with overtones of smugness colored the mental voice. Jacinth had to stifle the urge to ruffle Cat's thick fur backward.

Don't you dare! The feline voice sounded outraged, and Jacinth smothered a grin.

Douglas came in just then, and Jacinth began putting the dinner on the table, giving Cat's bowl to Benny.

"Benny, would you put this down for Cat?"

"Sure thing!" He carried the bowl carefully to where she'd indicated and put it down, then came to the table.

"Look, Dad, she's eating it!"

Douglas just chuckled, and Jacinth lifted Molly onto her booster seat. Douglas rescued the bowl of sauce from Benny's clutches, since the boy could hardly sit still for twisting in his chair to watch Cat eat. Jacinth broke a slice of garlic bread into small pieces and put it down for the cat, and watched with amusement as Cat bolted down a small chunk.

"She does seem to like it," Douglas commented. He took a bite, his brows raising. "And so do I. This is terrific, Jacinth."

Not bad at all, Cat seconded grudgingly. *I could get to like this.*

Jacinth had to hide her smile. Fortunately, Benny began to enumerate to his father all the items he stood desperately in need of. Jacinth mentally discounted such items as a personal computer, Nintendo, a hand-held PDA, and an autographed Lakers basketball.

"Lakers!" Douglas pretended to be outraged, and reached

over to knuckle his son's head lightly. "I'll have you know you're in New York now!"

Benny just grinned at him. It was obvious to Jacinth that the two were quickly developing a close rapport. She was glad of that; they clearly both needed the bonding. She worried about Molly, though. She was a little shy around Douglas, and still showed no signs of speaking. It had only been a few days since they'd picked up the children in California, Jacinth reminded herself, and they'd only been home for one day.

Cat must have either been listening in, or picked up on her unspoken anxiety.

The kit will be fine. She's happy. Kits need security, and you've given her that. Cat's mental voice was the kindest that Jacinth had heard from her yet. Maybe there was something of the human in her after all.

Cat had been sitting before the door washing her face with a broad paw, but now rose and meandered over to the table, stropping back and forth about Jacinth's legs... leaving red and brown cat fur on her clean white slacks. Oh, well. At least Cat didn't use the material to sharpen her claws.

Feeling a tug on her blouse, she turned to find Molly looking at her with beseeching eyes. She'd finished, and wanted down. Lifting the child to the floor, Jacinth saw that Douglas and Benny were just helping themselves to seconds. She glanced at Cat, wondering if she too wanted more. Cat shook herself, the long coat so thick hardly a hair moved out of place.

Douglas leaned over the edge of the table to get a better look at Cat.

"You know, I think she's a Maine Coon," he said. "But I thought they lost a lot of that heavy coat in summer. I'll ask Suzanne, my partner who takes care of the cats in our clinic, about it on Monday."

Cat's ears perked. *A veterinarian? Now that could be useful.*

Mindful of the children, Jacinth had to subdue her urge to ask how a veterinarian could be of use to a shapeshifter. Instead, she began gathering the dishes from the table. Cat scampered ahead of her to stand pointedly in the doorway between the kitchen and the front hall.

"All right, I get the message." Jacinth went to the front door and opened it, and Cat stepped gracefully out onto the front walk.

Thank you for dinner, Djinn. This is a good family. You should think about staying. The she-kit needs a mother.

Oh great, now she was getting advice on her life from a cat!

"Thank you," she said, trying to sound stern.

Cat was already walking off, and her long tail in the air waving gently. Jacinth wasn't sure if the cat was making a statement or not. She returned to the kitchen, to find Douglas and Benny clearing the table. Douglas shooed her out of their way.

"You're the nanny, not the housekeeper," he told her firmly, marching her into the living room. "You put your feet up and rest. You're going to need it, chasing these two around the mall this evening."

Jacinth dropped onto the sofa, making herself comfortable, and smiled up at him. "Well, when you put it that way... Although, you know Douglas, it's been a long day for the children. I couldn't get them to take a nap, what with Cat coming home with us from the park. Maybe we should put off the mall trip 'til tomorrow evening, and I'll make sure they get a nap in the afternoon."

Douglas sighed, rubbing the back of his neck with one hand. "I keep forgetting. It's only been a few days and already I'm screwing up."

His voice held frustration. Jacinth reached out to take his hand, pressing it between both of hers.

"Douglas, listen to yourself. It's only been a few days. And we've been traveling most of that. We've only been home one day. You're not screwing up at all. Don't be so hard on yourself. You love the children, and it shows. Right now that's the most important thing. The rest will come."

His harassed expression lightened. "Yeah, I guess. I just... I want to do right by them, you know?"

"You're doing fine. It's an adjustment for all three of you. Give it time, Douglas."

She gave his hand a last squeeze and settled back into the cushions, watching his broad shoulders as he disappeared into the kitchen. Molly came and crawled into her lap, and she cuddled the little girl close, nuzzling the golden curls, trying hard not to think of Cat's parting words.

CHAPTER 8

Douglas wiped his brow. Only two hours in the mall. He wished they had shopping carts in these places. He'd made three trips out to the car already, and both he and Jacinth were loaded down with parcels. But they'd finally left the last department store and were making their way to the nearest exit. Hallelujah!

"Look, Miss Jas!" Benny had darted a little ahead and had his nose glued to a store window. "It's just like that stuff in your bedroom."

He saw Jacinth press her nose to the window, much like Benny. When Douglas got closer he saw it was an imports shop.

"So it is." Jacinth sounded delighted. "Oh, look there, at that beautiful pillow with all the beads and embroidery."

Douglas sighed. It looked like they weren't going to get out of the mall that easily. He capitulated as both Benny and Jacinth turned identical pleading expressions to him.

"Okay, okay. But let's make it quick, okay?"

He followed them in, Molly cuddled in one arm. She was

sleepy, but fascinated enough by all the exotic furniture and knick-knacks in the shop to keep her eyes open.

"Dad, look!" Benny bounced with enthusiasm. "This is just like the teapot you have at home."

Jacinth shot Douglas a glance, the brown eyes dancing with mischief.

"So it does," she told Benny. "Except your dad's is real silver, of course."

"How do you tell?" Benny asked doubtfully.

Jacinth picked up the silver-toned teapot and turned it over, holding it for Benny's inspection.

"See here? There are no markings. Usually, real silver is stamped for authenticity. If there's no stamp, either it's not silver, or it's very, very old, made before silver was stamped."

"So maybe this is very old?" Benny asked with all the hopefulness of a six-year-old.

Jacinth laughter was like silver chimes.

"No, honey," she said, ruffling the boy's hair. "It's just a pretty metal."

"But how do you tell?" he insisted.

"The price, usually," Jacinth said somewhat wryly.

Douglas objected.

"You couldn't tell that by what I paid for... for mine." He caught himself just in time. He'd been about to say, "What I paid for yours."

Catching his almost-slip, Jacinth twinkled at him.

"Yours was a special price."

Benny was listening, alert. "Does yours have a stamp, Dad?"

"No. But I bought it in an antique store," Douglas explained. "You can tell from looking at it that it's very old."

Benny looked at the teapot in Jacinth's hands, and scowled.

"Well, that looks old to me."

Jacinth placed it back on the shelf.

"Yes, that's why you have to be very careful when buying antiques," she told him. "There are all kinds of ways of making something look much older than it is. So you have to make sure you're dealing with someone reputable."

Douglas bit back a smile as Benny nodded, serious as a judge. As if, Douglas thought, the six-year-old was accustomed to discussing the merits of antiques on a daily basis. Still, he saw the sideways glance his son gave first the teapot, then Jacinth. The boy was definitely suspicious. Time to change the subject.

"Tell you what," he suggested. "Let's walk across the street to the Baskin Robbins."

That did it. Even Molly woke all the way up, wriggling in delight.

"What's Baskin Robbins?"

Douglas turned to stare at Jacinth, as did the Benny and Molly. She looked back, blinking in clear puzzlement, before breaking into laughter.

"What did I say?"

Douglas cleared his throat.

"Baskin Robbins is an ice cream shop."

"Haven't you ever had an ice cream cone?" Benny asked in amazement.

Jacinth brightened. "Oh, I love ice cream cones! I had one of the very first ones they ever made. There was this big fair, and I met a man who spoke the old language. He was there making pastries to sell, and he'd roll them up..."

Douglas clapped his hand over her mouth, silencing her. The dark eyes above his hand danced with humor.

"Let's go," he said.

As Benny danced ahead of them, Douglas leaned over to whisper in Jacinth's ear.

"That World Fair was a hundred years ago!"

"Oops." The glance she gave him was both apologetic and amused, and Douglas shook his head. He caught her hand with his free one, and they walked together towards the mall exit in Benny's wake.

The hot, humid air hit them like a blow as they stepped outside. The late August heat was oppressive and smothering, and all of them were damp with perspiration by the time they entered the welcome chill of the ice cream shop.

"Thirty-one flavors of ice cream?" Jacinth sounded impressed, and Douglas nodded. He watched as she stared, round-eyed, at the dozens of containers of ice cream, and at the pictures of sundaes and floats on the walls behind the counter.

"What is this?" she asked, stopping before one section. Her brow was wrinkled in puzzlement. "Cheesecake? They make ice cream from cheesecake?"

"Naw, it just tastes like that," Benny answered. "They have cookie dough too, over here."

"Cookie dough? Really?" Jacinth peered through the glass.

"It has little bits of real cookie dough in it. Would you like a taste?" The teenage clerk behind the counter almost fell over himself in his haste to help her. Feeling invisible, Douglas rolled his eyes. She'd made another conquest, without so much as glancing at the boy.

Jacinth took the tiny pink spoon and slid it into her mouth. Fascinated, Douglas watched her lips close about the spoon. She closed her eyes, savoring the flavor of the ice cream. A trace of moisture remained on her lips, and he drew closer, fighting the urge to lean down and lick the sweet stuff away, to press closer and discover the sweetness of her lips, her mouth.

"Mmmm, that's good." Unaware, Jacinth handed the little spoon back to the clerk and moved on to the next section, trying the rum raisin, and a good dozen more flavors at least, the young man anticipating her every sign of interest. Douglas stared after her, feeling rooted to the floor, suddenly aware of the bright lights of the store and the presence of Benny and Molly. He'd been about to kiss her right here in public, in front of his children!

"Dad?" Benny tugged on his sleeve. "Dad, can I have chocolate chip?"

Douglas waved at the clerk, who left Jacinth with a good-natured grin.

"Sorry. What can I get you?"

A few feet away, Jacinth glanced up from the display case she'd been peering into with a slight frown. "Yogurt flavored ice cream?

Shifting Molly on his arm, Douglas stepped to her side. "No. It's actually yogurt that's been frozen, instead of ice cream."

She shot him a disgusted look. "Americans are strange."

She turned her attention to Molly. "Sweetie, what do you want?"

Molly pointed towards the end of the line of freezers. Douglas sighed, wondering if she was ever going to speak. He walked in the direction she indicated, though, to where the sherbets were kept separate from the ice cream.

"Rainbow?" he asked.

Molly nodded vigorously. Jacinth drifted along after them and looked curiously at the brighter colors in the freezer case.

"Sher-bay?" she read the label on the glass case.

"Probably," Douglas agreed. "But most people say 'sher-bet.' It's similar to ice cream, but made with a fruit juice base instead of cream."

Her face brightened. "Oh, *shorba*! I know this. We had it in my country even when I was a child."

"Where are you from?" The clerk, whose name tag read Brian, asked curiously.

"Persia." Jacinth pointed at a lemon sherbet. "Could I try that one?"

"Yeah, sure." Handing Molly her cone with a scoop of rainbow sherbet, the clerk hurried to get Jacinth a sample. "So are you from Iran or what?"

Jacinth took the spoon.

"Persia," she told him in a firm voice.

"There hasn't been a Persia for centuries," Brian stated in a definitive manner. Douglas guessed he was a college student. "Not since the Persian empire collapsed in three hundred something BC."

"There was a Persian empire in the middle ages," Jacinth argued. "Right up until the end of the twelfth century."

"Thirteenth century," he corrected. "And it wasn't Persian. That was the Seljuk Turks."

"True," Jacinth agreed. "But where was the capital of their empire?"

"Baghdad," Brian admitted, and Jacinth looked smug. "But it didn't collapse until well into the thirteenth century."

"Yes, it did," Jacinth compressed her lips with mulish insistence. "It collapsed in 1209 with the murder of the Wazir Nizam and the death of the ruler, Malikshah. It just took a while after that for the empire to fall apart."

Brian looked ready to argue the point, and Jacinth was clearly prepared to stay well into the evening. Amused, Douglas intervened before she could announce that she knew better, having been born in that time period. Benny was listening avidly, his bright eyes alert and filled with intelligence.

"Enough! We need to get going to get home and get all these things put away sometime tonight. Jacinth, what kind of ice cream would you like?"

She considered a moment.

"Vanilla."

"Vanilla!" Douglas couldn't believe it. "After you tried all these flavors, you want vanilla?"

Jacinth's mouth curved downward into a pout, but her eyes were teasing.

"I like vanilla."

Douglas rolled his eyes and sighed. "Fine."

"One scoop or two?" the clerk asked.

Jacinth brightened. "I can have more than one?"

"Uh... yeah," Brian admitted warily. "Up to three."

"She's new to America." Douglas hurried to explain Jacinth's odd lack of knowledge.

The young man accepted that, which Douglas thought a sad indication of the current generation of Americans' lack of knowledge of life outside their own country.

"I'll have two scoops," Jacinth decided.

"Do you want both scoops vanilla?"

She considered that, wandering along the cases again. She stopped and pointed.

"I'll have that one on top."

A long "ewwwwwwwwwwww" came from Benny, and Douglas didn't know whether to laugh or to make gagging motions like his son was doing behind Jacinth's back. "Watermelon sherbet?"

"It's a pretty color," she defended. "And I like watermelon."

"And you think Americans are strange," Douglas muttered.

Jacinth just laughed, accepting the cone from Brian with a word of thanks.

Douglas ordered rocky road for himself, and paid the total.

"Next time, try a banana split," the young man advised Jacinth. "They're really great."

"Banana split?" She looked interested.

Douglas wrapped his arm about her waist and drew her towards the door.

"We're going now," he announced, unnecessarily. "You can have a banana split next time. Say goodbye."

She twinkled up at him and looked back over her shoulder at the clerk as Douglas dragged her through the door.

"Goodbye!" she called.

Brian waved with enthusiasm. "Bye! Come back soon!"

"Not if I can help it," Douglas muttered.

An hour and a half later both kids were in bed and Douglas and Jacinth were still organizing the mounds of purchases spread across the sofa. While Douglas folded a stack of clothes to be put in Molly's room in the morning, Jacinth headed for the kitchen and opened the freezer, peering at the contents inside.

"I thought I'd make the pork roast tomorrow," she called. "What do you think?"

"Sounds good to me." Douglas sounded distant, rather abstracted, as if his thoughts were elsewhere.

She took out the roast to thaw, and went back into the living room, looking at him questioningly.

"How does it feel?" Douglas asked abruptly. "To be a genie... to live for so long? I mean, what do you do every day for nine hundred years? Don't you get... well... tired, sometimes?"

It was clear that he'd spent some time thinking over these questions; they didn't come out of nowhere. He wasn't looking at her, but instead was intently studying the small sweater he'd just folded as if it held the secrets of the universe.

Jacinth sat down on the sofa beside him, pushing a pile of bags aside, and clasped her hands together, frowning. She'd never had to explain being a Djinn before.

"It's not quite the same as with mortals, Douglas. I haven't exactly lived every day of nine hundred years... not like you mean. Time is different for us than it is for you. Just as a cat or a dog would experience an entire day quite differently than by your measure. And we can kind of... fold time, I suppose you'd say. For instance, if I was very tired, I could go into my vessel and sleep a full night, and wake up and rejoin you, and only a few minutes would have passed in your time."

Douglas' brow creased as he thought this over.

"You mean, when you go in your room for the night, you might not be sleeping?"

"No. Generally I read, or watch television, or even visit with other Djinn."

Amusement lit Douglas' eyes.

"You go teapot-hopping?"

Jacinth laughed.

"Not quite in the way you mean it," she said. "First, I'd never be gone from the house, not when I was responsible for the children, even at night. At least, not without telling you. But we have other means of communicating with each other."

"I'm almost afraid to ask." Douglas seemed to brace himself.

"Well." Jacinth relaxed back against the sofa cushions, settling herself more comfortably. "The metal of a Djinn vessel acts as a kind of conductor, through which we can hear... and see... each other."

"You mean, kind of like video-conferencing?"

Jacinth's delighted laughter filled the room. She leaned forward, her eyes shining with amusement.

"Video-conferencing!" She giggled. "Yes, that's just what it's like! Although Djinn tend to be very gregarious, we like to get together. But sometimes it's just not possible, for one reason or another. So using the vessels is convenient."

Douglas laughed. "The Genie Network. Gotta love it. So are all Djinn vessels silver?"

"No, some are brass, others copper. And some special cases have glass bottles. For instance, Julian... he owns Whimsies, the antique shop where you bought my teapot. He was spell-bound to the Djinn hundreds of years ago, forced to use his magical powers to grant wishes, as a Djinn does, until he was freed last year by Alessandra, who is now his wife, and he resumed a mortal life. His vessel was a blown glass bottle."

Douglas looked horrified. "That doesn't happen often, does it? I mean... the Djinn don't go around grabbing people and imprisoning them?"

"No, no." Jacinth reached for his hand, clasping it warmly, her smile one of reassurance. "We don't have the power... or the right... to do that. Our foremost law is not to interfere in human existence, with the sole exception of the wish-giving. No, I'm afraid the imprisonment was something Julian brought on himself. He was a powerful mage, but impatient, unwilling to wait for age and experience to hone his natural talent. So he cast a spell for unlimited power and ability. I admit that he had good reasons, and the best of intentions, but he was a little careless in the wording due to a certain arrogance and belief in his own infallibility, and the spell backfired, as you'd say."

"A mage." Images of werewolves and vampires returned to haunt him, and he firmly chased them away. "Uh.... mage is like, a magician? I assume you're not talking about the David Copperfield kind?"

A corner of Jacinth's lips quirked upward in a slightly guilty smile.

"I'm afraid not," she said, very solemnly. "He's a very powerful mage, too, which accounted for the strength of his spell. We were required to monitor him, of course, since he was temporarily one of us, and to try to guide him in the direction that would lead him to a resolution of the spell. I was one of those assigned to watch over him. It wasn't an easy task. A stubborn man, Julian, and proud even through it all."

Silently, Douglas vowed to make a return trip to that antique shop soon. A man... another human... who knew about the Djinn, someone he could talk to, ask questions... yep, he was definitely going to have to meet Julian soon.

Douglas became aware of Jacinth's hand, still tucked into his. Her skin was soft and fragrant, the scent of jasmine wafting about her. He knew that scent; when he was a boy his mother had been used to distill her own floral oils, and jasmine had been one of her favorites.

He studied her, as she gazed pensively out the front window. Heat coiled in his gut, a tension he knew well. How long had it been since he'd desired a woman? Not since his divorce, that was for sure, and he'd lost any feeling he'd once had for Lilian long before they'd split up. But this woman... Jacinth... had somehow crept under his skin. He remembered the kiss they'd shared just a few days ago, beside the carousel. It took no great leap of imagination to envision her in his arms now, her soft, full lips yielding softly as he kissed her until the slumberous, dreamy look in her brown eyes changed to awakening passion.

Happily unaware of his thoughts, Jacinth disengaged her

hand from his clasp and stood, gathering up the various empty bags. She cast a critical look around the room.

"We're going to have to do some more cleaning before your parents come," she decided. "How long do you think we have? I can run the vacuum and dust tomorrow, but what the whole house really needs is to be turned inside-out."

Douglas rubbed his nose, sighing. "I know," he admitted. "I'll call around tomorrow morning and see if I can't get someone out in the afternoon on an emergency basis, but it's unlikely I'll be able to get someone on short notice. But Mom and Dad are kind of, um, laid-back." No kidding! "They're not likely to mind a little dust."

Jacinth seemed unconvinced but nodded.

"I'll do what I can. I thought we'd spend the day at home tomorrow anyway, as the children need to settle in and start to get into a routine."

While the idea of having his house clean held great appeal, the last thing Douglas wanted was for Jacinth to feel like she had to do it herself.

"You let me worry about the house," he told her firmly. "The children are the most important thing, and it's an immense relief to know you're in charge of them. I can handle everything else."

Jacinth seemed to consider that.

"How about if I be in charge of making dinner every night?" she countered. "It would be hard on you to come home from work and immediately have to start getting dinner made. If I take that over, we can sit down to eat when you get home. And you and the children can be responsible for clean-up after."

"Deal." He closed on it. "I'll take over on weekends. And I'll get a cleaning crew in here as soon as I can, have them turn the place inside-out, as you so graphically put it. Once that's done

I'll have a housekeeper come in once or twice a week to keep things from disintegrating."

Jacinth's smile seemed to light the whole room.

"Okay, we've got a plan then! What about your parents?"

Douglas pondered that. "I figure they'll be here sometime Saturday. We should at least count on them for dinner, if not sooner."

Jacinth pondered that, her pretty lips pressed together thoughtfully.

"I think I'll plan on making spaghetti again. That way it'll keep if they come late, and it's easy to reheat. Could you drop by the store tomorrow on the way home from work, Douglas? We have most everything, but I'll need some more cloves of garlic, and olive oil would make it better, too. Oh, and a loaf of French bread."

"Garlic, olive oil, French bread. Got it. You can call me with anything else you can think of during the day."

Jacinth pulled out the cell phone he'd picked up for her on his way home from work, studying it intently. "I've never had one of these before."

"Here."

He took it from her programming in his number and the number to the veterinary clinic. "Just find the name you want in the contact list, then press the green phone icon next to the name. If you want to send a text, press this notecard looking icon."

She peered at the phone. "That sounds easy enough."

Taking it from him, she tapped his name, then the phone icon, and laughed merrily when his phone immediately rant.

"I like it!"

"You know," Douglas mused. "I've only got a few calls lined up to make tomorrow for work, I should be home by early afternoon. Why don't you make a list of anything else you think we need from the supermarket. Then I'll take the kids with me, get them out of your hair for a while."

"That's fine, although they don't bother me, Douglas. They're darling children, and I love being with them."

"You say that now," he said, slightly rueful. "We've only been home two days."

Jacinth's brown eyes sparkled with fun.

"And so much has happened already!"

"Don't remind me," Douglas said, rolling his eyes. "Between the hair-raising trip to the mall, a visiting shape-shifting cat, and a nine-hundred-year-old genie running amuck in Baskin Robbins, I think I feel my hair turning gray already!"

"And just think," Jacinth said cheerfully, her eyes twinkling in fun. "Your parents will be here day after tomorrow to add to the fun."

Douglas just groaned.

CHAPTER 9

The largest RV Jacinth had ever seen nosed into the curb and came to a halt in front of the house. Douglas' parents, already! How could they have gotten here so fast? It was only Sunday; they must have driven straight through from Florida without stopping. Hurriedly she put down the roasting pan she'd been rinsing out and dried her hands. Douglas had taken the children and headed for the supermarket, missing his parents by a bare five minutes.

She was curious as to what they were like. Douglas had refused to tell her about them, just laughing and shaking his head when she'd asked. He didn't seem overly concerned, though, so he couldn't be too worried about what they'd think of her. Full of curiosity, she went to the front door, opening it just as they reached the porch.

It was all she could do to keep her jaw from dropping. She knew she was staring, but she couldn't help herself. Standing on the porch, beaming at her, were two... well... flower children. Aging, yes, but flower children nonetheless.

From their long hair and daisy-chain necklaces to the toe-sandals on their feet, these were hippies. Jacinth smothered a laugh as Douglas' mother stepped forward, holding out her hand.

"You must be the nanny? Goodness, you're young." She smiled, her doe-brown eyes dancing merrily. "Douglas didn't tell you about us, did he? The naughty boy, he never does. He'll be so sorry he wasn't here to see your reaction."

Jacinth laughed and shook her hand, stepping back for them to come inside.

"No, he's gone to the store with the children. They should be back in a little bit."

Douglas' father offered his hand too. "I'm Blue," he told her, his eyes--which were indeed blue--alight with every bit as much mischief as his wife. "And this is Skye."

Blue and Skye. Jacinth had to laugh again.

"I'm Jacinth. Do come in and make yourselves at home. Would you like some tea or coffee?"

"Jacinth!" Skye dropped onto the sofa, kicking off her sandals. "What a pretty name. What does it mean?"

"It's an old word for a flower," Jacinth explained. "What you now call a hyacinth."

Douglas' mother seemed to sober a bit, exchanging an inscrutable look with Blue.

"So." Skye patted the sofa next to her. "Come tell us all about you."

Oops. This was going to be tricky. She made herself comfortable, and there was a brief silence while they all took stock of each other. Douglas had Blue's build and coloring, but he'd gotten his strong nose and high cheekbones from his mother, who had to be at least part Native American. Her hair was crow-wing black except for a vibrant silver streak down one side, and hung straight as an arrow past her waist, as long as Jacinth's. There was no gray in Blue's long locks, which were sun-bleached to a lighter shade than Douglas' toffee colored hair.

Skye and Blue looked at her expectantly.

"Well, as you know I like children," she began, feeling more awkward than she had since she was a gangly teen. She had to remember that she didn't look much older than a teen, either. "I haven't had a lot of experience as a nanny yet, of course, but I'm very responsible."

Skye patted her arm. "Of course you are. Douglas wouldn't hire someone who wasn't responsible to watch Ben and Molly. We don't want a resume, dear. We want to know about you... your family, where you're from..."

"Your political position," Blue put in, then "oofed" as his wife jabbed him in the ribs.

Oh, dear. Jacinth thought quickly, and decided to go for the heavily edited truth, and change the subject as quickly as possible. She hoped Douglas would get home soon.

"I'm an only child. My father died when I was young, but I'm very close to my mother." Speaking of whom, why Zahra hadn't dropped in on her yet? It was rare to go a whole week without hearing from her mother.

"As far as political positions," she winked at Blue. "I'm one hundred percent for world peace."

"Atta girl," he told her with a wide smile. "I thought you looked like a smart kid."

Kid? Jacinth smothered a laugh.

"So how are the children?" Skye asked the question casually, but Jacinth could hear the underlying worry.

"They're fine. Really. They weren't abused, or starved or anything. Although to hear Benny tell it, they've had their fill of pizza for a lifetime or two. They were neglected, though, especially emotionally."

Had Douglas told them about Molly? She racked her brain, trying to remember if he'd mentioned it. She'd rather leave it to him to explain, but they needed to be told before he came back with the children.

"I should warn you that Molly doesn't speak. She hasn't said one word since the social worker picked her up in California." She held up a hand, forestalling their startled exclamations. "We don't know why, and she doesn't seem traumatized. Benny hasn't told us much of anything that happened when they were with their mother, except that they ate lots of pizza. We haven't liked to press him yet, since they've only been home a couple of days. We wanted to give Molly a little time to settle in. We're hoping she'll find her voice on her own."

They all looked around at the sound of car doors slamming, and Jacinth looked around, eager to watch the children's faces when they saw their grandparents.

Benny was first through the door, of course. He may have been only four years old when he last saw them, but he had no problem remembering who the older couple on the living room sofa were.

"Gram! Gramps!" He flung himself at them, hugging them enthusiastically and clambering onto Blue's lap.

Molly hesitated in the doorway, and Jacinth held out a hand to the little girl.

"It's okay, Molly," she coaxed. "Don't you remember your grandmother and grandfather?"

Molly wasn't sure she did, and hung back, her cornflower blue eyes huge. She only moved into the room when Douglas, laden with bags, pushed her forward gently so he could come inside. Jacinth rose and went to take the groceries from him.

"You stay," she whispered. "I'll take care of getting the rest from the car and putting them away."

He cast her a grateful look, clearly eager to see his parents. He swung Molly up into his arms.

"I've got some herbal teas in the cupboard that I keep for when they visit," he told her. "Would you mind...?"

"No, of course not. You go on in."

With a nod he turned to the living room, and Jacinth retreated to the kitchen. She liked Douglas' parents, she thought, getting the rest of the groceries and putting the perishables in the refrigerator. She found herself chuckling quietly, and hovered over the tea kettle anxiously, wishing it would hurry and boil so she could get back to the living room.

By the time the tea was done, she found Molly cuddled in Skye's lap, playing with a strand of the daisy-chain necklace that had made its way around her own chubby neck. Benny, of course, was talking a mile a minute while Douglas, seated across from his parents in an armchair, long legs stretched out before him, watched the scene silently. A smile hovered about the corners of his mouth, and there was no mistaking his happiness. He looked up as she came in, and leaped to his feet.

"I'm sorry, I should have come to help carry these in," he apologized, taking the tray from her.

"It's no trouble," she told him. She passed a cup to Blue, who leaned forward to sniff the steam appreciatively.

"Chamomile," he said, taking a cautious sip of the hot brew and sighing with pleasure. "My favorite."

Skye sipped hers with equal pleasure, smiling at Jacinth.

"Douglas tells me you make an interesting kind of tea yourself."

Jacinth settled herself on Douglas' footstool and nodded.

"It's very simple, what we do in Persia. Take a basic strong, black Indian tea... full of caffeine," she added mischievously, and was rewarded by Skye's lilting laugh. "Then crush some clove and nutmeg into it, maybe a little allspice, and add sugar or honey."

"Clove and nutmeg." Blue pursed his lips and stared into the distance, deep in thought.

"Mom and Dad own a tea shop," Douglas explained. "Well... a combination tea shop, bookstore and craft shop."

"Really?" Jacinth looked with renewed interest at Douglas' mother.

"It's more quilting and embroidery than general crafts." Skye's dark eyes lit with enthusiasm. "We have tables for people to come and work on their projects, and we give classes in quilting and cross-stitch, that sort of thing. We carry mysteries and romances in the bookstore, and in the middle, between the books and the craft supplies, is the tea shop. We have a wide assortment of teas, plus a few pastries, croissants, that kind of thing."

"How fun!" It sounded fascinating, and Blue and Skye were clearly proud of their enterprise. "What do you call it?"

A mischievous look crossed Skye's face. "Cozies."

Jacinth couldn't help laughing. "Oh, that's perfect!"

She cast a glance at the clock and rose to her feet.

"I really need to start getting supper ready," she apologized.

"Oh, let me come help. It'll go quickly with two of us, and we can chat." Skye lifted Molly off her lap, kissing the chubby cheek as she set the little girl on the sofa. "Do you mind, sweetie?"

Molly shook her curly head solemnly, then reached up and grasped her grandmother's hand. Jacinth laughed.

"It looks like girls' night in the kitchen. Okay, come on."

Skye volunteered to peel potatoes, so Jacinth found her a

potato peeler and set about seasoning the roast. After sliding it into the oven, she began putting together a salad. They worked in companionable silence, Molly having decided things were too dull for her liking and wandered off to where Benny was showing off his bedroom to Blue.

After a while, Jacinth noted Skye aiming a sidelong look in her direction.

"So." Skye's light soprano was carefully casual. "Are you and Douglas having a... er... relationship?"

Jacinth choked, and nearly cut her finger along with the celery she'd been chopping.

"No!" she denied quickly. "No, I'm just here to take care of Benny and Molly. There isn't anything between Douglas and me."

"Well, I wouldn't mind if there was," was Skye's frank reply. "I can see you're good for him, and the children obviously adore you."

Jacinth was finding it hard to breathe from the odd pain in her chest.

"I know. I love them too. The children, I mean."

"Not Douglas, of course." His mother's eyes glinted with amusement.

"No, I can't... that is..." Jacinth stumbled to a halt, then began again. "I'm only here temporarily, until he can find a permanent nanny."

"Temporarily?" Quick dismay crossed the older woman's face. "You're not staying?"

"I have... other commitments. Even if I wanted to stay... not that I don't!" she hastened to assure Skye. "But I can't stay."

She was grateful when Skye changed the subject, and listened with interest to how Skye and Blue had come to open their tea-slash-book-slash-quilt shop. The salad done, she slid it into the refrigerator to chill, while Skye put the potatoes on to boil.

A distinctive cry floated through the open kitchen window, and Jacinth looked out the kitchen window to see Cat make a graceful leap onto the decorative white fence by the front walk. Beside her, Skye drew a quick breath.

"Oh, my! What a gorgeous creature!"

Jacinth dried her hands on a towel and went to open the front door.

"She lives somewhere in the neighborhood," she explained. "The children befriended her in the park, and she comes around now and then... usually at dinnertime."

Very funny, Djinn.

Jacinth allowed herself a silent smirk at the cat, and followed her into the kitchen, where the shapeshifter rubbed around Skye's ankles and purred. Skye knelt down to stroke the thick fur, looking up at Jacinth.

"This is beautiful fur, so long and heavy! What kind of cat is it, do you know?"

"Douglas said she's a Maine Coon," Jacinth told her, and Skye's eyes gleamed.

"Maine Coon," she murmured thoughtfully. "I've never heard of those."

Skye stood up, and carefully gathered the bits of long hair clinging to her fingers. She didn't seem to mind the cat fur, but she went into the living room and returned with her purse, which was more like a large carry-all. After rummaging through the contents, she triumphantly displayed a cat brush and a Baggie.

"Do you think she'll let me brush her?"

She carried a cat brush in her purse? Jacinth blinked. "Um... I don't see why not."

Cat seemed appreciative, leaning into the brush, and rolling over to have her tummy done. From time to time, Skye would clean the hairs from the brush and put them in the Baggie.

"Oh, what a good kitty you are," Skye was crooning. "Roll over now and let me get your other side."

She nudged Cat with her hand, who obligingly turned over.

"She has a lovely coat," Skye enthused, tucking some more fur into the plastic bag. "I do my own spinning, you know. This will make a lovely yarn for knitting something warm... a scarf and hat, or even a sweater if we could find out where she lives and have her owners save the fur for me when they groom her."

A sweater? Cat sat up with a snort, looking as disgruntled as a cat's features would allow. Which was pretty disgruntled. Jacinth stifled a giggle.

"I'll see what I can do," she told Skye, keeping a straight face as Cat stalked off, outraged dignity in every step.

Jacinth regaled Douglas with this story after dinner. They were sitting out on the porch swing, Blue having volunteered to do the dishes while Skye gave the children their baths.

Douglas laughed heartily.

"Better warn Cat to stay out of the way, then. Mom's nothing if not determined when it comes to collecting material for her spinning."

"So I saw." The whole situation tickled her funny bone. "It'll be interesting to see who wins out in the end."

Inside, they heard the "clunk" as the dishwasher was turned on, and a moment later Blue joined them, dropping onto one of the lounge chairs with a sigh.

"That was a fantastic dinner," he told Jacinth.

"Tired of sprouts?" Douglas asked with a wicked grin.

"Always were a mouthy kid," his father grumbled, then grinned at Jacinth.

"So! He treating you right? Union hours, overtime, that sort of thing? Vacation?"

She threw a teasing look at Douglas. "Well, he took me to Disneyland with the kids last weekend, does that count?"

Blue pretended to consider it, then allowed that Disneyland indeed counted. He drew in a breath, inhaling deeply.

"Smells like flowers. Fresh. Nicer than Florida, everything always has that fishy tang. Good thing you found the kids now, and not in the middle of winter with snow everywhere."

"I'm just glad I found them at all," Douglas sighed. "Two years is a long time. It seemed like forever."

"You have them now at least." Blue pinned Jacinth with a piercing gaze. "You're not likely to give the kids over to Lilian if she shows up, like that last babysitter, are you?"

Jacinth met his look steadily, but it was Douglas who responded.

"Now, Dad, that's not fair. Nobody knew what Lilian was going to do. Even if Annie had called and asked me if it was okay for the kids to go with their mother that day, I'd have said okay. There was no reason to think she was going to disappear with them."

"But we know now," Jacinth interjected. "And there's not a chance I'll let her have them."

Skye came down the hallway to join them.

"Molly's in bed, and Benny is reading one of his books," she said, sinking down next to her husband. "Jacinth, Benny said you've taught him how to read?"

"I don't know about that," Jacinth wrinkled her nose, thinking it over. "I started reading to both children when we were in the car coming across country and whenever we were having quiet time, and Benny seemed to pick it up pretty quickly. It's been less than a week, so I imagine someone was working with him on reading while he was with his mother."

"Must have been a babysitter, because God knows it wasn't Lilian," Douglas commented bitterly.

"Well, if you have any more problems with her, call us, and we'll come chase her off," Blue winked at Jacinth, and Skye laughed.

"Your father's going through his second boyhood," Skye told Douglas wryly. "He got arrested in San Francisco."

Blue leaned back in his chair with a sigh of immense satisfaction. "Anti-war rallies. Make love, not war. Crowds of peaceful protestors and armed riot police. Arrests in the hundreds. Just like back in the sixties with Baez and Dylan."

He appeared extremely pleased with himself.

"Without the drugs this time, I hope," Douglas put in.

His father snorted. "We haven't done that since before you were born, son. Anyway, we were just experimenting back then."

"The one time *I* experimented, Mom tanned my hide," Douglas told Jacinth.

"And rightfully so." Skye reached for her husband's hand, and the two exchanged a long look. "I got pregnant, back then in the sixties, doing the Haight-Ashbury scene. We'd tried just about everything, and didn't think anything of it. No one did, back then. But my baby... when she was born, she was what they'd call a drug baby, these days. She didn't live more than a few days."

Blue held her hand in a firm clasp, comforting. Jacinth could feel their sorrow, even after all these years.

"I'm sorry," she said.

The words seemed inadequate, but Skye smiled at her, slightly teary-eyed. "We named her Hyacinth."

"Mom, you never told me you had a baby before me!" Douglas appeared thunder-struck.

"It isn't something we were proud of," Blue said. "But it got us sobered up and cleaned up pretty quick. We were in our responsible phase when we had you a year later."

"Responsible? Dad, you lived in a commune!"

"There's nothing wrong with a commune," Skye defended. "Clean air, good healthy food, lots of people working together in harmony with the earth. And we *were* responsible. We named you 'Douglas,' didn't we?"

He snorted. "That didn't stop you from calling me 'Walks With Squirrels' the first seven years of my life."

"Walks with Squirrels?" The bubble of laughter welling up in Jacinth's throat threatened to choke her. These people just got better and better.

"And I don't think anyone would call gun-running, responsible behavior," Douglas told his mother sternly. He turned to Jacinth. "She smuggled guns and ammunition under her burgeoning, pregnant belly... that was me... to the Native Americans holed up in a church on the Wounded Knee reservation."

"Hah!" Skye's eyes sparkled with remembered satisfaction. "Right under the noses of the FBI and the GOONs, too."

"GOONS." Blue spat into the lilac bushes growing against the porch. "Guardians of the Oglala Nation," he said bitterly. "Bully-boys and sanctioned murderers, that's what they were."

"You're part Native American, aren't you?" Jacinth asked Skye, who nodded.

"Half. My mother was Lakota Sioux. When we heard what was happening on the reservation, we packed up everything in our VW bus and went to help."

"What did happen?"

"Time!" Douglas held up both his hands in a gesture of surrender. "Let's not get into the Native American politics right now, okay? We don't want Mom going ballistic."

Skye pretended to pout. "I will not."

"You always do," Blue told her. "I cast my vote with Douglas. Besides, I want to hear more about what's been going on with our grandchildren."

Douglas exhaled sharply, running his fingers through his hair in frustration.

"There's not much to tell, because we don't know anything except that Lilian moved around the country in hopes I wouldn't catch up with her... and that we already knew. Jacinth and I talked it over, and we decided to give the kids some time to adjust to being back. We thought it would be better to wait a little before pressing Benny for information; although if Molly doesn't start to talk in a few days, we're going to have to sit him done and ask what happened. And at that point, I may have to see about some kind of therapy."

Jacinth nodded, supporting his decision. "I honestly think Molly will come around on her own, once she feels secure. They've only been home a few days."

"Besides," Douglas said with a grin, "Benny talks enough for both of them."

Skye laughed merrily. "That's true. And they do love you, Jacinth. It was 'Miss Jas' this and 'Miss Jas' that, all evening long."

Warmth filled her chest, seeping through her veins.

"I love them too," she said. "They're darling children."

She noticed Blue and Skye exchanging quick, hopeful glances. Douglas didn't miss it either.

"None of that," he told his parents in a stern voice.

"None of what?" Skye managed to look the very picture of innocence.

"Matchmaking," Jacinth said, mimicking Douglas' mock frown. "I'm only here to watch the children for Douglas, as I told you."

Douglas caught that. "As you told her? Mom! You haven't been here two hours and you've already been grilling her?"

"I wasn't grilling her!" Skye said indignantly. "I was just asking, when we were making dinner."

Douglas rolled his eyes.

"I'm sorry," he told Jacinth.

"Save it," she advised, shaking her head. "Wait until you meet *my* mother."

"Your mother?" Douglas exclaimed, surprised into forgetting they had listeners. "She'll be coming here?"

"Um-hmm." Hopefully not until Douglas' parents left, however. The three of them together... now there was a scary thought!

"Why shouldn't Jacinth's mother come here?" asked Blue, at the same time Skye was saying, "Is she coming soon? Will we get to meet her?"

"No," Jacinth hurried to tell them, hiding her laughter at the thought. "I don't actually know when she'll visit. She's a little... unpredictable."

"Unpredictable?"

Beside her she could practically feel Douglas' interest peak. Maybe she should have used another word. Oh, well, it'd give him something to think about besides the growing attraction between them. Heaven knew she was having a hard enough time with that herself.

Time to change the subject.

"How did you get here so quickly?" she asked his parents. "We weren't expecting you until sometime tomorrow."

"Couldn't wait to see little Ben and Molly," Blue replied, his voice gruff with emotion. "Two years it's been. We took turns so we could pretty much drive straight through."

"We pulled off in a rest area a couple of times for a nap," Skye assured Douglas, who was looking anxious.

Blue concurred. "We're not that old, son, so don't go starting to think that we're not able to drive through the night now and then!"

"Besides, we have to leave by Tuesday," Skye explained. "I have someone to cover the shop for us for a couple days, but I teach a Tarot divination class on Wednesday afternoons, and I have to be back by then."

Douglas, who'd just taken a sip of his lemonade, choked, and came up sputtering. "Tarot!"

Jacinth helpfully thumped him on the back as he coughed.

"Thanks," he managed to wheeze. "Geez, Mom, give a guy some warning."

Jacinth wisely decided that now was not the moment to haul out her own pack of cards and engage Skye in a conversation about Tarot and comparison of the merits of their respective decks. She got to her feet, smiling at everyone in general and no one in particular.

"How about some more lemonade?" she asked brightly.

When she returned with a brimming pitcher, the talk had turned to plans for the next day.

"We don't necessarily have to do anything in particular," Blue told them. "We just wanted to get here and see our grandchildren. And don't feel like you have to entertain us, Douglas. We'll be fine, hanging out and playing with Ben and Molly."

"Is that lovely cat likely to come back?" Skye looked hopeful, and Douglas groaned.

"She will if she knows we're having spaghetti for dinner," he murmured in Jacinth's ear. She suppressed a giggle.

"Actually," she addressed herself to Skye, "We first saw Cat in the park just down the street. They have a huge play area for children and a wading pool, a pond with ducks, picnic benches, that sort of thing. Why not take Benny and Molly there? We've only been once, but the children had a wonderful time. I know they'll love to go back, and you might run into Cat while you're there."

"That sounds perfect," Skye assured her.

Blue rose from his chair and stretched, yawning.

"I'm ready to turn in. It was a long drive, and if we're going to be chasing Ben and Molly over the park all day tomorrow, I need a good night's sleep."

Skye opted to say goodnight also, and the two made their way across the dark yard to their RV. A light shone briefly within, then went out.

CHAPTER 10

ALONE AGAIN WITH DOUGLAS, Jacinth pushed at the ground with one foot to get the porch swing in motion. She breathed in deeply, savoring the night scents and the quiet. The neighborhood was a quiet one; mostly single-story homes set on large plots of land. Quite a few had horse pastures, the white fencing contrasting neatly with the brick of the houses. Douglas, too, had enough room for horses on his property if he wanted them, even with the large swimming pool she'd seen in his back yard. The moon wasn't up yet, but the darkness was broken here and there by the cheerful flash of lightning bugs.

Douglas must have noticed her watching them.

"We never had those when I was growing up," he said. "Not in the commune in California, or on the rez in the Dakotas. My grandparents on Dad's side lived in St. Louis, though, and sometimes I'd go spend a week or two in the summer with them. I used to catch them and put them in jars, hoping for my own personal night light, you know? But they didn't live."

Jacinth laughed, remembering her own childhood. "We had fireflies. I remember trying to catch them, too, they seemed so magical! But there were always so many of them. I've never seen so many fireflies since I was grown, and I've often wondered if Mother called more to the area, just for me to enjoy."

Douglas' dark brows raised in question.

"Can Djinn do that?"

Jacinth nodded. "We have a basic affinity with wildlife that allows us some communication... to attract or repel, on the most basic level, like with the fireflies. I hate mosquitoes at all, for instance, so you won't find any of those around while I'm here. I don't mind spiders, within reason. At least, I don't like them inside the house, but if you find spider webs in the bushes in the morning, sparkling with the dew, don't be surprised."

"As long as they don't string webs across the walkway so I get tangled in them getting to my car in the morning," Douglas remarked, his voice amused.

A silence fell between them as they sat, the porch swing squeaking a bit as it rocked gently.

Douglas found himself playing with the long strands of Jacinth's silky black hair that blew towards him. He rubbed one thick lock as it curled about his finger.

"Jacinth..."

Suddenly they were no longer alone. A stern voice spoke from the porch steps.

"What is this, Jacinth?"

Douglas struggled with the sudden flare of jealousy that sprang to life as Jacinth jumped up, running to throw her arms about the man... or more precisely, Djinn... who appeared out of nowhere.

"Kieran!" She turned to Douglas, beckoning him forward.

There was unalloyed joy in her face, a glow of affection in her chocolate eyes for the tall man who drew her to his side, an arm about her slim waist. And whose expression, Douglas thought, was neither warm nor welcoming. The air of possessiveness about the stranger caused Douglas to bristle. Jacinth was *his*… at least, for as long as she chose.

"Douglas, this is Kieran. My almost-stepfather." She glanced teasingly upward at her Djinn companion, her smile warm. "He had a thing for my mother."

Douglas didn't believe Kieran had ever had a "thing" for anybody, ever. A sterner face he'd never seen, as if carved from marble. Well over six feet, the Djinn's most remarkable feature was long white hair… not grey or silver, but a pure, shining white… sleeked straight back from his face to spill over his shoulders, streaming down his back. In distinctive contrast, black brows slashed over eyes of the purest azure. Douglas judged the man… Djinn… had about the same warmth and compassion of that unforgiving stone.

"Kieran, Douglas is my *Sahib*," Jacinth was explaining with her endearingly earnest expression.

"And does Douglas want to be more than that?" Kieran's voice was impossibly deep and menacing.

Jacinth stepped away from the Djinn, flushing. She raised her chin, apparently not intimidated.

"Whether he does or does not, such a choice is mine to make."

Douglas was both impressed and touched at her show of support. Kieran's cold eyes rested on his face, raking him. Passing judgment. Then the Djinn turned away in dismissal, addressing Jacinth.

"He is not good for you. He is mortal. Give him his wishes and return to us."

A flush of temper bloomed in Jacinth's cheeks.

"You're very rude, Kieran. Since when did any of us have to rush through the Wish giving? What business is it of yours if I tarry here?"

A flash of emotion crossed the Djinn's face, swiftly banished. He was not so much cold, Douglas realized, as controlled.

"I care for you." Kieran's deep voice softened, and he reached out to touch her cheek. "I don't want to see you hurt."

The screen door opened a crack, and Molly appeared in her nightgown, looking anxious.

"Molly! What are you doing out of bed?" Nearest to the door, Jacinth went to the little girl, drawing her out onto the porch. "Did you have another bad dream, sweetie?"

Molly nodded, leaning against Jacinth sleepily. Noticing the stranger, she looked up... and up, and up, to the Djinn's face. Her eyes widened, and with a rush she left Jacinth, the chubby arms locking around Kieran's leg as she gazed, apparently enchanted, at that hard face.

Kieran looked down at the little girl, then cast a flashing glance at Jacinth, his eyes no longer cold but blazing as hot and bright as fire.

"Why have you not helped this child?" He turned an angry, contemptuous gaze on Douglas. "Did the *Sahib* not wish to waste one of his precious wishes to help his daughter?"

The Djinn bent, lifting Molly easily in his arms. Molly laughed in delight, patting his lean cheeks and clutching a lock of long white hair tightly in one fist.

Douglas started forward, his own anger flooding over.

"Of course I wanted to help her! But we thought it best to see if she could come to terms with things in her own way."

"It was his first thought," Jacinth affirmed indignantly. "I was the one who told him no, that we should wait. You know some things are best left to heal naturally, Kieran. I judged that this was one."

Douglas reached for Molly, but his daughter clung to her new friend. Kieran in his turn seemed equally taken, the cold, hard line of his mouth softening as he murmured soft unintelligible words to the little girl he held so easily, stroking the golden curls with an oddly gentle touch.

Jacinth pulled Douglas away from the Djinn, taking his hand in hers with warning pressure. She tugged at his arm, and he leaned down.

"Kieran doesn't like children," she whispered into his ear. "Not even Djinn children. I never saw him hold one before. Never."

Kieran transferred his gaze to Jacinth, his expression gentler.

"The child will be fine," he said. "There's nothing terribly wrong. She should begin speaking in a few more days. It's good that she's with her father now, away from the mother."

By the darkling glance he cast at Douglas, it was clear the Djinn's admission was grudging. "Keep an eye on her, Jacinth. If you need me, call. I will come."

Bending down, he set Molly carefully on her feet but allowing the child to cling to his hand, seeming reluctant to let her go.

"Goodbye, Molly."

"Kieran!" Jacinth exclaimed sharply. She nodded at Molly. "Watch yourself."

Apparently, the Djinn had been about to disappear... or blink out, or whatever it was they did. Kieran nodded, however, and without another glance at Douglas, went down the porch steps and strode away.

A heart-rending wail came from Molly, who toddled towards the steps. Jacinth caught her and brought her to Douglas, but Molly refused to be comforted.

"Kayr!"

"What?" Douglas stopped rocking her, looking down in surprise. A pair of drenched gentian-petal eyes gazed back.

"Kayr!"

Ah, hell. For a week he'd tried everything to coax his daughter to talk, and the first word she said was the name of that arrogant icicle of a Djinn.

"Douglas! She spoke!" Jacinth launched herself at him, hugging them both in her excitement.

"Yeah," Douglas responded without enthusiasm. "She did."

"Kayr!" Molly demanded, her wail rising once more.

"Hush, baby." Jacinth took her from Douglas, cuddling her. "He'll be back to see you. You don't want him to see you crying, do you?"

Molly snuffled, thinking about that. The little golden head shook slowly.

"And you want your Daddy to be able to tell him what a good girl you've been," Jacinth prompted.

Molly's nod was more sure, and she squirmed to get down.

"Bed," she announced, tugging at Douglas' hand, the big eyes beseeching. She yawned and snuggled against Douglas' chest when he lifted her. "Sleepy."

Douglas cast an anxious glance at Jacinth, who smiled encouragement at him.

"She'll be fine. You can't expect her to babble like a brook the very moment she starts talking again. Take her on to bed, Douglas, and I'll lock up the house for the night."

"While you're at it, see if you can think up some way to explain Molly's sudden decision to talk to my parents in the morning," he grumbled as he disappeared down the hall toward Molly's room.

CHAPTER 11

"Morning."

Jacinth looked up from the batter she was stirring to see Douglas wander into the dining room, blinking sleepily. He was still in his pajamas, unshaven, his feet bare and his hair tousled just like Benny's. The striped pajamas hid strong, tanned, muscular arms, and his broad shoulders were just the right height for her to lean her head. She had to fight back the urge to go to him, to smooth back the thick, wavy hair from his face, and be enfolded in his arms.

She sighed, reining in her wayward thoughts. Why did Douglas have to be so... well... masculine? In all her centuries, she'd never been as attracted to any Djinn as strongly as she was to this man.

"Why the sad face?" Douglas wanted to know. He came into the kitchen, sliding his arm around her waist and dropping a kiss on her hair. Since he was dipping into the batter with his other hand, she wasn't fooled, and smacked at his hand with the spoon.

"None of that," she warned. "I've got lots of people to feed this morning."

He grinned, unrepentant, licking batter from a finger.

"Pancakes," he approved. "Want me to help? I can make the bacon. The kids are awake. I told them to get dressed, so they'll be here in a few."

He sighed, his eyes darkening with emotion. "Molly hasn't said one word this morning."

"It's early yet," Jacinth reassured him. "At least she made the break-through last night. It's been a big change for both of them, Douglas. Give her some time."

"Yeah, I know. It's just... I worry about her. You know?"

"Mmhmm." Her instinctive response to lean into the arm still about her, and with difficulty she restrained. "I saw your parents a little while ago. They went jogging, hand-in-hand like a pair of teenagers."

Douglas laughed, taking his arm from around her to stretch, leaning back.

"Yeah, that's Mom and Dad, all right. They've been billing and cooing like love birds for thirty years. Wish I were that lucky."

He turned away abruptly, as if regretting his words. Jacinth took a step forward, resting her hand on his arm.

"You could wish for that, you know," she said softly.

"What?" he asked, a slight note of bitterness in his deep voice. "That Jane Q. Public down the street falls wildly in love with me and we live happily ever after?"

"No." She felt his resistance, his anger, but she didn't understand where it was coming from. "I can't do that. But you can wish for the right person to come into your life, someone right for you and the children, and you're right for her."

There was a silence, as if he were struggling with himself.

"No. Thank you." He moved away. "I'll go get dressed, and see what's keeping the kids."

DAMMIT, dammit, dammit! Why couldn't she see it? Douglas ran his hands through his hair as he strode down the hall to his room. Why couldn't she see that *she* was the one he wanted... that she was perfect for him and the kids? And he was sure... so sure... that they were perfect for her as well. She was happy with them, content. He knew she was. More than that, though, he couldn't picture living his whole life through with anyone but Jacinth at his side... and he *could* picture that.

Douglas stripped quickly, swearing under his breath. What the hell was wrong with him? She was a genie, for God's sake. She didn't belong here, and certainly wasn't going to give up whatever it was she did as a genie to spend fifty or sixty years with him. He must be out of his mind to even be thinking about her.

With jerky movements he pulled on underwear and a pair of jeans. Maybe it was just... what was that word? Consanguinity? No. Propinquity, that was it. Maybe what he needed was to get out more. Yeah, that was it, he thought with a sigh, pulling his shirt over his head.

Of course, he had no idea how or where to meet women. He hadn't dated since his college days, when he and Lilian had first met. After his experience with his ex-wife, bars or nightclubs were definitely out of the question. Hell. Maybe he'd ask Troy, his best friend since middle school and one of his partners at the clinic, where he found women to date. Troy was single, maybe he'd have some ideas.

Too bad the idea of dating didn't hold much appeal. Not with Jacinth, sweet and womanly alluring, filling his home with the kind of love and laughter he'd always envisioned in a family. Having finished dressing, he went into the bathroom, where he stared at his reflection in the mirror and ran his fingers over the roughness of his unshaven chin. Hell with it. He didn't feel like shaving. If anybody didn't like it, they didn't have to look at him. That suited him just fine.

He stomped back out to the kitchen to find his parents had returned. Skye was squeezing oranges into a pitcher, but Blue poured a cup of coffee and handed it to him. He saw his mother shoot Jacinth a look, easily interpretable: What's wrong with *him*? Jacinth shrugged her pretty shoulders, looking bewildered.

Great! Just great! He could hardly go two minutes without thinking about her, and damn it, she didn't have a clue!

Benny came skipping into the room, Molly half a step behind him. After hugging their grandparents, Benny went to sit at his place at the table while Jacinth lifted Molly into her booster seat. Skye came from the kitchen bearing the pitcher of orange juice and two glasses.

"Who wants orange juice?"

"I do, Gram!" Benny bounced in his chair. "Please," he added as an after-thought.

Skye poured him a glass, leaning down to kiss his cheek as she set it beside him. "There you go, lovey."

She turned to Molly. "And you, my sweet girl?"

Molly nodded vigorously.

"What do we say?" Skye held the pitcher poised over the glass. "Oh!" She froze, her hand going to her mouth, glancing at Douglas in apology.

"Please." Molly's voice sounded clear and firm in the sudden silence.

There was a gasp from Skye, and a relieved exhalation from Blue.

"Well, you clever girl," Skye praised, filling the juice glass. She put the pitcher down and hugged the little girl tight.

Jacinth's eyes were glowing, and when she looked at Douglas, he saw the sheen of tears.

"She's going to be okay," she whispered.

He chuckled. "I'll probably look back on these days of silence with fond regret."

Beside him, his father guffawed, and clapped him on the back. "You may at that, boy."

After that the morning passed quickly. With breakfast done and the dishes washed, Blue and Skye bundled the children off to the park, and Douglas and Jacinth were alone.

"Wow!" Jacinth sank into the sofa with a sigh of relief.

"I know." Douglas groaned, sitting beside her and leaning back into the cushions. "It's so quiet... feels kinda weird. Like the eye of the hurricane maybe?"

"Enjoy it," she advised with a smile, her eyes sparkling. "Who knows when it may happen again?"

He chuckled. "You may have a point."

Douglas lifted a strand of her long hair, curling the silky stuff around his finger, and he caught the faint scent of lilacs.

"So, you have the day off today. Is there something you want to do? Can I take you somewhere? Or are you going to go vessel-hopping?"

She considered, sliding him a sideways glance.

"Actually, there is something I'd like to do... if it's possible. Could we go horseback riding?"

Her expressive eyes held a hopeful expression so reminiscent of Molly's silent pleading that he had to laugh.

"I think that can be arranged. There are some stables nearby, but let me give Troy a shout first and see if he's free to meet us at his place. He's got a few horses, and won't mind us taking them out."

"Troy?"

"Troy Shelton, one of my partners at the vet clinic. He was my best friend since we were kids. We went to college together, and met our other partner, Suzanne, in veterinary college. Troy's specialty is cats, and Suzanne takes care of the dogs. I do mostly horses but general livestock as well. Troy and Suzanne split up the miscellany that any clinic gets… rabbits, guinea pigs, and what-not. Troy lives out in the country, not far from the clinic. Sit tight, and let me call him."

Douglas' partner lived in a sprawling old farm house that looked like it had been there since the American Revolution. Past the house, in a well-kept pasture, half a dozen horses grazed. Jacinth stared at them as Douglas parked the car behind the house, her eyes wide.

"Douglas, they are huge!"

"Mmhmm," he answered, his glance lingering on the becoming flush in her cheeks, the sweep of her long black lashes, her sparkling eyes. "Used to Arabians, are you?"

"Yes. What are these?"

"Friesians. They're what we call half-draft horses. They're bigger than regular horses but not as massive as the full drafts, like Clydesdales. They were bred long ago in Europe to carry knights into battle, armor and all."

"Really?" Jacinth's eyes lit like stars. "I remember a movie I saw a long time ago. It was a man and woman who had been cursed… he turned into a wolf at night, and she was a hawk in the daytime. The knight had a horse that looked just like these… big and black, with that long rippling mane."

Douglas nodded. "That would be Ladyhawke. We have it on DVD at home, if you want to watch it again. And yes, that was a Friesian in the movie. They're gaited horses these days, used for dressage."

"Like the Lipizzaners," Jacinth said knowledgeably.

"Yes, exactly. Would you like to get out of the car and ride one, or do you want to sit here and look at them?"

She threw him a laughing glance over her shoulder, and reached for the door handle. "What do you think?"

A shaggy blond giant appeared on the back steps as they exited the car, calling out a welcome.

"Yo, Doug-man!"

He came up to them, his dark green eyes examining Jacinth. He whistled in appreciation.

"Your nanny? She's a child herself!"

Jacinth bristled, pulling herself up to her full five feet two inches.

"I am not!" she exclaimed indignantly.

Troy grinned, buffeting Douglas in their usual manner of greeting.

"Just teasing," he reassured her in a deep, rumbling voice. He held out his hand with a smile. "Troy Shelton, at your service."

Jacinth's small hand was engulfed in Troy's big paw. "Jacinth. I'm pleased to meet you."

Douglas wondered if he'd made a tactical error. With his large, muscular frame, his mane of dark blond hair and easy-going, laid back charm, Troy drew the ladies like flies. Jacinth was walking beside him, chatting up a storm about the horses, Douglas trailing along behind the two.

When they reached the paddock fence, Troy put two fingers to his mouth and let out an ear-piercing whistle. The large beasts raised ebony heads and, snorting, trotted to the fence. Amazingly, or maybe not so amazingly, Douglas thought with a grimace, they clustered against the fence, shoving each other to be the closest to Jacinth, who was laughing and stroking the black noses. The wooden fence groaned under the massive weight pressed against it, and Douglas slipped an arm about Jacinth's slender waist, pulling her a few steps back.

"We don't want them breaking the fence down," he told her when she looked up at him, the corners of her mouth drooping. He laughed at her disappointed expression, resisting the impulse to kiss those lush lips.

"Let's go riding," he told her.

She brightened immediately, the sparkle returning to her eyes.

"Okay."

Grooming and saddling the horses was quite an experience, since both horses kept doing their best to get as close to Jacinth as possible. They finally had to use the cross-ties to get the job done. Douglas went to help Jacinth mount the massive beast--her head barely came to her horse's shoulder--but she laughed at him and hauled herself up and over the horse's back, scrambling a bit until she was in the saddle. He grinned up at her, enjoying the sight of her flushed cheeks and flying hair.

"Not exactly the most graceful mount I've ever seen," he teased her, and her laughter rang in the rafters of the old barn.

"I'm up, aren't I? That's what counts."

Troy chuckled, and gave the nearest horse a friendly slap on the rump. "So it is. Well, I'll leave you two to it. Enjoy yourselves."

Douglas mounted with the smoothness of experience, and

they headed towards the door of the barn. Jacinth settled herself comfortably in her saddle, accustoming herself to the long, rolling gait, so unlike the quick, shorter steps of the Arabians she'd grown up riding. Together they turned their horses toward the woods beyond the pastures, riding side by side, close enough that their legs brushed.

"Is it always like that?" Douglas asked her once they were out of earshot of the barn and house.

"With horses? Yes, pretty much," Jacinth admitted. She leaned forward to slap the heavily muscled neck of her horse in a friendly manner, liking the feel of the rough hair, the long strands of mane tangling in her fingers. "I like horses, and they like me."

"Can you read their minds?"

"No. At least, nothing so specific. I can tell their mood, and if they are hurt, but that's all."

"Unless, of course, they're telepathic," Douglas said, tongue firmly in cheek.

Jacinth beamed at him, her eyes sparkling with amusement. "Cat. Do you know, I've heard all my life of shapeshifters, but I'd never actually met one until Cat... at least, as far as I know. They live among the humans, not like us Djinn, but they pretty much keep to themselves. They're very careful to keep their existence a secret."

"I can imagine so," Douglas remarked, his tone wry. "I can imagine what would happen if the world found out about them."

Jacinth mulled that over. "I suppose so. They don't have magic to disappear, like we do. Although I don't know how anyone could tell that someone was a shapeshifter, unless they were actually seen shifting. Still, it isn't news they'd want to get about. And we Djinn, at least, have the ability to erase the memory of any human we feel could be a threat to our own anonymity."

"I shouldn't think it was necessary, if you can just disappear into your teapot... or vessel, or whatever."

Jacinth shook her head vigorously. "But it's better for all concerned if humans, as a whole, have no knowledge of us. Besides those that would be looking for us to use us, just think of those who would claim we were actually demons. It'd be like the Inquisition again, everyone scrutinizing everyone else, looking for some kind of good luck a friend might have gotten from calling a Djinn, or blaming bad luck on a neighbor or jealous coworker having called a Djinn. No, we're better off as we are, mankind and Djinn alike."

"Can you stop being a Djinn, and become human?"

Jacinth regarded him with tolerance.

"Hollywood," she pronounced, nodding sagely. "Douglas, one cannot stop being Djinn. We are... what we are. Just as you cannot decide to suddenly stop being human and be a... a fish!"

"A fish?" Douglas couldn't help it... he burst out laughing. Jacinth's eyes twinkled responsively.

"But," he continued, "There must be some kind of relationship genetically, for a Djinn and a human to be able to have children together."

Jacinth wrinkled her brow thoughtfully. "There are old stories of very rare cases of a mortal becoming Djinn. I don't know if they are true. But a Djinn could never become mortal. Because of our fire, you see. We are made of fire, whereas man is made of clay. If the Djinn fire should leave us, we would cease to exist."

They had reached the cooling shade of the trees. Nearby a creek burbled, and a slight breeze moved the leaves overhead.

Jacinth brushed back the wisps of hair that clung to her face and neck, breathing a sigh of relief.

"Oh, this is nice."

Douglas was still thinking over what she'd told him. "Djinn fire? You mean... there's literally fire? Real, physical fire?"

Jacinth slid him a sideways glance, mischief dancing in her eyes. "Yes. Watch."

She touched her fingertips to her chest a moment, then extended her arms, palms up. Small blue flames raced down her arms, pooling in her cupped hands to form into a single cohesive fire the size of Douglas' fist. Jacinth laughed, watching it flare brightly, and lifted her hands. The flame disbursed, blue licks dancing between the slender fingers and zooming up and down her arms in blazing ripples, pausing at her shoulders to reach high as if licking at her cheek, like a puppy in ecstasies. The fire was playing with her, Douglas realized, interacting with a delight Jacinth obviously shared. It was fascinating.

"Is it alive?" He was almost afraid to interrupt the rapport between Djinn and flame, but curiosity was consuming him. "Is it... is it sentient?"

"Not sentient," Jacinth replied. She cupped her hands once more, gathering the flames there, then brought her hands to her breast once more and the fire disappeared, absorbed into her being. She smiled at Douglas.

"But it is alive. The fire and the Djinn have a sort of symbiotic relationship. The fire cannot exist without us, because it doesn't burn like the physical fire... it's more like," she frowned, searching for a way to explain. "It's more like a fire of the soul. It is our very essence, and the stronger we are, the brighter it burns. Those who are sad or tired, their flame diminishes, even to the point of banking, like you would do to embers. Then the Djinn may sleep in a kind of hibernation until their fire is restored. The oldest, most powerful Djinn, like Kieran, their fire is almost an inferno, such that you can almost see it."

Yeah, Douglas could see that. The guy practically smoldered. More like dry ice, though... so cold you'd be burnt if you touched it. He allowed himself an inward laugh, but was careful not to let it show. He didn't think Jacinth would appreciate the joke. She seemed unaccountably fond of the powerful elder Djinn.

The path they were following crossed the shallow creek they'd been riding alongside, and they came to a stop to let the horses drink. Jacinth dropped the reins on her horse's neck, and stretched, enjoying the breeze, the sounds of the forest and birds about them, the jangle of the bridles as the horses drank.

Douglas reached over to catch at the loose reins, but Jacinth shook her head at him.

"Oh, she won't go anywhere," she assured him. "Horses never bolt with me."

Of course they wouldn't. In fact... Douglas leaned down to stroke the neck of his horse, his brows pulling together in thought. Jacinth seemed to be able to do almost anything with the animals. Maybe... just maybe...

"Perhaps you could help me with a horse." He straightened in his saddle and fixed his gaze on her face. "The county raided a farm about a couple of weeks ago, and we rescued some animals. I've got a mare over at the clinic that no one can do anything with. She's terrified. She was abused and neglected. She's also pregnant, and I can't get near her to check on how she's doing, how the foal is doing."

Jacinth's eyes flashed dangerously, and her pretty lips thinned with indignation. "I hate when people abuse animals,

Douglas. I hate it! Of course I can help with her. Let's go right this minute."

They turned the horses, and she flashed him a sparkling grin. "Race you back!"

Troy appeared on his porch as they cantered up to the barn and hurried over to join them, concern etched on his face.

"You're back soon! Is anything wrong?"

"Nothing," Douglas assured him. "I'm taking Jacinth to see if she can help me with Lizzie."

Jacinth wrinkled her nose. "Lizzie?"

"After Lizzie Borden," Troy told her a bit grimly. He transferred his frowning gaze to Douglas. "Are you out of your mind? She's just a little bit of a thing. You shouldn't be letting her--or anyone else, either--anywhere near Lizzie."

Douglas swung down from the saddle and caught Jacinth as she slid off, setting her safely on the hay-strewn floor beside him. "Trust me, Troy. If anyone can help Lizzie, it's Jacinth."

"Dammit, Doug, that horse is vicious. Look at me, man." A large hand descended on Doug's shoulder, turning him to face his partner. "This is me... Troy. Your best friend, fellow vet and horse lover. She needs to be put down, and you know I don't say that lightly. She's going to hurt someone, Doug. She could *kill* someone."

Jacinth watched Douglas run his fingers through his hair, ruffling the thick waves. It was clear that deep inside he agreed with his friend, but he was unwilling to admit defeat, to give up on an abused animal.

Right at that moment she felt a small "thunk" in her chest, as part of her heart melted and she fell just a little bit in love with him. Not too much, she assured herself... nothing she couldn't deal with. Nothing she couldn't walk away from when the time came, when Douglas had made his third wish and it was time for her to leave. She'd granted hundreds of people wishes and disappeared from their lives forever over the last millennium. So why did she feel so empty then at the prospect of never seeing Douglas again?

"Look, I'll tell you what, Troy," Douglas was saying. "If Jacinth can't do anything with her, I'll put her down after the foal is weaned, or after its born if she's a danger to it."

Troy watched his friend closely, eyes narrowed. "Without risking your life trying to tame the beast?"

"Okay, yes! I agree. Besides," Douglas said, smiling a little. "I've got my kids now. I have to stay whole and healthy for them."

"Don't forget that, then," his friend warned. "I swear to God, Douglas, if I find you in her stall again, I'll... I'll..."

"Call me," Jacinth interjected, aiming a scowl at Douglas. "If the horse is truly that dangerous, he has no business risking life or limb... not with the children depending on him."

"She's vicious," Troy stated, not mincing words. He stepped forward to take the reins from them, jerking his head over his shoulder towards Douglas' car. "You two go on, I'll put these guys away."

"Is she really that dangerous?" Jacinth asked as Douglas backed the car around and headed down the drive.

Douglas sighed. "Yes, she is. But it's not hatred I see in her eyes when she looks at me, but fear. That's why I haven't been able to give up on her. She's terrified of all of us."

"Who's this Lizzie Borden that Troy mentioned?"

Douglas turned out of the driveway onto the paved road, his fingers flexing on the steering wheel. "Good old American folklore. According to the story, which may or may not be true, Lizzie Borden took an axe to her mother and father as they lay sleeping one night... oh, a hundred years ago. The staff started calling the mare that the very first day, because she was so savage. We don't know what name she had before."

The clinic wasn't far from Troy's farm, and within a few minutes they pulled into the driveway, passing the parking lot and circling the large, sprawling building to the back, where parking was reserved for the staff. Kennels ran the length of the back of the building, and dogs leaped at the fences, barking loudly.

"We board animals, as well as treat them," Douglas explained as they got out of the car. "These here are mostly boarders on this side."

Across the parking lot behind the main building was a traditional red barn, complete with white trim, double doors, and a massive hayloft. Jacinth surveyed the barn with interest, then nodded in approval.

"I like this older style," she said. "I don't like those new barns they make these days, there's no character to them. This is nice."

"That was one of the main considerations when we bought the place," Douglas told her. "We wanted separate wings for cats and dogs, and a barn for livestock. The barn was already here, but the rest was just a big, vacant lot, so we could build the clinic to suit ourselves. Troy already had his place, Lilian and I bought the house we live in now, and Suzanne, our third partner, married a veterinarian who was already established nearby. We all live within about a half hour drive of the clinic."

They'd reached the barn doors, and Douglas ushered her inside. Light poured in from the upper story windows, and whirling fans hanging from the ceiling moved the air, dispelling the heat. A young man and woman in overalls were busily employed in cleaning out stalls, while another young man, with a nod at Douglas, carried a bucket of oats into a stall further down the aisle.

Douglas led her to the far end of the barn, where the last stalls had been heavily reinforced with heavier wood and bars.

"A must in every veterinary practice that treats horses," Douglas explained. "Biters, kickers, truly vicious animals... eventually you see it all."

They came up to the bars and he heard Jacinth catch her breath at her first sight of the mare.

"Douglas! Oh, Douglas, she's so beautiful!"

She was at that, although he was surprised that Jacinth had seen that first off. Although the palomino mare was well-proportioned, with strong, clean lines, an arching neck and proud head, she was in disgraceful condition. Her coat was filthy, the long flaxen mane and tail so tangled and matted they'd need to be cut. Her hooves hadn't been trimmed or shod and were overlong, beginning to curl at the bottom. But underneath it all was a beautiful horse, one he was willing to fight to save.

Lizzie was backed into the far corner of the box stall, alarmed at their presence. She pawed at the straw, snorting loudly... a clear warning to them not to come closer.

Jacinth looked up at him, the sparkle of fun gone from her chocolate brown eyes.

"Douglas, will you leave me alone with her for a few minutes?"

No way. "Jacinth..."

She stopped him, putting a hand on his arm.

"Please. She cannot hurt me, Douglas. And I won't go inside until she will accept my presence."

Yes, he knew the mare couldn't harm the Djinn... after all, Jacinth could simply disappear, or whatever she called it. Still...

"You asked me to help you with her." Jacinth reminded him gently. "Now let me do so."

With a last uncertain glance at the mare, Douglas nodded and stepped back.

"I'll make sure no one comes near this end of the barn. Call me if you need me, if I can help."

Jacinth's attention was already on the horse, and he noted that the mare's snorting had already become quieter. Relieved, he turned away.

With his departure, some of the animal's agitation lessened. The pawing ceased, and the mare regarded Jacinth out of wide, wary eyes.

"Come on, girl," Jacinth coaxed, keeping her voice low and soothing. "You know I'm different. You know I won't hurt you."

In only a very few minutes, the fear in the mare's eyes had subsided, replaced by a spark of curiosity. She still dipped her head and snorted, but that, too, was more uncertainty than fear. Without seeming to hurry, Jacinth slid back the latch on the door and stepped inside the stall.

"Poor girl," she crooned. She held out one hand, but didn't approach the mare closer. "Such an awful name they gave you. We'll call you Firefly, which was the name of my first pony. Will that please you?"

The mare snorted again, bobbing her head, and took a tentative step forward. She stretched out her neck to its full extent, snuffling at Jacinth's outstretched hand. Another step brought the mare closer, and the golden muzzle hovered just inches from her fingers.

"There, you see? You want me to stroke you," Jacinth told her. She closed her hand, then opened it to reveal a few lumps of sugar. "One more step, sweet girl."

The mare took another step, and soft lips brushed across

Jacinth's palm, sweeping the offering up. Keeping her movements slow, Jacinth stroked the velvety nose, tracing the white blaze up to the mare's forehead. Firefly angled her head, and Jacinth obliged by scratching the broad forehead below the filthy, matted forelock.

"We'll get you cleaned up, too," she promised. "Not right away, but soon."

Firefly butted her with her head, and Jacinth laughed, spelling a carrot into her hand. She stroked the rough neck as the mare crunched happily.

"It's not your fault, you know," she told the mare. "Some humans are that way. But you're in fine hands now. Douglas will take good care of you, you'll see."

"Jacinth?" Douglas' voice was very soft as he called from some distance away.

"Come slowly," she responded. "Tell everyone else to stay far away."

When Douglas appeared at the half-open stall door, he looked at them for a long moment, and a smile tugged at his mouth.

"She's eating out of your hand," he said in a low voice. "I should have known."

"Of course you should." Jacinth gestured him closer. The mare paid him little attention. She glanced at him, but was calm under Jacinth's caresses, seemingly more intent on finding more treats in Jacinth's free hand. An apple appeared next, which the large white teeth bit cleanly in half.

"Come to her other side, Douglas. Let her smell you."

Finishing the apple, the mare snuffled at Douglas' chest a moment, then turned her attention back to Jacinth.

"I've renamed her," Jacinth told him. "She's going to be called Firefly."

"Firefly," Douglas repeated. "You got it."

He stroked the mare's neck and shoulders, amazed at the amount of trust and faith Jacinth had inspired in the horse in less than a quarter of an hour. He'd known she could do it, and yet it still hardly seemed possible. Even more, he certainly hadn't expected that the abused creature would so readily accept himself, from Jacinth's mere presence.

"Keep absolutely everyone else away from her," Jacinth cautioned him. "I don't know your people, and they might for some reason spook her with unexpected noises or movements. Care for her yourself so that you can create a bond with her, and I'll visit her at night, when there's no one here and I can... you know."

"Pop in," he said with a grin. "I've got no argument with that. What about the foal?"

Jacinth's brilliant smile seemed to light up the stall. "The foal is fine, and Firefly will be a good mother. The most important thing right now is to get her clean. It's way too soon to try bathing her, but we can start by getting her used to being brushed."

"Do you think she'll ever be safe to ride?"

Jacinth had cradled the velvety muzzle in both her hands, rubbing her nose against the mare's and breathing into the large nostrils. She glanced up, her eyes dancing with as much mischief as satisfaction.

"She'll be so safe you can put Benny and Molly up on her. You have my word on it."

CHAPTER 12

DOUGLAS AND JACINTH arrived home in triumph.

"You should have seen her with that mare, Dad," Douglas told his father. "Jacinth just stood there talking to her, in some kind of a kind of croon, and the next thing you know she was in the stall and the horse was eating out of her hand. Literally!"

"Dad! Dad!" Benny tugged at his hand, with news of his own. "We saw Cat, but Gramma kept brushing her. She followed her around and around until finally Cat ran away."

Jacinth burst into a peal of laughter. "I wish I'd been there to see it!"

She started for the kitchen, but Skye caught her sleeve and pulled her down onto the sofa next to her.

"And where do you think you're going, young woman?"

Jacinth stared at her. "Umm… to see about starting dinner?"

"No way." That was Blue. "We have to leave tomorrow morning, so we're taking the four of you out to dinner tonight."

Benny jumped up, punching the air. "Cool! Where are we going?"

"I saw a steak house down the road a bit..." Blue started, only to be interrupted by his wife.

"Blue! We're not going to any steakhouse. Remember your cholesterol."

"Chrissake, woman, once in a while isn't going to hurt me. I can take my son's family out for a steak dinner once in a while, can't I?"

His son's family. They'd included her in that family, Jacinth realized. A warm glow spread through her, fire coursing through her veins. She'd never been part of a family before. She'd had her mother, of course, but they'd been a very solitary pair even amongst Djinn. If only... she caught herself, cut off the thought before it went further. There was no use wanting what couldn't be.

AFTER SEEING Blue and Skye off on the next morning, the children were tearful and subdued. Jacinth rather missed them too. It was nice to have another woman around. Last night they'd sat on the porch and talked while the men tinkered with the RV, making testosterone kind of noises, their deep voices drifting across the yard to where she and Skye sat on the swing, rocking gently. It had been a long time since she'd had a woman friend, someone to sit and talk to, share secrets. There was Alessandra of course, but she and Julian needed time together to build their new relationship, their new life.

By Wednesday things were back to normal. The house was relatively quiet. Douglas had left for work, and the children were in their rooms, Benny reading one of his books, and Molly playing with her dolls. Jacinth settled herself into a deep cushioned chair and conjured up a cup of steaming Turkish coffee. She took a sip, savoring the rich scent and flavor with a sigh of pure pleasure.

Djinn.

The voice in her mind was very faint. Jacinth sat up and looked around, seeing no one. Cat?

Djinn, you're too far away for me to read you. If you can hear me...

It was Cat! Jacinth stood, concentrating in hopes of hearing better. The mental voice was faint, and thready with... pain? Fear? The voice grew slightly stronger, as if Cat called up all her energy in her cry for help.

I'm in the animal shelter. Dog in the park... attacked me. I'm all right... but the cage they put me in is small ... I can't shift. If you can hear me... please help. Cat's voice faded again abruptly. *Call Douglas.*

Douglas, of course! He was a veterinarian, he could get her out of there with no trouble. Jacinth ran for her cell phone where she'd lift it on the counter, but Douglas' number went straight to voice mail. Impatiently she scrolled down to the number to the veterinary clinic.

"Dr. McCandliss, please."

"I'm sorry, he's out on a call." The receptionist was apologetic. "Would you like to leave a message?"

"Um... No." Jacinth thought quickly. "It's rather urgent. This is Jacinth, I'm watching Douglas' children. What about Troy? Dr. Shelton?"

"Let me check."

There was a moment of silence, and a man's voice came on the phone.

"Dr. Shelton."

"Troy? This is Jacinth," she began.

"Yes? Is something wrong?" His response was quick and concerned.

"Not with the children." Jacinth bit her lip, trying to decide how much to say without saying too much. "There's a cat at the park nearby that the children always play with. She's very friendly and gentle. A dog attacked her today, and she was taken to the shelter. I don't have a car, and Douglas is out on a call. I need someone to go get her, make sure she's all right. The children would be devastated if anything happened to her... we all would."

"No problem," the deep voice assured her. "I'll run over and pick her up. What does she look like?"

"She's a long-haired calico tabby, lots of red. A Maine Coon, rather large. Call me right away if there's any problem, or... or if she's badly hurt, would you?"

"I have your number on my phone now, I'll give you a shout as soon as I've got her."

"Thank you," Jacinth told him, feeling deep gratitude. "We'll reimburse you anything it costs."

He chuckled. "No problem. I'll have it out of Douglas' hide, make him cover for me some Saturday."

His teasing made her smile, soothing some of her anxiety. He'd get Cat, and she'd be okay.

"We'll be waiting to hear from you."

She hung up, and immediately Benny came running to her, followed closely by Molly, their eyes wide and anxious.

"Miss Jas, we heard you on the phone. Is Cat going to be all right?" Benny wanted to know.

Molly said nothing, but leaned against her knee, the big eyes filling with tears.

"Yes, she'll be fine," Jacinth reassured them. "Dr. Shelton is going to get her now, and he'll take care of her. She's at the animal shelter, and they would have sent her straight to a vet if she was badly hurt. He's going to call us as soon as he's got her."

At least, she guessed they would have taken her to a vet if she was hurt. Maybe they wouldn't, or maybe they had vets at the shelter. She didn't know how these places worked. But it was important to reassure the children.

Benny was fidgeting again, a sure sign that his brain was kicking into high gear.

"How did... mmmphf."

Jacinth's hand clapped over his mouth, and she frowned at him, cocking her head towards Molly. He nodded, understanding, and she let him go. Molly, bless her heart, just accepted that Jacinth knew what was happening with Cat, as she accepted everything else. She was such a doll. Affection for the girl welled up, and Jacinth scooped Molly into her arms, planting kisses all over her face and hugging her until the little girl squealed. Benny joined in, wrapping his arms around Jacinth's neck, and they all fell to the ground in a tumble of laughter.

Jacinth emerged breathless, clapping her hands sharply.

"Okay. Listen up. Now Grandma and Gramps are gone, we've got to get on a schedule. First thing is to pick up your bedrooms."

"Aww." Both children whined, and she grinned at them, ruffling Benny's hair.

"Yes. Come on now."

Molly hung back, her rosy lips set in a mutinous pout. "I don't want to."

Jacinth pulled the little girl into a hug, glad that at least she was finally beginning to talk more.

"I'll help," she promised. "Okay?"

That satisfied the children, and she led them towards the

back of the house, mentally constructing a story that would explain how she knew about Cat being injured. A phone call, she decided, from a neighbor who'd been at the park, and ran home to call Douglas, having seen the cat hanging around the house before. That would work. But she was going to have to be more careful. It was starting to take a surprising amount of effort to hide the truth from Benny.

When the phone rang again not quite an hour later, Jacinth pulled it from her pocket and swiped it to answer, all but dropping it in her haste.

"Yes?"

"Hey, it's Troy. I got the cat just fine. Her shoulder and front leg are a little chewed up, and maybe a broken rib or two, so I'm going to take her home with me. I got hold of Douglas before I left the clinic; he said to tell you he's going to be out late on a call, or he'd bring her home himself."

"As long as she's safe, that's all that matters," Jacinth said, grateful that Cat was in good hands. She knew Douglas thought highly of his friend and partner. If anyone was qualified to take good care of Cat, it was Troy.

"I didn't have any trouble finding her," he reassured her in his deep voice. "She saw me as soon as I walked into the room and set up a howl, just like she knew who I was. She came out of that cage and clung to me like she'd known me all her life. She's a sweet little thing. She's cuddled up to me now here in the car, purring like mad."

Jacinth laughed, delighted, wondering what Troy would say if he knew what he actually had there.

"What's her name?" Troy asked.

Oops. She winced. "Cat. Long story. I'll explain sometime."

"Cat it is. Well, I'm headed for home now, get her settled in and head back to the clinic. I'll keep in touch and let you know how she is."

"Thanks. We all appreciate it."

She relayed the information to the delighted children, and promised them they'd see Cat again soon. She sent them back to work cleaning their rooms while she vacuumed. Not her favorite job, but it needed to be done, and with the children present she had no other choice than to do it herself. Djinn definitely had it made over humans, she reaffirmed.

Jacinth was just putting the vacuum away when Douglas arrived, looking anxious.

"I thought you weren't coming home until late?"

"I have a late appointment for this evening," he acknowledged, sliding his arm about her waist. He leaned down to rub his cheek against her hair in such an absent-minded manner she wasn't sure he knew he was doing it. "I didn't have much this afternoon though, so I rescheduled for tomorrow. Have you heard from Troy? I heard the news, but I haven't been able to reach him on his cell."

He'd taken time off work because he was worried about Cat? That was... sweet. She leaned into him, the encircling arm tightening about her. His shoulder was just the right height for her to lay her head, and she had to fight the compulsion to take advantage of that. She breathed in deeply, allowing his scent to encompass her, as rich and pleasant as the Turkish coffee she'd been enjoying earlier, with faint overtones of horse.

"Cat is fine," she reassured him. "Troy called, he said she had some wounds but would be okay. He's taken her home."

"That's a relief. Do the kids know?"

"Yes, they overheard me talking to Troy." She drew back, gnawing on her lower lip and wondering if she should confess. "Um... Benny asked me how I knew she'd been hurt. I told him a neighbor who'd seen her hanging around the house had been in the park and saw what happened, and called me, thinking she was ours. I don't know if he believes it or not."

Douglas thought about that for a moment. "Sounds reasonable to me. Why shouldn't he believe it?"

"Maybe because the phone hadn't rung?" Jacinth suggested. "Although they were in their rooms at the time, so..."

"Hey, Dad!" Benny's shout all but raised the roof, and the boy came barreling down the hallway. "You're home early, cool!"

"Just for a couple hours," Douglas replied, stepping away from Jacinth to catch his son up in his arms. Benny giggled madly as Douglas held him upside down.

"Are you being good for Miss Jas?" Douglas demanded.

"No!" Benny squealed as Douglas tickled his bare tummy. "I'm being bad! I'm gonna make her walk the plank!"

The shrieks of laughter brought Molly, who laughed as she flung herself into the fray, and the three of them fell to the floor where they wrestled around and growled a bit.

Finally Douglas stood, flushed and feeling a little sheepish. He threw a lopsided grin Jacinth's way. She just laughed at him.

"So what are we going to do now?" Benny scrambled up from the floor.

Douglas reached down to haul Molly to her feet.

"You two go get your suits on, and Miss Jas and I will teach you to swim."

"Aw-right!"

He laughed as the kids ran off to their rooms. God, it was great to have them back. Beside him, Jacinth cleared her throat. She leaned forward, fixing him with a serious look.

"*You* are going to teach them to swim, while *I* lay out on the deck and soak up some rays, as they say."

Douglas let his eyes linger over the creamy skin of her face, her neck and arms. She was beautiful just as she was.

"You don't need a tan."

"Whatever. I am not getting in the water."

She was perfectly serious. Douglas studied her a moment, frowning.

"Jacinth, what's wrong?"

"Nothing is wrong. I don't swim, that's all."

"In nine hundred years, you never learned to swim?"

"Hush!" She glanced past him, down the hallway.

He lowered his voice. "How could you have not learned to swim, in all that time?"

"I just didn't!"

"Okay, okay." He grinned at her. "We'll just have to teach you too."

Jacinth visibly flinched, shrinking away from him. She glanced past him at the shimmering blue pool beyond the patio and shivered, and for the first time since he'd known her, Douglas saw fear touch her dark eyes.

"I can't, Douglas," she admitted. "I am Djinn. We are made of fire, as humans are made of clay, and we carry fire inside us. Djinn cannot tolerate immersion in water."

His heart almost stopped beating at the thought of something happening to Jacinth. "Being in water will kill you?"

"No! Oh no! Of course, it cannot actually harm us." She touched the pink tip of her tongue nervously to her lips. "But it is incompatible with our fire nature, and as such, we have a... a natural aversion to being immersed in water."

"You didn't have any problem when we were caught in that thunderstorm the other day."

Jacinth dismissed that with a wave of her hand.

"Rain isn't any problem. Or showers. I even like a bath now

and then to relax, with some fragrant oils." She thought that over, then admitted, "I don't put in more than a few inches of water, though."

Douglas shrugged. "If water can't actually hurt you, then the fear is irrational."

She fixed him with a firm look. "I am not going in a swimming pool. Period."

"Why not?" Benny came back into the room just then.

With a glare at Douglas, she took the boy's outstretched hand. "Because I don't swim, honey."

Benny thought that one over for a minute, then burst into a wide grin.

"My dad can teach you," he announced. "You can learn with us."

Douglas couldn't help it. He burst into laughter at the horrified look on Jacinth's face.

"I don't think she wants to, Ben," he told his son, ruffling the tousled hair.

"But don't say anything in front of Molly, okay, honey?" Jacinth cautioned the boy. "If she's not used to being in the water, we don't want her to think there's anything to be afraid of."

Benny nodded sagely, as solemn as a wise man, and Jacinth smothered a laugh.

"Go get the sunblock," she told him. "I'll get you and Molly covered while your dad changes, okay?"

He ran off willingly and reappeared with Molly close on his heels. She took them both outside, and had just finished slathering them with lotion when the patio door slid open and Douglas stepped out.

She knew she was staring, but she couldn't help herself. Douglas was *built*, as they said in this century. His tanned chest was broad with a light dusting of curling light brown hair, narrowing to a trim waist and narrow hips, extremely well set off by the navy swim trunks he wore. His long legs were muscular and well-shaped.

Noticing her gaze lingering on him, Douglas grinned at her. "Want to spread lotion on me, too?" he offered, his voice low and seductive, one eyebrow waggling suggestively.

Jacinth ignored her quivering insides. "I don't think so," she retorted, retreating to sit on a lounge some distance from the pool.

"Dad's gotta have sunblock or he'll get a burn," Benny put in helpfully.

Douglas managed to look innocent and slightly hurt. "You don't want me to get burned, do you?"

With both children looking on, she didn't have any choice.

"Just your back," she told Douglas.

He grinned, sitting carefully on the edge of the lounge. She smeared a generous glob of the lotion across his shoulders, rubbing it in. His skin was smooth and warm to the touch. She liked the way his shoulders were muscled, strong but without the ridiculous bulges depicted on steamy romance novel covers. His masculine scent mingled with that of the suntan lotion, an incredibly pleasing combination, warm and earthy. She found her fingers lingering, exploring his back and shoulders. Shaking off the attraction, she finished spreading the lotion across his back, and handed him the bottle.

"You can do the rest."

Douglas looked over his shoulder at her, his blue-green eyes glinting wickedly.

"Want me to do you?"

"No!" Her breath almost stopped in her throat. "No, thanks, I'm fine."

She waved him away, gesturing at the waiting children.

"The swimming lesson?" she suggested in a sugary-sweet voice.

Douglas just grinned, and rose.

"Another time," he promised.

Her fingers still tingled with the feel of him. She didn't think she could take another time.

Holding Benny afloat while the boy kicked vigorously with his feet, the memory of Jacinth's touch, her fingers strong and soothing, remained. Wanting her was becoming a continual ache in his gut, the need to take her into his arms a growing compulsion. Odd that she was so afraid of the water, since it couldn't actually hurt her. She'd stayed well back from the pool, he remembered, when the serviceman came to clean the pool earlier that week, but he'd thought she was just staying out of the man's way. Looking back, in fact, he couldn't remember once in the several times they'd been in the back yard playing with the kids that Jacinth had come within ten feet of the swimming pool.

He set Benny to practicing his kicks from the side of the pool, and held out his arms for Molly. Glancing over at Jacinth, he almost laughed to see her sprawled on her stomach in the hammock, devouring a home and garden magazine. It just seemed so... well, so normal. June-and-Ward-Cleaver kind of normal. He shook his head, silently laughing at the thought. Normal? There was nothing remotely normal about having a genie in his life, much less in his backyard reading a ladies' magazine.

"Douglas!" Jacinth looked up just then, her brown eyes

glowing. "It says here there's something called a Princess of Wales rose. Could we get one?"

"One?" One what? Rose?

"A rose bush. We could plant it under Molly's window."

Molly looked up at him hopefully. "Please, Daddy? I want roses."

He tapped her nose. "You always want any flower, pumpkin."

"But this one is special," Jacinth insisted. "It was officially named in honor of Princess Diana. It says here it's ivory touched with pink. And 15% of the proceeds go to her memorial fund, to help people in need."

Douglas could no more resist the pleading in her eyes than the sun could resist rising.

"Okay, turn the page down, and I'll order it," he said.

The smile she turned on him was its own reward, but he noted her eyes were brimming with unshed tears.

"Thank you. It means a lot to me. I thought Diana was wonderful. When she was killed I could hardly believe it."

"You couldn't..." he glanced down at Molly. "There wasn't, uh... any way she could have been saved?"

Jacinth shook her head, sorrow in her dark eyes. "No interference, Douglas."

"Interference in what?" Benny piped up.

Douglas rolled his eyes.

"We'll continue this conversation later," he told Jacinth.

CHAPTER 13

"EASY THERE, NICE AND SLOW."

Douglas stroked the horse's muzzle as he checked the cross-ties attached to the halter. He nodded approvingly at Daniel, the gawky red-haired high school student who volunteered after school. "Good job on the grooming."

Apollo had been another rescue, although fortunately not in the same heart-breaking condition as Firefly. The bay gelding was going to his new home today.

"He l-likes being groomed," Daniel reported, running the stiff brush down the horse's flanks. "He'll stand still for hours as long as s-somebody's got a brush in their hand."

He had a slight stammer, and a nervous gulp that made his Adam's apple bob up and down, something Douglas judged would disappear with maturity and confidence. The boy was good with animals. Many of the high school students, bright-eyed and dreaming, didn't last long once faced with the darker side of veterinary practice, but Daniel had never flinched.

Douglas thought the boy would do well as a veterinarian, in time.

"You think he'll load okay?" Douglas asked the boy. He already knew the answer, but was curious to hear Daniel's opinion.

The boy nodded firmly, some of his diffidence vanishing. "Yes, Sir. He's fine with l-loading. We've been practicing loading him for a week now. He goes up the ramp s-smooth as pie."

A large blue pickup rolled into view, pulling a horse trailer behind it.

"Show time," Douglas told the boy, and stepped back to watch as Daniel took firm hold of the lead rope. The boy moved with smooth efficiency, without any hurried motions that might startle the horse. Together they moved forward from the darkness of the barn into the bright sunlight.

"Want to do the honors?" Douglas nodded to the approaching truck and trailer.

Daniel lit up like a Christmas tree, his eyes widening with anticipation.

"Sure thing, Dr. McCandliss!"

A tall, slender figure emerged from the clinic's main building and crossed the parking lot, clearly heading for him. He racked his brains for the name of the red-haired woman, a vet tech who worked with Suzanne. With relief her name came to him as she approached; it was so rude to forget the names of his own employees, although in his defense, she only worked inside in the wing reserved for the dogs. He'd passed her in the hallways now and then, but that was it.

"Good morning, Beatrice," he greeted her. "How can I help you?"

She handed him a sheaf of papers. "The receptionist asked

me to bring these out to you, the paperwork on Apollo." She looked past him at the horse who stood calmly beside Daniel. Another student volunteer hurried by to help open the back door of the trailer and let down the ramp.

"Oh, yes." Douglas took the papers, scanning them absently. "I could have printed out copies from here, but thank you."

Beatrice lingered. "You went to the Veterinary Conference last month?"

Raising his eyes from the papers, Douglas noted her eager expression. "Yes, in Michigan. I go every year."

"I've never been to one of the big conferences. I hope to go to one next year," she confided. "I'm trying to further my education."

"That's great," Douglas approved, making a note to check with Suzanne on the technician's performance. Maybe they could come up with a scholarship for her to go. Or maybe they could do a Tech of the Year award that came with a scholarship to the conference, and let the various techs and assistants compete for it. He'd bring it up at the next staff meeting.

"I was wondering," Beatrice continued, drawing his attention back to her. She tilted her head a little, sending a hesitant upward glance his way. "I would love to hear about the conference. Maybe we could get together after work and you can tell me about it? Over drinks, perhaps?"

Taken unawares, Douglas stared at her a long moment. His brain seemed to have turned off, and he couldn't think of a single thing to say.

"Umm..."

He was saved from his dilemma by Daniel calling him as they prepared to load Apollo into the horse trailer. "Dr. McCandliss, we're ready!"

"Be right there!" He called back, then turned back to Beatrice. "I'll have to get back to you on that," he promised.

Jogging over to the horse trailer, talking with Apollo's new owners and supervising as Daniel led the docile horse up the ramp and got him secured, Douglas found himself turning over the possibilities.

Well, why not? He'd been thinking of dating, and what would be a better way to ease himself back into the dating pool than a pleasant, stress-free meeting with a co-worker, talking shop? He could do this, he thought, pleased with himself.

After seeing Apollo off and sending Daniel back to the barn to his chores, Douglas strode across the parking lot to the clinic. Passing through the kennels, where dogs yapped eagerly for attention, he emerged into the relative quiet of the exam rooms. Beatrice was just coming out of one of these, a clipboard in one hand, looking cool and professional in pressed trousers and a light green tunic. She looked pleased to see him.

"Dr. McCandliss!"

"I've thought about your suggestion," he said, clearing his throat. He felt oddly nervous. It was just a get-together with a co-worker, he reminded himself. "How about we make it dinner, and we'll talk shop?"

For a moment her emerald green eyes seemed to sharpen in a way that seemed almost predatory. Then she smiled, her face lighting up, and the impression vanished. "Yes, I'd like that."

"Next Friday evening? Seven?"

"I'll look forward to it." From her clipboard she tore off a bit of paper, and wrote on it.

"My address and phone," she said, handing it to him.

He took it, sliding it into his pocket. "Okay! I'll see you Friday evening then."

Feeling weirdly relieved that that was over, he headed back

to the barn. He couldn't shake a sinking feeling, though, that this was a bad idea. *Why should it be?* He argued with himself. It was just dinner with a co-worker. It would be fine.

His next appointment was a show pony needing inoculations. Grabbing his bag from his office, he went out to his truck. He'd just pulled out of the drive onto the main road when the opening verse of Bruce Springsteen's "Erie Canal" filled the car. He laughed. Jacinth and the kids must have sabotaged his ring tone with the song Jacinth had taught them all on the long cross-country trip from California. Pressing the button on his steering wheel to answer, he spoke over the Bluetooth connection.

"Hello?"

"Dr. McCandliss, I'm glad I caught you." It was Barbara, one of the receptionists. "The Wallace's called to cancel their appointment. It seems the children caught the chicken pox... all three of them."

He winced in sympathy. "Ouch. Rough."

"Mrs. Wallace says she'll call back to reschedule when things calm down."

"Gotcha. Thanks for letting me know. Oh, and thanks for sending the paperwork for Apollo out with Beatrice."

There was a slight pause on the other end.

"Errr... I didn't?" Barbara ventured tentatively. "I thought you usually did that in your office in the barn."

Douglas shrugged. "Oh well, maybe it was Anna."

"Maybe." Barbara sounded unconvinced.

"I'm going to head home 'til my next appointment this afternoon."

"Have a good day, Dr. McCandliss."

"You too."

When he came to the highway, however, he hesitated, then

flicked the turn signal in the opposite direction of his home. There was someone he wanted to see, and since he wasn't expected at home, this was as good at time as any.

An hour later, he sat in his car looking across the crowded Manhattan street at the door of the antique shop, Whimsies. And that was another thing to add to the sudden bizarreness in his life. Each time he'd been to this shop, he'd gotten a parking space within a few yards of the shop. Either a space was sitting empty, or another car was just pulling out as he came up. In Manhattan. Downtown Manhattan. In the middle of the day. That just didn't happen.

As before, chimes rang as he opened the door to the shop. The dark-haired man he'd seen on his last two visits emerged from a doorway beyond the counter, pausing on the threshold. A gleam of recognition crept into the man's deep blue eyes as the two men took stock of each other.

Finally, Douglas stepped forward, feeling awkward. "You must be Julian?"

A grin split the man's face, and he came across the room, one hand held out. "Yeah. You must have gotten things figured out. Welcome to the dark side."

Douglas clasped Julian's hand, but grimaced. "This is unreal. One minute I'm a normal guy living a normal kind of life, and the next thing, there's a genie in my living room. I'm Douglas, by the way."

Julian led the way to the back of the store, currently empty of customers but crammed with antiques of all kinds. He gestured Douglas to an armchair in a small grouping around a table that held a hot plate and all the items needed for tea and coffee. He poured a cup of steaming coffee from a carafe, pausing with a questioning look.

"Black," Douglas affirmed, and took the cup Julian held out to him.

Julian sat across from him, leaning forward with his elbows on his knees. "So, what is it you want to know?"

Douglas took a cautious sip of the hot brew, appreciating the strength of it.

"I don't know that I have any questions, precisely," he admitted. "But suddenly there's genies... Djinn... and shapeshifters, and God knows what else, and no one I can talk to about it all."

The dark brows of the man across from him rose. "Shapeshifters?"

"Yeah, a housecat, if you can believe it, that they met in the park where Jacinth took the children to play, and she followed them home for dinner. She's a gorgeous thing, huge, with a long, heavy coat. I'm pretty sure she's a Maine Coon, looks purebred, too."

"Ah." Julian sat back in his chair, a twinkle in his dark blue eyes. "You've met Cat then."

"Cat, that's right."

"Did Jacinth tell you anything more about her?"

Alerted by the note in Julian's voice, Douglas looked at him with sharpened attention. "Just that she's a shapeshifter. Why?"

"Alessandra and I rescued her sister from a leopard shifter, in the woods up north a bit. That's how we first met Cat. In fact, that leopard is still hunting them, Cat and Melanthe. The sister and her children are staying with Alessandra and me for the time being. We don't see much of Cat; she has to stay away to keep the leopard from tracking her to us. You say they met her in a park?"

Douglas nodded. "According to the kids, she was laying on a park bench sunning herself, and they stopped to pet her. Apparently, the cat has... er..." he cleared his throat, wincing inwardly. "Telepathic ability, and talks mind to mind with Jacinth."

Julian was nodding. "Shapeshifters do, although only in their animal form."

Running his fingers through his hair, Douglas shook his head. "See? Telepathy. Shapeshifters. Genies. I know it's true, I mean, there she is, living in my guest room that she's got decked out like some kind of harem or something, and poofing cups of tea and stuff when the kids aren't around. But then I get to thinking about it, right? And it's like, completely impossible. It can't be real. But it is."

"Living in your guest room?" Julian looked interested. "How did that come about?"

Briefly, Douglas related the situation with his children, and his sudden panic at being reunited with them, and asking Jacinth to come with him. "So she's staying on for now, as the nanny, until I can find the right person to watch the children while I'm at work."

Seeming suddenly thoughtful, Julian held out his hand palm up and a steaming cup of coffee appeared in it. Douglas stared at him.

"I thought she said you weren't a Djinn anymore?"

Julian's sudden grin was strongly reminiscent of Jacinth when she was about to say something outrageous. Douglas braced himself.

"I was never Djinn. I was a Mage, bound to the Djinn bottle to fulfill wishes." He chuckled at Douglas' blank expression. "There is more magic in the world than Djinn magic. I have my own."

Mage. Magic. He stared at Julian, who gave a wry smile. "Although, after casting a spell that had me cursed--for lack of any better term--to grant wishes for six hundred years, the only spells I do these days are to conjure up tea or coffee, and help Alessandra's garden grow."

"Jacinth mentioned Alessandra. Was that the blonde with you the night I brought the teapot back?"

Julian laughed outright. "She loved that way too much! I had to step on her foot to keep her from laughing in your face. She'll be thrilled to hear all about what's happening. In fact..." He paused, his forehead creased as he pondered. "Alessandra would adore to meet you and your children, and to see Jacinth again. How would you like to come out to our place sometime? We can have a barbecue."

"That's a great idea," Douglas approved. "I like it. When do you have in mind?"

Julian shrugged. "Beats me. Have Jacinth call Alessandra and they can figure it out. Then you and Alessandra can compare notes on finding your home invaded by a genie." He grinned. "I'm sure we can keep the kids busy while you two talk."

"Works for me. I'd suggest my place, I have a swimming pool. I've been teaching the kids to swim, but..." Douglas paused, recalling another question that had been nagging at him. "Do you know anything about this aversion, or whatever it is, to water that Jacinth says Djinn have?"

Julian straightened, his expression turning serious as he nodded. "Oh, yeah. You're not going to get her anywhere near your pool, or near the shoreline at a beach. And yes, she's right, most Djinn suffer from that to some degree."

"But she says water won't actually harm them," Douglas argued. "So it's irrational."

"Perhaps. But the fear is quite real nonetheless. For us it would be like a phobia, except that this fear is pervasive through the race of Djinn."

A phobia. Well, okay, he could see that. "She became agitated just talking about it," he recalled. "As soon as the subject was dropped, she was fine again. She sat on a lounge on the deck, laughing and talking with the kids who were in the pool. She even tossed a ball to Benny a few times when it got out of the pool."

Julian nodded. "There you go."

Douglas had to laugh as a sudden thought came to him. "The big blue guy in the movie didn't have any problem diving into deep water after Aladdin."

Grinning broadly, Julian slapped him in the shoulder. "That's because they didn't have a Djinn on their production team, my friend."

Douglas groaned as the coffee in his cup refilled itself. "Oh man, this is just surreal."

"Just helping you get more accustomed," Julian said, looking far too smug. "Oh, hey. See if you can bring Cat along when you and Jacinth come over? I know Melanthe feels cut off from her, although they talk on the phone regularly. Jacinth can make sure your car can't be tracked, so it would be safe enough for her to come with you."

"Um, this leopard thing," Douglas advanced cautiously. Suddenly he sat up straighter. "Wait a minute!"

His mind leaped into action as things began to click. "You said you rescued Melanthe in the woods, north of the city?"

"Yes, why?"

Douglas reached behind him, pulling out his wallet. Opening it, he took out his business card and handed it to Julian.

Julian's lips pursed and he let out a slow whistle as he read it. "Damn, man. This is almost surreal, the coincidences stacking up here. Your clinic is where we stopped after we rescued Melanthe. Alessandra went inside and used the receptionist's phone to call Melanthe's sister... that would be Cat."

"We've gotten a few calls into the clinic with reports of large cat tracks, but no actual sightings of a big cat. We've got bobcats all over, and you know how people are... they see a bobcat track and suddenly rumor spreads there's a lion on the loose. We disregarded it, especially as there are no reports of any kills, and there would be if there was a big cat on the loose."

Julian looked grim. "That's because it's a shapeshifter, and its targets are other shifters. It's what they call a rogue. Apparently, when it moves into a territory--which this one has done--the first thing it does is clear out any other female shifters it might see as competition. It went after Melanthe, trapping her in the woods when she was pregnant, forcing her to take her cat form and have her children as kittens."

Douglas stared at him for a long moment. "I'm a veterinarian. Do you know how bizarre that sounds to me?

Chuckling, Julian nodded at the cup Douglas held. Looking down, he saw the cup was full again, steam rising from the hot brew. "Hell."

He sipped the coffee, his thoughts spinning. "Cat was attacked by a dog in our park. Could that be this... this rogue?"

Julian's lips tightened, betraying anxiety. "If your question is whether the dog could have been the shifter, the answer is no. Shifters can only take the form of one animal, the animal half of their nature. But it's possible that, since shifters are telepathic in their animal form, maybe she could have somehow controlled the dog. I'll definitely ask Melanthe about it. But I don't like this attack on Cat. Tell me more about it."

Douglas relayed what he knew. "But Troy, my partner, says she'll be fine. He's got her at his house out in the country, she'll be safe there with him. When I get home I'll confer with Jacinth as well. If nothing else we can get Cat to your place to see her sister now and then. No problem."

"That will make Melanthe happy, and to be honest, myself and Alessandra too. I know Jacinth has been trying to give us time to ourselves since we just got married. I don't think she realizes how much we miss her. She and Alessandra bonded together from the moment they met, and of course, Jacinth had been my mentor for centuries. She's an integral part of our family."

Repeating this conversation to Jacinth an hour later, he wasn't surprised to see tears spring to her eyes, clinging to the long, curling black lashes.

"Oh! I have missed them so much!" She smiled mistily at him. "I can't believe you went to see Julian! How wonderful! I'll call Alessandra right away."

A muffled voice sang from his back pocket. *I got a mule her name is Sal...*

Casting an accusing glance at Jacinth, he pulled out his phone. "Yes?" He listened a moment. "Yeah, okay. I'm on my way."

He shrugged in response to Jacinth's questioning glance. "Troy wants me at the clinic. I've gotta run."

"All right. Be sure to ask him how Cat is doing, will you?"

Douglas nodded, then paused, looking back over his shoulder. "I have a couple of appointments this afternoon, so I'll hang at the clinic until my next appointment. I may be late, so don't hold dinner for me."

CHAPTER 14

"Hey, Jacinth!"

Startled, she looked up from where she was washing up the lunch dishes to see Douglas standing on the front walk holding a large white file box. She glanced at the clock on the wall; it had scarcely been an hour since he'd left.

"I thought you were going to be at work until evening."

He shook his head. "Can you let me in? My hands are kind of full."

She went to open the door, giving the box a questioning look. "I thought you had receptionists who did the filing and paperwork."

He shook his head, grinning at her. "Are the kids here?"

"Well, of course! They're playing in their rooms, let me get them."

Douglas carried his box into the living room while she called to Benny and Molly to come. When they all had gathered curiously about, he lifted the lid from the box. In a nest of shredded paper, a small kitten was curled up asleep. It was a fuzzy, round little ball, its deep red fur with darker tabby markings sticking out.

Jacinth laughed. "Oh, isn't it darling!"

"Can we hold it?" Benny asked, while Molly just looked, wide-eyed and eager.

"For now let's take it a little slowly until he gets used to us. Here, Jacinth can hold him and you two can pet him. Gently now."

Douglas scooped it from the box. The little thing fit in his hand, and Jacinth felt her heart turn over as he held it out to her.

"Oh, Douglas."

The kitten stretched and yawned widely, and wide gold eyes opened to stare at her sleepily. The tabby markings were more apparent on its face than on its fuzzy body.

"Hey, it looks like Cat!" Benny noted.

Jacinth studied the little creature.

"He sure does," she agreed.

"Do you think this is her baby?" The boy wanted to know.

Caught unaware, Jacinth choked until Douglas had to pound her on the back.

"Uh... no, son. I don't think so," Douglas told the boy. "In fact, I know so for a fact. This is from a Maine Coon breeder who brought a litter in today for their shots. Troy called me to come see, and I bought this one from her."

"For us to keep? Really?"

"Yes, really."

Jacinth had to smile at the children's excitement. A pet was just what they needed. Benny had been stroking the kitten all this time, but now Molly moved closer, clearly wanting her turn.

"Come on, Molly." Jacinth leaned over to put one arm around the little girl, drawing her close. "Here, pet him like I showed you with Cat."

The kitten, apparently perfectly content with its new situation, yawned again, then struck without warning at the lock of blonde hair that swung down as Molly bent over him. Both children giggled as he captured a few strands in the minuscule claws and gathered himself for another attack.

Laughing, Jacinth put the kitten on the floor. "Go find a piece of string, Benny. Maybe he'll chase it."

Benny ran off to find some string while an entranced, Molly got down on all fours, letting her long curls brush the carpet for the kitten to pounce at.

Jacinth sat back in her chair, leaning toward Douglas.

"That was such a good idea," she whispered. "Just look at Molly."

"It hadn't even occurred to me to get her a pet," he confessed, looking guilty. "That would have brought her out of her shell days ago, wouldn't it?"

"It might have. But she's been coming around on her own anyway," she reminded him.

Douglas mumbled something, and Jacinth grinned, sure she heard something about "arrogant icicle" there in his *sotto voce* grumbles.

"Hey." Jacinth's grin was just short of wicked. "Think we should, you know, tell Cat what Benny thought?"

The look of horror on his face was priceless, and she laughed.

"No, I don't think!" He tugged lightly on her hair. "But it was the kittens' resemblance to Cat that had Troy call me to come take a look."

Jacinth glanced at the floor, where the kitten was now chasing the long hair ribbon... one of Molly's... that Benny had scrounged.

"What will we name it?"

"Ah." Douglas pulled an envelope from the box. "He's already been named and registered. The breeder had planned on keeping this little guy to show, but when I told her about Molly not speaking, and Troy explained about Cat and how much he looked like her, she agreed to sell him. His name is HavenCats Brandywine."

"Brandywine? How cute." Jacinth wrinkled her nose. "Kind of odd, though."

"Not at all." Douglas' eyes gleamed, pleased. "The breeder is apparently a Tolkien fan; Brandywine is a river in the Lord of the Rings trilogy. We can call the kitten Brandy, though."

Their conversation had caught Benny's attention, and he looked around from where he knelt on the floor.

"Brandy? Is that its name?"

At Douglas' nod, Benny let out a loud "Cool!" before returning his attention to playing with the kitten.

Jacinth rose to her feet. "Well, I'd better finish getting the dishes into the dishwasher, and then I'll clean out a cupboard for the cat food."

Douglas got up as well, nodding. "I brought food and a litter box... everything the little guy needs. I'll go get it from the car."

He brought it in. All of it. By his third trip from the car, Jacinth was laughing so hard she had to sit right down on the kitchen floor, while Molly and Benny, the boy carefully cradling the kitten, came to stare curiously.

"An 18-pound bag of kitten food," she gasped between spasms. "Douglas, he'll be full grown before he can eat half of it. And three... three! cases of canned food. The biggest litter box ever seen, and a 21-lb box of EverClean. Five furry mice, a cat scratching post... Douglas, you got just one little kitten, not the whole litter!"

Douglas seemed pleased with himself. "That's nothing. Wait until you see the *piece de resistance*."

He went out to the car and returned, puffing, a few minutes later, with a floor-to-ceiling cat tree, with perches and swings and hidey holes.

Jacinth dissolved into laughter once more, while the children shouted. Douglas set it up in a corner of the family room, then stood back proudly.

"Let's see how he likes it."

Benny brought the kitten over and deposited it on the wide carpeted base. Brandy gave the thing a perfunctory sniff, then turned away disinterestedly to wash his paws over his ears in a vigorous bath.

"Oh, wait, I know." Douglas went to fetch a brown paper bag he'd put on the table. "Here."

He pulled out a small plastic bag of catnip and cut it carefully open, then rubbed it on the base and lower platform of the cat tree. Everyone stood back to watch. Brandy's tail twitched, and the little body lowered to the ground as the kitten crept forward, intent. Jacinth giggled along with Ben and Molly as the tiny back end began to shimmy back and forth.

"See? He's getting ready to pounce," she whispered to the children.

And pounce he did. With a huge leap, Brandy launched himself forward, landing in the middle of the brown paper bag. Entranced with the crunchy sound and feel, he attacked the end that poked up. From the corner of his eye, he caught sight of the tip of his thrashing tail, and stilled, then with a great leap he twisted into the air to catch the moving object on the fly. Molly fell over in a heap she laughed so hard, while Benny collapsed into giggles.

Watching Douglas' crestfallen expression, Jacinth

snickered. "You certainly got him everything his little kitty heart could want."

He sighed, running his fingers through his hair, and smiled ruefully.

"Hey, maybe we can invite Cat to come over and play."

With a chuckle, he rummaged in his pocket for his keys. "Speaking of playing, my play time is over. I have to be at the Johnson's farm in half an hour, so I'd better get moving. See you later tonight."

The kitten was showing signs of sleepiness, yawning and stretching, and it was about time for the children's nap as well, so Jacinth got the children into their beds, while Brandy curled himself into a tiny bundle in a corner of the sofa, already asleep by the time Jacinth came back down the hall.

She'd loaded the remaining few pieces of silverware into the dishwasher and started the machine going, when the doorbell rang. Maybe this was Troy coming to bring Cat back, although he'd promised to call first. Well, at least the dishes were done. Wiping her hands on a towel, she went to answer the summons.

Jacinth's welcoming smile faded as she immediately guessed the identity of the woman standing on the porch. It was amazing how much the children looked like her, Molly in particular... the shining blond curls, the deep blue eyes. Except the children's eyes weren't tinged with red and crafty, darting here and there as if judging her surroundings, her opponent.

Oh yes, Jacinth thought, *you had best watch out, because you've never reckoned with a Djinn before.*

"Miss Jas, who is it?" Benny came running through the house, skidding to a halt in the kitchen doorway to stare at his mother. Without taking her eyes from the woman, Jacinth could feel his dismay, his sudden fear.

"Benny, go on back to your room," she told him calmly. "You're supposed to be taking a nap."

There was no way his mother could take him against Jacinth's will, but there wasn't any way the child could know that. It also wouldn't do to have Benny watching if she did any "funny stuff," as Douglas insisted on calling her Djinn powers. And, oh! She *did* want to put the fear of God into this woman. What Lilian had done to Ben and Molly, and to Douglas, was unconscionable... and for no other reason than spite. It wasn't as if she'd truly wanted the children, or cared about them. That much was obvious.

"Who are you?" Lilian asked, having looked Jacinth up and down. There was curiosity in her gaze, hostility held in abeyance; the woman would wait, Jacinth thought, until she found out whether she, Jacinth, would oppose her, before becoming nasty.

"I'm the children's nanny."

"I see." Lilian smiled, evidently pleased that someone so young and small was the only obstacle between her and the children. "I'm Lilian... Ben and Molly's mother. I've come to see them."

She took a step forward, clearly expecting Jacinth to invite her in. Jacinth didn't move.

"I'm so sorry," she told the woman. "My instructions are not to let anyone into the house without Mr. McCandliss' permission."

Irritation flashed across Lilian's face, quickly replaced with a friendly smile.

"Oh, I'm sure Doug didn't mean me. I'm their mother!"

"Perhaps not." Jacinth echoed the woman's smile with one just as friendly... and just as false. "But perhaps you should come back when he's here. Or you could call him at work and have him clarify for me."

Lilian's eyes bulged slightly, and the thin mouth tightened in irritation.

"This is ridiculous," she stated. "Ben and Molly are my children, and I have a right to see them. I've come all the way from California just to spend some time with my darlings."

Oh puh-leeze, Jacinth thought, resisting the urge to roll her eyes like Benny sometimes did. How pathetic could you get?

"Perhaps you could come back with a court order showing you have visitation rights on Wednesday afternoons," Jacinth suggested with her best guileless expression. "I wouldn't want to keep you from your legal right to see the children. In the meantime, if you'll call their father and ask what he'd like me to do, I'll be happy to let you in with his permission."

A surge of satisfaction flooded her as Lilian's face turned ugly. She wanted the older woman to be hot with temper, not in control and thinking coolly. Let her make just one move, and...

"Is there a problem here?"

Jacinth jumped at the deep voice behind her, and whirled in consternation. She blew out a breath of frustration at the sight of the tall, lean figure dressed all in black, a heavy cloak swirling about his booted feet, in stark contrast to the flowing white hair.

Kieran laid a heavy hand on her shoulder, his fingers curling warningly into her flesh. His cold gaze came to rest on Lilian, challenging, while Jacinth fumed. Darn him for spoiling her plan! Lilian looked delighted, however, her gaze moving from Jacinth to Kieran. Jacinth yearned to wipe the sneer from the woman's face.

"So, you're entertaining men while you're supposed to be taking care of impressionable young children? Wait until Doug hears about this."

Jacinth merely raised her brows. "Since this is my step-father, I hardly think Douglas would have any problem with his visiting. In fact," she took delight in rubbing it in, "my step-father is a particular favorite of Molly's. She just adores him."

An angry flush rose in Lilian's cheeks, and the blonde glared at them both measuringly for a long moment. Her thoughts were transparently clear as Lilian came to the decision that she wasn't going to be able to physically shoulder her way past Kieran as she'd planned to do with Jacinth. With a flounce, the woman turned and went down the steps.

"Step-father?" Kieran asked Jacinth with a lift of one mobile black brow as she closed the front door.

She grinned at him. "You would have liked to be. Close enough."

"It looks like I arrived just in time. You should have called me sooner."

Remembering how his appearance had foiled her plan, Jacinth scowled. "I didn't call you at all. Why are you here?"

"Keeping an eye on you. And what were you about to do, may I ask?"

She felt a guilty flush rise to her cheeks.

"Noninvolvement," Kieran told her sternly. "We don't interfere, except in matters of the wishes."

"She was going to try to take Molly and Benny by force," Jacinth said insistently, feeling mulish. She knew she was being childish, pouting like Molly when she didn't get her way. But she'd longed to come to grips with Douglas' ex-wife.

"And you weren't nudging her along to do that, of course."

She flushed more and glanced away. There wasn't ever putting anything over on Kieran. A fleeting touch on her cheek made her look up.

"Should she make any attempt to forcibly take the children,

you do what you must. But if such… confrontation… can be avoided, that is best."

"I know." She sighed. "You're right, it's probably better this way. I'll be good, I promise."

"She's gone!" Benny's shout echoed, and the little boy propelled himself down the hallway to launch his small body against Jacinth's legs. Right behind him came Molly, eyes alight with recognition.

"Kayr!"

Leaning down to lift Molly, balancing her carefully on his hip as she hugged him joyously, Jacinth had never seen Kieran so… well, so human. The hard lines of his cold, handsome face softened as he gazed at the child in his arms, listening to her tell him about her dolls and her new picture book with a surprising patience for one legendary for his goal-oriented directness and intolerance of frivolity or levity.

Benny pulled on Jacinth's hand, demanding her attention.

"That was Mom! She's not going to take us away, is she?"

"No, honey." Jacinth knelt, gathering the boy to her for a big hug. "Kieran and I won't let her take you, and neither will your father."

His lower lip stuck out so far she could have planted flowers on it.

"What if she comes again, when he's not here?" Benny nodded at Kieran. Jacinth hugged him tighter.

"I want you to trust me, Benny. No matter what happens, I can handle it. You and Molly are safe with me, and I don't want you to worry. Okay?"

"Okay."

Her word seemed to be good enough for him, and he squirmed to get free. She let him go and he raced off to play with his toys, confident in her ability to protect him and his sister. So trusting, she thought with a sigh, watching him go. If only more adults could have the kind of complete faith and trust, the easy acceptance that children did, the world would be a better place.

She turned to survey Kieran and Molly, hiding her smile. Molly's chubby little hand was on Kieran's cheek, turning his face towards her, holding his attention captive as she prattled away. Her fair ringlets fell across his shoulder, mingling with Kieran's pale hair like strands of gold against snow. Jacinth watched, storing up the image for remembrance. She could tease him about this for eons. It would be particularly satisfying to remind him of this whenever he went into his stuffy, overbearing, Lord-to-peasant *noblesse oblige* mode.

"I heard that."

Kieran spoke without taking his attention away from Molly, and Jacinth grinned. "You're not supposed to listen in on private thoughts."

"You were practically shouting your glee," he responded dryly.

That figured. Suppressing her emotions had never been one of her stronger points. She glanced at her phone with reluctance. Douglas needed to be told Lilian had shown up and tried to get the children.

"I'd better call Douglas."

He shifted the little girl in his arms. "I'll keep an eye on Molly."

Jacinth snorted. "I think she's the one keeping an eye on you!"

The cool blue eyes lit with unaccustomed humor.

"Go make your call," was all he said.

Douglas was not a happy camper.

"I can't believe she had the nerve to show up there!" He sounded angry and frustrated. "I'll come right home."

"No, no," Jacinth hurried to reassure him. "Kieran came and she left without even an argument. She can't take the children, Douglas. Not from me."

"You're right." But his voice was tight with anxiety.

"Douglas, it's okay. The kids aren't even upset. Benny's run off to play with his trains, and Molly is draped all over Kieran."

That surprised a laugh out of him.

"If I hadn't seen it for myself, I wouldn't believe you," Douglas admitted. "That is one scary dude."

"He is not!" Jacinth defended staunchly. "He's just... well..."

"Yes?"

She thought hard. "Intense."

Douglas' rich chuckle vibrated down the phone line. "He is that all right."

"I think you should call the police," she said, worrying. "I mean... she can't take them from me, but they need to know she's here and has made an attempt to get them. And Benny will be starting school soon."

Douglas swore. "Yeah, good idea. I'll get on it. Are you sure you don't need me to come home?"

"No. Kieran's here, and you know the two of you are like oil and water together."

He chuckled again. "Yeah, but if he's looking out for you and the kids I don't mind so much."

Jacinth narrowed her eyes at that, not sure if she should be insulted.

"I don't need anyone to take care of me."

"I'm well aware of that." Douglas' voice was rueful. "It's just that you *look* so damn small and delicate."

Jacinth sighed. "All my life, it's been a curse. But I can take care of myself, *and* Benny and Molly. So don't worry about us, okay, Douglas?"

"Got it."

Smiling, she put the phone down. She turned to find Kieran watching her, his face as cold and distant as she'd ever seen it. With a pat on the little girl's rosy cheek, he let Molly slide to the ground.

"I will go now. Call if you need me."

CHAPTER 15

GIVEN the events of the day, somehow Douglas wasn't nearly as surprised as he might have been when Jacinth's mother appeared that evening. In fact, he was proud of himself for scarcely blinking at the explosion of sensual beauty into his living room, enveloping them in a cloud of wafting perfume as exotic as she herself was. Taller than her daughter, with a sinuous elegance in marked contrast to Jacinth's open *joie de vivre*, Zahra was a sultry enchantress with dark red hair that fell in rippling waves to her waist, framing her lush curves. Slanted eyes of brilliant green, set off by black curving lashes, would have done credit to an Egyptian cat goddess.

"*Ya helwa.* My sweet." She swept Jacinth into her arms for a brief embrace, then straightened, looking across the room at Douglas, who had risen to his feet at her entrance. "And this is…?"

If Zahra had a tail, he thought, it would be a-twitch.

"This is Douglas. Douglas, my mother, Zahra." Jacinth spoke politely… in her 'nanny' tone, he thought with some amusement. "Douglas is my *Sahib*. As I'm sure you know from Kieran."

Zahra's emerald eyes glinted with humor. "Oh very well. I admit I'm absolutely dying of curiosity."

She extended one slender hand across the coffee table. He took her hand, understanding that the handshake formed as much a part of her judgment as the swift, keen scrutiny she sent him from under those incredible lashes. Her skin was cool and soft, lightly scented, not like Jacinth's, warm and pulsing with life.

Zahra moved away to seat herself in a chair set at right-angles to where Douglas had been sitting on the sofa before her abrupt arrival. She was dressed in an extremely chic tailored suit of cream linen, the jacket open to show a soft green silk blouse that echoed faintly the emerald glow of her eyes. Sheer nylons that Douglas had no doubt were grossly expensive encased her long shapely legs, and the high-heeled sandals she wore were of patent leather. Except for an air of maturity, and the sharp knowledge in the depths of her emerald eyes, she could have passed for a twenty-something fashion model.

"So, tell me everything," she invited Jacinth, settling herself gracefully in the armchair, her smile encompassing both of them.

"What if you fill her in," Douglas asked Jacinth, who had resumed her seat on the sofa, "while I make us all coffee?"

Jacinth nodded vigorously and launched into an account of the events since she'd come into Douglas' life. Douglas escaped to the kitchen, feeling a bit bemused. What had happened to his life? he wondered, measuring coffee into the basket. He'd been a simple kind of a guy, with the usual problems of the ex-wife and custody issues. Except for Lilian having stolen the children, everything had been pretty normal. Then suddenly here he was, with genies.... Djinn... popping in and out of his house. He had a nine-hundred-year-old Persian nanny for his children. Her mother, who looked scarcely older than her daughter, could rival Greta Garbo and Marilyn Monroe for sheer sex appeal, while his own daughter, who still rarely spoke, had formed a fascinated attachment to an ancient Djinn who looked like he ground mortals' bones to make his bread.

And he had a bubble of laughter in his chest constantly. He could hardly wait to come home every night to see what was going to happen next. The weekends were crazy, full of fun and excitement.

The coffee made, he poured three cups and carried them into the living room. He found Jacinth finishing her tale, and Zahra sparkling with indignation.

"How dare she!" The emerald eyes flashed angrily. "To come here and try to steal them away again! I hope you turned her into a toad."

"I had a better idea than that," Jacinth confided. "But Kieran came, and wouldn't let me."

Her mother sighed sympathetically. "Kieran can be so difficult."

Jacinth grinned in wicked enjoyment. "You should have seen him wrapped around Molly's little finger."

Zahra stared at her. Jacinth's grin widened. Chuckling, Douglas came to sit beside her on the sofa, enjoying her mother's reaction. Zahra turned that green gaze on him.

"Molly's your daughter? The little girl?"

He nodded, and she turned her attention back to Jacinth.

"Which Kieran are we talking about?" she asked cautiously.

"That one," Jacinth stated. "He stood and held her on his hip while she talked to him for half an hour. In this very room, too."

Zahra looked shocked to the core. She stared at them, speechless.

"Molly took one look and decided he was her soul mate," Jacinth said, relishing her mother's reaction.

"We had to practically peel her off him," corroborated Douglas. He grimaced in remembrance. "Not before he'd practically flayed me for not using a wish to make her talk."

"Yes, he told me a little about that part... the child not speaking," Zahra said, appearing to muse things over. A cat-that-ate-the-cream smile curved her lips. "Well, well, well."

"Hey, Dad!" Benny came charging into the room, and stopped short in surprise at seeing the visitor.

"You must be Benny." Zahra smiled at the boy, and he stared at her in fascination. "I'm Jacinth's mother. I dropped by to meet your family."

A quick frown came into Benny's eyes, and he glanced at the door. "I didn't hear the doorbell."

"I was in the kitchen and saw her coming up the walk," Jacinth ad-libbed quickly, to Douglas' complete admiration. They were really going to have to try to be more careful. Benny was sharp as a tack, and at this rate, what with Kieran popping in twice and now Jacinth's mother appearing out of nowhere, it wouldn't take him long to tumble to the truth.

Molly came into the room just then and was introduced. What with her obsession with Kieran, Douglas had almost expected her to launch herself at this Djinn also. But Molly was shy of the elegant stranger, and she peeked at Jacinth's mother from the safety of Douglas' side. Douglas watched as Zahra gently coaxed Molly to her, charming the little girl out of her shyness. The mother, Douglas thought, could charm the birds from the trees. It was almost unfair that she had the advantage of being Djinn as well.

Zahra shot him a sideways glance full of amusement, and he looked at Jacinth in alarm. Her expression was equally amused, from which he gathered that her mother could read his thoughts. He groaned aloud, and Jacinth giggled.

"Kieran also," she confided to him much later, after they had tucked the children into bed. "Only the strongest Djinn have that ability. And not all want it. I know I don't. It would be very unsettling to hear people's thoughts, I should think."

Once the children were asleep, the three of them had settled down in the living room with cups of fresh coffee, when the air shimmered, and a handsome young man... Djinn? ...appeared before them. He was slender and dark, with a wealth of waving black hair and snapping black eyes. Not seeming to even notice Douglas or Zahra, he addressed himself to Jacinth.

"*Salaam*, Jacinth. How are things with you? It's good to see you again."

Douglas bristled, but subsided at the wry smile Jacinth sent him, her fingers squeezing his with light pressure.

"It's nice to see you too, Samir. So good of you to come just to see me."

The Djinn smiled complacently, and slid a sideways glance in Zahra's direction. Suddenly Douglas understood. This was one of the mother's suitors. No wonder Zahra hadn't chosen a husband, if this specimen was representative.

The Djinn affected surprise. "Zahra! I didn't see you here."

Jacinth rolled her eyes, but Zahra greeted him with a gracious nod.

"*Salaam*, Samir. What brings you to visit my daughter?"

"Oh, well..." he floundered a bit, and caught himself, the smug look returning. "It's been some decades since Jacinth manifested in this world, and I wished to welcome her, and to renew our acquaintance."

"So kind," Jacinth murmured dryly.

Impervious to sarcasm, the Djinn preened himself, smoothing his short pointed beard. The glance he cast at Zahra, Douglas was sure, was to be sure she was admiring his fine form and handsome face. With difficulty, Douglas smothered a laugh.

"Since my mother has just arrived to visit me and to meet my *Sahib*," Jacinth suggested in a gentle voice, "perhaps you could come back to renew our acquaintance at another time?"

The Djinn took his dismissal in good part, merely casting one yearning glance in Zahra's direction before fading out.

Scarcely two heartbeats passed before another, older Djinn appeared. Elderly and white-haired, he was neatly dressed in a gray tailored suit, and carried himself with elegance and a quiet assurance that put Douglas very much in mind of a European aristocrat.

"Good evening, Zahra, Jacinth." He surveyed Douglas with bright, intelligent eyes. "Ah. You are the *Sahib* of young Jacinth?"

"Arthur!" Zahra appeared to regard this Djinn with a great deal of affection, rising from the armchair and extending her hand for him to bow over, which he did with a grace that made the old-fashioned gesture more effective than Douglas would have ever believed.

Even Jacinth smiled in welcome, conjuring a cup of coffee for their visitor and motioning him to sit on the sofa beside her.

"I will not stay long," Arthur assured them, sipping his coffee with a nod of thanks at Jacinth. "I could not resist the opportunity to visit with you both, although Zahra and I chat frequently. Your mother tells me you are looking after two young mortal children, Jacinth."

"Yes, Ben and Molly," Jacinth agreed. "Just until Douglas finds a nanny. I've become very fond of them. You would like them as well, Arthur. In fact, I wish you would come back in the daytime and meet them. Benny is quite bright... just six, and I think he is reading beyond his level. I would value your opinion."

"My dear Jacinth, I would be honored." Finishing his coffee, the Djinn set his cup down and rose. "Call me when it is convenient. I will hold myself available to you at any time. Until then."

With a bow to Jacinth and Zahra, and another nod for Douglas, Arthur vanished.

"Well, isn't that lucky!" Zahra exclaimed. She turned an inquiring look on her daughter. "Do you think young Benny is that advanced?"

"Enough that I have been wanting someone to ask about it," Jacinth admitted. She glanced at Douglas, apologetic. "I'd meant to talk to you about Benny before doing anything, but Arthur frequently withdraws from Djinn society, and since he was here, I wanted to ask for his assistance while I had the opportunity to do so."

"Arthur is a scholar," Zahra explained. "As with many of our elders, he feels strongly the weight of the centuries. Some, like Kieran, withdraw emotionally. Others remove themselves from the world physically, in a state rather similar to what you would call hibernation, until their fire renews and they can carry on once more."

"And some we have not seen for centuries," Jacinth admitted, looking unhappy. "I fear for Arthur. There is a shadow on him that I have not seen before."

Douglas frowned. "Shadow?"

"He is tired. I suppose you might call it soul sick. Sometimes

Djinn... well, never mind. Are you sure you can't accept him, Mama?"

One dark auburn brow shot up, and Zahra's green eyes gleamed with amusement. "Matchmaking, my daughter?"

Before she had a chance to respond, two more Djinn males appeared in Douglas' living room. It was clear that their simultaneous arrival had not been by design, as both glared at each other.

This time, however, Jacinth made quick work of getting rid of their uninvited visitors, firmly and not very politely requesting them to leave. Looking crestfallen, both complied.

"Arrrrgh!" Jacinth groaned a complaint. "Mama, how can you stand it?"

"They're good for a laugh," her mother responded, her dark green eyes twinkling.

"Well, I think it's enough!"

Jacinth rose to her feet. Lifting her arms above her head, she brought her hands together. The thunderous clap reverberated throughout the house, and Douglas could feel the ground beneath his feet literally shaking.

"Kieran!"

The shimmer in the air, now familiar to Douglas, heralded the great Djinn's arrival.

"You rang?" he inquired in a sonorous tone.

Had the imperious Djinn actually made a joke? Douglas could have sworn he heard overtones of the Addams' Family's funereal butler.

Kieran cast Douglas a sharp look from those silvery blue eyes, apparently having 'listened in' on Douglas' thoughts.

"No one could exist as long as I have without a sense of humor, I assure you," the Djinn told him. He turned his attention to Jacinth.

"You risk waking the children to call me like that." His voice was heavy with censure.

Jacinth's dark eyes flashed in annoyance.

"I shielded their rooms. But perhaps you'd prefer they get a different kind of surprise altogether," she said tartly. "The kind where they're awake and present when some Djinn pops into the room in front of them."

Kieran stared at her a long moment, his eyes narrowed as he considered this. His gaze then moved to Zahra, who shrugged casually, arching one brow in innocence.

"I'm not calling them," she said. "And I can't stop them. Wherever I go, they find me. You know that."

"You have to do something," Jacinth told him in a fierce voice. "I don't want my mother to have to stay away because the Djinn males won't stop following her around."

Zahra stood and glided to Kieran's side, putting a hand on his arm. She was almost as tall as he, and their eyes met, hers a warm green, his as blue and frigid as an ice cave.

"And I don't want to stay away. I'd like to be able to visit my daughter in peace, and to get to know Douglas and the children as well. I've put up with this for centuries without a word, Kieran. You know how distasteful I find their constant plaguing, but I've never asked you to intervene. I'm asking now. For the children's sake at least."

After a moment, Kieran nodded slowly.

"That's fair. I'll see to it that you're not disturbed while you're here."

"How about, or any other time," Jacinth muttered rebelliously.

Douglas noted with interest that the older Djinn's expression softened as his gaze rested on her small, flushed face.

"You know I can't do that," he told her. "In this case, it's imperative the children are protected, but that's all I can do. Your mother must fight her own battles."

"I appreciate it, Kieran," Zahra interjected swiftly. Douglas saw her nudge Jacinth surreptitiously. "Thank you."

He nodded, but addressed Jacinth. "The children are well?"

"They are fine," she reassured them. "Douglas brought them a kitten this morning, which I think has kept them from worrying overmuch about their mother's visit."

"Be cautious." The Djinn turned his head to look at Douglas, his stern gaze carrying a warning. "I had no difficulty in reading her this afternoon. She was angry at finding me here, but she discounts Jacinth. She is determined, and will try again to regain possession of the children. I did not find affection for them in her mind, nor concern for their well-being. She needs help, and until she gets it she will be a danger to you and to the children."

Jacinth's lips tightened. "I thought that also. I won't leave them alone for a moment. Although you know, Kieran, I would not anyway. Not when I have made myself responsible for them."

"I know." There was affection in the Djinn's faint smile. "Call on me should you have need."

He nodded to them, and disappeared.

CHAPTER 16

A DATE. Douglas was leaving his children with her, while he took some... some female out to dinner. Of course, it was none of her business who he went out with. He was a human, after all. A mortal, and she had no interest in him. It was just so tacky. Not to mention rude, to leave her at home while he went on a date. She scowled down into her tea cup. Well, whoever she was, the woman was welcome to him. Everyone knew human men were notoriously fickle anyway.

Okay, so that wasn't quite true. Her own father had never looked at another woman the rest of his long life after he'd lost her mother... but Omar had been an exceptional man in every way. Not like Douglas, who was apparently susceptible rather than exceptional. He'd take this female out to dinner, and then go back to her house, where she'd invite him in for a drink. Maybe he'd kiss her goodnight. Even... Jacinth kicked at the coffee table as she pictured him staying overnight, and kissing the woman goodbye in the morning.

She put her cup down and bounced up from the sofa,

calling for the children to come help her with dinner. With an effort, she pushed Douglas and his date from her mind. After all, she was just the nanny. It was nothing to her what Douglas did. Nothing at all.

Douglas pulled into the parking lot of the renovated brownstone that had been made into single apartments, forcing back a vague sense of guilt. What did he have to feel guilty about? He was single, unattached. Free to date whomever he liked.

To prove it, he parked the car and got out, slamming the door shut, and marched determinedly up the front walk. Beatrice opened the door of her first-floor apartment as soon as he knocked.

"Douglas." Her smile was wide and inviting as she stood aside for him to enter. "I'm almost ready, let me just get my shoes on."

It had been a long time since he'd dated--he and Lilian had married while he was still in college--but he recognized the ploy. He was supposed to admire the dainty ankles, the smooth curve of her calves as she slipped her feet into high heels. She bent over to buckle the straps, giving him the opportunity to admire more of her long legs as the short skirt she wore rose higher. She was casual about it... no sidelong glances meeting his, and she straightened as soon as the straps were buckled, but Douglas tugged at his tie, feeling suddenly uncomfortable. What the hell he was doing, anyway? He'd only just gotten his kids back, and the last thing in the world he wanted was to get involved with anyone. He wasn't ready for this.

Beatrice stepped to his side with a smile. She looked very

different than in the clinic, where she wore scrubs. He'd never noticed how elegant she was, tall and slender. Her hair was long and a pale red-gold, her face a narrow oval. Light green eyes were set off by the snug, curve-hugging dress of pale jade. It occurred to him that she'd be a natural for the leading role in a movie about the young Queen Elizabeth I.

He did his best not to recoil as she leaned forward, invading his personal space. Surely she wasn't expecting him to kiss her. Was she?

He cleared his throat, turning toward the door as if he hadn't noticed her close proximity. "We'd better go. The reservations are for seven."

She took it with good grace, smiling as she preceded him out the door. He closed the door and waited as she locked it. A slight frown creased her brow, and she pulled at the door.

"I can't seem to get the key out," she told him.

"Here, let me try." She stood back, and he grasped the key. It turned easily in the lock, but when he tried to remove it, the thing wouldn't budge. He wiggled it experimentally. He unlocked the door and opened it, and the key pulled smoothly out.

"Okay, I think it must have just jammed," he told Beatrice. "I've got it now."

He closed the door and locked it, and again the key refused to be removed from the lock. He stared at it in frustration.

"I guess I spoke too soon. Does this happen often?"

Beatrice shook her head, the pale red curls flying. "This has never happened before. I can't imagine what's wrong with it."

It took another five minutes, but about the time Douglas was ready to give up and have her call a locksmith, suddenly the key slid from the lock as if it had been greased.

"Well, that was just too weird." Beatrice slipped the key ring into her purse. "I wonder what was wrong. Thanks for getting it to work, Douglas."

"You're welcome." He frowned at the door another moment, wondering what he'd done differently on that last try. "If it does it again, you might want to get a new lock on that."

"You're right about that." Her agreement was heart-felt.

Douglas held the car door for her, then walked around to the driver's side. "I thought we'd go for steak, if that's fine with you?"

"Of course." Beatrice's smile was blinding, and Douglas again felt the stirrings of discomfort. This feeling increased during the short drive to the restaurant, as she kept finding excuses to touch him, reaching over to pat his hand as she leaned forward to emphasize some point. Once, when he'd removed his hand under the pretense of needing it on the steering wheel to make a turn, she'd even put her hand on his thigh. Douglas kept his face still, working to hide his shock... and his distaste. She'd never been this blatantly forward at the clinic. He'd never have asked her out otherwise.

Not even to prove a point.

Okay, so he did feel a little guilty about that, almost like he was using her. Even so, his invitation had been for dinner, damn it, not for a seduction. Beatrice was a cool professional at work, and he'd expected a casual evening talking about... well... stuff. The clinic. Animals. Whatever.

He consoled himself that once they got to the restaurant they'd be seated at a table, and there'd be some space between them.

Five minutes later, standing inside the restaurant's entrance, Douglas realized his relief had been premature. He fought down the stirrings of temper as he stared at the hostess.

"You lost my reservation?"

"Apparently so, sir. I'm very sorry. If you'd like to have a seat in the bar, we'll get you seated as soon as possible."

Since the apologetic young woman remembered having taken his reservation the day before, he assumed they really would give him first priority. With an inward sigh he bowed to the inevitable and led Beatrice into the small, darkened, and very intimate atmosphere of the bar. This evening was quickly assuming the proportions of a nightmare.

He picked a small table as the best of a bad bargain. They'd be in close proximity, but it wasn't as bad as sitting on the stools at the bar, where Beatrice would be close enough to crawl into his lap. Somehow he had the impression she wouldn't have much hesitation in doing so, given the slightest encouragement... or even none at all, if the opportunity presented itself.

"So." Beatrice leaned invitingly across the table after they'd ordered drinks from a waitress. "Tell me what you do when you're not working."

Kids. The kids. A man-eater like Beatrice was turning out to be wasn't going to be interested in a single father whose sole interest was his children. He'd bore her to death with talking about Benny and Molly. It wouldn't be a hardship, either. He was nuts about his kids. He grinned at her.

"Well, you know that I have two children that I just got back a few weeks ago after their mother took off with them and disappeared."

It didn't work. Douglas bit back a groan as he followed Beatrice and the hostess to their table some fifteen minutes later. Beatrice had hung on his every word, evincing total interest in his children. She claimed to be fascinated that he had a real live nanny (it had been all he could do not to roll his eyes), laughed at his (heavily edited) tales of the cat from the park who wandered by the house regularly to join them for dinner. For God's sake, she'd even expressed interest in coming over to meet Benny and Molly, dragging one long red manicured nail up his arm, all but purring seductively as she made the suggestion. He shuddered at the thought of bringing her home. Ben and Molly would think she was going to be their next mommy, and run away on the spot. He could hardly blame them. He was ready to run away, too!

Instead he was seating Beatrice at a large, beautifully appointed table, complete with candle. At least it wasn't a booth, he thought gratefully, and took care to seat himself across the table from her. Some of his tension eased as the familiar routine of eating out soothed him; settling in, looking over the menu, discussing the choices available. All too soon, though, their waitress came to take their orders, and left them alone.

"Now it's your turn. Tell me about yourself," Douglas said hastily, forestalling Beatrice's questions and suggestions. The ploy worked, as she leaned back in her chair, the red-nailed fingers playing with the stem of her wineglass.

"Well, I'm single, as you know," she told him, the sly look on her face telling him clearer than words that she assumed she'd succeeded in interesting him. "I grew up in Philadelphia. Last year my uncle died and left me his house here. I'd just gotten my vet tech certificate and it seemed like the smart thing to do to move here and establish myself. Almost like it was meant to be."

Aw, hell! She was laying another of those long, significant looks on him. Douglas began to mentally estimate how long it would take to get their dinners and eat, and get out of here. He had every intention of dumping her on her doorstep and fleeing for the safety of home the instant dinner was over with.

Douglas looked up gratefully as the waitress came by with their salads. Half a step behind her was the busboy, a pitcher of ice water in his hand. He wasn't certain exactly how it happened, but somehow the waitress and the busboy managed to collide while performing their separate tasks, and Beatrice let out a less than genteel shriek as icy water cascaded into her lap.

"Oh! Oh, I'm sorry!" The waitress almost wept with distress as Beatrice jumped from the chair, ice cubes scattering here and there beneath the table. With a brittle smile that was clearly a struggle for her to summon, Beatrice excused herself to Douglas and headed for the ladies' room, leaving the waitress and busboy to dry the tablecloth and collect ice cubes.

"I'm so sorry." The waitress, Nona by her nametag, apologized again.

"Don't worry about it," Douglas reassured her and the anxious-looking busboy. "Accidents happen."

Truthfully, he could almost have kissed her. The flash in Beatrice's eyes had given her away; she was absolutely furious. If this served to distract her from her attempts at seduction for the next hour, he'd be a happy man. Maybe he should leave the waitress an extra tip.

Beatrice was still cross when she returned, her dress mostly dry.

"Our dinners should be free," she told him, her eyes flashing spitefully. "First they lose our reservations, then this."

"It was an accident," Douglas soothed. "They do happen. It could have been worse. It was just water, after all."

She visibly fought for control, drawing a deep breath and summoning a smile for him.

"That's true. At least it wasn't my wine glass."

Ouch. "We can be grateful," he conceded. "Red wine would never have come out."

"No, and this dress is silk." She stroked the soft material across her thighs, sliding a glance at him sideways through her lashes. *Oh, no.* He managed to keep himself from groaning aloud.

Loud sizzling heralded the arrival of the steak fajitas they'd ordered for dinner. He bit back a smile as the waitress very, very carefully set Beatrice's skillet in front of her. She set Douglas' skillet on his side of the table and stepped back with a sigh of relief. Douglas leaned forward, sniffing appreciatively.

Without warning, the skillet burst into flame. He leaped to his feet, overturning his chair, and Beatrice screamed. Grabbing his napkin, Douglas began to beat at the flames. Restaurant employees converged on their table. Their waitress had untied her apron and was helping him, the flames having sparked over to the tablecloth. Someone rushed up and dashed a pitcher of water over the table, and the fire died as quickly as it had begun.

The commotion it had caused took a bit longer to settle.

"It shouldn't have caught fire," the waitress was insisting to the restaurant manager, backed up by the chef who had come out to add his support. "It was just fajitas. There wasn't anything in it that would cause it to go up like that."

Douglas narrowed his eyes, letting the argument rage over his head as his thoughts took another direction. The spilled water could have been an accident, but there hadn't been any reason for the fajitas to have caught fire. Nor for Beatrice's key to stick in her front door. No reason at all. Except, perhaps...

"Dammit! Kieran, if you're listening, tell Jacinth to knock it off, or I'm going to... to..." he mumbled under his breath.

"Um... Douglas?" Beatrice had returned from the restroom where she'd once more retreated to dry her dress, as some of the water thrown onto the table had splashed onto her.

"Sorry. I was just... um... taking some mental notes."

The manager, diverted from scolding the waitress, turned to them, suggesting a new table and a new dinner... on the house, of course. Given his strong suspicion that no one at the restaurant was responsible for the accidents that had occurred (and possibly their lost reservation as well), Douglas insisted on keeping Nona as their waitress. She was visibly distraught, and he hoped to preserve her job with a show of support. Over Beatrice's strong and rather shrill objections, he also insisted on paying for their dinners: Two swiftly prepared New York steaks, served with steaming baked potatoes and tender asparagus stalks in butter. Douglas rather thought it would be awhile before he ever ordered fajitas again.

"Enough," he told her, when Beatrice showed no sign of abating her argument against the restaurant. "It was an accident, nothing more."

Beatrice subsided, albeit a bit sulkily, and their dinner was finished in relative peace. Over dessert she showed a tendency to want to resume her seductive manner, but he rushed through his chocolate mousse--neither of them had been the least bit tempted by the restaurant's landmark dessert, Cherries Jubilee--and ushered her out of the restaurant practically before she'd put down her spoon.

Now, all he had to do was get her home... and then go strangle Jacinth. Not that she hadn't done him a favor, saving his butt from the man-eater most of the evening, but it was the principle of the thing.

Said man-eater was currently in seductive mode once more, having left off whining and complaining when they left the restaurant. Not, he reminded himself, that he blamed her. It hadn't been the most pleasant of evenings, for which he planned to kick some serious genie butt when he got home.

Beatrice seemed to share his opinion of their evening, and apparently had a plan to make things better. She leaned into him, so far as her bucket seat and seatbelt would allow.

"Why don't you come inside for a bit," she suggested as he parked in front of her house. "I'll make some coffee, and we can relax."

God! He hadn't even considered the possibility that she'd ask him in! He racked his brain for a convincing reason why he had to rush home, and couldn't come up with one.

"Um... that'd be nice," he managed, feeling his throat tighten as he choked out the words.

Okay, he'd rethink the kicking genie butt thing if Jacinth did something that'd get him out of this. Damn, why couldn't she be psychic like Kieran? And why hadn't she called him, anyway, to report on how the kids were doing? He'd thought she should at least do that, so he wouldn't worry about them. Then he could pretend to Beatrice the Vamp that he had to rush home. Or there could be an emergency at the clinic, or one of old farmer Higgins' mares could go into foal.

But his cell phone stayed maddeningly quiet, and every traffic light turned green as he came up to each one on the drive from the restaurant. Resigned to his fate for the next half hour at least, he turned the engine off, and got out to walk with Beatrice to her front door.

Except that the ground somehow felt squishy underfoot. They both looked down, to find the welcome mat sopping wet, a slow steady stream of water creeping from under the front door.

Douglas didn't need to hear Beatrice's horrified, "Oh, my God!" as she pushed open the door to know what had happened. A water line had broken, and the entire floor was awash.

He stayed, staunchly supportive, as Beatrice called a plumber, and helped her to get the most important items that were endangered out onto the lawn. Neighbors, seeing what was happening, came by to offer their assistance as well, and when the plumber arrived and began siphoning off the water, Douglas was able to make his escape at last.

"Thank you for dinner," Beatrice said, looking distracted. "I'm sorry for all this. Another time."

He just waved a hand as he walked to his car.

Not in this lifetime.

JACINTH WAS CURLED up on the sofa with a magazine. She looked up as he stood in the doorway.

"Oh, hi. How was your evening?"

He stepped inside the house, closing the door behind him, and stalked over to stand before her. She blinked at him questioningly with big, innocent eyes, not a shade of guile in the mahogany depths.

"I don't know," he uttered through gritted teeth, "whether to kiss you or strangle you."

"I already know you want to kiss me." She had the nerve to sound smug. "Why on earth would you want to strangle me? Didn't you have a good time?"

Douglas closed his eyes, counting to ten and praying for patience.

"No, I did *not* have a good time. As if you didn't know."

"How would I know? I wasn't there. I was right here, all the time," she pointed out in an oh-so-reasonable tone of voice. "With the children. Your children. Taking care of them. Just like I'm supposed to do."

Ut-oh. He could already see the direction this was going. Time to head her off at the pass.

"Setting my dinner on fire could have been dangerous," he told her as sternly as he could. "It spread to the tablecloth before we could put it out. You could have burnt down the whole place, or someone could have been injured."

Her eyes widened, and Jacinth clapped her hands over her mouth, clearly torn between concern and laughter.

"Oh, no!" she gasped. "Is that what happened?"

"Uh-huh," he agreed, settling on the sofa beside her. "Don't you keep an eye on your own magic? And how could you have known that I ordered fajitas, and to have them catch on fire just when they reached the table? You told me you weren't psychic, and I know you weren't there."

Jacinth looked chastened. "I'm sorry, Douglas. Truly. I never meant for anything bad to happen. I didn't do any specific magic, I just sort of... well... jinxed your date. That's all."

He couldn't help it. He burst into laughter. "Jinxed! That's what it was all right!"

She seemed to relax, leaning back into the cushions and crossing her legs under her, beaming at him.

"So what else happened?" she asked, eagerness in her voice.

"Let's see. First Beatrice's key stuck in the lock to her front door, and we couldn't get it out. When we got to the restaurant, they'd lost my reservation. Then the busboy spilled an entire pitcher of ice water in Beatrice's lap. She'd just gotten back from drying off her dress when our dinners arrived. My fajitas caught on fire, and Beatrice got doused with water again in the course of the fire being put out. Then when we got to her house, a water pipe had broken and the entire first floor was submerged in an inch or two of water."

"Oh." Jacinth digested that thoughtfully, looking anxious. "I hope nothing valuable was ruined. Was there?"

"Not too much. She had a tiled floor, so there was no carpet to be destroyed, but there was some damage, certainly."

She gnawed on her lower lip, contrition in the brown eyes.

"I'm sorry, Douglas. I'll do what I can to reverse any serious damage, especially anything valuable to her. I didn't mean to actually cause any harm."

"I know," he reassured her. "The worst that happened is that our waitress at the restaurant could have gotten fired from her job, so I insisted to the manager the fajitas incident was a freak accident. But to be very honest, you spared me a difficult evening, and possibly an unpleasant scene at the end, so it's hard for me to be as angry as I should be. "

Jacinth seemed a little put out. "You mean you weren't enjoying yourself anyway? I did it all for nothing?"

"That's exactly what I mean."

He watched with enjoyment as the generous pink mouth formed a pout, and she appeared to sulk.

"Why weren't you enjoying yourself?" she demanded.

As if, Douglas bit back a smile, he had no right not to be having a good time on a date she was determined to jinx.

"Because our efficient, professional veterinary assistant turns into a man-eating tiger when the lab coat comes off." Douglas grimaced in remembrance. "And I was apparently on tonight's menu."

The pout was erased as if by magic, and her face brightened.

"I thought the whole point was to prove that you needed to be around other women more."

Douglas stared at her in astonishment.

"How did you know that? I never said a word to you!"

She shook her head at him and reached over to pat his hand. Odd how he didn't mind that when Jacinth did it.

"Douglas, I haven't lived nine hundred years without learning something about how men think."

He tamped down a flare of annoyance. "How do I think?"

She tilted her head to one side, studying him for a moment. "Are you angry?"

He settled back against the sofa cushions with a sigh. How could he be angry with her?

"No," he admitted. "But I do want to know how you decided that was what I was thinking."

"Well." She wriggled around to sit sideways facing him, her back against the arm of the sofa, legs tucked under her. She began ticking points off on her fingers. "One, you're attracted to me, and you don't perceive that I'm attracted back. Then you became annoyed with yourself for being attracted to me. Next you decided that it wasn't really me you were attracted to--that is, not me as a person, but because I was a woman, and living in close proximity--that the attraction you felt was merely a matter of... what is the word? ...propinquity. Which led you to conclude that you needed to meet more women, and you'd be equally attracted to one of those."

She paused, the slender black eyebrows raised in enquiry. "How am I doing so far?"

"Just terrific," he mumbled. He glanced away, feeling unaccountably exposed. Jacinth's small hand slipped into his, squeezing gently, and he looked up.

"It's not that I'm not equally attracted to you, Douglas," she said, the dark eyes holding a troubled expression. "I am, but I am trying very hard not to be. It is not possible... you and I."

Douglas closed his fingers about hers, holding tight. "Why isn't it?" he asked bluntly.

Her eyes widened, as if he'd asked a surprising question.

"Because I am Djinn, and you are human."

Douglas shook his head. Did she truly think it was as simple as that? Or perhaps...

"Is there a law in the Djinn world against it?"

"No. Oh, no. I know any number of Djinn..."

Jacinth broke off, her teeth gnawing at her bottom lip as she stared up at him in dismay.

"I didn't think so." He slid his free hand around to cup her face, caressing the silken skin of her cheek with his fingers. "So why not you and I, Jacinth?"

Unexpectedly, the big eyes filled with tears. "You are human, Douglas, and I am Djinn."

He chuckled. "I think we've established that, yes."

"No, that's not... Douglas, humans die. Djinn are immortal."

His thumb caressed her cheek, wiping away the faint moisture as one tear trailed down. "I'm not blind to the facts. Of course I know that, and I've spent a great deal of time thinking about it."

She stared at him, blinking in surprise. "You have?"

"Mmhmm." He slid his hand down to her neck, over the curve of her shoulder, then down to her hand, entwining his fingers with hers. He brought her hand up to his lips, kissing her fingers. "There's nothing more I could want than to spend the rest of my life with you, Jacinth. And when it's my time... I know that you're still here to watch over Ben and Molly and the children you and I might have, and their children, and their children's children. It would become a kind of legacy, our love."

He watched the emotions... too many and too fleeting for him to interpret, but that it was an internal struggle was clear.

"But you'll be dead!" she finally burst out. "And I... I am the one left to grieve for you for eternity!"

With a sob she snatched her hand away and leapt off the sofa, all but running from the room. He heard her light footsteps grow distant, then the soft closing of her door.

He ran his fingers through his hair, wondering what the hell he was going to do now.

CHAPTER 17

Sunday mornings weren't Douglas' favorite. At least, not until Benny was old enough to push the lawn mower. Douglas ran his arm over his face, letting the cool cotton sleeve of his t-shirt soak up the sweat running down his face. Damn, but it was hot! At the sound of Jacinth's voice, he turned the mower off, grateful for the reprieve.

"What?" he yelled. "I couldn't hear."

The yellow curtain in the bathroom window was pushed aside, and Jacinth's face was framed in the opening.

"There's someone at the door. Could you get it? I'm giving Molly her bath."

"Oh. Sure thing."

Anything for a break. Even with the pool taking up a large chunk of the back yard, there was lots of grass left to mow. What had he been thinking of, buying a house with a yard this size? Maybe he'd have it dug up and make it into a big sandbox for the kids. Thinking pleasant thoughts of jungle gyms, he went to open the front door.

"Good morning. You seem in a good mood."

There, looking bright and chipper with a determined smile, stood Beatrice. Oh, God! It was all he could do to smother the instinctive groan that found its way into his throat.

"Beatrice! This is a surprise." He stepped back to let her in, which was the only option he had since she'd moved forward with a confidence that was unfazed by last night's events. "How's your apartment?"

Without waiting for an invitation, the redhead stepped into the living room, looking about her with interest. There was a kind of avid possessiveness in her gaze he didn't like, as if she were already envisioning making herself at home.

Benny bounced into the room as if shot from a catapult.

"Hey, Dad! Who was at the door?"

He halted at the sight of the visitor, his eyes wide.

"This is my son, Ben," Douglas introduced him to their unwanted visitor. "Benny, this is Beatrice. She works at the clinic with Dr. Anderson."

"She takes care of the dogs, right?" Benny had been evincing interest in the clinic's practice these last few weeks, and had begun to grasp the essentials; Douglas worked with horses, Dr. Shelton with cats and Dr. Anderson with dogs.

"That's right." Beatrice aimed a wide smile at Benny with that false cheer that some people seemed to reserve especially for small children and mentally handicapped persons. "So what grade are you in, Ben?"

Douglas cringed inwardly, awaiting his son's response. Benny had a particularly low idiot tolerance level, he'd discovered. Although shooting him a disgusted glance, the boy behaved.

"I'm starting first grade next month," he told Beatrice in his politest "company manners" voice.

Molly made her entrance, pink from her bath, her damp blonde curls clustered tightly about her head, Brandywine draped over one arm. Apparently asleep, the kitten dangled limp as a washrag. Douglas shook his head in amazement. He'd never seen such a laid-back animal in all his life.

Beatrice advanced on Molly, her smile firmly in place.

"And this must be your daughter, Molly. What a cute stuffed toy. It looks so real!"

As she drew near the kitten raised its head. The gold eyes grew wide, the oversized tufted ears sweeping back. Brandy's little back arched and he hissed at Beatrice, struggling to free himself and escape. Molly, herself alarmed at the kitten's behavior, held him all the tighter.

"Molly, let him go!"

Douglas started forward, afraid Brandy would scratch the child in his panic. Beatrice, attempting to help, tried to take the kitten from Molly. Spitting in fury, Brandy attacked the red lacquered fingers and squirmed in Molly's grip to launch himself to the floor, leaving deep scratches in Beatrice's fair skin. He raced away, down the hall, hissing and spitting as he went.

"Douglas, what in the world... Oh!" Still drying her hands on a towel, Jacinth appeared in the doorway and eyed their visitor.

Douglas was taking Beatrice's hands, examining the red marks with the tiny drops of blood oozing out. "I need to clean these. Jacinth, could you get some bandages?"

Jacinth peered at the scratches, and looked horrified. "Of course, right away."

She hurried down the hall to the far closet, where the first aid box was kept, and Douglas became aware of Beatrice's long fingers clenching tightly. He looked up, curious, to find Beatrice staring after Jacinth, her mouth tight, the green eyes glaring in a kind of baffled fury. She made an odd sound, eerily similar to the kitten's hiss, and took a step back, disengaging her hands from his.

"It's no big deal. Listen, I need to go. I'll... um... see you at the office, okay?"

Douglas trailed her to the door. "Are you sure? Those scratches need to be taken care of. I'm sorry, I can't imagine what made the kitten act like that, he's been very gentle since I brought him home for the children a few days ago."

Beatrice's smile was tight as she opened the front door. "It's no big deal. I have some peroxide at home. Well, it was nice meeting your family."

And she was gone. Still puzzled by her abrupt departure and Brandy's behavior, Douglas turned to find Benny and Molly still standing in their places, looking at him with round eyes. At least Molly was unscathed, he thought with a sigh of relief.

"I don't like that lady," Benny blurted out.

Molly edged towards her brother and clung to his hand, eyes wide. He wasn't sure if it was from Beatrice's visit or Brandy's unusual behavior, but she looked on the verge of tears, and more than a little scared.

"It's okay," he told them, gathering both children into his arms. "I don't think Brandy liked her either."

Benny snorted with laughter, but Molly just stared at him with huge eyes, and he gave her an extra tight hug.

"Don't worry, sweetheart. I don't think she'll be back."

Privately he was a little disturbed by the rage he'd glimpsed in Beatrice's face, but somehow he was very, very sure that she'd never return to this house again. All he could feel was relief.

"Did she go?" Jacinth had returned, laden with disinfectant and gauze. At Douglas' nod, she started to speak, then bit back whatever it was she'd been going to say, her eyes on the subdued children.

"So sad," she said brightly, eyes twinkling with mischief. "I was looking forward to dumping some iodine on her wounds."

Benny cracked up with laughter, while Douglas gave his nanny an admonitory look.

She gazed back innocently, the big brown eyes limpid. "What?"

He sighed and shook his head. "Never mind. Do you know where Brandy went?"

"Under Molly's bed, I think."

She shimmied to one side to allow Benny and Molly to dash past her as they raced for their pet, leaving Douglas and Jacinth to stare at each other.

"What in the world was that all about?" Jacinth asked.

Douglas didn't pretend to misunderstand. "Beatrice? Believe me, I have no idea. She walked in here like she owned the place... or planned to. She was absolutely furious when she left, and it was more than the kitten scratching her. She won't be back, I know that much."

They looked at each other for a long moment, then Jacinth stepped forward into his arms, and he held her tight.

"Jacinth," he groaned, burying his face in against her soft, thick hair, the sweet fragrance of jasmine enveloping him. "I didn't want her. I don't want anyone but you. What are we going to do?"

She stirred in his arms, resting her head on his chest. "I don't know," she whispered. "I don't know."

"What's wrong? Why can't it work between us, Jacinth? Talk to me."

He could feel her take a breath, and for a moment he thought she was going to answer him.

The phone rang. Damn!

"Dad!" His son bawled from the back of the house. "It's for you!"

Who else would it be for? He rose to his feet, and stood looking at Jacinth a moment.

"Hold that thought, will you? We need to talk, Jacinth, you and I."

He turned toward the kitchen and the phone, taking comfort in the fact that, while she didn't say she would tell him what it was that kept her holding him at arm's length, at least she didn't refuse to consider the possibility. He was making progress.

"Hello?"

"Hey, Doug-man. How'd the date go?"

Douglas grimaced, leaning against the wall. If Troy found out everything that happened last night, he'd never live it down.

"Let's just say, not good, and leave it at that," he suggested.

"That bad, huh?" His friend's voice was sympathetic.

"Yeah." In college, he and Troy had always compared notes on dates, but Douglas was mindful of the fact that Beatrice was an employee, almost a colleague, and discretion was necessary. "Besides... well, it just wouldn't have worked out."

There was a moment of silence on the other end of the line.

"I thought so. It's that outrageous nanny of yours, huh?"

Trust Troy to hit the nail on the head the first time.

"Pretty much," Douglas admitted. "Thing is, there are... reasons why it wouldn't work out between us."

"That's raw, man."

Douglas couldn't agree more and was grateful to Troy for changing the subject.

"Well, hey, the reason I called is this cat of yours is doing great. She's been wanting to go outside, so I thought I'd see if you wanted to come pick her up."

That was a good idea. The kids would like to see the horses, and Troy's collie had just had a litter of pups for them to ooh and aah over. He'd take everyone out to lunch, and they'd make an outing of it.

CHAPTER 18

CAT WAS glad to see them. She leaped into Jacinth's arms the instant the Djinn set foot in Troy's house and clung to her, purring like some mad motorboat. The children clamored around, reaching up to pet Cat's thick fur, while Troy still stood holding the door open, eyebrows raised a bit as he watched.

"She's always that friendly with me," he told Douglas in a low voice, "but she's done her best to chase off or ignore every other person I've brought into the house. Cherie, my collie, is scared to death of her and won't go near her."

Douglas wondered if that was because the dog sensed that Cat was a shapeshifter, or if Cat had managed to warn him off somehow, in either her cat or female form. Did animals recognize shapeshifters? Were they afraid of them, or did they feel a kinship? He'd have to ask Jacinth; maybe she'd know, or could find out from Cat.

Molly had left Jacinth's side and was pulling on his sleeve, looking at him with pleading eyes. "Can we see the puppies?"

"Oh, yeah!" Benny bounced over eagerly. "Puppies!"

"Sure thing," Troy said in his gravelly voice. He held out a hand to each child. "Come on, they're in the basement."

"They're not very old," he explained to the children as they trooped down the stairs. "Their eyes aren't even open. You can hold one if you promise to be very careful."

Douglas and Jacinth, trailing behind, exchanged smiles as both children promised Troy very loudly how careful they would be.

The puppies were adorable, six roly-poly bundles with damp noses and big eyes. Cat jumped down from Jacinth's arms and trotted over to inspect them as well. The puppies' dam, a beautiful rough-coat collie, whined anxiously when she saw the cat and leaned against Troy as if for protection.

Silly dog, Cat commented to Jacinth, her mental voice dripping with a mixture of scorn and amused tolerance. *I've told her I wouldn't hurt them. What a ninny.*

Jacinth pressed her lips tightly together to keep from laughing aloud.

"Cat says Cherie is a ninny," she whispered to Douglas, resisting the urge to lean against him. She was close enough to smell the masculine tang of his aftershave, to feel the heat radiating from his body in the close confines of the small basement room. His answering chuckle stroked her nerve endings like a caress.

"The poor dog is no match for a combination of female and feline."

He yelped when she retaliated by pinching his arm, then nudged her.

"Look at Molly hold that pup," he said, keeping his voice low. "And she's babbling away like a little brook. Maybe I should tell Troy I want one of them when they're old enough."

Jacinth considered that. "You've just gotten them the

kitten," she said, thinking aloud. "Molly is still very young, and you don't want to overburden Benny with responsibility. On the other hand... oh, Douglas, if we got a puppy, it and Brandy would grow up together. What could be better?"

"Although," she twinkled up at him mischievously, "You're going to have a full house, with two children, a cat, a dog, and a nanny."

"A pony, too," Douglas responded. "I always meant to get them one when they were older. My property extends on back beyond the yard to the field beyond. You can't see it beyond the trees, but it's enclosed with a stone wall. All I'd need to do is put up a fence behind the house, and a tack room."

"Then, of course, you'll have to have a horse for yourself," she teased.

He grinned down at her and winked. "Stick around and I'll get you one too."

The longing came from nowhere, hitting her like a blow to the gut. To stay, to be with Douglas and the children, being part of their lives. She could be a real mother to Molly and Benny. And she'd be Douglas' wife. Just thinking about it took her breath away. If only... *NO!* She pushed the enticing thought away and rose to her feet.

"The children are busy with the puppies," she told Douglas. "Let's go see the horses."

Outside, walking toward the barn, Douglas seemed silent, withdrawn a bit. A tiny crease between his brows indicated troubled thoughts. She yearned to take his face between her hands and kiss his cares away. He was a good man, and a good father, and deserved everything good that life had to offer. If only he would confide in her, perhaps she could help. Of course, being male, he probably wouldn't. He couldn't help it, she supposed... it seemed an intrinsic part of man's very nature.

Being female, however, she wasn't bound by that problem. She could just ask. And he still had the two wishes left, although he seemed to have forgotten about those. He never mentioned the wishes, never gave any indication that he was thinking of how he could best use them.

She was about to speak when Douglas himself broke the silence.

"Do you think I'm being too indulgent with them?"

What? Jacinth came to an abrupt halt and stared up at Douglas.

"Where did that come from?" she asked.

He shrugged his broad shoulders, looking uncomfortable, and dug his hands into the pockets of the khaki trousers he wore.

"I don't know. I just wondered, that's all."

Jacinth glanced about. To one side of the barn ahead of them was an old spreading oak tree, its wide branches providing shade for the rustic bench at its base. She took Douglas' arm and firmly guided him towards the bench.

Even on a wooden bench, Jacinth could make herself at home, Douglas thought, watching as she curled her legs beneath her. She gave him one of her bright, cheery smiles, the kind that lit up the sky itself, and patted the bench with a smile.

"Come sit," she invited.

He sat beside her, his thigh brushing her knee. Clasping his hands together, he stared at the ground, trying to make some order out of the nebulous thoughts that chased themselves through his mind. Jacinth laid her hand on his arm, her touch gentle.

"Talk to me, Douglas."

"She didn't take care of them," he blurted out, going right to the heart of the matter. "Lilian didn't buy them decent clothes, or toys. She didn't take them to the mall, or to the playground. They'd never been to the zoo or a circus or been in a swimming pool. She didn't bother to see that they had decent meals. Molly stopped *talking*, for God's sake, and she did nothing. I-I feel like I have to make it up to them. I want them to be happy, to know that I love them."

"They know that, Douglas," She tightened her fingers on his arm, giving a little shake. "You don't have to buy them things for them to know you love them. I don't have much experience with children, but I am sure that indulging them too much would be as bad for them, in its own way, as their mother's neglect."

"You're right," Douglas admitted. "But every time I think of what they went through, of what their life was like... I want to run out and buy them everything they could ever need, give them everything they want. I know it's wrong, but when Molly looks at me with those big blue eyes, or Benny pleads in that way that he has, I turn to putty."

Beside him, Jacinth laughed, a happy, infectious sound.

"I know. And, I might point out, they know it too. But you must resist, Douglas. Children need limits, and who will set those limits if you do not?"

"For someone who claims to not know much about children, you have a lot of excellent advice," Douglas said wryly.

"It's not so much knowing children, as common sense," Jacinth replied. "That, and seeing mothers in the stores with screaming, whining children in tow that makes me want to scream myself. You don't want Benny and Molly to be like them, do you?"

"God, no." Douglas remembered some of those incidents himself, and shuddered. He'd often wondered why those parents didn't exert themselves to discipline their kids, to put their foot down and insist on good behavior. No, he didn't want his kids to be like that, and he didn't want to be that kind of parent.

"Okay, you're right," he acknowledged. And yet... the puppy? "I feel like I'm giving in over the puppy... except, I'd always meant to get a puppy as soon as they were old enough. It's part of the normal childhood I wanted them to have."

"Ahh." Jacinth nodded, a wise look in her brown eyes. "That 'normal childhood' thing. Were you that unhappy, Douglas?"

"No!" The denial rose instinctively to his lips. He smiled, remembering the fun times with Blue and Skye. "No, of course not. It was wild and crazy, and fun too. But... it's not what I want for my kids, and it's not the kind of life I want for me as an adult, you know?"

"What kind of life do you want for you?" Jacinth asked, her voice gentle, her soft gaze inviting him to confide in her.

"A home." Douglas's response came without hesitation. He didn't have to stop to think about it. "One place that is mine, a place that, no matter how far we may travel, we always come back to. I want the kids to have stability, to feel safe, and loved."

"I guess it's what they call the American Dream." He shrugged his shoulders, feeling silly at saying the words. "You know... A house with a picket fence, two cars, a cat, a dog, and 2.5 kids."

Jacinth's laughter rang on the breeze like bells. Her hand slid down his arm and she wound her fingers between his, her hand soft and warm. "Well, I don't know how you'll get half a kid, but you're there, Douglas. If that's what you want, you've gotten there. As far as Benny and Molly, you're not spoiling them too much, at least not yet. It hasn't even been a month, Douglas. Give it some time. You're all three of you still adjusting, still learning to get to know each other. You're learning to trust your instincts with them, and they're learning to trust you. And you have good instincts, Douglas. Follow them."

He nodded, very aware of her hand in his. His palm tingled against the contact, spreading up his arm, warming the very essence of his being. Was she aware of it? Could she too feel the spark between them? They had something together, the two of them, and he wasn't going to just let her walk away from it, from them.

"It's your turn," he told her. No point beating about the bush, he'd waited long enough as it was.

Jacinth looked startled, her mahogany eyes wide as she stared at him.

"My turn?"

"Yes. Your turn to tell me what's bothering you. Why you won't admit to this attraction there is between us. It can't be just because I'm a human and you're a Djinn. There has to be more to it than that, Jacinth. I know it."

Sighing, Jacinth drew her hand away from his and raised her face to the slight breeze that sprang up, taking a deep breath. Tiny curls clung to her forehead in the moist heat of the day. Douglas reached out one finger to stroke them away from her face, and tucked a long silky strand of ebony hair behind one shell-pink ear. She smiled her thanks, and with some difficulty, he resisted the need to lean down and sample her enticing mouth.

"My father was a mortal." Jacinth was watching him steadily, a suddenly serious expression banishing the spark of fun that was her defining quality, that always seemed to make her larger than life.

"A mortal?"

Jacinth nodded. "A very famous one. Mother mourns him, even now."

Startled, Douglas raised his brows. "Nine hundred years later?"

With a chuckle that dispelled the uncharacteristic seriousness, Jacinth took his hand and gave it a quick squeeze, her cheeks dimpling enchantingly.

"Time is not the same as for you. To us that is not so long. One of the things Mother regrets most is that she had so very little time with him... no more than a few years. We had to leave him when I was very young, when she could not hide anymore that I was... different. He did not know, you see, that she was Djinn."

Douglas frowned, trying to sort this out. "You mean, she didn't come to him to give him three wishes?"

"Oh, no! Mother was never a Wish Bearer. She fell in love with him when she saw him out walking one night, when he was a very young man," Jacinth explained. Her eyes softened in fond memory. "She watched him for many years, as he grew, before she went to him. It was a very hard time then, you must understand, Douglas. The Turks and the Persians were warring, and life was chancy, even if one was favored at court, as my father was. If those who favored you fell from power, you would be perhaps met with enmity from those who took over. The Muslims were tolerant of the Christians and the Jews, but had it been known my father... an eminent scholar, an astronomer at Court... had married a Djinn... no, no, what trouble there would have been! It would have put his life in danger."

"So she never told him," Douglas mused. "But she married him, even knowing she couldn't stay with him?"

Jacinth nodded. "For some years she was able to hide who she was. We are able to take the appearance of growing older by human standards. But then I was born... and once I could walk, and speak, she could no longer use those means."

Her laughter rippled over him like silk.

"Djinn children can be... difficult," she said, her smile inviting him to share her amusement.

"I can imagine!" His agreement was heartfelt. "But you are half Djinn, then."

Those bright brown eyes twinkled at him. "No. I am Djinn. We are not the same species, Douglas. Djinn are magical beings. We are not humans with special abilities. No one knows how it is that Djinn and humans can have children, but such a child is born either human or Djinn. Not half. All human, and mortal, or all Djinn, and immortal." She paused, her look turning solemn. "I have been a Djinn for almost a thousand years, Douglas, and hope to continue for another several thousand more."

A thousand years. He'd be only a memory... a speck of a Kodak moment against ageless eons. The thought was disturbing.

Jacinth traced a pattern on her jeans-clad thigh with one fingertip.

"I remember him, you know. My father."

Douglas frowned in thought. "I thought you said your mother left him when you were young?"

She nodded her head vigorously, the ebony curls bouncing.

"Yes. I was four when we left Baghdad and went to the Djinn village. But we Djinn do not forget," she told him. "We remember every moment from our birth, not like humans. Once we learn a thing... like language, for instance... we never forget. Ever."

Her expressive face softened, her eyes warming with affection. "He would carry me on his shoulder, and call me his *katkuuta*... cute one. Sometimes we would go to sit in the desert all night, the three of us, well-wrapped in blankets, while he watched the stars and made his calculations. Later, when they thought I was asleep, he would recite poetry to her, and they would love each other."

"He wrote a poem just for me, not long before we left." Jacinth smiled, but the corners of her mouth trembled, and her eyes were misty. Feeling a bit bemused, Douglas watched as she conjured a dandelion from thin air and blew on its tiny fluffs, watching the white bits float on the breeze.

Oh, now wait a moment. Douglas sat up abruptly. Jacinth... the name was an old variation of hyacinth. Surely not... it couldn't be.

"*If of thy mortal goods thou art bereft*," he quoted softly. "*And of thy slender store two loaves alone to thee are left... buy one, and with the dole, buy hyacinths to feed the soul.*"

Jacinth looked up at him in delight. "You know it!"

"The world knows it!" He could hardly believe it. "Omar Khayyam. Mathematician, astronomer, and poet... he was born sometime in the first millennium, I think."

"1048," Jacinth nodded affirmatively.

"And that other famous poem, the one about the loaf of bread and jug of wine and thou... he wrote that was for your mother?"

"Yes."

She was silent a long moment, apparently remembering those days, so long ago that it might as well have been another world, Douglas thought. When she spoke again her voice was low, full of deep pain that he'd never heard from her before, had never suspected the joyous, fun-loving Jacinth carried within her heart.

"She loved him so much. It tore her apart to leave him. For decades she was so sad, watching him over from afar, unable to go to him, and when he died..."

Jacinth broke off, her gaze on the distant trees. "My mother is very, very beautiful, as you have seen. She has never chosen another mate even after all this time, although there are handsome, powerful Djinn who would court her in an instant if she allowed. But she shuns them all."

She looked up at him, her eyes dark and unfathomable. "I do not want that, Douglas. I do not wish to lose all joy in life, to long for what can never be. To live all my years, spend centuries, in regret for what cannot be changed."

He knew they were no longer speaking of her mother.

"Sometimes," he said, hearing his voice rough with suppressed emotion, "sometimes we have no choice. It isn't what I would have chosen, either, but... Jacinth, I'm in love with you."

She visibly paled.

"Douglas..." her whisper was a mere breath of sound. "No..."

"Yes," he insisted. He reached out, cupping one smooth cheek in his hand, stroking his thumb across her silky skin. "And you care for me also. You can't deny it, Jacinth. You care for me, and the kids, more than you know... or accept."

The dark eyes were wide with panic as she stared at him, frozen. "I don't."

"Yes, you do." He knew she did. "You belong with me. With us."

"I don't!" Jacinth leaped to her feet, her cheeks flushed and rosy, her eyes flashing with temper. "I won't!"

She stomped her little foot, and vanished.

"That's not fair," Douglas bawled furiously into the air. "You can't just blink out whenever we have a disagreement!"

"Deal with it!" a disembodied voice yelled back. And then there was silence.

Goddamit! Douglas fumed, staring up at the empty sky. What the hell was he going to do with her? Worse, what was he going to do without her?

He rose heavily to his feet and headed toward the house. With a bang the back door flew open, and his children spilled out.

"Dad! Dad!" Benny was almost incoherent with excitement. The boy ran to Douglas, pulling at his hand. "Uncle Troy said he'd let us have one of the puppies when they're old enough, if you say it's okay. Is it, Dad? Can we have one?"

"Pleeeeeeeease?" Molly drew the word out like it had a dozen syllables. She clung to his other arm, her big eyes beseeching him. "Please, Daddy?"

He melted. In the month she'd been home, even though she'd been talking since that first week, she'd never called him Daddy. Not once. He knelt in the dirt, pulling both his children into his embrace. God, he loved them! They were so precious to him. He couldn't erase the last two years, Lilian's neglect of them, but by God, he could damned well make sure he did right by them from now on.

"Of course you can have a puppy," he told them, his voice sounding unaccountably hoarse. "We'll go pick one out now, and Troy will let us know when it's old enough to come home with us."

A puppy was a little thing, hardly weighing on the scale in comparison with the hugs and kisses his overjoyed children bestowed on him before racing back to the old farmhouse, shouting and laughing as they disappeared into the kitchen.

Douglas paused as he followed in their wake, one foot on the stairs, and looked back toward the barn. Would Jacinth come back? Surely she would. How would he explain to the children, to Troy, if she didn't?

He breathed a sigh of relief when he found her in the living room waiting for him, along with Troy and the children.

"So I hear you're adding a puppy to the menagerie," Troy greeted him with a wide grin. "I knew it, man. You're a sucker for these kids."

Douglas couldn't help agreeing, which earned him a cheeky grin from his son. He was then swept, willy-nilly, back down to the basement to view the sleeping female pup his children had chosen. Cat sniffed at the tiny bundle of fur and sneezed in a show of feline disgust. Douglas chuckled. Figured. He watched as Cat trotted over to Troy's feet and stared up at him imperiously, quite clearly requesting... no, demanding... to be picked up. Troy obliged, scratching her absent-mindedly behind the ears as he nudged Douglas with his elbow.

"So, when you're ready for the pup should I send her over with Beatrice?"

Benny and Molly must have regaled him with the tale of this morning's fiasco. He was about to reply when suddenly Troy yelped and dropped Cat.

"She scratched me!"

Troy stared down at the cat at his feet, who stared back at him with accusing gold eyes. Douglas turned aside, choking back a laugh.

"Come on." He held out his hands for his children to take. "Time to go home."

They trooped up the stairs to where Jacinth waited in the living room. She didn't meet his eyes as she leaned over to receive Molly's exuberant hug.

Douglas looked down at Cat, who'd followed them upstairs and was sitting at Troy's feet, surveying them as if she owned the place.

"Cat's looking well," Douglas remarked to Troy. "Are we taking her with us?"

Cat's tufted ears swept back, and her muzzle wrinkled as she hissed at him. In a flash of red and brown fur, she raced past him into the hall and up the stairs.

"Uh... guess not."

Troy blinked after his feline guest, then turned back to them with a wry smile. "I think she understood you, man. Hey, I don't mind keeping her. She's a way cool cat. I thought someone might be looking for her, because she's been well cared for. Then again, no one's answered the ads I put in the paper."

"Looks like you've got yourself a cat." Douglas bit the inside of his cheek to keep the smirk off his face. Better Troy than him.

I heard that!

A muffled laugh nearby, hastily smothered, told him that Jacinth heard the cat's caustic comment as well.

"Okay, troops." Douglas glanced around at his children and nanny and gestured toward the door. "Time to get home and start dinner, so let's get a move on."

"Bye, Uncle Troy! And thanks!" Benny was still jumping with excitement.

Douglas chuckled. "I'd forgotten that's what he'd been used to call you," he told his friend.

Molly was no less excited, but still shy. "Thank you," she told Troy. She was adorable, her big blue eyes earnest. She was a tiny doll next to the giant vet, the top of her curly head barely coming to his knees. Troy hunkered down in front of her, and she disappeared into his huge hug.

"You're welcome, sweetheart." He planted a kiss on her cheek, then released her with a pat on the back. "You guys go on now. I'll take good care of your puppy for you."

"Okay!" Molly chirped her agreement, and scampered out the door Douglas held open for her.

Douglas waited while Jacinth shook Troy's hand and said goodbye. She passed him and went down the stairs and across the yard to the car, all without a word or a glance. She listened to the children's chatter, joining them in deciding on a meal for dinner, and making plans to go to the playground the next day. She neither looked at Douglas nor spoke to him. Not once.

CHAPTER 19

JACINTH AVOIDED COMING out of her bedroom the next morning until both children were up. It was childish of her to disappear last night as she had, and not much better to avoid being alone with him now. Still, that was better than facing him, than having to answer his questions, to look in his eyes and see the same pain that she felt. What was the use of talking about it anyway, she thought, feeling belligerent? There wasn't anything that could be done about it. She was Djinn, and he was mortal. That should have been the end of it. So why did she feel so... unsettled?

Without enthusiasm for the day ahead, she dressed and headed for the kitchen, where the children's voices were raised in gaiety. Douglas wasn't in the best of moods either, she noted. He looked rumpled and grumpy, and after pouring himself a cup of coffee he kissed his children goodbye and took himself off to work. Well, fine, if he wanted to be that way. She didn't want to talk to him anyway.

By mid-morning she'd worked off her bad mood, cleaning

the house from top to bottom in the human way. After lunch, she gave in to the children's pleas to take them to the park. It would be nice to get out of the house and smell the fresh air, to romp with Ben and Molly in the grass.

As she led the children towards the playground, a woman arose from a bench nearby and approached them hesitantly. Feeling real trepidation, Jacinth recognized Douglas' ex-wife. Benny and Molly fell silent as their mother approached, Benny hanging onto Jacinth's hand, and Molly clinging to Jacinth's leg with both arms.

Lilian stopped some feet away, her eyes on the children, but she didn't come closer. She cleared her throat, meeting Jacinth's eyes fleetingly.

"I-I don't mean to cause any trouble," the older woman stammered. "I thought maybe you would allow me to visit with my children and to play with them here. Just... just for a little while?"

Jacinth gnawed on her lower lip, not sure what to do. There was nothing to object to in Lilian's behavior, which was apologetic and hesitant, far from last week's histrionics. Somehow Jacinth was sure that Douglas wouldn't like this, but unfortunately, Douglas was not *here*. The decision was up to her. Lilian seemed sincere, and watched her hopefully. Jacinth turned her attention to the children. Benny looked equally uncertain, as did Molly, but neither seemed to object to the prospect of their mother playing with them. Perhaps they felt secure here in this public place. After all, there was nothing Lilian could do... not here in broad daylight with people all around.

But still, she hesitated. There was... something... lurking in the slightly bloodshot eyes, a shiftiness in the faded gaze. Lilian was up to something. For a moment Jacinth wished she had

Kieran's ability to read minds. Then again, what could the woman do? Still feeling reluctance, Jacinth nodded her permission.

Lilian smiled with relief, all but beaming in gratitude.

"Thank you so much. You don't know what it means to me, to be able to spend a little time with them." She held out long, manicured fingers to Benny and Molly, giving them a bright smile. "Shall we go to the swings, and I'll push you?"

The three of them walked to the playground, Jacinth watching carefully from the park bench a short distance away. She'd talk to Douglas the instant they got home. He wasn't going to be pleased, but what else could she have done? It wasn't like the woman had tried to kidnap them again. She just wished she could shake the feeling that something was afoot.

She stayed alert, watching for any sign of a cohort, someone whose task would be to distract her while Lilian made off with the children. Although the park was busy with other mothers with young children, joggers, couples walking hand in hand, no one approached her. Lilian seemed content to play with the children, pushing them on the swings, helping Molly up the steps to the tall slide, to kneel in the sand and catch the little girl at the bottom. Both Molly and Benny were laughing, talking to her unreservedly, enjoying the novelty of playing with the woman who called herself their mother. If only she'd been like this before, behaved like a real mother, Jacinth mused, Douglas would never have taken the kids away from her.

Hey, Djinn.

She took her eyes from the small group on the playground as Cat leaped gracefully onto the bench beside her.

"What are you doing here?" she asked, her hand automatically going to stroke the thick silky fur. Cat purred in appreciation, butting her head against Jacinth's hand. "I thought you were happy at Troy's?"

He had to go out of town. Cat sounded disgruntled, and Jacinth bit back a grin. *Some veterinarian conference. It's boring out there with just that stupid dog for company. I called a taxi and went home, then came here for a little company. I thought I might find you here today.*

The cat narrowed her eyes on the woman with the children.

Who is that with your kits?

"They're not mine!" The response was automatic, but Jacinth's gaze went to the children. She did think of them as hers, somehow. And was that jealousy she'd been feeling as she watched the children play with their mother? She chased those thoughts away and replied to Cat's question. "That's the children's mother, Douglas' ex-wife Lilian."

Cat snorted her opinion. By and large, Jacinth agreed.

Want me to shred her stockings?

At that Jacinth laughed aloud. "No, but thank you."

With a wide yawn that displayed a full set of sharp teeth that Jacinth imagined a great white would be proud of, Cat sprawled on the sun-and-shade-dappled end of the bench, disposing herself to sleep.

As you will. Let me know if you need any help. The gold eyes gleamed at her for a moment. *No one does retribution like a feline.*

Jacinth chuckled. She could believe that!

After another half-hour had passed, Lilian leaned down to hug the children, obviously preparing to take her leave, and Jacinth heaved a silent sigh of thanks that there would be no unpleasant scene. Lilian caught her eye and smiled, inclining her head slightly in thanks. She wasn't really so bad, Jacinth thought, watching the woman cross the grass to a water fountain near the farther parking lot. Maybe she'd finally realized what her drinking had lost her, and was on the right path now. That couldn't be a bad thing.

Jacinth gave the snoozing Cat a final pat and rose from the bench going to the children and holding out her hands for them.

"Time to go home and start getting dinner ready."

The kids took her hands, one on each side, bouncing with excitement as they related to her all their play. They were almost to the street when a shrill screech shattered the air. In horror, Jacinth looked over her shoulder to see Lilian running toward them, screaming, from across the park.

Gripping the children tightly she broke into a run, urging the kids faster across the grass, away from the woman. Had the woman gone mad?

No! An urgent voice shouted in her mind. Cat. *Don't run. That's what she wants you to do. It makes you look guilty!*

What? Guilty? Guilty of what?

"Stop her!" She heard Lilian screaming. "She has my children! That woman is stealing my children!

Jacinth skidded to a stop, fury rising as she turned. People began running towards them from every direction... the joggers and picnic-goers, mothers holding their children tightly. A crowd quickly surrounded them, the men looking angry and violent, the women no less hostile. Molly was sobbing, and Benny turned a white, scared face up to her. Jacinth knelt, holding both children tight as Lilian pushed through the crowd.

"How dare you!" Jacinth turned her angry gaze on the woman. "How dare you do this?"

"Molly! Ben!" Her mascara running in thick blobs below her eyes, Lilian gave a convulsive sob for the benefit of their audience, and reached for the children. They shrank from

Lilian, and Jacinth pulled them back, behind her, as she rose to her feet.

Lilian shrieked dramatically. "See? She's trying to take my babies from me. Give me my children!"

"They don't belong to you," Jacinth told her defiantly. "You have no right to take them. You have no right to do this."

"They sure look like her, girlie," a burly older man addressed Jacinth.

"I saw the three of them playing in the park for a long time," a woman put in. "This girl here was watching them from a bench all the time. She must have been waiting for her chance to grab the kids when the mother went to get a drink."

Angry mutters rose, and the older man looked down at Benny, pointing at Lilian. "Sonny, is this your mother?"

Benny nodded, wrapping himself about Jacinth fearfully as a murmur went through the crowd, which pressed closer. Jacinth found her arms gripped ungently, and Lilian darted forward to take Molly.

"No!"

"Just hold her," Lilian begged the people, artful tears in her faded eyes. "I don't want any trouble, just my children."

Molly screamed as Lilian pried her away from Jacinth. Other hands were on Benny, trying to pull him away too. He fought them, kicking and biting like a little tiger.

"No! I don't want to go with her! I won't!"

Jacinth found herself in a quandary. To use magic now... no, it was impossible. She could take care of this easily enough if she let Lilian take the children; she'd catch up in her own way, once all these people weren't around. But she couldn't do that, couldn't let them go. She couldn't allow Ben and Molly to think that she'd hand them over to their mother, no matter that they were safe enough. *They* didn't know that, and their trust would be shattered, thinking she'd let them down. It would be a betrayal. She couldn't do it.

"I'm the nanny!" She tried to make those nearest her, those holding her, understand. "Their mother doesn't have custody, she's the one trying to kidnap them!"

No one listened.

"Let the boy go," a man's voice ordered, harsh with anger. "Now!"

Fingers twined in her hair, yanking cruelly, and a fist struck her across the cheek with enough strength to send her reeling to the ground. She held onto Benny desperately, curling around him protectively as she fell.

Douglas shifted the bucket of fried chicken to his left arm, balancing it with the large bag of side dishes so he could unlock the door. Jacinth and the kids must still be at the park. Perfect. He'd have dinner all set out on the table when they got back. He'd forgotten to tell Jacinth this morning he only had a half day at the clinic, and rather than call, he decided it would be fun to surprise them by showing up early. This was even better than he planned, and he whistled as he began to unpack the bags onto the kitchen counter.

A strange thud sounded from the front of the house, like something heavy landing against the door. It was quickly followed by another. Douglas went to the door and opened it cautiously. Something large and furry streaked through the door, brushing past his legs.

"Hey!" He turned, to see a familiar red cat disappearing down the hall. She darted into the bathroom, and the door slammed shut behind her. Cat! What was she doing here? Had she smelled the chicken and come for dinner?

"Cat?" He waited outside the bathroom door. A moment later it was tugged open and a petite young woman with short tousled black hair and huge golden eyes emerged, clutching a bath towel wrapped tightly about her. She clutched his arm with her free hand.

"You've got to get to the park." She was breathing hard from her run, and her voice was tight with anxiety. "Your ex-wife is there, trying to take the children. She's claiming Jacinth was trying to kidnap them, and she's got a crowd gathered."

"Hell!" He started back down the hallway at a run, then remembered Cat was draped in the towel. He came back, going into his room.

"Here, have a t-shirt. We'll have to look for some pants in Jacinth's room."

She grabbed the shirt. "No time, no time. Do you have sweatpants, the kind with drawstrings?"

"Yeah, here."

He thrust them at her. She was already sliding into the t-shirt. One arm emerged and she took the pants.

"Go," she urged. "I'll be right behind you."

He went.

"WHAT'S GOING ON HERE?"

The press of bodies fell back, recognizing the voice of authority, and Jacinth gasped in relief as a uniformed policeman strode forward. She'd been overwhelmed by the sheer number of people, and they'd wrested Benny from her arms. The policeman shouldered his way through the crowd and bent down a hand to help her up.

"Are you all right, miss? What's all this?"

Outraged voices raised against Jacinth, but seeing his chance, Benny wiggled free of the hands holding him, and like a shot he was at her side. His arms clung about her waist, holding on for all he was worth. She bent over him protectively, noting that Lilian also was ringed in by the crowd, unable to escape with Molly, whom she still held. "It's going to be okay, now a policeman is here," she whispered to the boy.

Jacinth waited, pulling control about her with an effort until silence fell and the policeman's attention was on her. In a quiet voice, she explained the situation... the custody case, how Lilian had kidnapped the children two years ago and how they'd been found in California. Briefly, she told him of Lilian's earlier visit to the house, and that Douglas had filed a report with the police.

"She's lying." Lilian's voice was vicious. "Look at her. She's not old enough to be anybody's nanny. I was here with my children on the playground, everyone saw us. I went to get a drink of water, and she grabbed them and started running."

A dozen people began clamoring their support of her, that they'd seen Lilian playing with the children, and seen Jacinth leave with them while Lilian was at the fountain.

"I brought the children to the park." Although Jacinth took care to keep her voice calm and even, in marked contrast to Lilian's histrionics and convulsive weeping, inside she was shaking with outrage and the remnants of the paralyzing fear that had held her when they'd been surrounded and the children wrenched from her hold. "Lilian asked me if she could play with them here, and I let her because she's their mother."

Lilian scoffed. "That's just ridiculous."

Jacinth bent her energy on the policeman. All he had to do was decide to investigate without letting either one of them go, and things would be fine, because he'd find out the truth the instant he contacted the police station.

"Stop!"

The ringing shout had everyone turning. Jacinth could have wept with relief as she saw Douglas running towards them, a strange woman in baggy sweats on his heels despite a conspicuous limp. He would deal with the policeman, and Lilian too. She hugged Benny, tightly, aware she was clinging to the boy almost as hard as he was clinging to her, but unable to relax her tight grip on him.

"Miss Jas, she's taking Molly!" Benny pointed behind her.

As the crowd shifted, Lilian had seen her chance and began to run, gripping Molly's hand tightly as she dragged the little girl with her.

It was easy enough for Jacinth to make the woman trip. She winced, though, when Molly fell too, skinning her knee. The cop was already running after them, reaching Lilian before Jacinth.

"I guess that settles that," he told Jacinth, handing Molly over. Jacinth held the little girl, cradling her tight and shushing her deep sobs.

"I've got you now, sweetie. It's okay. It's okay."

At her side, Benny watched with wide, wary eyes as the policeman hauled Lilian ungently to her feet. Douglas reached them, out of breath.

"These are my children," he panted. "I have custody, and this is their nanny. My ex-wife was the one trying to kidnap them."

Quickly he ran down the story for the attentive police officer. Behind them, Jacinth was aware of the spectators moving away, silent now and chagrined at having been manipulated into helping Lilian kidnap the children. Well, so they should be, she thought angrily. They hadn't even tried to listen to her. They hadn't hesitated in condemning her unheard.

Suddenly Jacinth had had enough. Just... enough. Enough of Lilian's pathetic games, her complete lack of concern for the children whose welfare should have been her first priority. Setting her teeth, she aimed her thoughts at a cluster of bushes in the distance.

A sudden shriek ripped through the air, and Lilian leaped backward, screaming for all she was worth. The cop, who'd begun reading Lilian her rights, gripped her arm tighter, sighing with impatience.

"Look, lady..."

Lilian screamed again, her finger pointing. "My God! Keep them away! Keep them away from me!"

The cop looked in the direction she pointed. So did Benny and Molly. So did Douglas.

"There's nothing there," Benny said, puzzled.

"The elephants!" Lilian's face had gone sheet white, her eyes wide with terror, and she stumbled a few steps back. "Don't you see them? All those little elephants coming toward us! P-pink elephants."

The policeman's expression shifted. He leaned forward, sniffing experimentally. His gaze slid to meet Douglas'. "Alcoholic?"

Douglas nodded, and the burly officer sighed. "Great."

"Come on," he told Lilian, who'd begun shrieking that the elephants were getting closer. She appeared hysterical. At least this time, Jacinth thought with grim satisfaction, it was the real thing, not an act.

Douglas handed his card to the policeman.

"I need to get the children back to the house and calmed down. I have the custody order you'll want to see. I definitely want to press charges, and I'll be filing a restraining order. Can you come by after you take Lilian in, and take our report there?

The officer nodded, his hand going to his belt. He was reaching for his handcuffs, Jacinth realized. She shook her head urgently at him, gesturing towards the children. As badly as Lilian had behaved, Jacinth didn't want Benny and Molly to see their mother being handcuffed. The policeman understood, waving them away.

Jacinth turned, still holding Molly, to see the young woman who'd followed Douglas coming toward her, obviously favoring a lame leg. Jacinth took in the heart-shaped face framed with wildly curling short black hair, the pointed chin and great golden eyes, and smiled.

"Cat?" she mouthed silently. Douglas joined them just then and held out his hand.

"Thank you for coming to get me so quickly."

"Katerina," she said aloud.

Molly was still crying, holding out her arms to her father, and he took her from Jacinth, and they headed out of the park, Benny clinging to his father's side like a vine.

The two women dropped a few paces behind, speaking in low voices.

"I'm sorry I didn't read her in time to know what she was planning," Katerina whispered to Jacinth. "I saw that the children were happy, and that was enough for me. It wasn't until you started away and she started to come after you that I realized her intent."

Jacinth pulled the young woman into a tight embrace.

"It was enough. And you brought Douglas. I can't thank you enough."

Katerina returned the hug quickly, then stepped back, as if uncomfortable with the personal contact.

"You need to get the ki... the young ones home. I'll see you again soon."

She turned and walked away across the grass, graceful despite the disfiguring limp.

"Who was that?" Benny wanted to know. He was gripping his father's hand tightly, the anxiety not quite gone from his face. Jacinth smiled at him, sending waves of reassurance.

"A friend."

"Why was she wearing Daddy's clothes?"

Uh... Jacinth glanced wildly in Douglas' direction. He came to her rescue.

"She was swimming in the pool," Douglas nodded at the public pool not far away, "when she saw what was happening, and she ran all the way to our house in her swimsuit. She didn't want to stay behind, so I just threw a couple of things at her and we ran here."

"Okay."

But Jacinth noted Benny cast a strange look behind them, at Cat's disappearing figure. How long would it be, she wondered, before he began to put everything together?

Much later, after a visit from the police officer and a long consultation with his lawyer on the phone, Douglas came into the living room. Having settled Ben and Molly down for their naps, Jacinth was sitting curled in her favorite corner of the sofa, reading a magazine. She looked up as he came into the room. He stopped in the doorway, and she gave him a questioning look.

"Pink elephants?" he asked, his voice deceptively calm.

Jacinth became immediately defensive. "Well..."

"*Pink* elephants?"

He came forward, and she tried to make herself smaller on the sofa, biting her lip nervously as he towered over her. She stared up at him apprehensively for a long moment. Douglas sat abruptly, his head sinking into his hands, his shoulders shaking slightly.

"Pink elephants!" He raised his head, and Jacinth saw with immense relief that he was laughing. He laughed until he was gasping for air, holding his sides. "I can't believe it."

"Ut-oh."

Douglas only had time to blink in confusion at the odd remark, when a familiar figure manifested. Kieran. And he did not look like a happy genie.

"Jacinth!" The boom shook the ceiling, the Djinn's silver eyes stern.

Jacinth compressed her gentle mouth together in a stubborn line.

"She was trying to kidnap Ben and Molly," she defended, unrepentant.

With an impatient wave of his hand, Kieran dismissed her explanation.

"You'd already taken care of that. She was no further threat."

"She'd have kept trying," Jacinth retorted hotly. "The children were scared. No... they were *terrified*. That was a lynch mob Lilian gathered around her, and she dragged Molly from my arms by force. If a policeman hadn't been cruising by the park just then, she'd have gotten both children and taken off."

It seemed to Douglas that the Djinn's icy rage retreated a bit, the stern gaze softening minutely.

"Is Molly all right?"

Jacinth nodded, the dark ponytail swaying. "She's fine... now. No thanks to her mother."

"My daughter hardly let Jacinth out of her sight all afternoon," Douglas put in. "Not even to go to for her nap. Jacinth had to sit with her and hold her hand until she fell asleep."

Anger flared briefly in the silver eyes before Kieran paced to the fireplace, staring into the empty grate. There was a long silence as he seemed to struggle with himself. With a sigh he turned.

"It cannot be, Jacinth. You know the law... no interference."

"Look at her face!" Douglas shouted, angry with the Djinn's intransigent attitude.

That got his attention. Kieran strode to the sofa, staring down at Jacinth with narrowed eyes. She'd forgotten about the bruise where the man in the crowd had struck her, and she felt color rising to her cheeks. She put her hand to her face, turning her head away from the men, but Kieran brushed back the long ebony locks to reveal the dark purpling bruise on her temple.

"Who did this?"

"They were trying to take Benny from her, and she wouldn't let go," Douglas told him. "Jacinth said you can read minds. Well, read mine, and see what I saw when I arrived at the park this afternoon."

Kieran stared at him for a long moment.

"It is not mind reading precisely," he admitted slowly, as if reluctant to impart knowledge. "Flashes of thoughts that are foremost in the mind. There is a way, however."

Cupping his hands before him, a tiny blue flame appeared, much the same as Douglas had seen Jacinth call to her that day at Troy's house. But this blue flame grew, expanding into a flickering orb that hovered above the Djinn prince's hands.

"Place your hands on either side of the orb," Kieran instructed him. "It will not burn you. Then simply recall what it is you wish me to see."

Douglas glanced at Jacinth, who nodded at him, her smile reassuringly. He raised his hands, bringing them close to the blue orb. He expected to feel some kind of fire, not this curious warmth that came and went, almost like the flames were licking at his fingers.

"Now remember." The prince's deep voice encouraged.

The door to his house appeared in the orb, wavering, then steadying as he drew a deep breath, concentrating. The cat rushing past him in the doorway, then Katerina emerging from the bathroom, the towel draped about him as she gave him the urgent message. Their run to the park, the furious crowd that was gathered about as the policeman arrived, taking control. Jacinth struggling up from the ground, her arms tight around Benny. Lilian running, Molly's screams, her little face terrified as her mother made off with her.

"Enough."

The blue orb shrank, the flames giving a last tiny burst of light before vanishing. Fury flashed in the Djinn's glacial eyes. He turned away and bent over Jacinth, pulling her hand from the bruise with more gentleness than Douglas had seen him display yet, even with Molly. The Djinn cupped her face, laying his fingers across the angry purple marking. When he released her, the bruise was gone.

"Is that better?"

She nodded. "Yes. Thank you."

He nodded, and stepped back.

"About the other," Jacinth looked up at him. "I invoke the right of Firestorm."

The Djinn considered that, then nodded slowly. "Very well,

little one. I can accept that. Although, having seen Douglas' memories, you need no defense. It is disgraceful that this woman should have done such a thing."

Without warning he was gone, as swiftly as he had come. Douglas looked at Jacinth questioningly.

"What was that about? The invoking thing?"

"An ancient defense." Jacinth hesitated, choosing her words with care. "Djinn are creatures of fire, with all that entails... tempestuous and passionate. Emotional. We have our own laws of governing, separate from those of men. You know already that one of our foremost rules is not interfering in the affairs of mankind, aside from the wish-giving. But sometimes it happens that one of us may interfere because of something that's occurred to cause us some strong emotion, so that we are unable to refrain from responding. We can't deny that which is our very nature."

"And he accepted that," Douglas mused.

Jacinth dimpled. "Well, after all, I did use the magic in a positive way... Lilian will now get the help she needs. It's not like I murdered her or harmed her in any way."

"Or sent her to Timbuktu?"

Sobering, she nodded. "It wasn't because I didn't want to send her far away. I was so furious, Douglas. And scared. If you could have seen those people surrounding us... it was awful."

"Hey." Her distress was more than he could bear. Douglas reached for her, gathering her slender form into his arms. She clung to him, her arms tightening convulsively around him.

"If it had been just Lilian, I could have dealt with her." Her voice was muffled against his chest. "But with all those people as witness, there wasn't anything I could do... not magically. And they were so angry and violent, thinking I was a kidnapper. It's hard to blame them... after all, that's a parent's worst nightmare. But... they *wanted* to hurt me. It was truly frightening. Molly and Ben were crying, scared by all the confusion, and afraid Lilian was going to take them away again. They trusted me, Douglas, to not let her take them, but for those few minutes before the policeman came, I didn't see how I could stop her. Not without magic, and I couldn't do that with all those people around."

Douglas held her tightly, hating that she was shaking, that the joy that seemed intrinsic to her been dimmed, her unflagging optimism shattered by his malicious ex-wife's actions.

"I'm sorry," he whispered. "So sorry."

It seemed the most natural thing in the world to brush his lips across her cheek, where the ugly bruise had been. Sliding a finger under her chin, he lifted her face.

Jacinth didn't resist him, lifting her lips to meet his. Sensation overwhelmed her. His lips were soft and warm, his scent enveloping her. She'd never felt like this before, never felt this... this melting feeling, as if they were two halves, merged into a complete whole. The very rightness of it frightened her, but even as she stiffened in his embrace, her hands coming up to his chest in protest, Douglas retreated. He kissed the corner of her mouth, sliding his hands through her hair, one thumb caressing the skin where she'd been struck.

"I'm sorry," he repeated.

Jacinth relaxed, but stayed in his arms, her head resting on his chest.

"It's okay. Once the policeman came and got things under control, I was just determined that she would never, ever do anything like that ever again. That her attempts to get the children would end, one way or another. That was why I did it,

Douglas. Not to... to be mean, or to get back at her. It was the only thing I could think of."

He chuckled, rubbing his cheek against her soft hair, breathing in her scent.

"It was brilliant."

Jacinth drew back a bit to look up at him, her elfin face brightening.

"Really?"

Douglas thought of Lilian's drinking, of all the times he'd begged her to get help. How she'd refused even to admit that she had a problem. He pictured, not without amusement, a parade of pink elephants in the park, and Lilian's subsequent and, by the policeman's comments that evening, voluntary admission to an inpatient treatment and rehabilitation center... although still insisting she had really seen elephants.

"Yes," he affirmed. "It's perfect."

CHAPTER 20

JACINTH AWOKE WITH A START, alarm surging through her. Someone had her teapot! She scrambled out of bed, ready to rush down the hall, then forced herself to stop, taking a deep breath. That was a very human reaction, she scolded herself firmly. I can do better than that.

With a firm mental command, she sent herself into her Djinn vessel and peered out through the silver. Benny! What in the world? She rematerialized back in her bedroom, put on a robe, and padded down the hall.

"Benny?" She blinked a bit as she stepped into the brightly lit living room. "What are you doing?"

The boy jumped, and turned to face her. He'd opened the lid and had been peering intently inside.

"Miss Jas!" He looked amazingly guilty as Jacinth's gaze rested on the teapot in his hands. "I, um, was just looking at this."

"In the middle of the night?" She came forward and took the teapot from him. She turned it over, as if admiring it. "It is pretty, isn't it? Your dad bought it from an antique store last month. But why are you up in the middle of the night to look at it?"

Benny shrugged, clearly uncomfortable. "I dunno. I couldn't sleep."

Jacinth put the teapot back on the mantle above the fireplace.

"Well, go on back to bed and do your best," she suggested.

"Okay." He rushed off, as if glad to get away from awkward questions.

In the morning Jacinth regaled Douglas with what had happened in the night.

"He knows," she said glumly, cracking several eggs into a bowl to scramble. "He was looking for me in there."

Douglas objected. "He couldn't possibly know. Maybe he couldn't sleep and was wandering around the house picking things up."

Jacinth gave him her best do-you-think-I'm-stupid-or-what look.

"Get real," she suggested. "He snuck out of his bed in the middle of the night and dragged up a chair from the dining room just to get the teapot from above the fireplace so he could look inside it."

Concern warred with pride in Douglas' face. Pride won.

"He is a smart kid, isn't he?"

She shoved her fingers through her hair with a sigh. "Yes, he is. The problem is, what are we going to do about it?"

He shrugged. "Nothing, I guess. Hell, I don't know, Jacinth! I've never had to explain a genie in my house to anyone before. Much less to a six-year-old."

"But if we don't talk to him, he might say something about it to someone," she worried.

Douglas snorted. "You don't think anyone would believe him, do you?"

"Of course not. Although," she said frankly, "it'd almost be better if they did. They'll ridicule him, and make fun of him. You know how children can be. And even once he knows for sure, he won't be able to defend himself against the taunts, because he'll have to understand he can't tell anyone the truth. I don't want that for him, Douglas."

"Do you think he does? Know for sure, I mean?" Douglas asked.

That was a good question. "I don't know. I wish Kieran were here. There are times that mind reading can be helpful, and I think this is one of them."

Douglas tugged her into his embrace, his arms going about her to holding her close. She lifted her face as if it were the most natural thing in the world, and their lips met, lingering. He lifted his head with a sigh, resting his forehead against hers.

"I don't know what to do," he admitted. "Let's wait a bit, see if we can figure out how much he knows, or suspects, and then we'll decide."

"Maybe Kieran will pop in and we can ask him what he thinks," Jacinth suggested.

"Just what I need," Douglas muttered under his breath. "Your watchdog reading my lustful thoughts."

She giggled at that, standing on her tiptoes to press her lips against his chin.

"Do you have lustful thoughts?"

His mouth descended on hers.

"Absolutely," he whispered, before capturing her lips in a hard, fiery kiss that scorched the very air around them.

There was a spate of crackling pops, and Jacinth backed out of his arms reluctantly to tend to the bacon she'd been frying.

She knew her cheeks were flushed, and she tingled right down to her toes. The man could kiss!

Jacinth took a stack of plates down from the cupboard and handed them to Douglas to put on the table, her thoughts chaotic. She'd been kissed before. Not by a human, of course, but there had been Djinn males she'd loved before. Well, perhaps "love" was a bit strong... but she'd cared for them, slept with some. After all, she was nine hundred years old, it wasn't like she'd been missing anything along the way. Except... this was different, what she felt for Douglas. And all he'd done was kiss her! And that, only twice. Three times, if she counted that sweet, spontaneous kiss at Disneyland.

Jacinth found herself smiling at the memory. She supposed it was because there was a kind of seduction in feeling part of a family. She had few memories of her father, they had left him when she was so young. Although her mother had taken her to one of the Djinn villages to be raised, Zahra had been sad and withdrawn, and Jacinth had always felt a bit isolated, different from the other happy, carefree children. She loved being part of Douglas' family, loved darling little Molly and bright, precocious Benny. Perhaps that was why she felt so strongly attracted to Douglas.

She put her fingers to her lips, still throbbing from the searing pressure of that swift, passionate kiss. Then again, when Douglas touched her, all thoughts of Benny and Molly flew from her mind, and there were only the two of them, Douglas and her.

No way! She scolded herself, taking the bacon from the pan and pouring the scrambled eggs into the hot skillet. She must be feeling some kind of nesting urge... unusual though that was for a Djinn. That's all it was... all it *could* be, because there was no way, ever, that she would feel anything special for a mortal.

"Hey, Dad! Miss Jas!" Benny was in the living room watching television, and he sounded excited about something. "Come look! It's that lady who was at the park with Dad!"

What?

She exchanged a startled look with Douglas, and they both hurried into the living room, where Katerina's small, elegantly clad form filled the screen, the gold eyes in a triangular face staring scornfully out of the photograph being aired.

"...the missing Katerina Kazakis," the solemn anchor was saying. "While known to be reclusive, the eccentric fashion designer has never missed a presentation of her own collection. Employees are close-mouthed about the designer's disappearance, but admit they have no knowledge of her whereabouts."

Smoke reached into the living room, along with a strong scent of eggs, and Jacinth dashed back to the kitchen to rescue the eggs, now as brown as the bacon and rubbery. She sighed. That was the last of the carton of eggs, too. Now what? Glancing around to made sure she was alone, she returned them to an edible condition, sunny-side up, just like everyone liked. She laid the nicely done eggs on a plate just as Douglas and the children trooped in.

"I caught them just in time," she explained, avoiding Douglas' skeptical glance. "Was there anything else about Cat... Katerina?"

"No, but there was a number to call." Benny looked at her, a solemn expression on his young face. "Should we call and say we saw her in the park?"

Douglas gave a surprised "whuff" and looked at Jacinth, a pleading look that made her smile in response.

"No, Benny. I don't think we should."

She didn't think Cat would appreciate it in the least.

Although why she should have missed her show, when she was safe and well at Troy's, and obviously capable of getting around on her own, was beyond Jacinth's ability to determine.

"If she hasn't been at work, there's a reason she doesn't want to be there," she told the boy. "Even if we don't know what that reason is."

"But it's *her* company," Benny argued. "They showed lots of pretty clothes, dresses and stuff, that she made. And there were lots of people watching. She should be there."

"She was fine when we saw her in the park," Douglas interjected in a firm voice. "When she wants them to know where she is, she'll let them know. Now, let's sit down and have breakfast, and no more questions about Katerina, okay?"

"Okay." Benny seemed to accept the decree, but bounced back quickly. "So what are we going to do today?"

"I've been tracking that rose we ordered online, and it's supposed to be delivered this morning by UPS," Douglas interjected. "Why don't you find a spot to make a flowerbed and get it ready? Then I'll come home at noon, and we'll go to a nursery and get some more flowers to keep it company?"

Molly squealed with delight as her father lifted her onto her booster seat, and Jacinth exchanged a smile with Douglas. The little girl had a passion for flowers of any kind.

Benny, however, formed a pout.

"That's boring. Can't we swim? Miss Jas can watch us."

"Oh, no, Miss Jas can't," Jacinth told the boy firmly. "I can't swim, and that means if anything happened to either of you, I couldn't save you. In fact, if I tried, I might drown too!"

Benny shot her a skeptical look. Yep, the boy was definitely suspicious.

"When I come home from work this evening, we'll swim," Douglas promised the children, and Benny subsided, satisfied.

The day promised to be scorching, and was already uncomfortably humid. After breakfast, Jacinth changed into shorts and a loose, sleeveless cotton shirt, pulling her hair back off her face in a ponytail. Douglas chuckled as she emerged from the hallway, his briefcase in hand as he headed for the door.

"You don't look much older than Benny."

Jacinth stuck her tongue out at him, and he laughed. "That'll show me."

With a wink, he turned and left.

"Okay, kids!" Jacinth clapped her hands. "Everyone ready? Benny, you dig out the gloves; I saw some in the garage, in the cupboard under the workbench. Molly, honey, you bring some trash bags, and I'll get the tools."

By mid-morning, they had not one, but two flowerbeds cleared, the soil turned up and carefully mixed with potting soil, a bag of which Jacinth had found in the garage with the tools. At the little girl's insistence, they'd made a small flowerbed under Molly's bedroom window, and the other was against the wall at the far side of the pool.

They'd just finished digging the deep hole they'd need for the rose when the doorbell rang. Jacinth stood, brushing dirt from her bare legs.

"That must be the UPS man. What great timing, hmmm, kids? Brush the dirt off yourselves and come straight inside. We'll take a break and clean up a bit before we start lunch, okay?"

Opening the front door, it was indeed the UPS delivery man with her rose. Jacinth signed the slip and smiled at the uniformed courier as he handed her the carefully packaged plant.

"Thank you."

She was just closing the door when Benny yelled for her.

"Miss Jas!"

"I'm coming," she called.

With only a thought, the protective wrapping fell away and she cradled the small plant in her arms, touching the smooth, bare stalks that would one day be rough with thorns and blooming with foliage.

"Miss Jas!" Benny came skidding into the house, panic on his young face. "Molly fell in the pool!"

Fear gripped her by the throat, making it hard for her to breathe as she raced through the dining room to the sliding glass door that opened onto the patio, even as she sent a mental shout for help. *Kieran!*

She burst into the backyard, her eyes finding the small girl struggling feebly, submersed in the deepest end of the pool. Jacinth didn't hesitate but launched herself into the water. In a moment she had Molly in her arms. She didn't waste time trying to swim with the child, but commanded them onto the deck beside the pool. Molly was sputtering and crying, and coughing up water. Her small body was shivering, racked with sobs. Jacinth summoned a blanket, wrapping the girl warmly in its soft folds and hugging her close.

The next moment, Kieran appeared, his icy facade melting as he knelt beside them. He touched the curly blonde curls gently.

"Is she all right?"

Jacinth nodded. "Scared, mostly. And wet."

The little face lifted, and Molly's drenched blue eyes peeked out.

"Kayr?" She wiggled on Jacinth's lap, trying to free herself from the blanket.

"I'm here, sweetheart." Kieran took the child from Jacinth,

cradling her against his chest and tucking the blanket more closely around her.

An indrawn breath drew Jacinth's attention to Benny. He was standing watching them with wide, excited eyes.

"You really are a genie," he told her. "I knew it! And Kieran too! Cool!"

Now the fat was in the fire for sure. She looked instinctively at Kieran, who shrugged, tossing the problem back in her lap.

"Yes, we are." She took the boy's hand, drawing him closer to her. "But you absolutely cannot tell anyone, Benny."

"Nor you, Molly," she cautioned, her glance encompassing the little girl. "You can talk about it between yourselves, and with your father, of course. But not anybody else."

Molly nodded, accepting, but Benny's brain was already in overdrive.

"Why not?" he wanted to know. "You help people, don't you? And give them wishes!"

She blew out a breath. How to explain this so a child could understand?

"You know your favorite movie, Hunchback of Notre Dam?" she asked. Benny nodded solemnly. "Remember how the people acted when Quasimodo came down for the festival? Some of them laughed at him, some wanted to hurt him. And the bad guy, Frolo. Why did he hate the gypsies so much?"

"Because..." He couldn't answer. A six-year-old hadn't learned about hate yet.

"Because they were different," Jacinth told him. "Some people don't understand those who are different. Sometimes they just make fun of them. Sometimes they hate them, and want to hurt them."

"Nobody could hate you, Miss Jas," the boy said loyally. "And my dad wouldn't let anybody hurt you."

Jacinth's heart turned over in her chest, and she hugged him tightly.

"I know he wouldn't. But still, we can't have people knowing about us. We're only allowed to help the ones who find our vessels... like my teapot, and Aladdin's lamp," she clarified at his puzzled look. "Just think if everyone was running around trying to find a genie, instead of trying to solve their problems themselves. Some people might spend so much time trying to get a genie to grant them wishes, that they let their own lives fall apart."

She watched Benny turn that over in his head. It was a lot for a six-year-old to grasp, but a moment later she discovered she had underestimated him.

"You mean like Mom," he stated. "She was always drinking because she wanted to feel better, but she didn't feel better the next day and everything got worse because the drinking would make her lose her job, and we wouldn't have any money for food or to pay the rent, and we'd have to move again."

Jacinth lifted her eyes to meet Kieran's shuttered gaze. What could she possibly say? She cleared her throat.

"Something like that, Benny. Now." She fixed both children with a stern look. "Let's go to the embarrassing question of how Molly got in the pool in the first place. I told you children to follow me straight into the house."

"Molly wanted to ride her new bike to the door," Benny said. "I was watching her so she didn't fall, but then she got close to the edge of the pool. I tried to grab it and pull her away, but it tipped over and she went in."

Molly's damp curls bobbed as the little girl nodded agreement. Benny looked at Jacinth pleadingly.

"It was an accident. Honest! We don't have to tell Dad, do we?"

"Of course we have to tell him." Jacinth couldn't imagine keeping this from the children's father.

"Oh, man." Benny's drawn-out complaint was close to a whine. "He'll probably put us on restriction for a week."

Jacinth raised her brows. "What makes you think your Dad is the one to set the punishment? I'm the one you disobeyed."

Benny shrugged. "When Mom was here with us, before, she always said she'd tell Dad, and made him punish us."

Her lips tightening, Jacinth traded another look with Kieran.

The mother is not worthy of the name. The Djinn prince told her.

"Well, I'm not her," she told the children. "And it was me you disobeyed, so I'm setting your punishment. Neither of you are going to be swimming for a week."

She held up a hand, silencing their protests. "What's more, you're not going to the circus this weekend."

Molly began to cry, and Benny looked as if he'd like to. Kieran's brows lowered.

Oh, don't worry. Jacinth thought as loud as she could. She wasn't telepathic, but if he was reading her anyway, he'd hear the thoughts. *The circus is still going to be here next weekend, and your precious Molly will get to go.*

A glint of humor touched the piercing blue eyes, and one corner of his firm mouth twitched, proving her guess correct. Jacinth turned her attention to the crestfallen children.

"Molly could have died," she told them. "She might have drowned, or she could have hit her head on the edge falling in. This is very serious, and I want both of you to listen carefully. If either of you ever go near that pool again without an adult with you, your father will have the whole thing filled in with dirt, and you won't have a pool at all. Is that understood?"

And she would never, ever, leave them unattended again in the yard for a moment, she vowed silently. Not even if the house was on fire.

Benny kicked at the ground with the toe of his sneakers. "But you're a genie. Even if she drownded, you would have saved her, wouldn't you?"

Jacinth shook her head. "Not if she was dead before I got to her, Benny. My magic wouldn't have been able to bring her back to life."

"Not even if Dad wished for it?"

"No, honey, not even then," she said regretfully. "Even genies have limits to what they can do."

"Oh." He digested that. In typical Benny fashion, he bounced back. "So if Dad had three wishes, what did he wish for?"

Jacinth ruffled his tousled hair. "He wished to have you kids back."

"He did?" Benny's eyes glowed with pride. "Did you hear, Molly? Dad wished us back. But Miss Jas, he said it was just luck that the babysitter went on the Internet and saw us."

"Sometimes luck is only a matter of preparation meeting opportunity," Jacinth told him.

"Huh?" That was clearly over his head.

"What she means is," Kieran interjected, "your father made the preparations by reporting you missing and actively seeking you, so that your pictures were already on the Internet. The opportunity was that the woman watching you had a computer and was surfing the Internet. Jacinth made it possible for the two events to connect."

Jacinth nodded. "That's right. It wouldn't have been so easy if your father hadn't already had everyone looking for you. So a great deal of the credit goes to him."

"So what else did he wish for?"

She had to laugh. Benny was bouncing with impatience.

"Nothing."

Benny froze, staring at her in disbelief, and even Molly turned in Kieran's arms to look at her.

"Not a thing," Jacinth told them in a solemn tone. "He couldn't think of anything else he wanted but to have you two children back with him."

"Can he have more wishes?" Benny demanded.

"Two more. Just like in the fairy tale."

"You'll have to help your dad," Kieran told the children, not without a wicked spark in his cool blue eyes. "You can suggest things that he might want."

"Cool!" Benny exploded. "Maybe we could get an awesome monster truck!"

Molly stretched out her hand, pulling at Jacinth's sleeve.

"I know what I'd wish for," she said, her earnest expression adorable as she looked at Jacinth. "I'd wish for you for my mommy."

For a moment Jacinth couldn't breathe past the lump in her throat.

"Oh!" She took a step forward, hugging the little girl in Kieran's arms tight. "Oh, baby."

"I wish that, too," Benny declared, joining them.

Laughing, Jacinth reached down to hug him with her other arm.

"Group hug!" she declared.

Kieran looked less than happy at being involved in anything so plebeian and human as a group hug, but he encompassed Benny and Jacinth in his embrace, still holding Molly in one arm.

"What's going on?"

Douglas stood in the patio doorway, looking less than pleased to see Jacinth in what appeared to be another man's arms. She disengaged herself and went to him.

"We were having a group hug," she explained, wiping eyes that were somehow damp.

There was concern in Douglas' face, and he touched her hair with gentle fingers.

"You're wet."

She nodded, gesturing to the children. "Molly fell into the pool."

"You went in after her?"

His arm came around her, and she couldn't resist the need to lean into him, despite knowing Kieran was watching them disapprovingly. Now the danger was over, she felt definitely shaky.

"They know," she told him softly as Benny came dancing up to them.

"You should have seen her, Dad," he said excitedly. "One minute she was in the deep end under the water with Molly, and then she was there on the deck, like, Poof!"

Douglas' face paled, and he practically leaped the short distance to where Kieran stood. Molly went to him willingly, her chubby arms sliding around his neck.

"Molly!" He buried his face in her hair, holding her so tight she squealed.

"I'm sorry, Douglas," Jacinth apologized. She should never have left the children alone. "The doorbell rang and I went to answer it. I told them to follow me, but Molly's bike tipped over."

"We were coming in. She didn't go near the pool on purpose."

Jacinth wasn't sure if Benny was defending her, himself, or Molly.

"Miss Jas grounded us from swimming for a whole week," Benny confessed glumly.

"And the circus this weekend," she told Douglas.

His free arm snaked out and caught her around the waist, and he dragged her to him.

"Thank you," he choked out. "Thank you for rescuing her. I know how you feel about the water."

"I had to get us out with my magic," she confessed. "Since I can't actually swim, once I had her I didn't have much choice."

Douglas looked at his children, obviously at a loss.

"We promised not to tell," Benny told him, Molly nodding solemnly.

Kieran stepped back, his icy mask in place once more.

"Since I'm not needed here, I'll go now."

Jacinth touched his shoulder. "Thank you for coming so quickly when I called, Kieran."

He nodded absently and, flicking Molly's cheek with one finger, disappeared.

Douglas blew out a breath. "I am never going to get used to the way that guy does that."

Jacinth looked up at him mischievously. "I can do it too, you know."

He tweaked her nose. "I know you can. I'm just grateful you don't. Now, let's go inside and get you and Molly into some dry clothes."

CHAPTER 21

"Miss Jas?"

Jacinth looked up to see Benny standing outside her door. She smiled in welcome, and held out her hand. "Come on in."

He came to stand before her, his eyes big and uncertain. "I wanted to tell you something."

From his manner, the boy wanted to talk about the events of the day. It was nearly midnight and he should have been asleep long ago, so his thoughts had clearly kept him awake.

"Well, let's sit down then, and be comfortable."

She uncurled her legs and stood up from the chaise lounge where she'd been reading a novel, and led him to the low sofa against the wall. She sat, pulling him down beside her and tucking a silk throw about their bare feet against the air conditioning cooling her room.

"So tell me," she invited.

He fidgeted a little, then burst out, "So how old are you really?"

Honesty was best, even with young children. "Nine hundred years, give or take a bit."

Rather than reacting with the surprise she expected, Benny nodded sagely.

"I thought you were old. The ice cream cone was first invented at the World's Fair in 1904."

Sometimes, Jacinth mused, it was hard to remember Benny was only six years old. In the month she'd been with them, the boy had already learned to read, even though he hadn't been to school yet, and she knew for a fact that his mother hadn't made any attempt to teach the children anything. She made a mental note to check in with Arthur and remind him of his promise to visit with Benny.

Benny fidgeted a bit more. She sensed that there was something else he wanted to say, and waited patiently. These other things were just leading up to the real reason he was here to talk to her.

"You said Dad wished for you to find us for him," he said abruptly, not looking at her, apparently fascinated with the weave in the carpet under his feet.

"Yes, he did. In fact," Jacinth said, sensing the boy's need for reassurance, "I can tell you his exact words. I asked him if there wasn't something he wanted more than anything in the whole world, and your dad said, 'My kids. I just want my kids.'"

Benny didn't respond to that immediately. Clearly, there was something else bothering him. He fidgeted some more, before looking up at her with an anxiety that no six-year-old should have to feel.

"I wasn't sure he wanted us," he blurted out. "Mom said he told her to take me and Molly, but then I heard her tell a friend she thought he was looking for us and that's why we moved around all the time. But I wasn't sure... you know... if he really was looking for us. If maybe he was glad Mom took us, even if he didn't tell her to."

"Oh, honey." Her heart bursting, Jacinth pulled the boy into her arms, hugging him as hard as she could. "Your father was miserable without you. He could never have been glad she took you, and he missed you every single day. He loves you and Molly so much, getting you back was the only thing he ever thought of, the only thing he could think of to wish for."

"Of course," she added mischievously, "it took me a little while to convince him that I really was a genie."

Benny giggled at that, his little face beaming up at her.

"I bet," he told her.

He wriggled a bit, seeming pleased with himself. "I, uh... know about Miss Katerina, too."

Oops. She eyed Benny, who eyed her back.

"What do you know about Miss Katerina?" she asked cautiously.

"I know she's the cat from the park."

Well, she'd known he was bright. Still...

"How did you figure it out?"

Benny snorted.

"Her name. Katerina. Cat." He didn't say "duh" aloud, but the word was clearly audible in his tone. "And we'd never met her, but she brought Dad that day in the park."

Of course. There was no keeping up with the boy, and she smiled at him, feeling a surge of affection.

"Besides, her eyes are the same, and she was limping." Benny continued, as if that clinched the matter, which it did. "Cat limped too."

Yep, the child was bright.

"You're right," she admitted.

"What do you call someone like Miss Katerina?" he wanted to know. "She's not a genie, is she?"

"No. She's a shapeshifter, able to change between cat and human forms."

His little face was alight with excitement, and she could practically see the wheels turning in his head.

"Can she change into anything she wants?

"I don't think so. I don't really know that much about shapeshifters, Benny. There aren't many of them, and Cat is the only one I've ever met."

"So are there really such things as vampires and werewolves too?" Benny wanted to know, his eyes bright with excitement.

Jacinth laughed, ruffling his hair. She pulled him against her for a big hug.

"You sure are like your father. No, Benny, I'm sorry, there aren't.

He looked so disappointed, she was almost sorry there weren't. Although she was sure the world could very well do without werewolves and vampires and the like.

"Mom told us there was," the boy said unexpectedly. "She said there were bad things that would get us if we didn't behave. Molly cried for Dad and her dolly all the time at first, and she kept asking when we were going home. So Mom locked her in the closet and said the boogie would get her if she didn't stop whining. Molly would scream because she was so scared, and Mom would get mad and leave her in there longer. That's how come Molly stopped talking."

Jacinth was speechless. The very idea of locking a child of any age in a closet was horrible, and Molly would have been only about two years old then. She hoped suddenly, fiercely, that Lilian was still seeing the pink elephants. She hoped pink elephants were crawling all over her skin.

"I let Molly out once, when Mom went out," Benny confessed, not meeting Jacinth's eyes. "But she came back and was mad, and she locked me in the closet too. So I never did it again."

Jacinth's heart broke, and she pulled the boy onto her lap, rocking back and forth, holding him fiercely.

"Not your fault," she told him, struggling for words to lessen the boy's feelings of guilt. She found she could barely speak. "Not, Benny. You were so little. Her son. She should... she should love you. Treasure you and Molly."

She found that her cheeks were wet with tears that would not stop at her command. She drew back and, holding Benny's face tightly between her hands, kissed him on one cheek, then the other.

"You are a good boy, Benny. So bright, so good. Don't carry this burden, or be afraid to talk about it with me, or with your father. No blame is yours. You did what you could, and you love your sister. It is enough. And you are safe now, you and Molly."

Benny looked up at her, curiosity replacing the troubled expression. "How come you're talking kinda weird, Miss Jas?"

"Oh! English is not my first language. Sometimes I forget it when I become emotional..." She smiled down at him, shedding the sadness with a shake of her head. Standing up, she set him on his feet. "Come on," she said. "Time for you to get to sleep now. I'll tuck you in, okay?"

"Okay."

She got Benny in bed and kissed him on the forehead, and was heading back to her own room when she heard the faint sound of Douglas' phone ringing through the door to his bedroom. A few minutes later Douglas charged from his bedroom, barely clad in half-zipped jeans, still struggling to button a loose cotton shirt. He stopped, surprised at seeing her in the hall. Jacinth nodded at Benny's door.

"We were having a late talk. What's wrong, Douglas?"

"Troy called from the clinic." He finished buttoning his shirt and tucked the ends into his jeans. "He's been there with a couple of patients he operated on earlier today and happened to take a quick look into the barn, and found Firefly in labor. She's been at it a while, he says. I want to get right over there, just in case."

"No, we don't want anything to go wrong," she agreed.

Not quite knowing why she did so, she went to Douglas and, leaning up on her tiptoes, kissed his cheek.

"I know you'll take good care of her. We can bring the children to see the foal in the morning, they'll be so thrilled!"

Douglas encircled her slim waist with one arm, holding her close a moment. He inhaled deeply, savoring the lilac scent that was so much a part of Jacinth. He wished he didn't have to rush out and spend the night in a barn. He'd so much rather carry Jacinth down the hall and spend the night making beautiful love to her.

And she'd probably put a hex on his private parts if she had an inkling of what he was thinking. With a sigh, he drew away.

"Take care."

"Oh! Wait." She held up one shapely hand, and a digital camera appeared on her palm. With a stern look, she handed it to him.

"Bring back pictures," she commanded.

He knew that tone of voice.

"Yes, ma'am."

"There's nothing more we can do."

Dawn was approaching, early light streaming into the barn from the windows high above the center aisle. The mare's head lay listlessly on the straw, eyes dulled from pain, her breathing coming in heaving gasps.

Troy wiped the sweat from his face with his forearm, leaving bloody streaks behind.

"Yeah, I know. She's got nothing left to give. Even if we finally succeed in turning the foal, Doug, I'm not sure she can push it out."

Douglas was panting from the exertion of trying to turn the foal's convoluted body about in its mother's womb, sweat running unchecked down his face, stinging his eyes. His fists clenched as he surveyed the exhausted mare. He knew she wasn't going to make it. She was going to die here, the foal with her. He could maybe save the foal, but...

"Dammit!" He roared, the sound echoing in the wooden cubicle. "Dammit, she hasn't even had a chance. We'd just gotten her turned around. She was accepting us... hell, she followed Jacinth around like a puppy, even let the kids near, let them pet her."

"I know, man. I know." Troy's voice was rough with sympathy. "I'm sorry, Doug."

Douglas patted the mare's drenched, sweaty flank. "I'm sorry, girl. I wish... I wish..."

For a moment he could hardly breathe as he looked up to stare at Troy across the mare's rotund belly. "My God, that's it!"

"What's it? What are you talking about?"

"A wish. I can make a wish." Douglas stood up, stripping the bloodied gloves from his hands.

"Jacinth!" He shouted into the darkened barn. "Jacinth! I want to make a wish... right now!"

Troy gaped at him as if he'd lost his mind. "Doug..."

"What is it, Douglas?"

Jacinth stood in the deep straw by the stall door, her petite figure draped in a long silk caftan of vibrant jewel colors. Her eyes widened when she saw Troy, and the color rose in her cheeks. Then she looked past him to the mare, laboring on her side in the straw, and her expression changed.

"Oh, no!"

A moment later she was dressed in jeans and a T-shirt with a dancing Snoopy on the front. She approached Firefly, ignoring Troy's disbelieving stare, and dropped to her knees by the mare's head.

"What is it, Douglas?"

"The foal is twisted around in the womb. Not just breech but sideways. I can't turn it, and even if I could, Firefly doesn't have the energy or the will left to push it out. We're going to lose them both unless you can save them. Can you do that?"

"Yes." Her answer was firm, confident.

"Then I wish for you to save this mare and her foal."

"All right." Jacinth sat down in the deep straw, lifting the mare's head onto her lap. "Go ahead and turn the foal, Douglas."

He hesitated. "Benny and Molly?"

"I put a safety spell on the house, and sent a message to my mother." She closed her eyes a moment, then opened them with a reassuring nod. "She is with them now."

"Okay, great. Troy, toss me another pair of gloves from my bag."

Troy visibly pulled himself together, tearing his gaze from Jacinth with obvious difficulty.

"Uh... yeah, sure thing."

The gloves on, Douglas again reached into the birth canal. The foal slid easily, as if oiled, as he maneuvered it into position.

"There! I've got it! See if you can get her to push."

Jacinth stroked Firefly's sweaty head, murmuring softly. The mare's eyes were brighter, Douglas noted, the spark of life returning.

"Come on now, Firefly," Jacinth crooned. "Help us get your baby out into the world. You're almost there, and then it'll be over."

The mare whickered softly, and the muscles in her abdomen contracted.

"Here come the forefeet," Douglas announced. "And the nose!"

He wiped the tiny muzzle free of membranes as soon as the head was free, and the rest of the foal's body slid out easily a moment later.

"Yes!" he cheered. "You did it! It's a filly, and she's perfect."

Troy began to applaud, still looking a bit shell-shocked, and Jacinth laughed from her seat in the straw, leaning down to hug Firefly. After a moment the mare scrambled to her feet, the slender legs trembling a bit, but she was up, turning to nose her baby and washing it with a broad tongue.

Douglas reached down and grabbed Jacinth's hand, hauling her to her feet and into his arms.

"You did it!" He kissed her hard and fast, then hugged her tightly. "You did it, you did it!"

"Hey, I get to hug her too." Troy butted in, taking Jacinth from him. He delivered a kiss to her cheek, and gave her a big hug. He looked over her head at Douglas. "I'd give her a proper kiss too, but I'm not sure I want to take such liberties with a... genie?"

Douglas cleared his throat. "Well, um... Jacinth, I'm sorry."

Jacinth disentangled herself from Troy's embrace, dimpling up at Douglas' friend. "We prefer to be called Djinn. It's okay, Douglas, but let's all be glad this happened in the middle of the night, and not in the daytime with a barn full of people."

"I think we can be glad for that," Troy stated. He was scrutinizing Jacinth carefully. "I swear, if I hadn't seen it for myself, I'd never have believed it."

"Get used to it," Jacinth muttered somewhat cryptically. Before Douglas could ask what she meant, she looked past them, and a brilliant smile lit her face. "Oh, look!"

Firefly had her baby on its feet, finding its first meal.

"Yeah!" Douglas cheered, and held his hand up for a high-five from Troy. "That is one healthy, happy foal. A palomino, too, like her mommy."

CHAPTER 22

Douglas pulled into the driveway with a sigh of relief that the week, which had seemed hideously long with everything that had happened, was over. He had the weekend off, thanks to his partners. He called down silent blessings on Troy, Suzanne and Mac, who were taking extra shifts Saturday and Sunday to give him this weekend with Benny and Molly. He'd tried to object, but Suzanne stopped him.

"You've only just gotten your children back after two years. You need this time to be with them. Let us do this for you for a few weekends, Douglas. Later on, you can repay the favor when any of us need it." She smiled, her eyes dancing. "Mac and I are going to be trying for children soon. You'll have your chance, believe me."

Douglas laughed, giving in with good grace. He couldn't wait to tell Jacinth and the kids. Letting himself in the front door, he paused. It seemed eerily quiet.

"Jacinth? Ben? Molly?"

Well, maybe they'd gone to the park, although they were

usually home by now. He headed for the dining room just as the patio door slid open and Jacinth entered, followed closely by her mother. Jacinth's face lit up, her dark eyes sparkling.

"Douglas! You're home early!"

"No big deal," he said, holding out his hand to shake with Zahra. He still didn't quite know how he was supposed to greet her, a thousand-year-old Djinn. Zahra, however, stepped close to him, presenting one perfumed cheek for him to kiss. He did so, feeling a bit awkward, and she laughed at him.

"You're family, you know," she told him. "None of that formal handshake thing."

Jacinth looked at him with an apologetic expression. "I'm sorry, I didn't realize it was so late. I haven't even started dinner."

"Actually, maybe that's a good thing. Suzanne and Troy thought I should spend more time with my family, and kicked me out of the clinic for the weekend. Maybe we could go out to dinner to celebrate. And you as well, of course, Zahra."

Jacinth shot him an amused look.

"Mother's complaining because I didn't think to tell her that the children knew I was Djinn," she explained.

"Ah." Douglas couldn't help chuckling at the thought. "Did they give you a hard time?"

"Well, they certainly had some very creative questions," Zahra told him, dimpling in a way that reminded him very much of her daughter. "Especially Benny. I hope you don't mind, but Arthur is here. He's out in the back yard with the children, reading to them. I must say, Douglas, he is quite impressed with young Ben."

Douglas noted that Jacinth was looking almost as proud as he felt. Dammit, she already was a part of his family. Why couldn't she see that? He wished suddenly, fiercely, that they could have some time alone, just the two of them. No children, no shapeshifters or parents or Djinn popping in and out.

As if to mock his thoughts, the doorbell rang. Why was his home suddenly Grand Central Station?

He went to open the door, then groaned, stepping back.

"Well, don't fall over for joy at seeing us," Blue advised.

"Besides, we're not here to see *you*," his mother interjected as she walked past him into the hallway. "We came for our darling grandchildren."

Douglas rolled his eyes. "Oh, lord."

"Did I hear someone say grandchildren?"

Panic struck him, and time seemed to slow to a crawl as he turned. How could he possibly explain Zahra to his parents? Zahra, who looked no more than a few years older than her daughter. He actually felt beads of sweat forming on his forehead. Then Jacinth's mother came into his line of vision, and he blinked and looked again. She seemed older somehow; still as beautiful as ever, but with faint lines at the corners of her eyes, the red hair a shade less vibrant. A woman still in her prime, but old enough to be the mother of a grown daughter. Douglas sighed with relief, ignoring the amused look she shot him from those clear green eyes.

"Mom, Dad, this is Jacinth's mother. Zahra, this is my mother, Skye, and Blue, my father."

"I'm so pleased to meet you," Zahra enthused, a cloud of exotic scent wafting past him as she came forward to extend her hand to Skye. "The children are in the back yard with an old friend of mine, reading."

Skye looked positively thrilled, her eyes bright with curiosity. Douglas watched, bemused, as the two women bonded before his eyes before strolling off toward the kitchen, arm in arm, chatting a million words a minute.

"You're in trouble now, boy." Blue clapped him on the shoulder. "Those two are matchmaking, take my word for it."

"As if I didn't know," Douglas muttered, somewhat resentful. He didn't *need* any matchmaking help from his parents or anybody else. What he needed was some time alone with Jacinth. If only she wasn't so stubborn, refusing to even talk about the possibility of a relationship. Surely things could be worked out. Other Djinn had married mortals before, not just her mother. It stood to reason that some of those relationships had to have been happy. But he wasn't going to get anywhere with her if they didn't get some time to themselves.

The duet in the kitchen had expanded to a trio with the addition of Jacinth, and when Douglas and Blue joined the women, they all headed in a group for the back yard.

"Dad!" Benny called, then noticed the new visitors. "Gramma! Gramps! Look, we're reading the Arabian Nights with Miss Jases' friend!"

Remembering Jacinth's comments about Arthur earlier, Douglas studied the older Djinn carefully. Actually, he thought Arthur looked a little better than he had the one time they'd met, a couple of weeks ago. His white hair was a little disheveled, and his eyes were brighter, and he seemed more animated. Then again, being around Benny and Molly would animate anyone, Douglas thought with a chuckle.

"These are charming young ones, Douglas," Arthur told him, standing up as the group of adults reached the small table where he'd been sitting with the children. Introductions were made all around.

"Dad! Dad! Guess what?" Benny tugged at his hand, bubbling over with proud excitement. "Did you know that Shah... Shahar... that lady who said the Arabian Nights to the guy, did you know that she was really a..."

Douglas clapped his hand over Benny's mouth, luckily anticipating what he was about to say in time to stop him.

"Secret!" he hissed in the boy's ear, nodding toward his parents.

"Oops." Benny glanced up apologetically. "Sorry, Dad. I forgot."

Douglas ruffled Benny's tousled hair in affection. "S'okay. We'll talk about it later."

They'd have to have regular pep talks with both kids, he decided, to stress the importance of secrecy.

"Nice catch." He hadn't heard Jacinth approach, but she stood beside him, her eyes alight with amusement. It was all he could do not to catch her to him and press a kiss on her wide, inviting mouth, but with all these people here, he figured that would be a bad move. Even if the only one who would be disapproving would be Jacinth herself. He resisted the impulse.

Taking advantage of the visitors... Djinn and human... being entertained by the children, he took the opportunity to ask her about what Benny had started to say.

"What's this about Sheherezade?"

"She was a Djinn," Jacinth replied, shifting slightly so that Douglas was between her and the others to ensure she couldn't be overheard. "The world was much smaller back in that time, Douglas, and there were many stories of Djinn and magic. It was only a matter of time before our existence would no longer be stories, but widely believed. Sheherezade was in no danger from the king, of course, and I'm told she grew to love him as he did her. But she created the tales as a cover... the Thousand and One Nights stories to be told and repeated through the centuries, magical, fantastical tales of things that could never truly be. So reports of Djinn passed into myth, and we remain a secret to all but a few, as it should be."

Douglas grinned at the narrative style in which she explained it, as if it was a text that she had memorized to be recited.

"Djinn History 101?" he suggested.

Her rippling laugh filled the air and she nodded, then moved off in response to Arthur, who was beckoning her.

Skye had apparently been waiting for her chance to get him alone, and she sidled over to him.

"I know there's something you're not telling me."

Douglas looked at his mother in alarm, and she laughed, shaking her head.

"Don't look so horrified. I haven't discovered her secret, Douglas. But we... your father and I... have talked it over, and we want you to know that whatever it is, we don't care. Jacinth is a perfectly wonderful young woman, and we thoroughly approve of her... Secrets or not. It's easy to tell the two of you are in love, and as for Benny and Molly, well, they couldn't possibly have a better mother to bring them up."

"I... uh..." Douglas struggled for words. What could he say? *Hey, Mom, just so you know, Jacinth's a genie and she's nine hundred years old and immortal, but I plan on asking her to marry me anyway*. Uh-huh. That'd go over great.

Skye smiled at him in what she clearly considered understanding... she didn't have a clue!... and patted his arm.

"It's all right, dear one. To give you a better chance to get to know each other, your father and I have decided to abscond with the children for the weekend! And besides, we thought it would be nice to do something with them, you know, grandparents and grandchildren together, before Benny has to start school. It'll give you and Jacinth some time alone together, which is very important."

"Very important," Douglas echoed automatically. A dozen

scenarios rose in his mind's eye... most of them involving Jacinth and himself alone together. For a whole weekend. No children, no other people around. Just the two of them. He cleared his throat, trying to concentrate on his mother's words.

"New York... Statue of Liberty... Rockefeller Center..."

He couldn't quite make out what she was saying, but he nodded agreeably, distracted by a vision of Jacinth kneeling in the middle of his bed, laughing, her glorious hair tumbling about her shoulders...

"Douglas?"

"What?"

A hand was shaking his shoulder, and his mother's face peered intently at his. "Dear, are you all right?"

"Yes... I'm fine," Douglas managed to assure her. Was that sweat he could feel dampening his forehead?

"So we'll have the children back on Sunday afternoon," his mother continued blithely, thankfully unaware of the direction his thoughts had taken.

"That's fine, Mom," Douglas managed to say, clearing his throat. "Benny and Molly will love it."

At least, he hoped they would. He'd never been that thrilled with being dragged around a strange city, made to suffer hours of boredom in stuffy museums and wait in long lines to get near to some display that made the adults around him "oh" and "ah" in pleasure. He suppressed a shudder at the memory, and sent silent sympathy to his unsuspecting children, who were going to be so happy at the prospect of going away for a weekend with their grandparents. Little did they know!

"...is going with us."

That brought his attention around quickly. "What?"

"I said, Zahra is going with us," his mother repeated in a patient voice. Her face lit with animation. "She's just lovely! We hit it off right away, and she obviously adores the children. We'll have a splendid time, and there's plenty of room in the RV."

This was the worst idea Douglas had ever heard. Zahra was a Djinn, for heaven's sake, and Benny and Molly knew it. How in the world were the three of them going to keep the truth from Skye and Blue... also no slouches in the mental department... over a whole weekend spent in such close quarters?

"That's great, Mom." He tried to inject enthusiasm into his voice, and began edging away. He'd better have a word with Zahra.

She saw him coming a mile away. Waiting by the pool, with a glint in her green eyes that wasn't quite malicious but still a far cry from angelic. He was absolutely sure she'd been reading his mind.

"What are you thinking of?" he hissed as soon as he was close enough for her to hear. "The kids have zillions of questions, Benny especially. How are you going to keep him quiet for a whole weekend, with my mom and dad right there, when he's dying to ask you all about being a Djinn and all?"

Zahra lifted one elegant brow. "You think I can't keep the situation under control for two itty bitty days?"

Well, perhaps she could at that. Still...

She patted him on the arm.

"I can certainly keep young Benjamin from letting the cat out of the bag, so to speak. Don't worry about a thing, and you two have a nice weekend. I'm counting on you, Douglas. We all are."

She walked away, leaving him staring after her. Did she mean what he thought?

CHAPTER 23

THE AFTERNOON WAS WELL advanced before the RV was stocked with food and the kids packed up and inside, but finally it rolled off down the street. Standing side by side, Douglas and Jacinth waved goodbye to children and parents.

"Whew! I thought they wouldn't get out of here before midnight," he admitted, dropping onto the porch swing with a groan. Jacinth sat beside him, one toe on the floor rocking the swing gently back and forth. She looked equally relieved that the frantic pace of the last few hours was over. With a quick look up and down the street to be sure no one was watching, she conjured up two cans of soda and passed him one.

"So what time are you supposed to meet Troy?" she asked, popping the top of the can and taking a drink.

Douglas followed her example, enjoying the sweet fizz of the cola, the chilled beverage in pleasant contrast to the late afternoon heat. "I said I'd call after they left. I'll give him a shout after I've had a chance to catch my breath."

"You might want to hold that thought," Jacinth commented,

her eyes on a bright red SUV that was turning the corner onto their street. "I think we're about to have more company."

He watched the vehicle approach. "I don't know that car."

"I'm pretty sure that's Alessandra's new one. Julian insisted on buying it for her after her old Volkswagen beetle broke down in a bad part of town, and she almost got killed by a mugger."

Douglas whistled. "Whew, that's bad!"

"It was. She was saved by a policeman who shot the mugger, but himself was shot. He was on the brink of death when Alessandra called Julian and used her third wish to save the policeman." She paused, smiling. "That broke the spell that bound Julian to the Djinn bottle, because she had used all three of her wishes for others."

The SUV rolled to a stop along the curb before the house, and a moment later Alessandra and Julian emerged, Alessandra waving at them.

"We thought we'd take a page from Jacinth's book," Julian said as they reached the porch, reaching out to shake Douglas' hand as he submitted to Jacinth's embrace. "And drop in on you unannounced."

"Besides, we want to meet the children," Alessandra put in, hugging Jacinth.

"Oh! They have just left with their grandparents," Jacinth told them. Her eyes held a bright, inquisitive glow. "What is this 'my book' thing?"

Julian laughed. "An Americanism. At least, I think it's American?"

He glanced at Alessandra, who shrugged and grinned at them. "Beats me. But it means to do like you do. You would come by to visit when we weren't expecting you, so now we're doing the same."

Jacinth laughed and hooked her arm through Alessandra's. "We're glad you did! Come inside, and we will show you about."

Douglas hesitated. "I'm supposed to meet my friend, Troy. He called earlier, wanting to meet up."

"He just found out that Djinn are real," Jacinth put in with a mischievous twinkle. "He's traumatized."

Alessandra grimaced expressively. "I can relate to that!"

Grinning, Julian slid his arm about his wife's waist. "But look how it turned out."

She smiled up at him, the love in her eyes clear. "Yes, it did."

Douglas had been thinking fast. "I told Troy we'd meet him at Rudy's Grill, a few miles from here. Why don't you come with us? I bet Troy'll appreciate all the support he can get."

"Especially as he has Katerina living with him as Cat," Jacinth put in mischievously, "and he doesn't know shapeshifters exist yet. The more he can get used to the idea of Others now, the easier it'll be when he finds out about Cat."

"This sounds fascinating," Alessandra said, her eyes gleaming with interest. "I want to hear more!"

Sliding a glance to the men, Jacinth leaned in close to Alessandra. "Oh, the things I have to tell you!"

Alessandra grinned. "What are we waiting for? Let's ditch the men!"

"Hey!" Douglas objected, while Julian laughed, but Jacinth was struck with a notion.

"Wait!" She commanded. She stood thinking while they all watched her. After a moment she looked up. "I've got it! You two, Douglas and Julian, you go to meet with Troy. Alessandra and I will call Katerina to come and we'll have girls' night here!"

"Yes! Pajama party!" Alessandra cheered.

Jacinth had her phone out and was looking up Katerina. She

glanced up. "Oh! Yes, I'll tell her to bring jammies. Come on, let me show you my room."

Bemused, Douglas and Julian watched as the two women wandered off down the hall. Julian began to laugh, and slapped Douglas on the shoulder.

"Well, call your friend Troy. Looks like we've been turned loose for the evening."

An hour later, Douglas was ensconced in a secluded corner booth in the crowded sports grill with his oldest and his newest friends.

"And she was just there," Troy was recounting to Julian his experience in the barn. "Her hair was done up in all these intricate braids, and her jewelry! Man! She was loaded with jewels that were glowing even in the dim stall... rubies, emeralds, sapphires, opals. She looked like something out of a dream, or the Arabian Nights or something. I hardly had time to even blink, and then suddenly she was in tattered jeans and a t-shirt and sneakers, with her hair up in pigtails, like some teenage kid who'd wandered into the place."

Julian grinned. "She always knew how to make an entrance."

"I'd have fallen on my ass if I hadn't already been sitting down." Troy took a deep swig of his beer, then paused, looking at the glass he held. "That's my third. I better knock off for the night."

"Go for it," Julian told him. "I'll be designated driver. You two probably need it more than me. After all, I've had six hundred years to get used to it."

Troy, who'd just lifted his glass to take another gulp, choked and sputtered as he struggled not to spew Sam Adams across the table.

"What the...." he coughed, and Douglas pounded his back helpfully. "What the hell?"

"I take it Douglas hasn't gotten around to tell you."

"Hell, man, I'm still struggling with it all," Douglas defended.

"I'm from the fourteenth century," Julian told Troy. "I was a mage... an alchemist," he specified in answer to Troy's questioning look. "I was in Genoa when the Black Death first came from the Crimean Sea. To make a long story short, I cast a spell for the power to be able to help all the people who were dying, and wound up spell-bound to a Djinn vessel, granting wishes for six hundred years. Alessandra was the one who freed me."

Troy's brow creased as he thought that over. "Alchemist? Like in that Harry Potter movie?"

"Yes, but she didn't make that up. Alchemists have existed for centuries, pursuing the Philosopher's Stone, which is not, in fact, a stone at all but an elixir. Or *al aksir*, in Arabic. There was even a Nicholas Flamel in fifteenth-century France; although whether he was actually an alchemist is a subject of heated debate."

"Mages. Alchemists. Djinns." Troy took another swig.

Douglas nodded in sympathy. "Welcome to my life. And if you think Jacinth was something in all her Djinn glory, wait until you meet her mother."

Julian arched a brow. "You've met Zahra?"

"Oh yes! And an unending stream of her suitors into my living room, until that Kieran put a stop to it."

Both black brows went up. "Kieran too! I'm surprised he intervened. He's not known for doing so."

"Because of the children." Douglas felt obliged to defend the elder Djinn. "Zahra wanted to be able to visit with us, and spend time with Ben and Molly and not be worrying about her suitors popping in and out uninvited. Although now, of course, the children both know she's a Djinn after Molly fell into the pool and Jacinth rescued her."

Troy sat up straight, alarm in his face. "Molly fell into the pool?"

"Yes, but it's okay." Briefly, Douglas explained.

"Maybe you should put up a fence," Troy suggested, looking worried. Beside him, Julian nodded his agreement.

"That was my first thought, too," Douglas told him. "But Jacinth has put a barrier around it... it's invisible, but there. It's active if I'm not present. Or her, of course."

"Damn. I can see she's handy to have around," approved Troy.

Julian grinned. "So am I." His fingers moved in a discreet intricate pattern, and frost appeared on their beer mugs. Douglas had to laugh as Troy's jaw dropped open.

"You get used to it," he told his friend, but turned a questioning look onto Julian. "I thought you didn't have magic anymore."

"Not the Djinn magic," Julian agreed. "But I'm still a mage. Plus, I think some of the Djinn magic rubbed off onto my own, after so long. I wouldn't have been able to do something like this, before." He gestured to the chilled beers.

"Mage magic," mumbled Troy, lifting his glass and taking a deep swig.

Julian just laughed. "So how are things going with Jacinth?"

Douglas looked down, studying his still-frosty beer glass intently, as if seeking the answer in the golden liquid.

"It's great. It's like I've known her all my life, you know?

Like she's been a part of the family forever. She's great with the kids, they adore her. She's smart and funny, and cheerful..."

"But?" Julian prompted.

"But she's going to leave. After I make my third wish, she'll go back to Qaf, or wherever. And... I don't want her to."

Julian seemed to ponder. Troy said nothing, but his gaze held sympathy.

"You know," Julian said slowly. "Alessandra made a fourth wish."

That got their attention. Douglas sat up attentively, his eyes on Julian. "I never heard anything about four wishes. Jacinth always said it was three, and only three. Like that's one of the rules."

"That's true. But one night, shortly after I was freed from the spell, Alessandra said there was one more wish she regretted she hadn't made. And there was the zing of magic in the air, as if a wish was activated. I could not mistake it, not after six hundred years of using Djinn magic."

"What did she wish for?" Troy asked curiously.

"That's just it. She said Jacinth was so special, that she deserved someone who could see her as she was, and love her. She wished for that."

"And here we are," Douglas said slowly.

"And here we are," agreed Julian.

"Except, I'm not the one holding up the program," Douglas pointed out. "She's so determined she's not going to fall in love with a mortal that she refuses to accept that we belong together. She loves me, I know she does. It's... it's in her eyes, you know?"

Julian looked thoughtful. "I only saw her for a few minutes back at your place. It seemed to me she was different. A kind of content about her, I don't know how to explain it. Happy, but it was more than that. The best I can tell you is to give her time.

Jacinth has always been stubborn." He grinned. "Outrageously so. And once she wants something, she goes after it with everything in her. All you have to do is wait until she realizes what she wants is you."

Douglas thought that over. "It sounds reasonable," he admitted. "But... what if she doesn't realize it?"

"She's stubborn, not stupid. She'll figure it out eventually."

"So patience is the name of the game."

"Let's have a toast." He raised his glass, clinking it against Julian's, then Troy's. "To patience!"

Troy shook his head, grinning. "Man, this is some crazy stuff. Who knew?"

JACINTH JUMPED up from the sofa when the doorbell rang. "That's Katerina!"

"Unless it's the pizza," Alessandra said.

As she opened the door, Katerina breezed in, walking past her into the living room with a jaunty step.

"I'm here!" she announced.

Jacinth blinked at her, then burst into laughter, as did Alessandra.

"Cheshire cat pajamas?"

Katerina grinned, raising one foot and wiggling it for their inspection. A large plush pink and purple cat grinned back at them. "With matching slippers."

Alessandra pouted. "I didn't know we were having a pajama party, or I'd have brought some too."

"That's not a problem." Jacinth grinned happily. "What do you want?"

"Hmmm." She thought it over. "Lounge pants and a top."

"Color?"

"Green."

A moment later, a set of clothes, neatly folded with a pair of satiny ballet type slippers on top, sat on the coffee table before her. Laughing, she rose, and headed down the hallway.

"Djinn are so handy to have around," Katerina commented.

Jacinth just smiled.

Alessandra returned in a few minutes, garbed in satin lounge pants in a brilliant emerald green and a soft top of a lighter shade. Her long hair was loose, spilling down her back in waves. She flopped down on the couch beside Katerina.

"Hey, what about you?" she demanded, looking at Jacinth, still dressed in jeans and t-shirt.

Looking mischievous, Jacinth made the famous wiggly-nose with the tink-a-tink-a-tink sound from the old TV show, and a moment later she was wearing pajamas. Both her friends took one look and dissolved into laughter.

"Onesies? Seriously?"

Alessandra was doubled over. "Blue flannel with sheep! Jacinth, you are so nuts!"

Jacinth looked pleased with herself, and with a flick of her fingers, a fire roared into life in the fireplace.

"It's July!" Katerina protested. "It's 90 degrees out there!"

"With, like, 90 percent humidity," Alessandra agreed. "We'll melt."

"Djinn climate control!" Jacinth announced happily. Suddenly the air was cooler, even with a slight nip, just enough that the fire was welcome.

"Awesome," Katerina said, and Alessandra nodded, laughing.

"We ordered pizza," Alessandra told Katerina. "They should be here soon."

The shapeshifter put her Cheshire-cat-covered feet up on the coffee table. "Did you order anchovies?"

Alessandra rolled her eyes. "Yes, just for you!"

"We also got a pepperoni with double cheese, one with ham and pineapple, and a supreme, with the works," Jacinth put in.

"Four pizzas?"

"Well, we couldn't decide," Jacinth grinned. "So we got everything. The men can polish off what's left when they get home."

"Ugh, cold pizza." Katerina wrinkled her nose. "That's just gross. But guys will eat anything. Do you know when he was having a barbecue at his house, Troy put baked beans in the crockpot to heat? And nothing else. I mean he just opened a can; no onions, no brown sugar, no nothing."

"I'm lucky," Alessandra told her. "Julian's a fantastic chef."

Jacinth giggled, plopping down onto the floor to sit cross-legged facing her friends. "Douglas is more like Troy. He's great at grilling meat but that's about it."

"Unless you count pouring cereal from a box?" Katerina asked with a grin, and Jacinth laughed.

"Exactly!"

The doorbell rang again, and Alessandra jumped up. "I'll get it."

She came back a minute later with a stack of pizza boxes, and Katerina sat up, taking her feet off the coffee table as paper plates and napkins miraculously appeared.

"There are sodas in the refrigerator," Jacinth said, standing and heading to the kitchen door. She returned with three 2-liter bottles of different sodas along with glasses and a bucket of ice.

"Oh yeah, this is great," enthused Katerina, sliding a piece of pizza onto a plate and taking a bite with clear enjoyment. "We need to do this again."

Jacinth grinned at her. We've hardly gotten started with this one!"

"So are we going to watch movies or what?" asked Alessandra.

"I think we should play board games," Katerina said, pouring herself a glass of soda. "I haven't done that since I left home for college."

"Oh, I like that!" Alessandra applauded. "Jacinth?"

"Douglas got a ton for the kids when we went to the mall," she said, rising to her feet and disappearing down the hall. She returned a minute later with a stack of boxed games. "He went a little crazy, some of these the kids won't be old enough to play for a decade."

"Wow!" Katerina stared at the games. "No kidding! Masterpiece? Clue? Monopoly?"

"Julian and I play Monopoly," Alessandra put in. "He's a killer at that one."

"Scrabble, Life, and Parcheesi," Katerina peered at the boxes. "Also, Yahtzee and Boggle."

"Oh, Parcheesi!" Jacinth smiled in fond memory. "We had a very similar game when I was a young girl, in Persia. It originated in India, you know."

"Well, let's do Parcheesi then!" Katerina looked at Alessandra, who nodded and opened the box while Jacinth set the others aside.

Three games later, they voted for a break.

"I can't believe you always win," Jacinth grumbled at Katerina, who looked pleased with herself.

Alessandra stood up, grabbing a throw from the sofa. "I think we need another log on the fire."

"And we need hot chocolate," Jacinth said, adding a log to the fire without moving from her spot.

"We should make s'mores," Katerina said.

Alessandra whooped. "S'mores!"

Jacinth looked interested. "What are s'mores?"

"Oh my god, you haven't ever had s'mores?" demanded Katerina.

She and Alessandra shared A Look.

"We'll go get what we need," Alessandra said to Jacinth. "You stay here."

They went to the kitchen, scrounging through the cupboards.

"Graham crackers!" Alessandra announced.

Katerina emerged victorious with a bag of white puffs. "I got the marshmallows, but I don't see any Hershey bars." She stuck her head out the kitchen door. "Jacinth, do you all have any Hershey bars?"

"Yes, they're over the refrigerator," came the response. "We had to put them where the children couldn't get to them."

Alessandra opened and shut kitchen drawers. "Ah-hah! I found the skewers!"

They trooped back into the living room, and a few minutes later all three were busily roasting marshmallows over the fire. Jacinth bit into the gooey treat, humming in pleasure as the combined flavors of the chocolate melted against the hot marshmallow, sandwiched between graham crackers.

"Ohhh," moaned Jacinth. "Why did I never know about these?"

Alessandra smirked. "You had to have been a Girl Scout."

Lots of s'mores and cups of hot cocoa later, the living room was a fine mess. Jacinth cleared that up with a wave of her hand, and produced sleeping bags and pillows.

"Let's watch movies!"

"No way," Alessandra objected. "I want to hear about you

and Douglas. Especially the whole story of what happened that night."

Katerina, who'd been crawling into a sleeping bag, sat up, looking inquisitive. "What night?"

Jacinth grinned, fluffing up one of the pillows. "I had my teapot... my Djinn vessel... at Julian's antique shop, Whimsies. Douglas bought it and brought it home. When I first appeared, he didn't believe I was a genie, which of course was to be expected. He thought I had snuck into his house, and he threw me out."

The other two giggled and, eyes dancing, Jacinth continued her tale. "That didn't work, because of course I poofed right back inside before he even had the door closed. When he was finally convinced, he asked me to go back in my teapot, and then he took it back to Whimsies."

Katerina turned wide gold eyes onto Alessandra, who snickered. "We'd just gotten back from dinner when he came stalking up to the counter. We hadn't even known it had been sold; a part-time employee had been watching the shop while we went to dinner. Anyway, so Douglas says something about full disclosure. When Julian said we didn't give refunds, he snarled at us about not wanting money, and left."

Jacinth nodded vigorously. "He got about three blocks before he saw my teapot in the passenger seat."

"So back he comes," Alessandra said. "He didn't say a word to Julian and me, he just put the teapot on the counter and said 'Stay!' and walked out."

Jacinth was clutching the pillow to her stomach, laughing so hard tears were running down her cheeks. "But when he got back to the car, my teapot was there again."

"By now I was about half dying," Alessandra told Katerina, who was rolling on the floor laughing. "Julian was shushing me when back Douglas comes in again and tells us he absolutely does not want to see the teapot in his car when he leaves. Then he gives it to Julian and heads out, and that's the last we saw of him. I've been dying to know what happened when he got home."

"I was waiting for him, of course," Jacinth said, her eyes sparkling with mischief. "He turned to walk out, saying he was going to a motel, but I grabbed his hand and pulled him back inside. I asked if there wasn't anything he wanted more than anything else in the world, and he said, 'My kids. I just want my kids.'"

Katerina let out a low whistle. "What happened? That ex-wife?"

"Exactly." She turned to Alessandra, who was looking lost. "Douglas had custody of the children, but his ex-wife had kidnapped them, and he hadn't seen them, or even known where they were, for two years."

Alessandra looked horrified. "Oh no! How awful!"

Jacinth nodded. "Yes, so that was his first wish. I did my thing with the magic, and while Douglas was getting ready to throw me out again, his phone was ringing with his private investigator calling to say they'd been found." She grinned like the cat that ate the canary. "The thing is, they were in Los Angeles. The children had only been two and four the last time he saw them, so Douglas panicked and asked if I'd come along with him to get them. Of course, I said I would, and we settled on it that I'd be the nanny. That night we caught a late flight--a redeye--to California and got the children, and here we are!"

After they all had a good laugh, Alessandra asked curiously, "What else did he wish for?"

"Well, there was Firefly." Quickly Jacinth related the story of the abused mare and the difficult labor.

Katerina snickered. "You should have seen Troy when he got home. The poor man didn't know what hit him. He tied one on pretty good with a bottle of Scotch... the really expensive kind... while he told Cat all about it."

Jacinth's eyes danced. "Did he really?"

"Mmhmm." She slid a sideways glance at Jacinth. "So you're only staying until Douglas finds a new nanny for the kids?"

Fidgeting with the zipper on the sleeping bag she was sitting on, Jacinth couldn't meet her friends' eyes. "Well, yes. But I mean, there's no hurry. Of course Douglas wants to find just the right person, and that takes time."

She looked up in time to see Alessandra and Katerina exchanging glances.

"What?" she demanded, feeling almost cross.

"You're different," Alessandra said gently. She reached out to take Jacinth's hand. "In all the time I've known you, you've been restless, bored. Moving from one thing to another quickly. As if you were seeking something but you didn't know what. Just in these couple of hours tonight I can see the change in you. You're content and happy, completely comfortable here in this house, a part of this family. I haven't seen you much with Douglas yet, but..."

"I have," Katerina interrupted. "It's clear you care deeply for him. Watching the two of you interact, it's like you're attuned to each other, as if you had known each other for years. And then there are the children. You're as fiercely protective of them as a lioness with cubs. Can you really just walk away?"

"I... I..." Jacinth stammered, feeling tears spring to her eyes. "I don't want to. But I know I have to."

"Why?" Alessandra asked bluntly.

"Because he is a mortal, of course," Jacinth replied,

surprised. "And I am Djinn."

Katerina humphed. "Is there some kind of law against that?"

"I thought your father was human," Alessandra added. "You told me that, or Julian did."

Jacinth drew her legs up and wrapped her arms around them. Even now she could remember the lost feeling she had as a child, the loneliness as her mother withdrew into herself. Being different, she and her mother apart from the happy, laughing families in her village.

"He was," she said, though the words were hard to speak through the lump that seemed to rise in her throat. "Yes, he was human. My mother left him and took me to Qaf when I was only four. He did not know we were Djinn, you see, and my magic was beginning to manifest. And she has grieved for him ever since. She still grieves, will not choose another mate."

She looked up at her friends, feeling wetness slip down her cheeks. "I do not wish this. I do not wish to spend eternity mourning my lost love."

Clearly sympathetic, Alessandra reached out to squeeze her hand, but Katerina looked thoughtful.

"Nine hundred years is an awfully long time to mourn someone," she observed. "Have you considered that maybe there was something else going on, something you don't know about the situation?"

"Well, no," Jacinth admitted, feeling slightly defensive. "She has never talked about it, never talked about him."

Alessandra suggested, her voice gentle, "Perhaps you should talk to her, then."

Jacinth looked at her friends impatiently. "Whatever she might say, that doesn't change the fact that Douglas is going to get old and die."

"You're not going to get any sympathy from us," Katerina

observed in a wry tone. "We're going to grow old and die, too. Do you not want to be friends with us now, because you'll miss us when we're dead and gone?"

"Of course not!" Jacinth stared at Katerina, feeling horrified.

Alessandra frowned. "That was harsh," she said chidingly to Katerina, who shrugged.

"For humans and shapeshifters, that's how it is. We live, and we die, and loved ones are left behind. It's a fact."

"I-I..." Jacinth stammered, looking at her friends.

"It's all right," Alessandra assured her. "Katerina was just giving you perspective. And consider that old adage about it being better to have loved and lost, than to have never loved at all. Is that really what you want, to live an eternity never having loved anyone for fear of losing them?"

"I could fall in love with a Djinn," said Jacinth, feeling obstinate. "Nothing says I have to fall in love with a human."

"But you have fallen in love with him," said Alessandra gently.

Jacinth stared at her a long moment, letting the truth of that sink in. She did love Douglas, whether she wanted to or not.

"How could I have let this happen?" she wailed.

Alessandra laughed softly, reaching out to pat her hand. "Love isn't something you can choose, or turn on or off like a light switch. And yes, Douglas will grow old and die, but don't you see? He's going to do that anyway, Jacinth. Wouldn't you rather have those years with him, at his side, than off in Qaf all alone?"

"We're not telling you what to do," Katerina added. "We're suggesting that you be open to the possibility, that's all."

Alessandra nodded her agreement.

Jacinth drew a long, quivering breath. "Okay," she said. "Okay, I'll think about it."

CHAPTER 24

LATE THAT EVENING, their friends having gone home, Jacinth sat with Douglas on the swing out on his front porch. Although it was still quite warm, the ferocious heat and stifling humidity of the daytime had let up, and the night air was stirred by a soft breeze. They were far enough away from the city that the stars overhead twinkled brightly. Jacinth lifted her face to the breeze, inhaling deeply.

"It's lovely in the evening. I can smell the honeysuckle from the fence, can you?"

Douglas chuckled. "I remember when I was a kid, pulling off the flower and licking the little drops of nectar from the ends."

"Oh! I did that also!" Jacinth beamed at him. "I had forgotten. When the children come home, let's show them."

"Also how to make s'mores?" Douglas cast a teasing glance at her, and she laughed, her eyes sparkling with delight.

"I never knew of s'mores before! It was so much fun!"

"I'll be eating leftover pizza for a week," he complained.

She only grinned at him and handed him one of the tall glasses she's brought from the kitchen, brimming with an icy beverage the color of red Kool-Aid. Douglas took a tentative sip, and raised his brows at the rich, fruity flavor.

"*Kerkade*," she responded to his unspoken question. "Dried hibiscus leaves steeped in hot water, much like you do with tea, then sweetened and cooled, and served over ice. It is a favorite drink where I grew up."

Douglas remembered his recent Internet searches on the Djinn. "Would that be... Qaf?"

Jacinth beamed at him, her pleasure apparent. "You've been doing research!"

He shrugged his shoulders uncomfortably. "Just a little, on the Internet. At first, it looked like there was a lot of information, but there wasn't actually very much. A lot of repetition, variations of the same information over and over."

"Well, most of what is there is nonsense," she said frankly. "And lots of it is very ill-informed. Like that part about evil Djinn being ugly. What nonsense!"

Uh... "There really are evil Djinn?" he asked cautiously.

Jacinth eyed him with amused tolerance. "Of course. We are not perfect, Douglas. There are bad Djinn and good Djinn, just as there are bad and good humans, or animals or... or anything."

"However," she went on, "the Djinn are not handicapped like humans in our ability to tell good from evil. We can look into the hearts of man and Djinn."

Which reminded him. "Most of the information online about the Djinn seems to come from the Muslims... the Qur'an."

"Yes, and quite accurate as far as it goes," Jacinth nodded, her ebony curls bouncing about her shoulders. "But it is not the whole story, Douglas. We are mentioned, although briefly, in many passages, yes, from which Islamic scholars over the centuries have deducted much about the Djinn. It is not the Qur'an in error, for that is the Word of God, but it is the deductions made by man. And only part of what is known to mankind about the Djinn is told in the Qur'an. For instance, the good Djinn. The Qur'an states that Djinn were created, like man, with free will. They have the ability to choose the right path or the wrong path; the good versus the evil. But then it goes on and talks at great length almost exclusively about the evil Djinn, as if most Djinn are evil. In truth, there are far more good Djinn than bad, the same as with men."

"I do remember that, about the free will. There were also folk tales about the Qaf and villages. Do you really have Djinn princes?"

"Of course." She dimpled enchantingly, her eyes mischievous. "You've even met one."

"Kieran," Douglas deduced unerringly, biting back a groan. That figured.

Jacinth giggled. "Yes. He is the prince of our land. Not just my village, but for many miles around."

Douglas held up his hands. "Wait... back up a minute. Your village? I thought you lived in your teapot."

"Only when I am actively granting wishes. Mother and I have a home in our village. We don't spend a great deal of time there now, mostly only Djinn families with children live there all the time. But there is a... an attachment. It is difficult to explain, Douglas. Think of it as a kind of tribal affiliation, although it is a little more complicated. I belong to my village, even though perhaps I have not been there in a century. It is my home, and when I return it is as though I have not been away at all. I told you before, our time is not like time for humans."

She sipped her drink, studying him over the rim of her glass as if turning an idea over in her mind. Putting the glass on the table at her side, she turned to look at him in an oddly hesitant manner.

"Would you like to visit Qaf?"

"Could I? They won't mind if you bring a human?"

"Oh no. Humans come through now and again. Of course," she added, her eyes sparkling with fun, "they don't know we are Djinn. They think only that they have found an old, traditional bedouin tribe, living the life of our ancestors."

"But I would know," Douglas pointed out.

"Yes. You are more than *Sahib*, Douglas. You are what we call *Sahib karim*... one that is a friend, not merely master." She wrinkled her nose. "I hate that term, Master. It does not truly describe the relationship between the Wish Bearer and the Wish Maker, but it is easiest for a human to understand. Oh, I am digressing. Although unusual, still a *Sahib karim* would be welcomed at a village of a Djinn."

"Here." She took his glass from him and put it aside, then took his hand in hers. "Close your eyes."

HEAT. Scorching hot, the dry air encompassed him, as if he were wrapped in a warm roll fresh from the oven. Almost stifling, the heat wasn't actually overbearing... far different from the heavy humidity of New York which sometimes made him feel as if it were hard to breathe. It wasn't hard to breathe here. In fact, it was invigorating. Scents enveloped him... rich floral aromas, and the smells of cooking and campfires, of goats and sheep and horses.

"Now look," Jacinth's voice encouraged him. "Open your eyes, Douglas."

They were standing on a dirt path in the midst of a multitude of simple black wool tents. The sky was a shade of deep blue so intense it was almost unreal. Greenery, lush and exotic, grew in abundance around them, and date palms swayed lazily overhead in the slight breeze. Far above, a hawk soared, its silhouette dark against the azure sky. Between two nearby tents, Douglas caught a glimpse of blue... a small lake, judging by the distribution of the palm trees, which he assumed would surround the water. This was an oasis. He felt as if he'd somehow strayed into a Discovery Channel special.

"Jacinth! Jacinth!"

With cries of delight, a horde of children of all sizes converged on them, surrounding them to chatter away in what must be Arabic. The younger children hung on Jacinth, all but climbing up her side, clinging to her legs and arms. She must have changed when she brought them here, as she now wore a long, simple dress of cream cotton, prettily embroidered with flowers. She laughed as she greeted them, bending to lift the smallest in her arms, her pretty face alight with joyous affection.

"Yes, yes, I am here to visit you," she said in English. "I have brought a guest who does not speak our language, so you must be polite."

Douglas found it interesting that none of the children seemed at all shy of a stranger... and a foreign stranger at that... in their midst. The older children smiled readily at him and began shooting questions at Jacinth. A little dark-haired girl tugged at his trousers, clearly begging to be lifted up.

"That is Lilah," Jacinth told him as he bent to pick the child up. "She is too little to have learned English yet."

That didn't seem to bother the little girl, who seemed

perfectly happy in his arms, and began talking to him in Arabic with great animation. He couldn't help chuckling, as a picture came to mind of Molly talking to Kieran in exactly this way.

"She's a cutie," he commented, examining the little girl's curly black hair and the black eyes, darker than Jacinth's. The ebony hair and eyes contrasted markedly against skin the same dusky gold as Jacinth. She wore a long rose-colored dress, and many gold bangles on one arm. All the girl children wore such bangles, he saw, looking around.

"*Ya 'awlad!*" A woman came toward them from the direction of the lake. Her dark, seamed face under a bright black and red scarf brightened as she saw Jacinth. "Jacinth! *Ya habibti, kayf hallik?*"

"It is Khadija, an elder of the village. She asks how I am," Jacinth whispered to Douglas, and responded to the older woman.

He noted with interest that Jacinth's own English had suddenly become more heavily accented, and he ducked his head toward Lilah to hide a grin.

The older woman, Khadija, listened to Jacinth for a moment, then turned to him, wreathed in smiles.

"You are welcome to our village, young man. We are pleased to receive any *Sahib* of Jacinth's." She clapped her hands together. "Children! Come, let Jacinth show her guest around. You can talk with her later."

Other adults, presumably hearing the ruckus, began emerging from the tents. Most of the women were dressed like Jacinth, in long flowing embroidered dresses, then men in long white shirt-dresses like those seen on Arab men on the television and in National Geographic. A few were dressed in Western clothes, while others wore loose trousers and tunics that Douglas thought vaguely may be Indian.

They crowded around, as eager, it seemed, as the children to greet Jacinth and meet her *Sahib*. Jacinth's voice making introductions was lost in the hubbub, but the men extended warm welcoming handshakes. The women were more openly curious. Douglas gradually became aware of some speculation in the glances aimed at him and Jacinth, and in consternation, he remembered Jacinth telling him that some of the Djinn could read minds.

A dry chuckle at his side had him turning. Firm hands took Lilah from where she had cuddled herself into the crook of his left arm, and a tall woman smiled at him, white teeth gleaming against skin the color of darkest night.

"None would be so rude as to 'read' a visitor, an esteemed guest," she assured him. She raised one finger. "And no, I did not read your thoughts. We Djinn can see strong emotions, however, and I caught your flash of panic. You have nothing to fear amongst the Djinn."

The little girl redirected her lilting babble at the newcomer, who let the child slide to the ground with a fond pat.

"Even our Lilah likes you."

Douglas didn't have a clue why that should matter, but it seemed to him that the woman now regarded him with more respect than curiosity. With a stately nod she turned, swaying gracefully back along the path behind him.

Turning his attention to Jacinth, he saw that the crowd had begun to disperse. Jacinth's hand found his, and she slanted an upward glance toward him.

"My people," she said simply, her big eyes shining in obvious affection.

"They are wonderful," he admitted. "I expected at least a little suspicion, along the lines of 'what is *he* doing here?'"

She laughed merrily.

"I told you that you would be welcome! We Djinn are very hospitable. They have gone to cook a welcome feast for you."

"No kidding. A welcome feast? For me?" Douglas could hardly imagine it. He was just a visitor who'd popped in with Jacinth, and they were cooking him a welcome feast! Wait a minute. "Cooking? They're actually cooking?"

She gave him another of those looks, the amused tolerance. "Yes, Douglas. One can't live by conjuring anything we want all the time. It is pleasant to cook, to do things with our hands, and learn skills."

Her eyes sparkled in fun. "And of course, it is so easy to correct when we make a mistake."

He laughed at that. Jacinth tugged at his hand, and he followed her through the maze of tents to a section of the village where the tents were not so closely placed. This area seemed quieter, and looked the littlest bit less lived in.

He didn't have a clue how Jacinth knew which tent was whose, since they all looked basically alike. But at the far end of the village, set slightly apart from the others, stood a small tent. It wasn't so small in and of itself, perhaps, only in relation to the others in the village. It was to this that Jacinth led him.

She held the flap open for him, and he had to duck his head to enter. The cool air hit him like a blow after the extreme heat of the outdoors, and he took in a deep breath gratefully, reveling in the slight chill against his skin. It took him a moment to fully take in his surroundings.

He could feel his jaw drop, and his breath left him in a startled "whoosh." This... was a tent? More like a mini mansion, he thought, gazing about in wonder. Where was the dirt floor, the cloth sides and top? There were rugs covering the floor, certainly; glowing rugs, rich with color, but the floor they covered was marble. Piles of pillows in every color known to man... and a few still unknown, he suspected... were scattered invitingly along the periphery of the room. The walls also appeared to be marble, although hung with woven tapestries and mirrors. Candles in wall sconces and a massive chandelier hanging from the ceiling lit the room.

It took him a full minute to realize that the room was at least three times the size of the tent as he'd seen it from outside. Douglas shook his head, trying to make his confused brain come up with an explanation for the discrepancies.

A low laugh caught his attention, and he turned his head to look at Jacinth as she patted his arm.

"It's okay, Douglas. The inside of a Djinn tent reflects the Djinn's vessel. It is one of the magical properties of Qaf. Djinn villages exist in both the real, human world and also on Qaf, which is mystical, at the same time. Thus we appear mundane from the outside, but the inside is pure Qaf."

Although still feeling a bit stunned, his brain was beginning to turn again.

"I thought you said humans come through the village, unaware," he reminded her. "What if someone looked inside the tents?"

She nodded solemnly. "A good question. But this is Qaf, Douglas. A human could not enter it without the Djinn being aware. Each village has elders... a *majlis*, or council, if you will... responsible for greeting stray visitors, alerting the Djinn living in the village, and keeping our true natures secret."

Kicking off the leather sandals she wore, Jacinth reclined gracefully on a pile of pillows, then reached up to pull him down beside her. Douglas was surprised at how comfortable it was. He'd seen this kind of... furniture, for lack of a better word... in Jacinth's bedroom at his house, but he hadn't sat on it before.

Shifting a pillow out of his way, he put one arm about Jacinth's shoulders, drawing her closer to him. She came to him willingly, snuggling within the curve of his arm, her head resting on his shoulder with a sigh of pleasure.

He breathed in deeply the scent that wafted about her, a light cloud of lilac that made him think of springtime. Her body was soft and pliant against him, her hair silky under his cheek.

"Is this where your mother brought you? When you were young?"

"Mmhmm. Most Djinn raise their children in a village. Everyone helps with the children. We have teachers who live here, and elders. Some stay always, others come who have special areas of knowledge, to teach those who wish to learn. We have very skilled Djinn in the arts, as well as other fields such as medicine."

Djinn medicine? Before he could follow this up, a light chiming rang through the tent, like harp strings being strummed in a rippling wave of sound.

"Come!" Jacinth called. Douglas smothered a grin. Genie door chimes?

The older woman he'd met when they first arrived entered, balancing a silver tray with glass cups as she held the tapestried flap open for little Lilah, who carefully held a steaming coffeepot with both hands, well-swathed in thick cloths.

"We brought coffee for you and your guest," Khadija told Jacinth. A small mother-of-pearl inlaid table appeared before them, and the tray and pot were carefully placed on its polished surface. The tray also held a plate of dates and thin slices of what appeared to be pound cake of some kind.

"*Alf ash-shukr*. A thousand thanks," Jacinth told her, glowing with pleasure. She glanced at Douglas. "No one makes *qahwa*, coffee, like Khadija."

"*W-ana! Ana!*" Lilah ran to Jacinth's side, reaching up to pat her cheek insistently. Jacinth laughed, and lifted the child to her lap, listening to her chatter.

"Yes, and you, sweetie. Douglas, Lilah wants you to know she has been learning to make the Turkish coffee."

"Already?" He was startled. "She doesn't look to be more than three or four."

Khadija reached over to stroke Lilah's curly hair, her eyes crinkling in a smile. "All Arab children, even Djinn children, learn to make coffee and tea early. It is so much a part of our culture, and an especial matter of pride to be able to make good coffee."

With a nod at Douglas, Khadija lifted the child from Jacinth's lap and departed. He stared after her in wonder.

"How can they accept me so easily?" he asked Jacinth. "For all they know, I might go back and tell everyone about the Djinn, or sell my story to National Enquirer or something."

She touched his cheek fleetingly, her fingers soft and cool.

"Of course you won't, Douglas. If I thought for one minute you would do something like that, we would not be here. We Djinn know who can be trusted and who cannot. Even were I not here with you, any Djinn would know you are an honorable man, Douglas."

Her praise warmed him as much as the affection in her brown eyes. For a fleeting moment, he wished things could remain as they were now, forever. The two of them living alone in this tent that wasn't a tent, in this other-worldly paradise for as long as they lived.

He shoved the tantalizing vision away. He was a father, with two children he adored. He couldn't spend forever with Jacinth, but this life would be waiting for her when his time with her was done. If she cared for him, if she could love him, and be a part of his life for as long as he lived, that would be all that he could ever want.

A young voice, Lilah's, raised up from outside.

"Jacinth, *yela! Yela bina!*"

Beside him, Jacinth chuckled softly, rising to her feet. "Roughly translated, that means, come on, let's go."

"Go where?" He asked, standing up as well.

She slid her soft hand into his, smiling at him. "The feast. It is ready."

No sooner had they emerged from the tent than a half dozen children swarmed to them, chattering away in Arabic. They led the way through the clusters of tents, Lilah clinging to Jacinth's hand the whole way. The tents gave way to a wide, open area that stretched between the village and the shimmering surface of the lake. A series of long, low tables was laid out under the shade of towering palms, with cushions on either side. The tables were loaded with enough food to make Douglas' eyes widen. Huge platters of rice, glistening brown with spices, and chunks of meat alternated with platters of rice and whole roasted chickens. In between were bowls of dates and other fruits, as well as plates of sweets, most of which were unfamiliar to him. Incongruous in this setting were the carafes of presumably tea or coffee, with tiny cups set about.

Jacinth chose a cushion and lowered herself to it, tugging Douglas down at her side. All about them the other Djinn were doing the same. She lifted a carafe and filled two of the small cups, handing one to him. He regarded the thick greenish colored liquid suspiciously.

"What is it?"

"Coffee, but bedouin style, we add cardamom."

He sipped cautiously, then choked at the bitter flavor, even though it was heavily sweetened. Seated on his other side, Khadija laughed.

"It is what you would call an acquired taste," she told him.

Across from them, an older man with a neat, pointed beard, dressed in a long, flowing robe over loose trousers, addressed Douglas.

"*Marhabban*, welcome. I am Ahmed. I am told you are the *Sahib karim* of young Jacinth here?"

Young? Douglas wondered, even as he acknowledged his status with a nod. At nine hundred years old, Jacinth was considered young?

"A *Sahib*?" A boy down the table from them looked over, his expression eager. He seemed to be in his pre-teens, Douglas judged, dark haired and dark eyed. "You are a *Sahib*?"

A bit taken back by the urgency of the question, Douglas nodded. The boy's eyes were wide with excitement.

"I'm going to be a Wish Bearer one day," he announced importantly. "And I will have a *Sahib* and grant wishes."

"Of a certainty, Boutros," Khadija smiled at the boy but shook one finger at him. "Once you have learned there is a time and a place for mischief."

Jacinth leaned close to whisper, "Boutros is always into mischief. He is a handful, that one."

Douglas chuckled. "I can imagine. So what is this... Wish Bearer? I remember you've mentioned it before. I'd meant to ask more about it, but forgot."

"Ah. The Wish Bearer."

She sipped her coffee. Douglas took another sip of his, prepared now for the bitterness of it. Rather to his surprise, it didn't seem so unpleasant, and the exotic taste lingered on his tongue.

"Not all Djinn are Wish Bearers," she explained as she

piled rice and lamb onto two plates, placing one before him. "Only those who wish to, and for them it is a... a..."

She paused, seeking the right word.

"A calling, or avocation," put in Ahmed from across the table.

"Yes, exactly!" She beamed at the older man, nodding her head in agreement. "Usually we feel the call to be a Wish Bearer at a young age. I was just about Boutros' age when I knew. Then when we are older, we are given special training, and we work with a craftsman and have our vessels specially created for us."

"So it's not like in Aladdin... the movie," Douglas specified. "Where you're bound until someone wishes you free?"

All about the table, heads were shaking, and he saw lots of smiles.

"That movie!" Khadija exclaimed, with tolerant amusement.

"It has its uses," Jacinth put in. "It has made it much easier to convince a new *Sahib* that we are real when we first appear."

"True," others chimed in from down the table.

"A Djinn cannot be bound against his will," Ahmed told Douglas. "Even the Wish Bearers may remove their vessel from the human world at any time, until they are ready to grant wishes once more."

Again, there was a general agreement on this around the table.

"Of course, we can be summoned by sorcerers," Jacinth added, watching Douglas with a mischievous gleam in her eyes.

"Sorcerers?" Douglas struggled not to choke on the mouthful of aromatic spiced rice he'd just taken. Okay, that did not sound good in any way. "Like... er..."

"Black magic." Beside him, Khadija nodded, her face set in

stern lines. "We are hard to summon; it is far easier for such magicians to call a demon than a Djinn, but it can be done."

Ahmed spoke up. "We are also far more difficult to control and to command. Djinn are mischievous; that part of our nature is well-established; the dark side to that is that we can also be tricky, deceptive. Such a magician would have to be supremely skillful in his control to succeed in his goals, because a Djinn held against his will is going to do everything in his power to turn the spell back on its creator."

"Plus, we are family," Jacinth added, her eyes flashing with anger. "No Djinn, summoned unwillingly, fights alone. This is the other reason such magicians leave us alone and concentrate on demons. Demons are solitary by nature. Not so with the Djinn. If you fight one Djinn, you fight all his family."

Khadija's lips curved in a satisfied smile. "Usually it does not end well for those who seek to invoke a Djinn against their will."

Well, that made sense, and he was aware of relief. The thought of Jacinth being summoned away, held against her will and used for black magic, made him distinctly uncomfortable. He was glad when the conversation turned general. Jacinth lifted a nearby carafe and refilled his cup of tea. Setting the carafe down, she slipped her hand into his.

"Don't worry so, Douglas." She leaned close, her cheek coming to rest against his shoulder. Her smile as she glanced up at him was warm with understanding. "It could never happen to me. And such things are very rare anyway."

"There's so much more to it," he said, a sense of wonder filling him. He gestured with one hand at the lively people lining the tables, the palm trees overhead, the nearby rows of black tents. "So much more than the brief Internet articles I read even hint at."

Her eyes danced with humor. "A whole new world," she agreed. "Just like the song."

Douglas had to laugh. "So true."

When everyone seemed to have finished eating, more carafes of hot Arabic style coffee were brought to the table and passed around. Douglas nearly fell backward off his cushion when, with no warning, all the platters and dishes of meat and rice disappeared, although the bowls of fruit remained.

Jacinth giggled, and leaned over to whisper, "Someone has sent it all back to the central kitchen tent. Then later, they will gather what is left over and leave it for those who come later."

"That's a handy trick," Douglas admitted. "Where were you Djinn when I was a kid and had to do the dishes every night?"

She laughed merrily. "Well, that happens here, too, when we're not having a big feast like this. Most mundane chores are done by hand. And it teaches the children responsibility and accountability."

No one seemed in a hurry to leave, he noted. Men and women lounged on their cushions, chatting idly, while the children ran about.

"Oh!" Jacinth straightened on her cushion, and her smile widened. "Atif and Farhan are coming."

He looked around to see two young boys, perhaps a couple of years older than Benny, rather awkwardly carrying a small, cream-colored baby camel between them. As they neared the table, the boys set the creature on its feet, steadying it with great care as the long legs wobbled a bit, then found their balance.

"Such long eyelashes," Jacinth crooned, stroking the shaggy little head.

Douglas reached out to run his hand down the long, curved neck. "It's soft," he said, surprised.

"Because it is baby," one of the boys told him. "Only one day old."

"*A* baby, Atif," Jacinth corrected.

The boy nodded. "It is a baby," he repeated obediently.

"This is my *Sahib karim*," she told them. "He is a veterinarian... like a doctor, but for animals."

"Horses mostly," Douglas added.

The boys looked suitably impressed, although whether it was from his being a veterinarian or a *Sahib karim*, Douglas couldn't tell. An older woman descended on them, scolding in Arabic. Beside him, Jacinth seemed to be struggling with amusement.

"She says they should not have taken the camel from its mother," she whispered into his ear.

Chastened, the boys moved off with their baby camel toward the tents, tenderly supporting it on either side. Watching them, Douglas began to laugh suddenly.

"I just had a vision of Benny with those boys," he explained in response to Jacinth's questioning look. "The three of them hovering over that camel like three hens with one chick."

She laughed also. "Oh, yes! I can see them together. They would like Benny."

"And Lilah and Molly." He grinned. "She'd go nuts over the baby camel, too."

Jacinth found that she had to stifle a twinge of regret. She also could see Benny and Molly running about here, laughing and playing with the children, the animals, being spoiled by the adults. If she was a real part of their family, they could all come here to visit regularly... weekends and holidays. They could bring Julian and Alessandra as guests, perhaps even Katerina. The children could run about and play, with the whole village to look after them. They could... She brought her thoughts to a halt. This was not possible. It wasn't fair to the children, either to Benny and Molly, or to Lilah, or Atif and Farhan or the others here in the village, to bring them and let them grow to be friends. She would leave when Douglas made his third wish, and the children would never see their friends again.

"Jacinth?"

Douglas' voice, warm with concern, brought her out of her reverie. He was watching her, concern in his eyes.

"What's wrong? You looked so sad all of a sudden."

She discovered her eyes were brimming, and she blinked back the tears that threatened.

"Nothing. It is nothing." She slid her hand in his and rose to her feet. "Come. Let us return to my tent."

CHAPTER 25

THE OTHERS at the tables stood also, and came to bid them farewell. She watched Douglas' bemused expression with enjoyment as the farewells took almost a half hour.

"How do you ever get anything done?" he asked as they finally disengaged from the crowd and threaded their way through the maze of tents.

She grinned, sending him a sparkling glance. "Fortunately, we are not bothered with deadlines or any particular sense of urgency."

Douglas shook his head in humorous bemusement. "I can see that!"

They reached her tent and she smiled as Douglas held aside the flap for her.

"Such a gentleman, even when roughing it in a tent," she teased.

"Roughing it," Douglas said with a snort of disbelief. He looked around at the sumptuous carpets and draperies, the brass and crystal. "Right."

With a laugh, Jacinth sank onto a sofa, drawing him down beside her.

"I'm not going to ask if you want anything to eat or drink."

"God, no," he groaned, patting his stomach. "I may explode. Do they always eat like that?"

"Oh, no," she reassured him, tucking her feet up beneath her. "Only for feasts to celebrate special occasions. Of course," she added, dimpling at him, "we always look for an excuse to celebrate."

His laugh was a deep rumble in his chest, and his arm came around her, pulling her against him. She lay her head on his shoulder, which was placed perfectly for her to use. His warm lips pressed against her forehead, lingering, and she hummed in pleasure.

"Are you tired?" he asked. "It's been a long day."

Jacinth had to laugh, glancing up at him through her lashes. "Even longer since it was already late evening in New York when we left and it was morning here!"

"So it was! Good thing I'm off tomorrow, and with the kids gone we can both sleep in."

"Mmhmm." She snuggled closer, liking how she fit against him, his shoulder strong and muscular beneath her cheek, his arm holding her close. Contentment filled her, and a feeling of rightness. As if she belonged here, with this man, in his arms. They fit together as if... as if they'd been made for each other. She felt him stroking her hair, his fingers coming through the long strands, and she sighed in bliss. When his hand slipped beneath her chin, lifting her face, she didn't resist. Her pulse began to pound as his lips hovered above hers, then descended slowly to claim her with a searing kiss.

She slid one arm about his neck, her eyelids drifting shut as she lost herself in his embrace, his kiss. No one had ever made her feel like this before. It was as if some part of her, deep within, had been missing and she'd never known it... until Douglas. The ragged feeling of frustration, the edgy impatience, of something always just out of her reach that kept her moving from place to place, unable to settle down... all these faded to nothing when Douglas was near.

She'd felt it from the very start, that first night, preparing the children's rooms before leaving for California. Being with him felt so right, so natural, it had become a daily struggle to hold herself aloof when she wanted nothing more than to melt into his embrace. She was tired of fighting it, of denying what her heart already knew: Douglas was her mate, her Chosen. And she desired him as she had never desired any other.

She drew back, her hands cupping his face. She traced the strong line of his cheekbone with her fingers, her thumb brushing the crease at the corner of his wide, well-shaped mouth. Raising her gaze to his, she saw the longing in his face, the desire. The love.

"Can't you feel it?" Douglas turned his head, seeking the palm of her hand with his lips, lingering on the sensitive skin. He could feel her responsive quiver, the quickening of her breath. It was heaven holding her, soft and pliant, in his arms.

"There's something between us, Jacinth. The connection is so strong, I know you feel it, too."

"I do," she admitted, her voice soft. "It feels right, being here together."

Douglas closed his eyes, letting out a long breath. At last, she admitted it.

"Jacinth," he whispered against her cheek. The dark lashes fluttered closed as she lifted her face, the lush, curved mouth seeking his. Her arms clung to him, her body pliant as he lowered her to the pillows, the ebony hair fanning out like a dark flame about her.

The chandeliers and sconces flickered and dimmed until light and shadows were all that could be seen, the satiny glow of her skin, the dark flash of her eyes in the low candlelight.

"Douglas." She spoke his name in a low murmur, her husky voice seductive, full of longing. Her hand crept behind his head, pulling him down to her. "Love me."

DOUGLAS AWOKE in the night to moonlight pouring through his bedroom window. He raised himself up on one arm and blinked, looking around, and realized they were back at home, in his own room. In his bed. Jacinth slept beside him, her long slim legs intertwined with his. Her face peaceful in the moonlight, her lashes black against the creamy skin of her cheek.

He brushed a lock of hair away from her face, letting his fingers linger, enjoying the silky smoothness of her skin. She was so beautiful, so perfect for him. The sight of her in his bed, curled trustingly against him, brought a tight feeling to his chest. There had to be a way to work this out. There just had to be. He wouldn't accept any other option.

She stirred, her eyes opening slumberously. Her lips curved up in a smile as her gaze met his, and she traced the line of his jaw with a gentle touch.

Douglas dipped his head to capture her mouth. He lingered savoring her sweetness.

"I love you," he whispered against her lips. "Love me."

Her reply came on a soft breath as she reached for him.

"I do."

THE SUN SLANTING across his face woke Douglas. The other side of the bed was empty, the sheets cool. Jacinth must have gotten up with the birds. *Jacinth.* A flush of warmth stole through him as he thought of their night together. She was incredible... everything he'd ever wanted in a woman, and hadn't thought to look for. Funny, cute, cheerful... and sexy as hell. If he searched the world over, he wouldn't find another woman like her.

Stretching, Douglas kicked the covers off and got up. He'd take Jacinth out for breakfast, and then plan a day together, while they still had the chance to be alone. Their parents would be back with the children tomorrow, but they still had today... and tonight. He couldn't wait longer, he had to know. He'd take her somewhere quiet for dinner, someplace romantic, and he'd ask her to marry him. He'd tell her he loved her, and ask her to stay with him all his life.

The house seemed awfully quiet as he headed for the kitchen. No Jacinth. The range was cold as well; usually, whoever got up first in the morning, put on the tea or coffee.

"Jacinth?"

No answer. Douglas began to get a very, very bad feeling. He strode back down the hallway. Jacinth's bedroom door was closed. Sniffing experimentally, there was no scent of incense in the hallway, which was odd. He could always smell her incense in the hall. He tapped on the door.

"Jacinth?"

Again there was no answer. A sinking feeling in his stomach, Douglas turned the knob and opened the door. The room was bare, except for the muted wall-to-wall carpet. No bed and hangings, no sofa and cushions. No brass lantern or incense brazier. Douglas raced to the living room, to find the shelf where her silver teapot stood. The shelf was bare.

She was gone.

CHAPTER 26

YAWNING, Troy was heading up to his room, Cherie his faithful shadow and Cat leaping up the stairs ahead of him. His cell phone rang, and he reached into his pocket for it as he reached the landing. Sitting on the end of his bed, he swiped the screen to answer. "Yep."

"Troy?"

The voice on the other end of the line was a woman's voice, older. She sounded vaguely familiar.

"Yes, this is Troy."

"Troy, it's Skye, Douglas' mother."

He sat upright, every nerve on alert. "What is it? What's happened?"

"Blue and I took the children to D.C. for a few days, we came home this afternoon. Douglas and Jacinth weren't here. We didn't think anything about it at first, because they weren't expecting us back until tomorrow, but it's been hours. And Jacinth's room is empty. The children are upset, and my husband has been out looking for Douglas everywhere. We thought you might know something... or have an idea where he might be?"

"Ah, hell." He ran a hand through his hair. "Hang tight. I think I know where I can find him. If not, I'll come by and we'll decide what to do next."

"Thank you." Her voice quavered. "We haven't known what to do."

"No problem. You just stand by."

Hanging up the phone, he shook his head.

"Ah, hell. Man, that just sucks."

Taking the stairs two at a time, he went upstairs and changed quickly into jeans and a pullover. He knew exactly where Douglas would have gone. Back in their college days, there was a bar not far away from the campus where they'd gone to shoot pool, chase girls and make their plans for what they would do when they finished veterinary school. Back then, it had been just a dream, veterinary school itself only a hope for the future. But if Douglas and Jacinth had argued, if she had gone back to that lamp, or teapot or whatever it was, Troy knew just where to find him.

He stopped just inside the doorway of the bar. Man, he hadn't been here for years. It seemed smaller than he remembered, darker and dingier. He took a step forward, his sneakers crunching on the peanut shells strewn about the floor, and he smiled. Yep, this was the place. It hadn't changed, after all.

At the bar, hunched over a half-full glass, he found his friend.

"Hey, man." He grabbed Douglas' shoulder, shook him gently. "Hey, man, this isn't the way to do it."

Douglas looked up at his old friend. "She's gone," he

mumbled blearily, his fingers curling around the glass he held. "She left me. Went back to Qaf. Beautiful, friendly Qaf."

"That's rough. But you can't do this, man. You got kids."

"They love her too." He stared into his drink. "How'm I going to tell Molly and Ben? What do I tell them?"

"You tell them that she loves them, loves all of you, but that things just didn't work out."

Douglas shook his head. "They know. Troy, they know."

He could feel the grip on his shoulder tighten as Troy realized what he meant.

"They know? The kids know that she's a..." Troy cleared his throat. "...a genie. Djinn. Whatever."

Nodding morosely, Douglas took another swig of his drink. "Last week Molly fell into the pool, and Jacinth had to rescue her. Jacinth can't swim, so she had to... you know."

"Eeeeyah. And Ben was there too?"

"Yeah." Douglas raised his head, looking straight at his oldest, his best friend. "She saved her life. Jacinth saved Molly's life. And now she's gone. They'll never understand."

"Then you can tell them the truth," Troy told him. "Tell them that she can't stay because she's a Djinn. She had to go and do Djinn things. Whatever. Are there laws against Djinn and human being together?"

Douglas shook his head. "No. She didn't want to love a human... didn't want to be sad when I died." He lifted his glass, took a deep drink. "She took me to her village. To Qaf."

"Qaf?"

"Djinn live in villages, out in the desert, beyond the horizon."

"Beyond the horizon?" Huh?

Douglas belched. "It's complicated. Believe me."

"But she took you there."

"Yeah. The village where she grew up. Man, a whole village full of Djinn... men, women, children. It was unbelievable. Like this huge, close family. So friendly, welcoming, even though they knew I wasn't one of them. She had a home there. Well, it was a tent, but it was her home. She took me there. And we..."

He seemed unable to go on. Troy's hand was firm on his shoulder.

"I get the picture."

"The next morning I was home, and she was gone." Douglas gazed into his glass. "I loved her, you know."

"I know, man. I know you did. Do. But you need to come home now."

"Why?" Douglas picked up his glass, drained it without a blink. "It's empty. I couldn't stay there. Too quiet."

Troy took the glass from him, sliding it down the bar. "Not anymore it's not. Your parents are home with the kids."

"The kids?" Douglas straightened on the bar stool, and looked around at Troy. "The kids are home?"

"They came back this afternoon, and your dad has been searching for you ever since."

"My kids are home, and I wasn't there to greet them." Douglas seemed about to relapse into sorrow, and Troy shook him.

"Man, look at you. You haven't shaved, or washed, and you smell like the inside of a bottle. You have to pull yourself together. Come to my place and get cleaned up before I take you home."

The fog in his brain seemed to recede, pushed away by sudden alarm. "God, yes. I can't go to them like this. Not after Lillian."

Troy took his arm in a firm grip. "Come on, then."

The drive was made in silence, Douglas struggling to pull

himself together. He had to think what he was going to say to Ben and Molly, but somehow the right words wouldn't come. At Troy's house, he got out of the truck and stood a minute. The fresh air helped, clearing his head some. Following Troy into the house, he stopped abruptly, seeing Cat wending her way to them across the hardwood floor.

"Cat," he pronounced. He bent to pet her broad head with a heavy hand. "Jacinth left me, you know."

"Um... what are you doing?" Troy wanted to know.

"I'm telling Cat about Jacinth."

Cat prowwed in a low cat voice, stropped herself against Douglas' leg. He pet her some more.

"Thanks, Cat."

Troy took Douglas arm and pulled him toward the staircase. "Up we go. Shower time."

Half an hour later, showered, shaved, and somewhat baggily dressed in some clothes of Troy's, no more than a couple sizes too large, Douglas was ready. When he came downstairs, looking considerably better, Troy had a steaming cup of coffee ready for him.

"I called Skye. I thought they should know right away that you're okay and would be back in a bit."

"Thanks, Troy," Douglas said. "I appreciate it."

Cat wound herself around his legs, her golden eyes wide as they fixed on his face. He heard her unmistakable voice in his head.

"Take me with you. My presence will help the kits."

Holding out his arms, he staggered a little as she leaped into them. She wrapped her large paws bout his neck, shoving her head against his jaw in that peculiar way only cats did.

"Can we take her with us?" He addressed Troy. "She understands."

Seeing the concern in his friend's face, he belatedly remembered that Troy didn't know about shapeshifters, and hurried to add, "It'll help soften the blow; Ben and Molly love Cat, and if she's there it might... well... help."

Troy's response came immediately. "Of course."

The drive was spent mostly in silence. As they drove past the park where Jacinth took Ben and Molly to play, Douglas spoke at last.

"How am I going to tell them? She's only been with us for such a short time, and yet, she was there from the minute I got Ben and Molly back. We... we were a family. She loved me, and she loved Ben and Molly too, and they love her. To them, it'll be like she abandoned them."

"You said they know she's Djinn, so you can be honest with them," Troy advised. "Just make sure they know you love them too; that you don't love them less, now that she's gone."

"God, no!" Douglas exploded. "Of course not! Ben and Molly are my whole life!"

"Then let them know that."

"Of course I will! I just..." A groan seemed to be wrenched from him. "What are we going to do without her?"

"You're going to do what you have to do," Troy said, firmly.

"Yeah," Douglas said, sounding defeated.

When they went inside the house, though, they discovered that Ben and Molly had already gone to bed, and were fast asleep.

"I thought it best," Skye told them, catching her son in a tight embrace. "We told them that you would be home late. We did close the door to Jacinth's room so they couldn't see she wasn't there. Since we didn't know why she left, we thought it best to leave it until you came home.

Douglas nodded, glad not to have to face his children tonight. "Tomorrow will be soon enough."

He looked around to where Cat was perched on the sofa back, watching them with her big, intelligent eyes.

"Can we keep Cat for tonight, Troy? Then she can be here in the morning when the children awake, and she'll be a comfort to them when I tell them about Jacinth."

Cat purred at Troy, rubbing her muzzle along his hand. He sat on the sofa, accepting a cup of coffee from Skye, who'd gone to the kitchen and returned with two steaming cups. "Of course you can keep her. Anything I can do, man."

"And we'll be here too," Blue told his son. "We'll stay as long as we're needed."

Leaving his coffee where his mother had set it on the table, Douglas walked down the hall to check on the kids. Molly was asleep, her golden curls spilling over the pillow. He left the room quietly, moving on to Ben's room. At first, he thought Ben was asleep as well until he saw the faint sheen of tears on the boy's cheeks.

"You awake?" He asked softly.

He waited, letting Ben decide if he wanted to talk or pretend to sleep. A smothered sob reached his ears. He sat on the edge of the bed, not sure how much his son knew or guessed. In the faint light shining in from the hall, he saw Ben's eyes open, fixing on his face. He opened his arms, and Ben sat up, reaching for him. He held his son close, words failing him.

After a bit Benny drew back, sniffling. "She's gone, isn't she?"

"Ben..." His voice choked up as he tried to think what to say.

"Her teapot's gone. And the stuff in her room." Ben clung to him, burrowing into his shirt, and Douglas held the boy tighter. "Doesn't.... doesn't she love us anymore!"

"Of course she does!" The denial came instantly. He pushed Ben back, gripping the boy's shoulders. "Of course she loves us... you and Molly, and me. She just... it's difficult, Ben."

"It's 'cause we're not Djinn, you mean?"

"Yes... no! Not exactly." How could he explain to a six-year-old? He reached over to turn on the lamp on the nightstand. Ben scooted back to sit cross-legged on the bed facing him. He was wearing a pair of Aladdin pajamas, big blue laughing genie faces scattered on it, but his eyes were swollen and red-rimmed.

"The thing is, she *is* a Djinn," Douglas began. "For a Djinn to make a commitment to a human family, it's a pretty big deal. And for her, maybe it's a little scary, too. She came to grant wishes, not to fall in love. She needs some time to think."

Benny thought about that a minute, then looked at him, his eyes shining with hope. "Then you think she'll be back?"

Douglas looked at his son, seeing the love there, the need. His mind went back over the last weeks, of Jacinth hugging the children, playing with them. Fighting her terror of water to save Molly from drowning. Their last night there in Qaf. Suddenly he knew. He didn't know how he knew, he just did. A smile curved his lips, and the heavy weight that had been like a stone on his chest lifted. He reached out to ruffle his son's hair.

"Of course she'll be back," he said with absolute certainty. "She loves us. We need to give her a little time to think things over, to work it out for herself. Be patient, Ben. She'll come back to us. I'm sure of it."

CHAPTER 27

JACINTH HUDDLED into the silk comforter on her lounge, crying softly into the billowy folds. *Douglas*. She hated leaving him. And Ben and Molly... what would they think when they got home to find her gone? She hated thinking of it, of them hurting, wanting her, and she wouldn't be there for them. She wouldn't be there to see Benny off for his all-important first day of school. And Molly had just started talking normally.

But how could I stay? She asked herself for the thousandth time, perhaps the millionth time. Douglas was mortal. He would grow old and die, and she'd never see him again. All her life, she'd determined she would never love a mortal man, to mourn him for all eternity. She wouldn't do it. She wouldn't stay, and let herself fall in love with him! She would *not* wind up like her mother!

Except, she *had* already fallen in love with him. With him and his two wonderful children. And little Brandy and the puppy Douglas hadn't even brought home yet. She loved the large, comfortable house and yes, even the detested swimming pool! What was she going to do?

She reached for a Kleenex, and discovered she didn't have any. Feeling suddenly cross, she conjured a box and blew her nose.

A shimmer in the air heralded a Djinn's arrival. Zahra, of course. No one but her mother could enter her teapot without an invitation. Jacinth straightened as her mother appeared, wiping her eyes surreptitiously. Not that it did any good.

"Oh, Jacinth." Zahra sighed, frowning down at her. "What have you done?"

"I never meant to fall in love with him," Jacinth defended. "I never wanted to, it just... happened."

"Well, of course you fell in love with him. He's a wonderful man."

Jacinth stared at her, the Kleenex falling from her fingers.

"What?"

"*Ya helwa.*" Zahra sat down beside her, the green eyes sympathetic. "My sweet, what's going on here? Why have you left Douglas to come here? You seemed so happy."

"I *was* happy! But... but I fell in love with him!" Jacinth wailed, burying her face in Zahra's shoulder as her mother's arms came around her. "I didn't want to, but I did. I couldn't help it!"

"So what's the problem?" Zahra asked, as if puzzled. "It's perfectly clear that Douglas loves you too, and the children simply adore you. It was almost as if you were made for each other."

Jacinth raised her head to stare at her.

"What's the problem? He's *mortal*!" she all but shouted. "I don't want to love a mortal, to spend all my life grieving for him!"

"But you love him," her mother protested. "What's so wrong with that?"

For the first time in all the centuries of her life, Jacinth felt a flash of impatience with her mother.

"You know what's wrong with that. No one knows better than you!"

Zahra's brow creased, the dark red eyebrows drawing together in a frown, her eyes steady on Jacinth's face.

"Perhaps you'd better explain what you mean, because I do *not* understand."

With a sigh, Jacinth sat back against the lounge.

"I saw what it did to you when we left my father. For years and years, I could not make you smile, no matter how hard I tried. You would disappear inside your vessel and stay for so long... I knew you were watching Omar, helping him in secret ways, making sure he was safe and that he did well. I was always afraid one of the Council would find out, that they would send you away as punishment and separate us. Then when Omar died... Mother, I lost you for so long!"

Alarm filled her as her mother's eyes filled with tears. She leaned forward, taking Zahra's cool, slender hands between hers, pressing them gently.

"I'm sorry, Mother. I didn't mean to make you remember. I was simply explaining, you see, that I knew, even though you never said anything to me about it. But I saw what it did to you. You've never been happy since... not really happy. And you've never loved anyone else in all these centuries. I... I didn't want that for myself. I didn't want to love someone who would die, and then spend the rest of my life mourning him."

"Oh, my darling." Zahra closed her eyes, taking a long breath. Her fingers returned the firm pressure of Jacinth's grip.

"I'm sorry. I'm so sorry. We should have talked about this, long ago. I had no idea you thought..."

She broke off, as if uncertain as to how to continue. Puzzled, Jacinth waited. Finally, with a sigh, Zahra began again.

"I had no idea you thought I was mourning Omar all these years. Of course I grieved over his death! But it was less his death that I mourned than my own lack of faith, my own cowardice. I was so young, Jacinth, when I first came into my powers, and I knew so little of the world. I never ever regretted loving Omar. Not for one minute. What saddened me... desperately... was that I didn't have faith in our love. I was too afraid to tell him that I was a Djinn, too afraid of what his reaction might be. I was afraid of his anger, that he would cast us off. But I also feared his acceptance just as much, because that would have meant facing the world at his side, always fearing discovery."

She sighed, leaning back against the cushions. "It was years before I realized that Omar would never have reviled me, or you. That wasn't the kind of man he was. Together we could have found a way. But by then it was too late. Too late to go back. What I regretted... what I still regret to this day... is the time lost. We could have had so many wonderful years together, if I'd had the courage to go to him, to confess what we were."

Zahra pressed Jacinth's hands tightly. "If you love Douglas, live out those years with him. Savor each and every moment. Be there for Benny and Molly... such darling children... as they grow. You'll be there and watch over their children, and their children's children. And you and Douglas will have children, too. Don't do what I did," Zahra urged. "If you leave him now, you *will* spend a lifetime of regret, like I have spent."

Jacinth blinked back her own tears. "I never knew, Mother. You never told me..."

"No, I didn't. I was trying to protect you, I suppose."

"From what?" Jacinth demanded, indignant.

Zahra released her hands, making a helpless gesture.

"I don't know. Looking back, it seems foolish of me. At first, of course, you were too young to be talking with you about these things. And later... well, I confess, it was hard to admit to my own cowardice. And I'd robbed you of your father as well. Then when you were old enough for me to explain, I told myself that it was water under the bridge, that you'd grown into such a wonderful young woman, there was no need to dredge up old, hurtful issues that had no bearing on your life, after all. But I didn't know you thought I'd spent my life regretting having loved your father. Never that, my darling. Never, ever that!"

"Oh, Mother, I've made such a mess of things!" Jacinth wailed. "I left without a single word! What if he can't forgive me? I didn't even say goodbye to the children! I don't even know how long it's been since I left."

Her cheeks were dried with a soft tissue, and cool lips touched her cheek.

"It's been five days in the human world since you holed yourself up in here, and of course Douglas will forgive you, silly girl. He loves you."

"But... what will I say to him? How do I explain?" Jacinth sniffled, and reached for another Kleenex.

"You'll tell him the truth of course," Zahra replied briskly. "Remember, this has been difficult for him as well. He can't have envisioned falling in love with a Djinn, after all. He's bound to have some reservations also. But that's something you and he can work out. Together."

She fixed Jacinth with a pointed glance. "You can't work it out with you over here hiding out like a child."

"I wasn't hiding!" Jacinth defended vigorously. "I was... I was..."

"Sulking?"

"No! I was... well... missing him," Jacinth confessed. "And the children. And feeling a little sorry for myself, I guess."

"Jacinth!" Both of them jumped when a thunderous voice echoed from outside, anger reverberating through the receptive silver sides of the teapot. "Invite me in!"

It wasn't a request.

"Kieran." Zahra seemed smugly satisfied for some reason. "I wondered how long it would take him."

"Enter," Jacinth called, and Kieran's tall form shimmered into substance before them. Apparently ready to deliver his reprimand, he paused when he saw Zahra.

"So, you're here too, are you?"

"Yes." Zahra raised her chin in defiance. "And I'm not leaving."

"Fine," he snapped. "I assume you're aware of what your daughter has done, then?"

Jacinth bristled, indignant. "It's not against the rules to fall in love with a mortal!"

"Of course not." Kieran waved that away with a gesture of his hand. "I don't have any argument against that."

"You don't?" Jacinth was momentarily diverted, as was Zahra, who stared at Kieran with her mouth open. "I thought you didn't approve!"

Kieran frowned in impatience.

"Of course I don't approve. But then," he added, the cool blue eyes glinting with sudden, unexpected humor, "I don't have to approve. It's not my life. It *is* yours, however, and it's in shambles, which I suggest you pull together quickly. Very quickly."

It was Zahra who caught his meaning first, looking concerned, and then the significance of his words dawned on Jacinth. She sat up in alarm.

"What do you mean? What's happened?"

"I mean that young Benny has run away. To look for *you*."

"Oh, no!" Jacinth kicked off the comforter and scrambled to her feet. "Benny!"

"Not to worry," the Djinn prince reassured her. "He's safe enough; I'm keeping an eye on him. He's in that place you and Douglas are so fond of taking the children to shop... the mall, I think it's called."

"The mall?" Jacinth asked, incredulous.

"The mall?" Zahra echoed. "What in the world is he doing there?"

Jacinth stared at Kieran in perplexity. "I thought you said he was looking for me?"

"He is." An expression of bemused distaste crossed the Djinn's usually impassive features. "I believe he's engaged in looking inside teapots."

Jacinth gasped, as did Zahra.

"Teapots!" They cried in unison, then burst into laughter.

Jacinth leaned down to hug her mother tightly. "I'd better get there right away. Thank you, Mother."

"You're welcome, darling. And I'm sorry. About... everything."

Jacinth nodded, and disappeared. Zahra and Kieran were left looking at each other.

"Do you care to explain what that was all about?" Kieran asked, his mild tone unusually polite.

"Not really," Zahra admitted. "I've made some... mistakes... in not having some mother-daughter talks with Jacinth. A mistake that's been rectified now."

Kieran sighed. "What is it with these mortals, that so many Djinn have to go fall in love with them?"

Zahra hooked her arm through his.

"If you don't know, I can't explain it to you," she said, twinkling up at him. She arched one brow. "And just how did young Benjamin get to the mall all by himself, a child of his age?"

A faint smile touched the corner of his mouth, quickly banished.

"How should I know?" He replied blandly.

Zahra laughed at that. "Well, then. Shall we go make sure Jacinth and Douglas get it right this time?"

"We'd better," Kieran said with a sigh. "At least from now on, Douglas will have the job of watching after her."

Jacinth materialized carefully in a vacant dressing room in a department store. She found she was trembling slightly, anxiety gripping her chest. Kieran said he was looking out for Benny, and of course she trusted him, but she couldn't be easy until she had the boy was safe.

She had no trouble emerging from the dressing rooms, as the store was filled with shoppers. Instinct led her feet to where she somehow knew she would find Benny. She paused outside the Bombay Company and looked through the wide plate glass windows. Two anxious looking clerks hovered near the back of the store, and she had a pretty good idea what was making them anxious.

Bells chimed as she entered the store, and one of the men turned in her direction. She gave him her most charming smile.

"I believe you have someone here looking for me," she told

the man, her gaze going past him to a tow-headed boy arguing earnestly with the other salesman.

At the sound of her voice, Benny whipped around, his blue eyes sparkling with hope.

"Miss Jas! You're back!"

He charged through the store, to fling himself at her. Laughing, she bent to catch him in a hug.

"Yes, I'm back. But what are you doing here, Benny? You know I'm not here."

"Your teapot was gone," he told her in a subdued voice, his blue eyes solemn. "I thought maybe if I could find it, I'd buy it and you'd come back."

"Oh, honey." She wanted to cry, but hugged him again instead.

"Ahem." One of the salesmen cleared his throat. "Miss, you, ah, know this boy?"

Benny looked up at the man, one hand firmly clutching Jacinth's. "She's my nanny. She was lost, but I found her."

There was a muted snicker from the other sales clerk, but the first one nodded sagely. "I see."

Jacinth stood up, encompassing both of them in her smile.

"Thank you for watching out for him."

Once outside the shop, Jacinth fixed Benny with a stern look.

"You should be ashamed of yourself, running away from home like that. I'm sure your father is worried sick. Awful things could have happened, Benny."

"But nothing did. And I found you," the boy pointed out. "Besides, I knew you wouldn't let anything bad happen to me."

Jacinth thought perhaps it would be better not to go into that right now.

"We'd better find a phone and call your father," she

decided. "He'll want to know you're safe, and he can come pick us up."

At least, she hoped he'd pick both of them up. She hoped Douglas still wanted her, that he hadn't changed his mind since she'd left him. Perhaps he would be angry... what if he refused to talk to her, or...

"Jacinth!"

Her breath caught in her throat, and she looked about for the source of the masculine shout.

"Jacinth! Benny!"

"It's Dad!" Benny shouted, pointing. "Up there!"

She followed the direction of the boy's finger, and saw Douglas, Molly in his arms, on the floor above them, leaning over the low wall. He managed to look both relieved and glad and fiercely angry at the same time.

"Don't you move!" he shouted down, ignoring the interested attention of the multitude of shoppers around them. "We'll be right down."

He headed for the escalator. Looking around, Jacinth edged out of the stream of foot traffic into the center of the mall, to wait at the edge of the concrete fountain that created a restful atmosphere for tired shoppers.

Douglas charged down the escalator, brushing people aside in his haste to reach his son... and Jacinth. Then she was there, before him. He caught her in his arms, not even pausing to put Molly down in his haste, but he managed to pull Benny into his embrace as well, brave Benny who had brought Jacinth back to them.

He kissed her fiercely, letting her taste his desperation, his fear. His love for her. Molly began to squirm, caught between them, and Benny was giggling. Reluctantly Douglas drew back, and leaned down to set Molly on her feet, then took Jacinth's face in both hands.

"You came back," he managed, his voice husky. "You came back to me."

"I had to come back." Jacinth's beautiful smile was tremulous, uncertain, but the truth was there in her lovely eyes. She loved him, and she had come back to him. "You didn't make your third wish."

"I didn't, did I?"

She shook her head, wide brown eyes twin pools of dark chocolate.

"I wish..." Douglas drew his children close, hugging them tightly. "*We* wish... for you to stay. To be my wife, and Ben and Molly's mother. But only if you wish it too."

"I do," she whispered. Tears threatened. "I wish it so much, Douglas."

With a triumphant shout, he scooped her into his arms, whirling her in a circle as she clutched his shoulders for balance. Ben and Molly were jumping up and down in their excitement. Douglas' beloved features blurred a bit, and she blinked happy tears away.

"Say you'll marry me," Douglas demanded, and kissed her.

She broke away, laughing and breathless. "Yes."

A loud roar rose about them, and Douglas turned in surprise to find they were surrounded by people... shoppers... all cheering and applauding. Half the mall must be here, he thought, and broke into laughter. Jacinth beside him was laughing too, and his children were dancing with delight. He flung up their clasped hands.

"Heard and witnessed!" he shouted to the crowd.

"Heard and witnessed!" A hundred voices echoed the cry, the sound ringing off the high vaulted ceiling.

Cheers turned to laughter and catcalls as Douglas pulled Jacinth back into his arms and kissed her soundly. They broke apart as the children tugged at their hands, and Jacinth bent with a smile to lift Molly.

"Group hug!" she declared.

Both children clung to her, and she held them tight, delighting in their soft arms clinging about her neck, the slightly damp kisses landing on her cheeks. Douglas joined in, gathering them all into his embrace.

"How did you know I was here?" Jacinth asked him.

"Your mother came to let me know that Benny had come here and that Kieran was watching over him to be sure he was safe."

"I found her!" Benny announced proudly, and Douglas grinned down at his son, pinching the upturned nose.

"This calls for celebrating," he announced. "Where shall we go?"

Jacinth looked thrilled. "Really? Right now? All of us?"

At his nod, her face lit with eagerness.

"Let's go to Baskin Robbins!"

Ben and Molly yelled their approval, and Douglas shouted with laughter. No one else, he thought. No one else would choose to celebrate her engagement at an ice cream shop.

Only Jacinth.

FOR MY READERS

I'm always happy to hear from you! I can be found almost everywhere on social media (but particularly Twitter), and I'd absolutely love for you to add me! My website where you can see what's upcoming and what's current is www.AllieMcCormack.com

Sign up for my monthly author's newsletter at http://www.alliemccormack.com/Newsletter-Signup

I announce new and upcoming releases, news from the writing front, excerpts of works in progress (there's always at least a couple in progress), maybe a giveaway now and then, and a Recipe of the Month from my family's old tried-and-true recipes, some of which have been handed down for generations!

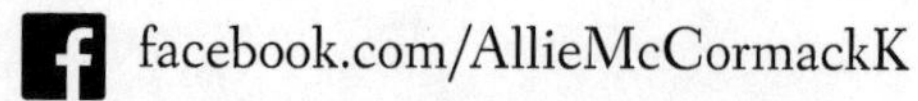
facebook.com/AllieMcCormackK

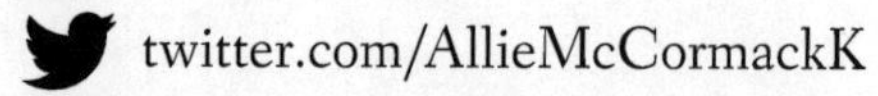
twitter.com/AllieMcCormackK

instagram.com/alliemccormackk

pinterest.com/allie9227

patreon.com/alliemccormack

Made in the USA
Middletown, DE
28 December 2022